WHITE POWDER

To Carol,

Hope you enjoy!

Mary Thru Dawson

WHITE
POWDER

MARY SHARON
PLOWMAN

Goodfellow Press

With special thanks to the following:

Dave Morrison, founder (est. 1981) and supervisor of the Eastside Narcotics Task Force of Bellevue, Washington.

Sergeant Judy Munday and Officer Rick Hubl of the King County Department of Adult Detention, Seattle, Washington.

Corey and Kara Salmela of the United States Biathlon Association, Lake Placid Olympic Training Center, New York.

Bill Aaron, director and producer of the video "Intro to Biathlon," Auburn Ski Club Regional Center of Excellence, Soda Springs, California.

Craig Ackley, Pilot for Cascade Helicopters of Wenatchee, Washington.

A Goodfellow Press, Inc. Publication
16625 Redmond Way, Suite M-20, Redmond WA 98052

Edited by Pamela R. Goodfellow
Cover illustration by David Hartz
Cover photography by May Thompson
Book design by Scott Pinzon
Chapter art by C.J. Wyckoff

Printed on recycled paper in Canada.

Dreams aren't unrealistic, some are just unrealized.
—Rachel Aldridge

To my family and friends, for keeping my dream alive.
To my critique group, for helping to shape
the dream until it was the best it could be.
And to my editor and mentor, for the countless hours
spent making this dream a reality.

Thanks for dreaming with me.

ONE

THE SECRET OF Last Chance Chute lay buried beneath the surface. The slope was primed for a disaster. Megan Jeffers knelt in the snow pit and ran her gloved hand down the icy wall. The variation in the layers, from hardpack to slush, was striking. Six inches of powder had fallen the night before, but it was the thin band of ice over the buried surface hoar that worried her the most. In half a dozen years with the Okanogan Forest Service, she'd seen the same conditions only once before. The day Thia died.

Setting the shovel down, Megan wiped at the perspiration forming on her brow. Though the Control Center would try to second-guess her, it was time to take action. She crossed to the snowmobile and switched on her radio hand set. "Joe?"

"That you, Jeffers? Go ahead."

"I recommend we close the Last Chance run today."

"Again?"

"Yes." Her jaw tightened. "Add it to our recording. Put a news flash out on the Internet."

"Megan, are you sure this isn't personal?" She heard him clear his throat. "It's only been a year. It will get easier."

He was wrong. One week short of a year. But that was irrelevant. This was her job and she was damned good at it. She lifted her chin. "The avalanche risk is too high, Joe. Incohesive layers. The boundary, depth and resistance data is logged and verified, per your request. I'll issue a detailed report when I get in."

"You can bet your ski boots you will. The District Manager will have your ass, mine too, if we close it prematurely. Every skier who comes up here wants to see the view from Devil's Elbow."

"And that's more important than saving lives?"

His sigh of exasperation was clearly audible. "All right, tell me what you have."

She stared out across the slope as she relayed her findings. The location and height of the various bands, the shape of the ice crystals, the hardness of the snow. Elevation. Wind and temperature conditions. He let her give the full account before objecting.

"Let's rate it 'Moderately Unstable.' That should be sufficient to keep people away."

A lump formed in her throat. That wording would never work. Nothing short of full slope closure would deter the true die-hards like her sister Thia. "Not enough teeth."

"I can't do it. You haven't given me sufficient data."

"I'll get more. I can dig a second pit closer to the run." Megan swallowed before continuing. "I'll get the proof, Joe."

Another sigh. "Okay. Call me back."

She replaced the handset. It would take at least another half hour, maybe longer, to give him what he wanted. Skiers from the nearby towns of Snagtooth, Mazama and Winthrop would be appearing by then and her morning training run would be pushed further behind schedule. Memories of Thia had delayed her. Again.

The avalanche report couldn't be filed late. To make up the time, she would cut short her morning circuit by skipping target practice. She needed the endurance training more, to bring her heart rate up to biathlon standards.

She chose a second site, picked up the shovel, and started again. Over and over she lifted the heavy mass of snow and flung it to one side. Hopefully she'd picked a location with stronger evidence of instability than the first snow pit. She hadn't time to dig a third.

With each thrust, she remembered Thia's passion for taking risks. Her sister had placed the love for skiing before all else, including common sense. That attitude had earned her a violent, early death at the base of Devil's Elbow.

Thia had made the decision to ski the Chute that afternoon, not Megan. She had recommended closure. A week from tomorrow it would be exactly one year since the accident. That was why her patience was so short. Perhaps the resurgence of guilt would pass when the grim anniversary was over.

Leaning on her shovel, she stared into the pit, chest heaving. The band of ice was barely visible in the second pit. She reached for her pocketknife, opened the blade and slowly ran the edge down the wall, testing the resistance of the snow. The extremes in the layers, both hard and soft, were faint. The slope would remain open.

The whine of a helicopter overhead broke her concentration. Megan shielded her eyes against the brilliance just beginning to show through the morning fog layer. She frowned and checked her watch. Seven A.M. The chopper was earlier than usual, traveling south from the Pasaytan Wilderness. That particular airspace was seldom used. Didn't the operators care about the bank of dark clouds forming to the west, or had today's wealthy clients bribed the pilot to ignore the marginal conditions?

Straightening, she threw down her shovel. She crossed to her snowmobile and rummaged in the backpack for binoculars. Adjusting the lens, she brought the copter's logo clearly into view. High Mountain Adventures. Yesterday she'd spotted the same outfit on

Phantom Peak, but later in the morning. What was their hurry today? She jotted down the name of the charter company on a pad of paper. It might come in handy if an incident report was needed later.

Skiers were about to hit the slopes. She would reword her report, downplay the second snow pit, get Joe to agree. That would have to be enough.

❄   ❄   ❄

A combination lock secured the door to the back country hut at Desolation Point. Reynold Harrison Moore III reached for it and stared at the dial. Strange. According to his business partner, detail-fanatic Dave Edwards, these huts were supposed to be open during the day for use by the general public.

It was mid-morning. The three of them had been on the slopes since eight A.M. and badly needed a rest stop. Despite the delay the lock was causing, Rey smiled. His sister, Ali, would badger Dave about the mistake. And Dave, with his steady-as-you-go attitude, needed a good dose of badgering now and then.

Ali huddled closer to him. "What's the hold up? I'm freezing my butt off."

"I doubt it. You had enough sense to cover that part of your anatomy." He tugged at the loose hood of her jacket. "It's your head that's cold."

"Forget the hat. Get us inside." Her teeth chattered. She'd been skiing with a headband instead of hat and hood, not wanting to flatten her hair. No doubt her behavior was linked to Dave's presence. Despite a complete lack of encouragement, Ali held romantic notions.

She stomped her feet on the snow-covered step and glanced around. "Where's our fearless leader?"

"Visiting the outhouse."

Alison raised her eyebrows. "Now that's what I call freezing your tush."

Rey smiled. "And after that, he'll check out the next slope."

"Good. By the way, why isn't this shack open?"

"I don't know. The proper term is 'hut', not shack. See that large flat area over there?"

She looked where he was pointing and nodded.

"That's a landing pad. Commercial outfitters bring skiers in by helicopter. They can use these huts during the day for lunch, to outwait a storm or to spend the night. I have no idea why it's not open today." Rey focused his attention on the lock.

"Maybe we're breaking into the wrong place."

"I'm not breaking in. This is definitely it." He pointed to a wind-swept slope to their right. "That's the Last Chance Chute. Devil's Elbow is below it. It's quite popular. This hut is probably used often."

He glanced at the darkening sky. The cloud bank was increasing. There were no trees at this elevation to break the harsh, icy wind. He flipped the padlock over. The metal loop wasn't actually inside the hole. A column of ice was the only thing holding the ends together.

Ali shivered. "Do something."

"My pleasure." With a quick twist Rey broke through the ice. He slipped the lock out of the latch and handed it to her. "Here, hold this." Squeezing hard on the handle, he shoved against the wood. The hinges groaned, but the door swung open. Icicles fell and covered his ski boots. He kicked them aside. With a grand sweep of his hand he waved her in.

Ali stared down into her glove then looked at him. "Very impressive, big brother." She preceded him into the hut. "If you ever get tired of manufacturing ladies' underwear, maybe you could take up safecracking."

Rey laughed. "You always were an obnoxious baby sister."

"You loved me anyway."

"Yes, I did." He raised one eyebrow. "Past tense."

Despite the freezing temperature, the room emanated warmth. Honey-colored curtains framed the double-paned window on the opposite wall. Twin-sized beds, adorned with patchwork comforters in varying golden hues, sat against the far wall. Next to the bed were two high-backed chairs carved from tree stumps. Their seat cushions coordinated with the quilt and their sides were sanded to a fine finish. Each tassel on the throw rug on the wood plank floor was primly tied with a yellow knot. Rey knocked the snow from his boots and entered.

Alison followed. "Is this place for real? Looks as if we've stumbled onto the set of *Country Home and Hut* magazine."

"Yes, it's real."

"But your pictures from last year's trip . . ."

"Those huts were east of Winthrop. According to Dave, the western ones are legendary for their homespun touches." His tone softened as his gaze took in the hand-crafted doilies, embroidered pillows, and well-worn Bible complete with frayed satin ribbon bookmark. "Seeing this, I have to agree."

It reminded him of his childhood dreams, of a place where kids could mill around the kitchen waiting to lick a mixing bowl clean. Where family members could fall asleep to the quiet clicking of a grandmother's knitting needles. He'd wanted an environment like that for Ali. And for himself.

She pulled off her headband and goggles. "Can you imagine Mom trying to crochet something? Anything?"

"I think the seat cushions are knitted."

"You're an expert?" Ali laughed as she stuffed her headband into her pocket. "Picture her with Great-Grandma's Chippendale

rocker firmly lashed to the deck of Father's yacht. He would be sitting at her feet, of course, carefully holding her skein of yarn away
from his cigar."

Rey smiled at the image. "No, I can't see it. I would have liked to,
though." He shrugged out of his parka.

"Hello." She waved a hand in front of his face. "Is my brother
in there? The one who lives in the Seattle high rise? Condo dweller,
surrounded by metal and glass?"

She was right. He'd done no better than his mother. But neither he nor Ali spent much time there anyway. He'd turned it over
to the decorator he was dating at the time. She'd wanted more
from him, but he'd been content limiting their activities to select-
ing coffee tables and engaging in occasional sex.

Relationships were too confusing. He was never sure whether
women were interested in him or the Moore millions. It was easier to start and stop a casual friendship than to end an intimate relationship. He sighed. "Let's get the water boiling."

"Good idea." Ali slipped off her backpack.

"I'll start the fire." Reaching into his pack Rey retrieved a single burner stove. A gallon can of white gas sat in the corner of the
room. For ill-prepared skiers, no doubt. He set the camp stove on
the narrow table. A bit more rummaging produced coffee, spoons
and powdered milk.

Alison picked up the bundle of single-cup coffee bags and
arched her eyebrow. "No espresso? Some ski trip this is." She
tossed her gloves onto the table. The corporate insignia on the cuff
drew Rey's attention. He should be used to it by now, but the sense
of pride that came over him warmed his soul. Moore Comfort was
his company. His and Ali's.

Above the embroidered name was a decorative 'M' forming the
shape of a mountain. The day he chose Alison's design for his new

corporate logo, she'd almost burst with excitement. Her drawing was more clever than the sketches he'd commissioned from a commercial artist. His deeper intent had been to restore another piece of his sister's self-esteem, a task he'd been working on for the last two years.

The windows rattled. Rey crossed the room and looked out. The cloud bank had grown darker. Was that noise thunder? He raised his voice. "We may have to wait for the storm to pass."

"Stay here? With outhouses, no water to speak of and absolutely no privacy?" She glanced around the room again. "And only two beds. Mmm. Yes. This place has definite possibilities." She grinned. "If this turns into an overnight, you'll have to find your own place."

"Very funny."

The door opened and Dave entered. The burst of wind accompanying him shook the lamp shade. He quickly closed it behind him. "There's a helicopter out there. I'm surprised they're still flying. Should we ask for help?"

"Definitely." Rey grabbed his jacket. "I'll go."

His partner frowned. "This snow has me worried."

"It's everywhere, Dave." Ali smiled as she positioned the camp stove square on the table. "Which flake was that in particular?"

Rey noticed that instead of sparing a glance her way, Dave continued undeterred. "It was sticking to our skis earlier. We'll have to keep an eye out for other avalanche indicators." He rubbed his hands together and blew on them.

"A bit cold out there for you?" Alison sauntered over to where he stood. There was a trace of mischief on her face. "Too bad the construction crew didn't place the planks in the outhouse walls a little closer together." She pointed to the gloves he had clipped to the zipper pull on his coat. "How were you planning to test our new line when you treat these as accessories?"

The muscle near Dave's jaw line briefly clenched. Rey shook his head. His partner was too serious for his own good. Ali viewed it as a personal challenge.

Dave's tone was slow and steady. "Is your role on this trip defined to be the official thorn-in-my-side, or are you planning to serve some useful function?"

A smile curved her lips. "Actually, I'm designing a new fly. One specifically for back country skiers. Did any great ideas come to mind while you were out there?" She looked directly at him. "Tell me, quick, before you warm up and forget."

Rey had never seen Dave blush before. He stepped in, trying not to show his amusement. "Both of you, take your corners. I'll be right back." He zipped his jacket, then ran his hand over the outer shell. "What temperature range did we design this model for?"

"Twenty below." Dave and Ali answered simultaneously.

Despite their bristling and poking, the two made a great marketing team. "Good. It's at least that, the way the wind is howling out there. This will be a good field test." Rey fastened his hood and slipped on his gloves. Both the gloves and the parka were made from Thermex, Moore Comfort's new insulation material. "Let's hope we were right."

Alison held up the small aluminum pot. "Mind filling this with snow while you're out?"

"Sure."

She smiled sweetly, handing him the container. "Make mine white, please."

The Thermex padding was just thin enough to allow Rey to tweak her nose.

❊   ❊   ❊

The blades of the helicopter threw pellets of corn snow in every direction. Rey moved back against the side of the building. By waiting until the pilot cut the engine, he would avoid a direct blast to his face.

The seconds ticked by. The blades didn't slow. Weren't the skiers getting out? He secured the Velcro flap under his chin and around his wrists, then pushed off from the wall. He ran headlong into someone, knocking the man over. Odd. He wasn't carrying skis. The only items he toted were a large back pack and a rifle, each slung over a different shoulder.

"Sorry. I didn't see you." Rey stepped closer.

The man on the ground raised his head. His hood had fallen back, revealing a hand-knit purple and red scarf. He was a kid, hardly old enough to shave. What was a kid doing on a mountain top with a rifle instead of skis?

"Let me help you." Rey extended his hand. "I wasn't looking. The wind . . ."

The boy wrenched his arm away. He grabbed his rifle and pointed it directly at Rey. "You're not supposed to be here. The boss will be pissed."

Rey stepped back. His heart pounded. He'd done nothing. Why was the kid pointing a gun at him?

A second man came around the corner. He was a huge man, taller and at least a foot wider than the boy. In his hand was an empty burlap sack. The butt of a gun protruded from one pocket. He wrapped his scarf more securely around his face. It wasn't high enough to fully cover his unruly, carrot-colored beard. Unusual color.

He yelled at the boy. His overgrown eyebrows were knit almost together. "Get up." Intimidating man.

"But, Lute." He motioned the barrel toward Rey. "What about him?"

Rey flinched at the rifle's movement. Who in the hell were these people?

"Shut up." The man gestured toward the three pairs of skis leaning against the wall. He stepped away, shouting at Rey. "Get back inside with your friends."

"Hey, where are you going?" The kid scrambled to his feet, slinging the rifle over his shoulder. "I'm coming. But what about our job?"

"I said, shut up." The man kept moving. He reached the aircraft first, yanked open the door and pushed the boy inside.

They were leaving. Thank God. Rey could breathe again.

He clenched his fists. They'd threatened him. What innocent skier would they harass next? He needed to get Ali and Dave away from here. When they reached safety, he would call the authorities.

Shielding his eyes from the wind, he tried to catch sight of the pilot. A woman, judging from her profile. After glancing his way, she quickly pulled her goggles down and began twisting the controls. The helicopter lifted off without the side door being fully closed.

Rey gripped the aluminum pot in his hand tighter. A shiver of fear ran down his back. The men had expected the building to be empty. If this were in fact private property, that would explain the padlock. What "job" had the gunmen been there to do?

He glanced back at the hut. They'd better forget the coffee. Rey made a mental note of the advertisement affixed to the side of the departing helicopter. Mountain High Adventures. When they arrived at the bed-and-breakfast where they were staying tonight, he'd call the authorities. Give descriptions of the men and the aircraft.

His gut instinct was telling him to leave, storm or no storm. Most of his successes were due to trusting his own intuition. He wouldn't ignore it now.

He entered the hut and sought Dave's eyes. The word trouble must have been successfully communicated. His partner glanced at Ali, then joined him near the door. Oblivious to his concern, his sister hummed a rock song as she rummaged for snacks.

Dave stood close and lowered his voice. "What happened?"

"They weren't interested in helping." He pointed toward the door's ice-frosted window, then unzipped his jacket. They both looked out. The helicopter headed due west, toward the dark cloud front.

Dave watched for several moments before turning to him. "What did they say?"

"Not much. They pointed a rifle at me, then took off." He made sure his back was to Ali. "The strange thing was they gave no clue they were at the wrong place. This is a public ski hut, but when we arrived it was padlocked. These guys expected it to be empty. I'm worried."

Alison walked toward them and reached for the pot Rey still held. "Okay, hand it over."

Rey turned the pot upside down. "Sorry. Slight change in plans. We'll have coffee later."

She raised her eyebrows. "I hope you're prepared to suffer the consequences."

"I'm serious, Ali. We need to get moving." He put a hand on her shoulder. "Let's pack."

Dave was already returning the cook set to its original tight stack. Ali stood motionless. "Why?"

He tried to keep his tone light. "The men in that chopper weren't here to ski."

"Knock off the intrigue and tell me what happened."

He paused. "Can't you simply trust me on this one?"

She shook her head. "I can't help if I don't know. Stop protecting me from bad news."

"All right." He swallowed. "There were two men." She stared at him as if waiting for the punch line. He wanted to keep the distress to himself but needed to convey the urgency. "One pointed his gun at me."

"My God."

He nodded, glad she was taking him seriously. "Let's go."

"No argument from me." She crossed to the table. Grabbing the pouch, she tried jamming various pieces inside. It was a stark contrast to Dave's precise movements. Metal containers clanged together. A spoon fell to the floor.

Dave picked up a piece near her feet, then took a second one from her hand. "We'll be fine. Why don't you put away the snacks? Carefully, unless you want the energy bars to turn into crumbs."

Rey watched his sister slow her movements. Dave's words had more of a calming effect than his own. Within minutes, they were out the door and back on their skis, leaving the hut and all its mystery behind.

❄   ❄   ❄

Rey braced himself against the wind as he came around the hut and scanned the horizon. It was almost noon. They needed to descend as quickly as possible. The dark clouds, earlier in the west, were now directly over them. New snow fell on their hats and jackets. The harsh wind blew ice crystals against their cheeks.

Dave held out an arm and caught snow samples against the black fabric of his parka. "The crystals are needle-shaped."

Ali peered at them. "So?"

"They won't bond together. That's a bad sign."

Rey sidestepped toward them. "What do you recommend?"

"Let's stay as high as we can and traverse single file. Last Chance has a history that's worrisome, even on a good day. Two skiers died

19

just last year." Dave pointed to the lower end of the slope. "That's Devil's Elbow. The cornice above is an accumulation of drifted snow. They might have closed the slope this morning. Damn, I wish that helicopter would beat it. They're not helping. Let's head for the trees on the far side."

Ali lowered her goggles and cupped her hand around the side of her face. "Where? I can't see five feet in front of me."

"You've fogged your goggles. You're right, though, the landmark is hard to spot from above. But it's there. The skiers who died last year missed it." Dave scrounged in his pocket, producing a piece of treated flannel and gave it to Ali. "We'll proceed slowly and listen for sounds of cracking."

Rey adjusted his hood. "I'll go first. It makes the most sense."

"I have more experience."

"I know, but I want you last. Watching." He wanted to say more. Ali was off to one side, working on her goggles. He wasn't sure if she was listening or not.

She side-stepped over and handed the cloth back to Dave then glanced toward the pile of gear. "I'll get the rest of my stuff. Be right back."

Rey adjusted his collar to better shield his neck. When his sister moved out of earshot, he leaned toward Dave. "I've never dug anyone out of an avalanche before, only read about it. I'd hate for my first attempt to be rescuing you." He paused, looking directly at his partner through the darkly tinted shades. "Keep a close eye on her for me."

Ali returned, hoisting her bag on her back. Rey bent close to be heard above the wind. "You'll be second, after me. Turn your transceiver on."

She did, then watched him for a moment, chewing nervously on her bottom lip. When she finally spoke her voice was unsteady. "This gives me the creeps."

He wrapped an arm about her shoulder. "When we're sipping

hot chocolate around a blazing fire, you'll be wishing spring would never come."

"Right."

He pulled her in for a hug. "Dave knows what he's doing. Listen to him."

"Okay."

"No grief?"

Alison looked up at him with a forced grin. "For that, big brother, forget the chocolate. Promise me mulled wine."

"We'll see." He released her. After a parting thumbs up for good luck, Rey pushed off.

❊   ❊   ❊

Seated inside the chopper, Lute unwrapped his scarf. Ice and snow stuck to his beard. Folding the empty burlap sack, he stowed it in one of the helicopter's mesh side pockets. The ride would be bumpy due to the storm. Hopefully Rookie wouldn't puke.

Keeping his movements as slight as possible, he avoided looking at Cowboy seated across from him. No explanation would be good enough for his boss. He didn't tolerate screw-ups.

Being this close to Cowboy made Lute's palms sweat. He was a cold, calculating son of a bitch but an excellent judge of character. Collected weak men with greedy souls. Men like Lute, himself. He swallowed and focused on the damned fool skier on the ground.

Where in the hell had he come from? Lute tried to think. He needed to find a way to minimize the damage. For Rookie's sake. The kid didn't know any better. There wasn't time for training anymore. The speed with which Cowboy's organization picked these young punks off the street and lured them into action was sickening. They were used and disposed of. Most didn't last until pay day.

Lute gave Rookie his helmet. The kid was afraid of heights. The helmet, complete with stickers, was his security blanket.

He grabbed his safety belt and clicked it shut. The copter was circling the hut, gaining altitude, but the kid still wasn't buckled. He was too busy peering out at the scenery below. What did he think this was, a fucking chair lift? Cowboy sat, arms crossed, not moving a muscle except to press the transmit button next to his thumb. His voice came over the headset. Smooth as bourbon.

"Fill me in."

The words sounded like a request, but he knew better. Time for a full accounting. The fact that Cowboy was along today was adding to Lute's stress. Usually he and Rookie handled the pickups alone. The shipment must be huge for Cowboy to want it this badly.

He looked at his boss, trying not to show fear. His eyes were hidden beneath the rim of his dark Stetson. Lute was glad. He'd caught a glimpse once. Once had been enough.

He cleared his throat. "We ran into someone. A ski bum is my guess. Either he broke in or the delivery boys forgot the lock." He flexed his shoulders. He hoped the movement was inconspicuous. It helped relieve the tension.

He was almost out. Retirement. This shipment was a big one. His cut would set him up for life. He'd worked too hard to throw it all away now.

"Which one was it, Lute?"

"I'll find out."

"Do that."

"Hey, I think I know." Rookie pulled off his gloves and rubbed his hands, blowing into his palms. His voice was pitched higher and faster than usual. Lute wished again the kid was smarter. Intelligent enough to fasten his belt and shut up. Instead, the boy rambled on. "I got a good look at the guy."

"You did?" Cowboy tipped his Stetson a fraction of an inch in Rookie's direction. "Tell me."

The kid grinned. "He had dark bristly hair, a straight nose and no scars. Not yet, anyway." He laughed. Lute winced.

Cowboy nodded. "You saw his face."

"Got a real good look."

"And he saw yours?"

"Right down my rifle barrel."

Lute clenched his jaw. The brim of Cowboy's hat was still. Deathly still.

"From the looks of his fancy threads, I'd say he's got money to burn." Another laugh. "And remember there were two more pairs of skis. Maybe the others had bucks they could part with also." Rookie patted the rifle still slung over one arm. "You know, given the right encouragement."

Lute grimaced.

"There were others?" The question was chilling.

"Yeah." The boy nodded with excitement. "Two more." He turned toward Lute. "You saw the extra equipment, right?"

"I didn't see nothin'." Lute snarled his words at the boy. "A scarf covered my face the entire time."

Even with the continuing whine of the chopper's blades, Lute felt the weight of the silence. Cowboy would reach his decision on Rookie any minute now.

Lute called all the punks Rookie. It was simpler than learning their names. Though this one was dumber than most, he'd taken a liking to him. The boy treated him as a pal, looked up to him in an almost paternal way. Pathetic. Endearing. Lute wouldn't make the same mistake with the boy's replacement.

Suddenly the kid started forward, scrambling to his knees. "Hey, that's them now. I'd recognize that flashy coat anywhere."

Lute saw Cowboy's hand signal and leaned forward to take a look. The skiers were crossing Last Chance Chute, single file. He remembered that slope well. Steep enough for an accidental burial.

"Well?"

Lute turned. Cowboy's gaze was fixed on him. "Could be them." He had no choice but to stick by his story.

"Snow conditions?"

"Good."

The pilot's voice came over the headset. "Where to, boss? Original flight plan?"

"Circle west. Near the trees below Devil's Elbow."

Cowboy reached into the pocket of his leather jacket. Lute flinched. The boss never did the job himself. Cowboy retrieved a toothpick, bit down on the stick and began chewing. He nodded at Lute. "First, the trees. Then we'll circle back."

His heart pounded. The "we" said it all. He would be pardoned this time. It was a simple choice. Cowboy was giving Lute a chance to show whose side he was on. He should have been relieved but part of him felt sick. Wouldn't lose it, though. He'd passed this test before. He was surprised, and thankful, that it still bothered him. He drew his .22.

"What do we do now? Go get 'em?" Rookie glanced at Lute, his trainer and mentor. He stared at the barrel pointing at him. His excitement faded. His eyes were huge, his mouth open. He turned and looked pleadingly toward Cowboy. "But . . ."

"You let him see your face. I told you, never let them see your face."

The boy made it easier for Lute by exposing the entire length of his neck. He shoved the nose of the gun behind the kid's ear-lobe and pulled the trigger. It was over in a split second, probably before the feel of cold metal registered. Neat, too, the helmet trapping the gore.

The chopper circled low over the thick fir trees. They were a slope away from the Desolation Point hut and the skiers, well hidden from view. As the pilot banked left, Lute reached over, opened the door, and pushed the boy out in one smooth move.

It was done. Over. Once again, Lute was still alive.

He put the safety on and stowed his weapon. They were all young, the runners. The fall guys. He'd be replaced by another rookie, one just as hungry for quick cash. The kid's name had been Charles. No use remembering that now. As he'd stopped counting the killings so he'd forget the faces, too. Lute sighed. The boy had been a good sidekick, better than most.

Cowboy's softly spoken question interrupted his thoughts. "Princess?"

She turned. The pilot was a beautiful woman, despite the fact her broken nose had healed slightly to the right. She was also a survivor. She'd learned her lessons, as Lute had, years ago. It wasn't smart to cross Cowboy.

"Where to?"

"Back to Last Chance, honey. Take us in real low."

❄   ❄   ❄

They were halfway across the clearing when Rey heard the second helicopter. Or was it the same one as earlier again? He stopped and scanned the sky. The chopper was flying low above the tree tops to his west, but not low enough for a landing. Not circling, either. As it headed his way, it dropped steadily in altitude. Strange. Maybe the group from Mountain High Adventures was returning to help.

Rey shifted both poles to one hand and waved with the other. The aircraft changed course and hovered downhill, kicking up snow. The slope was a thirty degree incline, maybe forty. Not suitable for landing.

Below was Devil's Elbow. Was the surface flat enough to serve as a helipad? And if not, what were they doing?

The sound of the blades was deafening. The wind beating against his face burned his skin. He glanced to where his sister and partner waited for their turns across the slope. Were they waving at him, or signaling to the helicopter?

They were shouting but he couldn't make out the words. Maybe if he moved on, the chopper would return to the hut and land. Ali and Dave could be picked up first. They would figure out a way to get him on board later, after his traverse.

The helicopter dipped lower. He heard a cracking sound followed by a *whomp*. The surface beneath his feet moved, jolted and began to slide.

Dave's words echoed back to him. Remain calm. Dump your equipment. Swim. Rey dropped his poles. He struggled to keep upright as he squirmed out of the pack's harness. It fell just as the snow slid out from under him. He toppled over, feet first, nose down against the hill. He tried several strokes as he slipped further, starting with a crawl. It didn't help. The snow was heavy and fluid—moving over his back and neck.

Feet first, face up. Was that correct? If so, he was half right. Rolling, he fought to keep his head above the snow.

His neck cramped. Though his lungs were bursting, he held his breath. His chest ached. Continuously replace your air.

He chanced another gulp and realized the sky was still visible. Thank God he was riding the surface, or close to it. He yanked his goggles off and looked upward. Snow crystals burned his eyes. He closed them, fighting on in the dark. Dave had seen him fall, that and the transmitter he'd faithfully turned on would be his lifesaver. If he remained near the surface, a dig-out should be no problem. Unless, of course, he was headed over the Devil's Elbow drop-off.

Abruptly he stopped moving. Pain shot through one leg. The rock ledge? Thank God he hadn't gone over. He put his hands in front of his face as the snow covered him. Pain made him grit his teeth. Black dots danced before his eyes. He couldn't give in now.

Hands cupped, he pushed against the drift settling over him, carving out an air space. It worked. He could still breathe. The freezing mass around him stopped shifting.

He couldn't roll, couldn't move. Couldn't relieve the pressure against his buckled knee. Gritting his teeth, he sucked in new air, fighting for every breath. He needed to preserve his air supply. No way to know how long he'd have to wait.

Lifting one arm he burrowed upward. Time passed slowly. At last his hand was free, or so he guessed. He couldn't feel the wind because of the glove he was wearing, but there no longer seemed to be any resistance.

The black dots danced closer together. He couldn't shake them, couldn't move his head. Not even a fraction to the side. The cramp in his neck might become permanent.

He tried wiggling his fingers. Were they waving in the air or digging in the snow? The feeling in his extremities was fading fast.

Great gloves. Moore Comfort gloves. Maybe he should manufacture a new avalanche-style model. Thinner, so air could be sensed through the fabric. Maybe little windows. Stupid. Fingers can't see.

He opened his eyes. He couldn't see either. Was the self-made cave really this dark or had the dots danced together into a sea of blackness?

His neck still ached. So did his head. Was the neck actually part of the head? Probably. If so, his complaint was redundant. He had to focus. Be patient. Focus on patience. Focus on anything.

If the gloves had Velcro flaps on the index finger, then his thumb could flick it open. Trapped skiers would be able to sense the difference between air and snow. He tried experimenting with the bit of feeling he had left. Yeah, that would work. Perfect. Maybe two flaps. Thumb and finger. No, Ali would say that was overkill. She was always saying that. He could almost hear her voice: sometimes less is more.

She said plum would be next year's hot color. Some blue-ish version of purple. Purple windows. He'd have to remember to ask her opinion on that.

Oh, God. Ali. Her voice was no longer in his memory. He couldn't bring her face into focus, either. If he didn't survive this grave, would Dave take care of her? And if so, for how long?

Dave. He couldn't see his face either. Someone. Had to come. Someone. Anyone.

Please help. Please come.

Quick.

TWO

MEGAN GLIDED TO a stop beside her snowmobile. God, she loved racing. The exhilaration of the wind scrubbing her cheeks and blowing her hair was indescribably good. Her new ankle-high boots had performed well. Unfortunately not all aspects of the run had gone right. Her pulse was too fast, probably two hundred beats per minute. She glanced at the wrist monitor. The face of the watch was fogged over from body heat. She pulled off her glove and ran her finger over the digital display. 195. Too high.

She breathed deeply and made an unhurried cool down loop through the trees. Still at 180. Her goal was to drop her pulse rate thirty beats in thirty seconds to allow firing between heart beats and indrawn breaths. Her aim would be steadier, her accuracy higher. She couldn't hit the side of her shed at this rate. She would never be able to trip a target fifty meters away.

She'd lost her concentration and pushed too hard, that much was obvious. When? During the last mile? Fast as a rabbit, steady as a rock. Thia's favorite Biathlete Creed. Megan sighed. Another failure.

Anger at Joe's refusal to close Last Chance had distracted her. That and the helicopter buzzing overhead. The outfitter shouldn't be flying, not with the storm front increasing. But neither distraction was the real reason. Thia. The Control Center hadn't closed the slope that day, either.

Frowning, Megan returned to her snowmobile. She popped her bindings, stepped out of her skis and placed them in the upright holder. Her rifle and shoulder harness were the next to come off. She retrieved her woolen coveralls, unzipped the ankles and slipped them on over her light weight training suit. Temperatures like this gave the term 'cool down' a new meaning.

She ran her hand over the vehicle's smooth, black finish. The sleek Vmax 500 DX was all hers. Although the Forest Service had issued her a standard snowmobile, she'd ordered the tricked-out black Yamaha for her own private use. It was an indulgence she'd never regretted. It made her job easier, as well as more enjoyable.

Her radio crackled to life. She frowned. Normally her calls were outbound unless it was an emergency. She reached for the handset. "Jeffers."

"We've had a report of a slab avalanche on Last Chance. Big. Maybe ten by fifty meters. We believe you're the closest."

She bit back an 'I told you so' and zipped her coat. "I'm ten minutes away."

"It's yours then. Call if you need help."

"Where's Rachel?"

"Out on a practice drill."

Megan felt her jaw tighten. Even if they weren't going to close the slope, the warning should have been passed on to the rescue team. It hadn't been. Rachel wouldn't have ignored it. "Okay. What do we have?"

As she listened to the details, she checked the bungee cords to make sure her gear was strapped down tightly. With the coming storm, the ride could get rough.

"It's a private party. One man down. Less than a meter under. The other two dug him out."

The heli-skiers, no doubt. At least what the skiers lacked in weather sense they compensated for in avalanche training. "That guy should buy lottery tickets."

"What?"

"Never mind." She pulled on her regulation parka and zipped it to her chin. "Did they have to resuscitate?"

"No. He's awake. Speaking but groggy. There may be a leg injury. He can't ski out."

Megan slipped her helmet on and stepped onto the running board. She plugged the radio cord into her headset. "You still there?"

"You're loud and clear."

She replaced the hand-held unit and adjusted her chin strap. Her movements were brisk and mechanical. When she realized she was rehearsing a lecture on the value of mountain reports for the stranded skier, she stopped herself. It would be a waste of breath. She hadn't persuaded Thia from skiing in weather like this; why did she think she'd have better luck with strangers? The engine roared to life. "I'm off. Who called in the report?"

"One of the skiers."

"What?"

"Surprised me, too. The victim's cellular phone apparently survived. They were high enough above the tree line to call it in."

Yuppies. She shook her head. "Guess they never heard of flares."

"Get this. They say there were a couple of guys with rifles. Near Desolation Point."

She amended her earlier description. City-dwelling-yuppies. There were many plausible reasons for carrying weapons up here. As long as the owners knew how to use them, she didn't care. She revved the engine. "I'm on my way."

"Good luck."

Megan frowned at that comment as her vehicle sped across the snow. When would Joe and the others around the Okanogan accept the basic truth: when it came to mountain survival, luck had nothing to do with it.

❄   ❄   ❄

The snowmobile glided easily along the track. When the path veered south, she left the trail and cut through a thick stand of trees. She clutched the grips as the ride turned bumpy, avoiding stumps and undefined shadows on the ground. The morning sun was disappearing under the onslaught of the storm. Her skin felt chapped from blowing ice crystals.

When she emerged from the forest, Megan spotted the small party only a hundred yards away. Devil's Elbow. The slide had almost taken him over. She braced herself and continued toward them.

A man and woman knelt before a second man, well out of the way of the avalanche debris. She steered toward the group and cut the engine, welcoming the momentary silence. As she pulled off her helmet, she could hear the woman crying.

The man with wire-rimmed glasses stood. "Dave Edwards." He pointed to the downed man. "This is Rey Harrison. Alison is his sister."

"Megan Jeffers. Forest Service." She crossed to the other side of the victim. Kneeling beside him she brushed snow from his ski pants and jacket, looking for broken bones.

Dave spoke again. "Thanks for arriving so quickly."

"It's my job." She forced a smile. "We'll get you to safety as soon as possible."

He extended a hand and pulled Alison to her feet. When the young woman leaned against his side, Dave wrapped an arm around her shoulder and smoothed the hair back from her face. Megan forced herself not to sigh. Here she was, rescuing this stranger, when she hadn't been able to save her sister.

These two people were distracting her efforts. She addressed Dave. "My cabin is a little over five miles from here. The snowmobile carries two. Since neither of you are injured, the quickest way out of this storm is to ski to my place." She gave him the directions.

"Thank you." Despite his words, defiance flashed in Dave's eyes before he stepped away. Maybe her tone had been too sharp. Tough. The risk of hypothermia was high. Politeness would have to wait. They should be gone in minutes. She turned back to the victim.

"Tell me where it hurts." She ran her hands slowly along his leg, checking for injuries.

"My left knee. Would you've kept searching if I hadn't told you?"

Laugh lines crinkled the edges of his eyes. He was flirting with her. Amazing. She couldn't remember her last brush with flirtation. The attention both pleased and surprised her.

"Here?" She gave his right thigh a sharp squeeze.

He jumped at the unexpected pressure. "No. The other leg." Rey drew a deep breath, no longer grinning.

"Oh, yes. You mentioned that." It was her turn to smile.

"Quite a grip you have."

"It comes in handy in my line of work."

He tilted his head toward her snowmobile. "And the rifle?"

"It motivates my patients to behave."

"I'm convinced."

"Good. Now please open your jacket."

He was staring at her. His eyes were green. She'd expected them to match the chestnut hair curling from beneath his ski cap. His lashes were dark and laced with snow crystals. His gaze didn't waver as he pulled the zipper of his coat down. Its intensity made her heart pound. He was a nice looking man.

She continued her examination, moving her hands quickly over his arms, chest and ribs. Pulling off a glove, she placed one hand on his neck and took his pulse. "Are you experiencing any dizziness? Headaches?"

"I've felt worse." Rey grimaced. "But not lately."

He was cracking another joke. The man had no sense of timing. Didn't he realize how close he'd come to sliding over Devil's Elbow?

A gust of wind piled a fresh drift of snow next to them. She pulled the edges of his jacket together and grabbed her space blanket. After securing the reflective material around him, she reached for the roll of elastic bandaging and the collapsible splint. She extended the frame until it was bent at the desired angle then tightened the screw.

Ice pellets blew across her face. She wiped the cuff of her sleeve over her eyes then positioned her body to protect him from further blasts.

He spoke again. She couldn't make out his words. "Would you repeat that?" She leaned closer, her ear to his mouth.

"The splint. Dave thought I'd need one."

"He did, did he?" She glanced toward the trail. The others were almost out of sight. She didn't need advice from an amateur. "If your friend is such an expert on mountain rescue, why did he steer you across Last Chance? People die there, needlessly. If you'd have bothered to check the conditions, the layering would have shown you the slope was unstable."

"There was a helicopter."

"They shouldn't have been flying." She slipped the device under his knee. "Your pilot was reckless. Ditto, you and your friends." She tugged at the side straps. "Next time you might not hit a rock, simply continue over the edge." Her words came faster. "We'd find you at the bottom. Take pictures of you lying prone in a body bag." A lump caught in her throat. Her fingers trembled as she fastened the Velcro. Tears burned her eyes. He didn't know. Couldn't know. She kept her head down.

His hand covered hers. "I'm sorry."

Though the two surfaces were separated by his glove, she felt warmed, connected somehow. She took a deep breath then let it out, feeling drained. "Sorry, for what?"

"For whatever happened before."

It was bad enough that she was an emotional mess. Now she'd taken it out on a stranger. "I should be the one apologizing." She looked out across the slope. "It's not you. It's me." She glanced in the direction of Devil's Elbow. "My sister died here, almost a year ago. I'm not handling it well. Sorry I exploded."

The silence intensified her embarrassment. What could she say after an admission like that? She climbed to her feet and helped him stand. "Let's get moving and beat this storm."

❄   ❄   ❄

Despite the bitter wind whipping his face, as far as Rey was concerned the ride to Megan's cabin could go on forever. Her snowmobile had a raised second seat, comfortably affording him a place behind and above her. His injured leg rested across her thigh. Her idea.

This woman had an intriguing bedside manner. Drill sergeant voice, a Florence Nightingale touch. Competent, independent. Hurting. Deeply hurting. Her outburst had come from nowhere, seeming to surprise her as much as it did him.

The trigger had been her sister's death in the same area as his accident. In his experience, resolving grief required the support of friends and family. He sensed she was a loner. Ali came to mind.

His sister had needed stability and purpose after the trouble she landed herself in. That was why he'd insisted she move into his condo. She was one of the main reasons he'd chosen to start his own firm despite doubts about being a CEO. Now her life had focus. Her creativity and energy were funneled into designing ski wear. And he realized that having her buzz around his place, bossing his housekeeper and questioning everything, added new zest to his own life. It was a lot more exciting than simply managing the Moore family inheritance.

So, where was Megan's family?

His knee hurt but the rest of his body was merely stiff and sore. He moved closer against her, arms secured around her waist, as she raced the storm. The field test was supposed to have doubled as a vacation. Now he was riding through a storm at breakneck speed with an injured knee, thankful to be alive.

The impact of the avalanche was just sinking in. Hell, he could have died, buried under the snow. He tightened his grip on the woman in front of him. Time to learn the fine art of relaxation. His injury would be the catalyst.

As agreed, Dave had introduced him as Rey Harrison, the name he'd been using for twenty years, whenever he traveled. Using his middle name lessened the threat of abduction and increased his chances of being treated as a person rather than a bank account. He'd learned the hard way that there was never a lack of women once they found out he was heir to the Moore millions.

This one didn't seem to care who he was. Megan called things the way she saw them. He liked that. As direct as the Okanogan storm buffeting them.

Took herself a little too seriously, though. Maybe he could change that. And then perhaps she'd smile again, just for him.

❄   ❄   ❄

They approached her cabin from the uphill side. Ali and Dave should be no more than a half hour away. Rey spied the roof and chimney through the worsening storm. It wasn't until they turned the corner and headed downhill that he realized it was a two-story structure, complete with deck and daylight basement. A wood shed stood to one side. It served as a wind break as they pulled up, for which he was instantly grateful. A large place for just one person.

Megan switched off the engine. He was the first to speak. "This is impressive. Cabin hardly seems the right term."

"Thank you." She drew off her helmet and secured her knitted cap against the wind. He followed suit. After hooking both helmets over the handlebars, she lifted his left leg up and off her knee. She stepped down, then turned to assist him.

His leg felt numb. He vowed not to look foolish by stumbling. "Do you live here by yourself?"

"Sometimes." She put his arm around her shoulder and helped him stand.

He waited for her to elaborate. She didn't, so he tried again. "Is this one of those times?"

"No, it's not." They stepped into the wind.

A very direct answer, the type he appreciated in the boardroom. Short and sweet, not overloaded with details. No details at all, in fact.

Before he could decide what to ask next, she glanced at him. "You're here, aren't you?"

The humor surprised him. From their initial encounter, he'd assessed that it wasn't her specialty. Maybe she was out of practice. He found he was looking forward to the next few hours.

He used her shoulder as a crutch, leaning with each awkward step. Her arm beneath his was firmly around his back. She was strong. A result of her job, no doubt. If Ali were here, she'd be smirking.

Rey tried to ignore the personal side of it. Assisting him was part of the task, that was all. Why, then, was he so aware of the fact the top of her head was at approximately the same level as his mouth? And only inches away. He faced forward and tried to concentrate solely on hopping.

He leaned more fully against her as they approached the cabin along the shoveled path that led toward the deck. When they reached the stairs, he used the hand rail to maneuver his way up solo. Megan preceded him. But instead of opening the door, she looked off into the distance. A scowl wrinkled her brow.

His gaze followed hers across the snowy landscape. A quarter mile away, a man in a calf-length coat moved about in front of a second cabin. He was unpacking a long duffel bag from a brilliant red snowmobile. To one side of him a burst of yellow incongruously edged a frozen lake.

"One of your neighbors?"

She nodded. "Sort of. Grandma Grace lives there. The man, Eric Mitchell, is new in town. He'll be boarding at Granny's for several weeks, I think."

Town? What town? He refrained from smiling. "What's that yellow area on the ground, to his right?"

"Flowers."

"This time of year?"

"All year long. They're Granny's." She was still staring. Rey watched, too, wanting to know more but anxious to be indoors. "Is something wrong?"

"Not yet. Let hope it stays that way." She looked at him. His confusion must have shown on his face. "Granny agreed to let him stay. Went against my advice. He's supposedly here to do research on repopulating the Okanogan with grizzly bears."

"And?"

She sighed. "It's winter. Do you see any grizzlies?"

He hadn't seen a town, either, but decided against mentioning it.

Megan exhaled. "Sorry. Let's get you inside." She unlocked the front door.

He followed her to one of the kitchen chairs. She positioned a second one for his injured leg. Within minutes their jackets, hats and gloves were hanging on a rack near the entrance. There were empty pegs for at least ten more. "You have plenty of room here."

"Sometimes I need it." She removed his boot. "I'll get the fire going, then we'll take a look at your injury. How are you feeling?"

"It aches like hell, but I think I'll live. I've wrenched this before."

"Sports injury?"

"Something like that."

She knelt in front of the fireplace, moving aside the wrought iron screen. "This place is a bit large for one, but I put the space to good use. The cabin doubles as a bed-and-breakfast."

"Do you do it for the company?" He wanted to keep her talking. "It's desolate out here."

"Not desolate. Wonderful. And I prefer it quiet. When a party of more than three or four makes reservations, I usually want to move out before the night's over." She wadded paper, tossed it onto the grate and sorted through the kindling. "My place is part of the hut-to-hut system. Skiers have a choice of self-service, or pampered B&B living, or something in between. To the east, the back country huts are named after the local wildlife. Quite rustic. They're at one end of the comfort scale."

He nodded. "Dave mentioned those. Said the ones on this side of the highway are very different. Exquisitely furnished."

She sighed. "Granny's mission in life." There was a touch of affection in her smile. "Still, they're not much better than camping out. No running water, no toilets."

"We had reservations at another place. I've forgotten which one." Rey checked his pockets. "Dave would know. Near Lost River, I think."

"Lily's Lost and Found?"

"That's it."

Megan's expression became unreadable. "A local favorite. Notorious for late night parties." There was a hint of sarcasm in her voice.

"And yours is not?"

She lit the fire and stood. "I'll notify Lily about the situation and call the local doctor. Would you like to contact your physician?"

"Yes. Maybe he will refill my pain prescription locally."

"Good." After wiping her hands on a towel, she crossed to the kitchen. "As soon it's warm in here, I'll help you off with those pants."

It took a generous portion of his self control not to grin.

He glanced around the room. The main area of the cabin was stark, but very livable. The utilitarian decor gave him the feeling she didn't spend much time at home. A bookcase below the picture window was crammed with reference books, but lacked novels. No television. There was probably a radio somewhere. But other than a few magazines beneath the end tables, there wasn't much for indoor entertainment.

Megan reappeared with a large patchwork quilt in varying patterns of blue and green. Teal, Alison would say. It was similar in design to the one he'd seen in the hut earlier. He frowned as he recalled the distinctive pattern and the events that followed. He should tell her about the locked hut, about the men with guns instead of skis. There was no way to know if their first warning was passed on. She would know the proper authorities to notify.

Megan glanced down at the blanket. "Is there a spot on it?"

"No, it's just that I saw a similar quilt this morning."

"What color?" She tossed it onto the couch.

"Gold. Why?"

"That tells me where you were." She knelt in front of him and began untying the stays securing the leg brace. "Desolation Point. In this stretch of the Okanogan, the huts are named after the closest mountain peak. Grandma Grace decorated that one in shades of gold."

Grandma Grace. That explained the homespun touches.

She stripped away the fasteners, padding and splint from his knee. "Smuggler's Peak hut is pink. She used red for the Needles. The list goes on. I like Snowy Lakes best."

"Why is that?"

"Apricot is one of my favorite colors."

"More orange than peach, not too much red."

Megan looked at him. "Yes."

She was trying not to smile. He wished he could call the words back. He and Ali played this game. Ali used exotic names for the colors on her new palette, sometimes inventing names for them herself. "My sister claims I'm still in training. Calls me color blind when it comes to current trends."

"I wasn't able to say much more than hello to Alison. Maybe we'll have time to talk later."

"She's great."

"Then you're close?"

"I'm all she has." He hadn't meant for that to slip out, but it was easy to talk to Megan. Something had clicked between them. Maybe she would feel comfortable enough with him to share more about her sister's accident, if he were here long enough. The thought of staying awhile pleased him.

She watched him a moment, as if considering a response. Refolding the hinged metal brace, she set it aside. He read her expression. Back to business.

She was looking at him. At his pants, to be more exact. "Stand up. Hold onto the table for support."

He followed her direction.

She knelt and pulled upward on the zipper tab by his ankle. As he watched, her blond hair glided across the dark nylon of his ski pants. He fought the urge to run his fingers through it. His breath caught in his throat. He tried concentrating on the notes hanging on her refrigerator.

He drew a deep breath. Padded long johns next season, he vowed. Not thin, form-fitting underwear like the ones he was currently wearing.

Since his hands were occupied holding himself upright, Megan assumed command. Her thumbnails slightly grazed the skin at his waist before slipping beneath the correct layer of fabric. He closed his eyes. Padded in front. Padded with steel.

She had barely slid the ski pants over his backside when the front door opened. Other people present would be a welcome relief. He sat down hurriedly. The extra fabric bunched in his lap. Despite feeling out of breath, he managed a greeting. "Dave. Alison. Glad you finally arrived."

"I bet you are." There was the smirk he'd expected earlier.

Dave glared at Ali. Her smug grin transformed into an outright laugh.

Rey's silent plea for help got through to his partner. Dave crossed immediately to where Rey sat, heedless of the tracks his snow-covered boots left on Megan's wooden floors. "Let me help."

Megan lifted her chin. "I can manage."

"I'm sure you can. But has it occurred to you that some things are not cross-gender activities?"

She stared at Dave for a moment, then stood and turned to Rey. He couldn't refrain from nodding.

"Oh, for heaven's sake." She exhaled loudly, hands resting on her hips. "All right. Off with the pants, all layers, then hobble to the couch." She turned to Dave. "Cover him. When he's decent, call me so I can finish my job."

"I will." Dave stepped back and shoved his hands into the pockets of his coat.

"One more thing. That sofa pulls out into a bed. I want Mr. Harrison up here with me tonight. I don't want him negotiating stairs. You and Alison are bunking below. If he doesn't feel safe or wants a chaperone, tough."

She shifted her gaze to Rey again. "You got that?"

People didn't normally make decisions for him. Strange feeling. Memorable, the way her gaze intensified whenever the sparks flew. He nodded meekly.

"Good." She directed Dave's attention to the far wall. "The steps leading down to the bunk room are behind that door. Feel free to take your backpacks out of my entryway."

She turned on her heel and walked out of the kitchen. The door at the end of the hall shut with an emphatic slam.

Dave slowly unzipped his coat. "Wow."

"Wow is right." Rey smiled slowly. "How long are we staying?"

❄   ❄   ❄

Eric Mitchell slid the duffel bag from his shoulder. It was still snow-covered, despite his attempt to brush it off outside. He dropped it onto the closest bed.

The storm had raged for a good part of the day. At least he was dressed for it, not shivering as he'd done on the streets this past year. Staying at Grandma's house would be quite a change.

He flexed his right hand. The muscles were stiff, but at least today they were working. Maybe now that his primary mode of transportation was a snowmobile, the strength on that side would return. Strength was a secondary concern, though. Dependability was first. The lack of which caused continual nightmares.

He cursed. Self-pity could wait for later, after the mission. Unzipping a flap of the bag, he reached inside and withdrew a stack of jeans and T-shirts. The trappings of his new personality. Behind him stood an antique dresser. He shoved the clothes into an open drawer.

The room needed to look lived in, as if work occupied his every free minute. Grabbing an assortment of phony research materials, he scattered them across the quilted comforter. He tossed a pen on top of the mess. Each time he passed a window, he paused as if on stage. Darkness had fallen hours ago. The bedside lamp was switched on. Let them look. In a community this tight, word would spread. They would get used to his face and the sooner the better.

Snagtooth. The name amused him, reminded him of a cartoon character from his childhood, when life had been simple and the bad guys always wore black.

Two cabins were visible outside his window, across the lake. The residents would be chummy, living this far from town. Chatty. Dependent. Watchful. He was counting on his presence in Grace's house to generate some interest. If he did his job right, that could work in his favor.

After a final pass around the room, he strode toward the doorway. The hall was clear. His landlady was muttering to herself. Preparing dinner, from the sounds he determined to be ladle-hitting-pan. He closed and locked the door. Ten minutes, tops.

He pulled a phone from the outer pocket of his bag. Flipping open the cover, he sat on one of the beds and dialed. He used the wait time to pull the shade closed. The performance was over, for now.

Logan, his partner, picked up on the second ring. "Are you in position?"

"Yes. Clear view of the other two homes. Front doors face the lake."

"Survey the other exits?"

"Tomorrow. At first light." Scoping out the town had con-sumed more time than he'd allotted. But scripts were made to be modified, no matter how carefully prepared. He would orchestrate his movements closely until he was viewed as harmless. Eccentric, like Grace herself. It would take time.

"Any sightings?"

"This morning. One chopper. Our side of the border."

"Time?"

He had the notepad out and open. "Eight A.M." That was the great thing about teaming with Logan; they could read each oth-ers thoughts. Most of the time. Except for one huge, ugly secret. He flexed his right hand. The muscles were already stiffening. "What's on the air?"

"An avalanche. Routine. We're checking it."

"Add another item to your list." He stood and began pacing. "Remember the tickets I used last night?"

"Court-side seats, you dog. I would forget that?"

"A reentry perk. To assist me with the transition from the streets back into polite society." He smiled. "What can I say?"

"Go on."

"Guess who bought popcorn at half time?"

"Madonna."

Another smile. "Close. Cowboy, without the Stetson." Pausing in front of his duffel bag, he set down his notepad and pulled out a handful of rolled socks. "He was buying for a young guy in a wheelchair. Late twenties."

"He went all out."

"Sure did. They were with an older woman. Sixties."

"This lowlife has family? He's not a test-tube experiment gone bad?"

"Guess not."

His partner was silent for a moment. Mitchell used the time to pitch socks at the open dresser drawer from behind an imaginary free throw line. All air, no rim. Lucky he'd learned to shoot baskets left handed. He cradled the receiver. "Are you thinking what I'm thinking?"

"This could be the chink in his arrest-proof armor."

"Exactly. I'll fax you the pictures."

"We'll nail his identity. Researching the kid, too, might make tracing Cowboy easier, depending on how recent the boy's accident was. What did the guy have, a broken leg?"

"No. Our luck, he's a quadriplegic." Mitchell winced, rubbing his hand over his eyes. He'd become as stone-hearted as Cowboy. "God, did I really say that?"

"I got the drift."

Another entry for the self-pity list. Focus now on the drugs, the wasted lives. The rest could wait. "Look for records. Ongoing therapy. I'm sure the bastard spares no expense."

"Dry your tears, Mitchell. Cowboy's not on the list for sainthood. I checked."

Grace called to him up the stairs. Was she really bellowing the words beef stew? She'd warned him, as she laid down the house rules earlier, that there'd be no tolerance for tardiness. Nor for rudeness, sloppiness or untruthfulness. Three out of four wasn't bad. "Gotta go, partner."

"Tomorrow?"

"Yes."

He switched off the phone and tucked it into a bedside drawer. Once he set up the rest of his stage equipment, the phone wouldn't look so out of place. The aroma of fresh baked bread brought him up short. Too many years on the street. He followed the scent downstairs. Unpacking could wait.

❄   ❄   ❄

Lute glanced around the flop-house room. Cowboy hadn't uttered a word during their long flight across the Okanogan Forest. Instead of dropping him at the Lost River airstrip as usual, Cowboy had taken him to their base camp in Everett.

He'd find out why in due time, if he lived long enough. His boss didn't know yet that the skier had seen not only Rookie's face, but also Lute's. Maybe he suspected it. Maybe he had special plans for eliminating him, something less merciful than a quick bullet to the head.

He'd held out for one shipment too many, but had no one to blame but himself. His greed, and his god, were finally catching up with him. Forget those warm breezes off the Gulf of Mexico that he loved to dream about. Forget Cancun, the bikini-clad girls and the crates of fresh seafood. He would see his last days on earth right here.

The flimsy door to his room swung inward. A pock-marked man ten years his junior motioned for him to follow. Great. Now he had a fucking escort, after two full years of faithful service.

The bodyguard walked him past what could only be a coke kitchen. Saucepans sat on top of the stove, others were on the counter cooling. Plastic bags and wooden spoons lay scattered about. Yesterday's shipment was being converted to crack.

The chemical process needed nothing more than common everyday ingredients. Cooking it took twenty minutes and resulted in one of the most addictive drugs around. Probably the most profitable, too. Kids, like Rookie, were the victims.

A bottle of dark rum stood behind the pots on the counter. That meant some of the product was going to the cooks. Replacing all or part of the water with rum made better crack. Maybe it affected the taste, he didn't know. He'd never been a user.

"Stop gawking." Pock-face shoved Lute toward a long hallway, guarded by kids not yet past their teens. He trudged by them. Barely old enough to vote. Far too young for the assault rifles they carried. Glazed expressions and sniffley noses.

At the end of the hall, they shoved him through a partially open door. He landed knees-first on a tattered rug. The room was narrow, with a single high window at the far end. Cowboy leaned forward in his chair, elbows braced on an oak desk.

Lute scrambled to his feet as the door closed behind him. He brushed off his pant legs and waited for Cowboy to speak.

"We needed that shipment."

"Yes, sir."

Cowboy puffed on his cigar. "What went wrong?"

"No idea. Bad luck, running into that skier."

"I'm tired of accidents."

That makes two of us, Lute thought, but kept silent. His heart beat rapidly.

"What's our next move?"

Lute blinked. Not only was he still alive, but Cowboy was asking him for advice. Maybe he could still grab the stash and get out for good. Maybe he would taste that Gulf shrimp after all.

He cleared his throat. "I'll initiate emergency procedures. By tomorrow night, we'll have it in our hands. I swear."

"Have you fully communicated the plan?"

Lute nodded. "Weeks ago. At the point of my gun. Told Rusty to keep the huts clear."

Cowboy tapped the desk. "Then I'll hold you personally accountable."

Lute swallowed hard. He'd walked into that one.

"I'll stall the next delivery until you retrieve this one." His voice dropped to a whisper. "I hate schedule changes."

That was an understatement. Lute stood silently at attention while Cowboy leaned back in his chair.

"Tell me about the man who saw you."

"Not me." Oh, God. Did he know somehow? Lute tried not to stammer. "Like I said before, he didn't get a look at me."

"I'm trying to be reasonable." Cowboy leaned forward, slamming his fist onto the desk.

He flinched. Cowboy's tone was as sharp as a razor blade sliding across a glass mirror. Lute wiped the beads of sweat from his forehead with his sleeve. "He's dead. He's gotta be dead. And Rusty will bury it under a mound of paperwork, like he did the others."

"And if the man's alive?"

"We saw him go under."

"Verify it." Cowboy stubbed out his smoke.

Lute nodded.

"You'll need some help."

Scapegoat, would be more accurate. "No problem. I've been working that angle. Ahead of time, just like you said." Lute added a touch of certainty to his voice. Cowboy seemed to look for that. "There's a street punk who's been flashing too much cash lately. Been bragging about his connections. Bringing him in would satisfy his itch to be a big shot. Reduces our exposure, too. The punk's name is Billy. Perfect material."

"Will he be missed?"

Lute snorted. "Not a chance. We'll make him a great offer. Let him pick his own replacement from down the food chain." He grinned. "I'll even help with the final interview, so to speak."

Cowboy nodded and pushed a button on the base of his phone. The bodyguard opened the door. "Tomorrow night, then."

"Less than twenty-four hours, boss." Pock-face tried to grab his arm. Lute wrenched himself free. Cowboy reclined his chair again, watching him, this time hooking his thumbs under his belt buckle. From that angle his eyes were more visible than usual. "There's a lot riding on this, Lute. Come through for me."

Lute turned and left, shutting the door softly.

❄   ❄   ❄

"How can I help? Should I load the dishwasher?"

Megan glanced at Alison. "Do you see a dishwasher?" No written report filed. No target practice. Nothing to show for the day but three unexpected guests and dinner dishes. One injured, one helpless, one who drove her crazy.

She couldn't help but notice that their parkas, hung side-by-side on the coat rack, practically matched. Rey's was black with teal piping, Dave's had magenta instead of teal. Alison's combined all three colors. Cute. Triplets.

But it was the stylized mountain embroidered chest-high on each jacket that caused her to roll her eyes. It would have been less trouble if these bar bunnies had chosen a downhill resort, instead of wandering into her part of the Okanogan.

Dave's voice drifted from the living room. He'd been getting on her nerves throughout the evening: hovering while she checked her patient, offering useless suggestions, being a general nuisance. Was his role in life Rey's personal bodyguard?

He was by the couch again, about to sit beside Rey. Megan called to him. "Please bring the rest of the plates to the kitchen." Dave stared at her. She opened a drawer and tossed him one of Granny's aprons, just for fun.

Alison turned toward the sink, grinning. Megan sighed and handed her a sponge. "I didn't mean to snap at you earlier."

"No problem. I know we're underfoot. It doesn't help that neither Dave nor Rey is used to being idle." She smiled. "I, however, have tons of practice. After a day at the office, it's headphones and the couch for me." Alison ran the sponge under the water. "Why do you run a B&B if you'd rather be alone?"

"My equipment costs money."

"What's it all for?" Alison glanced sideways at her. "If you don't mind my asking."

"Biathlon." Megan shrugged. "A pipe dream. But it keeps me in shape, if nothing else." She switched subjects. "I know you and Rey are brother and sister, but what's your relation to Dave?"

"Talk about pipe dreams. Dave is mine." Alison shut off the water. "Someday I hope to have him see me as more than just Rey's little sister." She proceeded to wipe down not only the table, but the microwave and counters without any coaching. Alison might not know her way around the kitchen, but she wasn't a slouch.

Alison and Dave. Maybe she'd misjudged the young woman. She was funny, intelligent, and obviously returned her brother's affection many times over. She'd sat near him, cross-legged at the foot of the sofa bed, most of the afternoon. Her only break had been when the doctor stopped by. She'd made Rey laugh with one story after another, helping him pass the time. It just might take a woman like her to soften Dave's spine.

Megan allowed her gaze to move toward Rey. He was an excellent patient. Asked for nothing. Stayed off his feet, as she'd requested. Actually, it had been closer to a threat. Either way, he'd made the prudent choice.

When the clean-up was over, Ali asked permission to turn on the stereo. Soon she was swaying to jazz blues. Megan considered retiring to her room, but instead joined the group near the fire. She'd been anti-social most of the day. She'd try to put on a better front for the rest of the evening. The fire was dying. She knelt to stir the embers, listening in on their conversation.

"A fun Saturday night, big brother. You sure know how to show a girl a good time."

"That I do." He smiled.

She flipped another page of her magazine. "Say, didn't you promise me hot mulled wine by the fire?"

"If we made it through safely."

"Oh, I see. Let me get this straight." She lowered her copy of *Wildlife Today* and glanced at him sternly. "Since you only managed to go halfway down the slope on your feet, you think you're off the hook."

He nodded. "Something like that."

"Well, think again."

"Alison, don't badger him." Dave stopped pacing. "It's the last thing he needs."

Rey interceded. "It's all right, Dave. This is how we communicate."

Alison smiled sweetly. Dave glared at her, then stepped back.

Megan decided she could be sociable another night. Even if Rey didn't need a break, she did. She stood and set the fireplace poker aside. Alison's remark about her pipe dream came to mind. An idea formed, one she was sure the young woman would like.

"Our patient needs some rest." She tried to maintain a straight face. "Alison, maybe you two could find a way to pass the time downstairs."

Alison's gaze met hers for an instant before it moved to Dave. Rey yawned, as if on cue.

After a significant pause, Dave nodded. Alison stood and walked toward the pull-out couch. Bending, she laid her cheek next to Rey's. "Good night. If you need anything . . ."

"I know." He ruffled her hair. After a moment Alison stepped back. She joined Dave by the bunk room door and linked her arm within his. She winked. "Sounds like bedtime for us, Bonzo."

Dave's eyes met Rey's. Megan held her breath, waiting for an objection. Rey smiled. Alison waved a cheery good-bye and led Dave down the stairs.

Megan closed the door. The noise level dropped to zero. It would be at least an hour before she could dispense another round of pain killers. Now what? They could sit and talk.

She glanced toward the sofa. Rey was watching her. Suddenly the silence seemed intimate. She cleared her throat. "May I fix you something? Hot tea?"

"I thought you wanted me asleep."

"It's herbal. It will help you relax." That sounded inane, even to her own ears. He couldn't sleep with a mug in his hand. How could she think when he was looking at her like that? She'd have to settle for the truth. "Actually, I needed a break from your cohorts. Your next dose of medicine isn't until ten."

After a moment of silence, he laughed. "You're honest."

"It's just . . ."

He raised a hand. "No, it's all right. She takes getting used to." Smiling, he shook his head. "When Alison first moved in, she used to follow me from room to room chattering. I didn't mind. Still don't." He shifted his position against the pillow. "I listen as long as I can and let the rest roll off my back. Sometimes I forget the effect she can have on others."

It wasn't Alison, she wanted to say. The urge to correct him dissipated, though, as the true meaning behind his words sunk in. To be loved like that, for exactly who she was, with no other expectations.

"Do you have siblings to deal with?"

His voice brought her back. "Yes. A brother." She cringed at her error. Crossing to the far end table, she picked up the framed photo. She stared down at the picture. It was taken a year ago at Christmas. "Scott is three years younger. Next to him is Cynthia. We called her Thia for short."

"Your sister."

"She was the oldest." Megan swallowed as she looked at her, bundled in a university jacket. Thia wore the scarf Granny had knitted that particular Christmas. It coordinated with her school colors.

"When did she die?"

Megan glanced up. "A year ago next Sunday." She felt awful having left Thia out of the sibling count. But she really didn't have a sister. Not any more.

"I'm sorry." He handed the photo back. "I lost someone close to me, too. Twenty years ago. The pain fades, but the feeling of loss never really goes away."

"Who?" She wanted him to keep talking. To fill the awkward silence.

"My father. May I tell you about him?" He pushed aside the stack of magazines. Megan sat beside him on the bed.

Rey relaxed against the pillows and crossed his arms overhead. "Dad worked too hard and cared too much. He gave his employees flex time and job sharing before it was fashionable. He brought work home instead of missing a family dinner. And when he was in town, he tried hard to make it to my ball games."

"Heart attack?"

"No." Rey's voice was softer. It barely crossed the distance between them. "He was shot."

Megan drew a quick breath. "How?"

"During a rescue attempt." Rey closed his eyes.

Policeman? Security guard? Neither fit the nine-to-five office profile he'd just described. There were a million questions she wanted to ask.

"Ali was a baby. Mom couldn't face it. I was only fifteen and took on as much as I could. But I wasn't there when Ali needed me most." He opened his eyes. "I'm trying to make up for that now."

"It wasn't your responsibility."

"Sure, it was. That's what families are all about." He inched lower until his shoulders disappeared beneath the blankets. "I think I'll go to sleep. It's been a long day."

She stood, feeling as if she'd been dismissed. What was there to say after such a testimonial? That whoever wrote his version of The Book of Family Rules had never circulated a copy in Snagtooth? At least not where the Jeffers family could find it. She headed toward the kitchen. She'd leave the medicine bottle and a cup of water on the night stand in case he needed it later.

"Megan?"

She turned.

"You're a good listener."

Thank you, she wanted to say but knew she'd never be able to force the words past the lump in her throat.

THREE

THERE WERE MANY contenders for her concentration this morning, primarily the man who'd spent the night on her sofa bed. In the pre-dawn light, Megan had studied the long, dark lashes resting against his cheek. Heard his low, steady breathing. Could almost feel the beard-stubbled jaw. A man on her couch was quite a departure from her usual solitary existence or the loud groups that sometimes rented her cabin. Tiptoeing by him, she'd suppressed the urge to check his forehead for fever. But since he hadn't been running a temperature the night before, she really had no excuse.

Enough. Reminiscing further might cause her to veer off the trail by accident.

She crossed the make-shift finish line and let her skis glide for a moment. Several inches of new snow covered the trails, left behind by last night's storm. Shifting both poles to one hand, she quickly checked her wrist monitor. One hundred sixty beats per second. Well within the developmental endurance zone. Her arms felt good. Her legs, strong. She was back on track. So what if the first four kilometers had taken twenty minutes? No use fretting the slow start.

Poles back in position, she reduced her reach and stride gradually. The final stretch around Desolation Point had taken fourteen minutes flat, a new personal best. Concentrate on that. She would reload her clips tonight and attempt a combination run tomorrow while the momentum held.

She eased her pulse toward resting rate, a step she couldn't skimp on. Inhaling deeply, she allowed herself to enjoy the scenery. The early-morning sun highlighted the Okanogan's rugged peaks, casting shadows on the deep valleys. All was silent except for the slight whistling through jagged cracks and crevices. To her left the fresh snow swirled across the slope like small white dust-devils attempting an escape. Gliding past, she smiled at their antics.

South of her was Snagtooth Ridge, the town's namesake. Row after row, the indigo peaks stood brilliant against the clear sky. The strands of low-lying clouds would surely burn off soon and the solitude would be destroyed, as usual, by the slicing noise of chopper blades. She glanced skyward, her smile fading.

Where would the outfitters take their clients today? There was no way to predict the route. Most charters promised their weekend guests ten thousand vertical feet. That meant four, maybe five, runs per day. Thank goodness traffic slowed on weekdays. She was one ranger who looked forward to Monday mornings.

Executing a wide turn, she headed back toward the Vmax. Time to return home and check on Rey. What was it about having him in her cabin that made her want to slip off her shoes and relax by the fire? Maybe it was the warm tone she'd heard in his voice as he teased his sister after dinner, or the tenderness she'd seen as he ruffled Alison's hair. Both lingered in her memory.

She didn't want to like him, but his carefree manner and quick wit put her at ease. No other guest she'd hosted had ever had that effect on her. It would help immensely if she could pigeon-hole him as a footloose playboy and thus dismiss him from her mind. But she couldn't. Not yet, anyway.

He and Ali had the sibling relationship she had always wanted. The one she would build with her own brother if only he would let her. Maybe Scott would drop by later simply to surprise her. Right. That hadn't happened in months.

Her grip tightened on her poles as she drew to a stop. Actually, this evening would be bad timing for a visit. Russell was coming to question Rey about the two men he'd spotted with rifles. She'd suggested he drop by during the day instead. He'd seen through her ruse and specifically asked for a time when she would be present.

She'd seen the copter, too, but could tell him little about the accident, only the rescue. He could read her report if he were really that interested. She pulled off her ski hat and gloves and rubbed her temples. Enough about Russell.

Rey and his party would probably be with her for a while. She would broach the subject of how long when she took him into town later for an exam. Short of the doctor recommending an airlift home to Seattle, maybe Rey would consider canceling his other reservations. He could continue on at her place instead. After all, he was already unpacked. It made sense.

She glanced east toward Snagtooth. Sharing her cabin usually made her uncomfortable. Rey staying longer, though, didn't bother her at all. Having company would prevent her from facing the anniversary of Thia's death alone. The fact she was attracted to him, made it all the better. She quickened her pace back to where she'd parked her snowmobile, suddenly anxious to be home.

❄   ❄   ❄

The Okanogan was as beautiful as it was cold. Eric pulled the hood of his parka tighter around his face, thankful he still sported a beard. It had been a small but important part of his cover. None of the homeless he'd met would have confided in an addict who was clean shaven.

From his perch amid a cluster of boulders, west of Desolation Point, he could see forever. He raised his binoculars and scanned the morning sky. There hadn't been a sign of Cowboy's Canadian partner yet. He'd been in position since sunrise. The plan was to watch the drop, then move closer and observe the pickup by the Americans. In between there would be lots of time to wait.

Damn. Company. He scrunched down further behind the rock. There she was, sporting a rifle on her back. It could only be Megan Jeffers. He'd been expecting her. Her vehicle was parked at the edge of the open terrain near Desolation Hut. His was close by hers, but hidden in the trees.

Logan had warned him to stay out of her way until he had his research down cold. She was a sharp one. Would probably quiz him until he blew his cover unless he was prepared.

She sped by, less than forty feet below. Smooth, sure strokes. Long, powerful reach. Never wavering, never varying. All-out effort. She was so engrossed in exercise that she ignored the raw beauty around her. Rugged peaks reaching skyward so rough and steep even a mountain goat would have to reconsider. The sterility of the air seemed to cleanse him somehow. Maybe it would scour the filth collected in his soul.

He'd seen too many years of sitting on sidewalks, waiting for handouts as he listened to the street talk. Since a single lead could potentially put Cowboy out of business, he'd sat and listened, just as he was sitting again now. He'd ignored the greasy spoon cafes venting heavy steam on him, the street vendors who shooed him aside in order to set up business on his piece of turf. On some days, he could actually feel the edges of his heart hardening.

He'd never go back, a decision not solely his own. He flexed the fingers of his right hand through the layers of glove and insulation. Pay-back time. He'd nail Cowboy's organization and get on with his life while he could. Before any more harm could be done.

Jeffers raised her arms suddenly, letting her skis glide. Her actions resembled an athlete crossing the finish line. Hands on her knees for an instant. Then off with the gloves as she checked her pulse. He smiled. Her dreams must include gold medals. She turned the corner and glided out of sight.

The sound of an approaching helicopter focused his thoughts. He raised his binoculars skyward. He willed the pilot to turn the aircraft, wanting a good look at the logo. Only one other chopper had gone past, dropping off legitimate customers as far as he could tell. The Canadians were later than his sources had indicated. The chopper was flying extremely low, barely skimming the treetops east of Devil's Elbow. Then it headed north. Desolation Point.

He waited until the logo came into view. Mountain High Adventures. A pickup. Following yesterday's flight path. What the hell? Cowboy was changing his pattern. Eric kicked the rock next to him.

As the pain from that stupid reflex action registered, he paused. The chopper wasn't landing. Circled back, instead. Cowboy must have called off business at that particular hut for now. Jeffers' vehicle was parked much too close to chance a landing.

A small consolation, perhaps, but it would buy Eric additional time. Hopefully, before their next attempt at the same hut, Logan would come up with a theory as to why the Canadians had missed today. Because he, personally, didn't have a clue.

❄   ❄   ❄

Megan skied toward her snowmobile parked off the trail beneath the grove of spruce. As she approached, she noticed tracks leading from her vehicle into the trees. Strange. She hadn't gone that way herself. Though the snow field around her was pristine, the area close to the Vmax was trampled.

Great. Now she could add vehicle tampering to the list of headaches she was accumulating: low flying copters, avalanche rescues, a houseful of guests. She popped the hood latch and examined the small engine. Nothing seemed amiss. No bombs, no out-of-place wires. She was becoming paranoid. Maybe. Maybe not.

One more thing to discuss with the sheriff. She sighed, then began removing and storing her gear.

❄   ❄   ❄

She was barely through cleaning her rifle when there was a knock on the door. Megan wasn't expecting anyone. The cabin was crowded enough. Before she could answer, Rachel burst in, jarring two coats from their pegs as the door hit the wall.

"Good. You're here." Her friend rushed into the kitchen. "There's been an accident. Yesterday sometime."

"I know. I was the one who radioed it into the Control Center. Relax." She pointed toward the couch. "The skier is here, having coffee. Doing quite well considering the circumstances. Come on." She steered Rachel towards her guests. "I'd like you to meet them."

Rachel stood firm. "Listen."

Ignoring her, Megan introduced Rey and Ali. "Feel free to ask them about the avalanche. I'm sure they'd answer your questions."

Rey put down the trail guide he'd been reading. "We'd be happy to."

Pasting on a grin, Rachel put her hand on Megan's shoulder and dropped her voice to a whisper. "Listen to me, my friend. The man I'm referring to is dead." She tilted her head toward Rey. "So it's not likely him, is it?"

Dead? That had her attention. There were ski injuries each year. But death was rare. Except for Thia. Her heart pounded. "Where?"

Instead of answering, Rachel looked at her oddly. Megan was no longer sure she wanted to know.

"Let's discuss this alone." Her friend smiled at the guests. "Please excuse us a minute."

Megan allowed herself to be ushered down the hall and into her bedroom. After the door was firmly shut, Rachel turned. "The man was killed twenty-four hours ago. Sheriff Russell hasn't filed anything official yet. Details are being withheld for some reason."

"They could be looking for next of kin." She winced at the ugly, yet common phrase. So final. So impersonal. It stripped the sense of family, reducing the relationship to a statistic.

"No." Rachel stood in front of her. "I think it's more than that."

She put her hands on Rachel's shoulders. It was hard to react objectively, but they had to. "I'm sorry. For him and for his family. But the man knew the risks. That's part of being a thrill-seeking, back country heli-skier." She swallowed hard. "As much as we might want to, you and I can't change that."

"You're not getting it. Here, look at this." Rachel fumbled in her pocket and produced a photo then shoved it into Megan's hand. "This guy wasn't a fun-seeker. It looks as if he tried to commit suicide. Twice."

"That's not funny." Frowning, Megan rotated the snapshot until it was right side up. "Oh, my God." From the odd angles of his limbs and torso, she knew it had to have been a fall. From a ridge, judging from the depth of the snow around the body. The area didn't look ski-able, surely it had been roped off. Wait.

Her hand trembled. Devil's Elbow was in the background. It was distant, but recognizable. It was too familiar. Thia. Pete. A line of sweat broke out across her forehead.

"You can say a prayer of thanks that I took this picture before I removed this kid's helmet." Rachel grimaced. "The right side of his head was blown away."

Megan walked toward the bed, sat, and stared at the image. How could this have happened? He looked no more than twenty. Maybe not even that old. It was his hair, though, curling over the edges of his scarf that really got to her.

Her heart beat an unsteady rhythm as she looked up at her friend. "Thia's school colors."

"Exactly. Grandma could have knitted it."

Megan swallowed and stared again at the picture. Wanting to make sense of it. "They're common enough colors."

"Right." Rachel sat next to Megan. "Look here. Does that marking look like the top half of a 'J'?"

"As in 'Jeffers'? I can't tell."

"Neither can I, but it made my skin crawl anyway."

Megan shivered. The word murder was so ugly. So final. But there were few other options. Surely he hadn't jumped from the ledge and shot himself on the way down. Firing, then jumping, was also out of the question. This kind of reasoning was a waste of time. Think.

What could be so important in her one-road town to warrant a murder? It had to be an accident. She couldn't accept any other explanation. And who knew better than she and Rachel how easily accidents could happen?

Megan held out her hand, wanting her friend to take away the photo. Willing the memories of last year to fade again into oblivion, into the blissfully thick fog where they belonged.

Rachel stood. "Keep the picture. I have others."

"I don't want it."

"We'll have to ask questions. Given the location, there's a chance that someone might have seen the kid earlier in the day."

Megan had difficulty forcing her voice to cooperate. "Rey."

"What?" Rachel frowned.

"The site of Rey's avalanche was Last Chance Chute, right above Devil's Elbow. I thought you knew."

"I heard, but I didn't make the connection." Rachel looked toward the door separating them from the living room. "That guy on your couch hardly seems like the murdering type to me, though."

Megan straightened her back. "That's not what I meant. Rey, Dave and Ali were in the same vicinity. And earlier in the day, they saw two men with guns."

"Could be just a coincidence. It could also be a lucky break." Rachel snatched the photo from Megan. "Let's find out."

❅   ❅   ❅

When she opened the bedroom door, her three guests were watching her. Alison perched on the foot of the bed, Dave stood guard with arms crossed, Rey reclined against the sofa cushions. He didn't appear relaxed.

In general, Megan hated sugar-coating bad news, but Rey had been through enough in the past twenty-four hours. She would compromise by feeding the information to him slowly.

"Rachel leads the Snagtooth Rescue Patrol. The second accident was near yours." She paused to introduce Rachel to Dave.

Rachel greeted him. "Sorry we're meeting under these circumstances." She stepped forward and held out the photo. "Do you know this man?"

Dave glanced at Rey, who nodded slightly.

Strange. Why did a guy like Edwards, with a personality suited for running the world, need permission? Megan watched as Dave took the picture and studied it. Crease lines formed above his brow.

After a few moments he shook his head. "Sorry." He returned the photo. "It might help if more of his face were showing."

"Unfortunately, part of it was blown away."

Megan cringed. Rachel was known among the Rescue Patrol for her hard edge, but this was bringing out the worst in her.

Alison uncurled from her spot on the bed and stood. "He was murdered?" She was pale.

Megan stepped in. "For now, let's just say that he died. Until we know more." She touched Rachel's arm. "Tone it down."

Rey sat forward. "Maybe I should take a look."

Alison put her hands on her hips. "Rey . . ."

He watched her silently for a moment. "All right. Let's look together." Alison moved to stand next to him. She put her hand on his shoulder. He covered hers with his for a moment then accepted the photos from Rachel.

He was treating Alison as if she were a hot house flower. If someone did that to her, she'd set him straight. Megan paused. That was just a wild guess, of course.

Still, she couldn't resist butting in to some degree. "There's nothing in that picture your sister couldn't see on Seattle's nightly news. The city's jails are packed." Megan spoke directly to the younger woman, softening her tone. "I'm guessing that's where you're from. Am I right?"

Ali seemed to hold on tighter. Ignoring the photos for a moment, Rey looked up at his sister. "Seattle, Alison. Megan wants to know if you're from Seattle."

She nodded slightly.

Rey focused again on the top picture. "Yes, I've seen him."

Alison glanced at her brother. "When?"

"He was at Desolation Point yesterday."

"This baby-faced kid was the one who pointed the rifle at you?"

65

"Yes."

Megan had neglected to ask Rey about the gun-toting men he'd seen. She'd figured she'd wait and hear the facts tonight when Russell visited. Thia, again. Her obsession with the similarities to her sister's accident were impacting her ability to be thorough. "The sheriff will be by later. I'll let him know beforehand that there's been a twist in events."

Dave stepped forward. "We were concerned about the hut being locked. Desolation Point is supposedly open to the public."

"I've never known it to be locked." Megan turned to Rachel. "Have you?"

"No."

Rey tapped the picture. "All I know is that this kid, and the red-haired man with him, were at the hut. They left immediately after they saw me." His eyes met Megan's. "Now the kid's dead."

"You're sure it's the same person?"

"The scarf is easily recognizable, don't you think?"

Her heart seemed to beat in her throat, in her ears. Her head pounded from the noise. "He was wearing it?"

"Yes. At the hut."

"Did you see any distinguishable markings near either end? Something that might resemble initials?"

"I don't remember. He might've had it tucked inside his jacket."

"This entire conversation gives me the shivers." Alison walked toward the kitchen, her boots tapping against the wooden floors. "Mind if I make tea? Coffee? Anything?"

Megan called after her, trying to restore normalcy to her voice. "Help yourself. You'll find whatever you need in the cabinet nearest the stove." She accepted the photo back from Rey. Murder. In her woods. Where she practiced everyday. A scarf hauntingly similar to Thia's. There had to be an explanation.

"Let's not make too much of this yet." State the facts. Stop thinking about the what-ifs. Steady and logical. "Making a wrong turn while skiing isn't that unusual. Visibility was low yesterday."

Dave spoke up from across the room. "The kid wasn't skiing." He joined the group by the sofa and pointed to the photo still in her hand. "Look at his footwear. Not Nordic or Alpine. Common hiking boots." Dave leaned closer in. "The chopper reappeared just as Rey was crossing Last Chance. My opinion is they buzzed the bottom of the slope on purpose, causing the slide."

Megan glanced from one man to the other. "But why? You said that you were in the process of leaving."

"I don't know, but I wrote down the name of the charter. I can have it checked out." Rey reached beneath the quilt as if searching for his pants pocket. He reddened, then re-adjusted the covers.

Megan looked away. She'd been watching his actions too intently. Earlier, she'd seen the fleece pants that matched his sweatshirt folded neatly, under the end table on the far side of the couch. He must have been too warm under all the blankets she piled on him.

Rey continued on as if nothing had happened. "I'll get the name for you later. It was Mountain High Adventures, I think."

"I saw them, too, at first light yesterday. It's actually High Mountain Adventures." She frowned. "Didn't that group bring the three of you in?" She felt heat rise to her face.

Rey shook his head. "We flew in the day before. Private charter."

Megan watched him. "But I thought . . ." She swallowed. "Sorry for the lecture."

"Actually, I didn't hear it yet. I bet it's a good one." His grin was slow; his eyes crinkled in the corners.

She didn't let her gaze lower, didn't slink away. "I owe you an apology."

"And I owe you my thanks. Let's call it even."

She nodded and returned his smile.

Rachel stepped forward, clearing her throat. "If you two are through, we have an investigation to launch." She turned toward Megan. "You'll call the sheriff?"

Megan sighed. "I'll brief him today at noon. We'll be in town getting x-rays."

❋   ❋   ❋

Lute was almost to the Everett landing strip, heading back with Princess and four empty burlap sacks. Cowboy would be pissed, but there was no way they could have landed with a snowmobile parked that close to Desolation Point. Impossible. It would blow the entire operation. Surely Cowboy would take that fact into consideration.

Yeah, right.

Lute turned off his headset. His stomach clenched; he wanted to puke. The least he could do was ride the rest of the way in audio peace. He'd use the time to sit back and think about his miserable life. It might be his last chance to do so.

❋   ❋   ❋

Megan stepped onto the wooden planks in front of the Snagtooth General Store and checked her watch. Two P.M. She'd stopped by Sheriff Russell's but he had been on the phone. Waiting in the lobby for him to finish was the logical choice, but her dealings with the sheriff were seldom logical. A phone call would suffice. After all, she would see him tonight during the interview.

Though not avoided, the confrontation was at least postponed. She quickened her step. Rey would be at Doc Brown's for at least an hour. There could be no better way to spend the free time than with Jeri. They were long overdue for a heart-to-heart conversation.

Foot traffic at the store where Jeri Hurst worked was usually slow this time of day. Megan entered and glanced around. After waving to a few of the regulars, she pulled out a chair and sat at one of the small gingham-covered tables. The scent of burnt chili and over-baked bread filled the air. She smiled. Practically home. Granny's home, anyway.

Jeri emerged from the back room and after seeing her, made a beeline her way. "Megan. Hello. How's the morning treating you?"

"Fine." Megan smiled, then tapped her wrist watch. "Actually, it's afternoon."

"Already?" She brushed her bangs from her eyes with a sweep of her hand. "I'm rearranging stock in the back room. I guess I lost track of the time."

"Can you take a quick break?" Megan indicated the empty chair. "I haven't seen you since . . ." She changed course. "In such a long time." That was a good place to stop.

"I'd love to. My official lunch is in fifteen minutes. I'll check with Hazel to see if I can take it early."

Hazel Cooper, shopkeeper and gossiper-extraordinaire, agreed to let Jeri off early. Within minutes they were seated across from each other. After ordering a sandwich to share, the younger woman brought her up to speed on the happenings in Snagtooth. The recap took a full five minutes.

Afterward there was an awkward pause. Jeri broached the subject first. "So," she averted her eyes. "How is Scott?"

Megan waited until Hazel had passed by their table. She kept her voice low, her tone consoling. "You see him more often than I do. He still comes to dinner on Tuesday evenings, but other than that, we rarely cross paths."

"He stops in for lunch several times a week, but never says more than a few words." She sighed. "A month has passed since I moved out. We can't be together for more than a few minutes without him losing his temper."

"It's his problem, not yours. He snaps at everyone." She decided against pursuing that line of thought any further. "I usually overlook it. He hasn't adjusted to your leaving yet."

"That's not it." Jeri stared at the table. "I really can't say more."

"I don't intend to pry. It's his business. I'm concerned because it's had such a negative effect on him. He's dropped weight, has no interest in family activities. He's basically lost hold of those things that were uniquely Scott. Even Granny has mentioned it." She forced her shoulders to relax. "As long as he's not willing to accept help, he'll have to deal with it alone."

"And I'll continue to keep my distance." Jeri picked up her napkin and twisted it. "It hurts too much to argue with him."

Megan covered the other woman's hand with hers. This would be hard. "Please take this advice in the spirit that it is intended."

Jeri groaned. "I don't think I want to hear this."

"You need to. Waiting is not the right approach. You and Scott might never get back together." Jeri sat straighter in her chair; Megan rushed to finish. "Get on with your life. If that means another man, or another city, then so be it." She gave Jeri's hand a squeeze.

"I already heard a version of this from Mom and from Hazel. If Russell consoles me next, I'll scream." She smiled, though pain still showed in her eyes.

Megan kept the tone serious, not wanting to shelve the conversation just yet. "You were good for Scott, never doubt that."

She dabbed at her eyes. "Think so?"

"I do. And when he does reconsider, you may or may not be available." Megan added a touch of humor to her tone. "He'll just have to take his chances."

"Right." Jeri laughed. "There are so many eligible bachelors here in Snagtooth, I may be swept away any minute. Speaking of which, Rachel stopped by yesterday."

"Oh, no." Megan took a bite of her sandwich.

"She told me about the man on your couch."

Megan waited.

"Let's see. What was her phrase? A hundred and eighty pounds of testosterone, just waiting to recover."

Megan coughed and took a drink to clear her throat. "You might as well learn early in life, never quote Rachel. Not in public, anyway."

"You're not denying it." She scooted her chair forward. "It must be true."

"He's staying with me, yes." Megan dabbed at the corners of her mouth, trying to stall as Hazel passed by again. She couldn't think of one plausible thing to say. She stuck with the facts.

"His name is Rey Harrison. He's here in town with me today, having his knee examined. That's all. His sister and a ski partner of his are also staying with me. It's not as if we're alone. He's leaving as soon as he recovers."

Jeri appeared ready to ask another question. Megan cut her off by reaching for the bill. "I'd better go. I'm late picking him up."

"This one's on me." Jeri snatched the check from her hand. "And thanks for the words of encouragement. I needed them."

"Sure. I'll get it next time." Both women stood. Megan gave her friend a quick hug. "See you soon."

"I'll hold you to it. And as far as next time?" Jeri winked at her. "Bring your house guest with you."

FOUR

ERIC CLIMBED THE stairs quickly, knowing Grace's pot of water would boil in less than five minutes. In another ten, the spaghetti noodles would be ready. He'd have to hurry if he wanted to squeeze in a phone call to Logan without risking a demerit for tardiness. Grace's rules reminded him of elementary school. Somewhere she must have a wall chart and a packet of yet-to-be-earned gold stars.

He shook his head recalling the reason he was behind schedule. She wasn't the typical grandmotherly-type at all. Her impassioned stance on the government's plan to repopulate the Okanogan with grizzlies had run on and on. He would have to actually read some of those bogus research papers he'd brought if he hoped to hold an intelligent conversation with her.

He closed his door and dialed quickly. "Sorry for the delay. What do you have?"

"Whoa, not so fast. Did tea time set you back?" Logan's tone made Eric bristle. "Or were you and Granny watching Oprah?"

"Cut the shit."

"My, my. You're in a nasty mood. Maybe she should put more bran in her muffins."

Eric remained silent.

Logan sighed. "All right, so you're not up for humor tonight. Here's the scoop on Arthur."

"Who?"

"Arthur F. Turnople. 'F' as in fuck-head, is my guess. Alias Cowboy. You with me?"

"Finally." Papers rattled on the other end of the line.

"The wheelchair victim is a younger brother, Jimmy. The woman, Jimmy's caretaker Mrs. Dodge. A touching story really."

"Give me the condensed version."

"It happened over twenty years ago. Head-on collision. Both drivers died. Jimmy was the lucky one."

Eric refrained from comment.

"He's just been released from a foster home. Lived with a family called Dodge. Get the connection?"

He searched his memory. Nothing but Grace's bear facts came to mind. "No."

"Too much soft living. Get the doilies out of your ears, partner. Dodge. Mrs. Dodge?"

"Oh, right. The caretaker." He made a second note and underlined it.

"After his release from the hospital Jimmy went to live with Cowboy, who needed money, big money. When it started to pour in, he moved to a larger place and brought the old woman in to take care of little brother."

"Do you know where?"

"Of course. Nice digs. A big spread in the Mukilteo area."

"Selfless bastard." Eric frowned. "Wonder if little brother knows how dirty the money is?"

"That's the next step. We'll see if he's part of it. I'll send a couple of men."

"Wait." Eric switched the receiver to his other ear and picked up his hand exerciser from the dresser. "I'll go myself."

"No way."

"Hear me out." He began his routine. He tried to fit in three, maybe four sessions a day. He'd been told it might help. An awfully big might. "I'll use the local poker game as my excuse for going into town. I've been wanting to stick my nose into that anyway."

"Why? There are a dozen agents who would handle it for you. I'm one of them."

"I've been tailing this guy too long, Logan." He squeezed harder.

"Don't let it get personal."

It already was. Each time his hand failed to perform, the desire for revenge increased. "I want this one bad. I'm close. I can feel it."

"Correction. We're close."

"Right." He tossed his exerciser onto the dresser. "Send the plane. You'll be busy. I need you to check out something else."

"What."

"Remember the pusher I referred to as Curly?" He swallowed hard.

"You meet lots of punks. You fret over every damn one of them."

Eric refused to defend himself. Everybody dealt with senselessness in their own way. "This kid's the one who led us to Cowboy."

"Yeah I remember. Go on."

"Dead. They found his body this afternoon."

"How about the skier caught in the avalanche?"

"He's still alive. Staying at the Jeffers' cabin. Don't know his name yet. I'll snap the pictures; you run the trace." Eric paced the floor. "Back to the kid. He's dead but no one's looking for him. No noise on the airwaves."

"A hit?"

"That's my guess." He forced his tone to stay flat. "Most of his brains were blown away."

"I'll get right on it." Logan lowered his voice. "Are you all right?"

Eric's laugh was sharp. "Yeah. The ironic part is the kid's scarf was hand-knitted."

"Who the fuck cares?"

"Granny Grace made it. There's a tag in the corner that matches the quilts in each of the ski huts."

"How do you know?"

"I borrowed it from Russell's evidence box."

"The dead kid wearing Granny's scarf." Logan cursed. "What's the tie-in?"

"Don't know yet. That's what I'm here for, buddy." Eric glanced in the mirror and frowned. Dinner at Grace's practically had a dress code. He reached for his comb. "One more thing."

"I'll need a bigger notebook."

Eric grinned. Logan complained only when he was approaching the limits of his patience. Office work was getting to him. His partner was a good field agent, deserved to be on the front line. Unknown to him, they'd be switching places after Cowboy was brought in. "Check out the weather conditions north of here, as they were between six A.M. and nine. Anything that might have interfered with the Canadian partner's ability to lift off."

"You didn't spot them?"

"Not a blue bird in sight, except for Cowboy's half of the operation."

"Have any good news?"

"Fresh out." Eric bent his knees in order to see the top of his head in the dresser mirror. Since when had he developed a cowlick? "I don't believe in pattern changes. Something's up."

"Maybe you watched from a bad spot."

"Not a chance. I was sitting so high, I was looking down on Saint Peter."

"All right. I'll get on it."

Eric picked up a spray bottle next to the ivy plant. He unscrewed the cap, sniffed it and shrugged. His cowlick would soon be history. "Send the plane."

"Will do."

"Thanks, partner."

Logan sighed. "Be careful."

❄   ❄   ❄

Megan leaned forward in her chair and switched on the computer. While the machine booted, she retrieved a file folder from her bottom drawer and began composing her day's avalanche report.

It was past eight P.M. Russell would be here soon. She'd called him after returning home from town. He'd been pissed that she hadn't visited him in person to relay the news about the dead body. Hopefully his mood would pass before he arrived.

Too bad Rachel wouldn't be here, Megan could use her support. But Rach had her own report to do and her task would take longer. She had to describe the accident victim. Megan vowed to refer to him as that until murder could be proved.

The sofa bed creaked again. Rey must be restless. The aged mattress was lumpier than a mogul field and not nearly as exhilarating. Add to that a bed several inches too short for his six foot two frame and he had all the makings for a very uncomfortable night.

A knock on the front door rattled the glass. Russell. She sighed. Might as well get this over with.

She entered the living room. Rey was alone. Dave and Alison were still downstairs. He yawned and seemed instantly embarrassed.

"Don't worry. Sheriff Russell has that effect on most people." She smiled at him as she headed for the entryway. "We'll make this short and sweet, okay?"

He maneuvered into an upright position, propping the pillows behind him. "Should Dave and Ali join us?"

"No. They didn't see the victim or the other gunman."

"All right. We'll wait until Russell asks."

She paused before opening the door. "Stay with the basic facts. Don't let the sheriff steer you onto a tangent."

"Sounds as if you have him pretty well pegged."

"No one knows him better." She took in the expression of discomfort on his face. There was nothing more she could do. The second day was always the worst for sore muscles. The doctor's x-rays had confirmed nothing was broken. He'd simply have to wait it out.

She'd given him only half a dose of the pain killers after dinner, not wanting him to be groggy for the interview. Apparently Rey had been the only one to see the young man alive. Russell had a right to talk to him as much and as often as he liked, a privilege he would take full advantage of, no doubt.

Megan first checked the peephole, then quickly opened the door. "Scott, I was hoping you'd come, too." Grasping his arm she led him inside, ignoring Sheriff Russell standing behind him.

He pulled away. "This is not a social call. I'm here for official reasons." Scott stepped aside, allowing his superior to enter.

"That's right. We're going to double-team this one." Russell touched the rim of his hat. "Good evening, Megan. It's always a pleasure. I don't get out this way very often."

Thank goodness, she wanted to add. If she looked hard enough, there were still traces of his youthful good looks, his quicksilver charm and his quarterback physique. She made it a habit not to. She stepped to one side.

Russell followed her, standing only inches away. "No telling, really, what's involved in this one yet. It could get nasty." He leaned forward. "It could take a very long time."

"Nasty is exactly the same word that came to my mind. Coincidence, I guess."

"Funny." Sheriff Russell inserted a gloved finger between his teeth and pulled, freeing his hand from the leather.

She grimaced and took a step back. "You're late."

Russell lowered his voice. "Jealous of where I might have been?"

"Drop dead."

"Someone else already has." He raised an eyebrow. "I'd watch myself, if I were you."

"Don't threaten me." She glanced pointedly at her watch. "Let's get started. Rey, this is Sheriff Carrol Russell." He hated his name. She used it as often as possible. "With him is Deputy Scott Jeffers, my brother. Sheriff, Scott, meet Rey Harrison."

After pleasantries were exchanged, Megan excused herself and walked into the kitchen. Scott and Russell shrugged off their jackets and hung them on the back of the same chair.

"Over there, gentlemen." She pointed to the other coats, hanging on a row of hooks above the floor mats. Scott frowned at her as if embarrassed, but she didn't relent. He moved both jackets in silence.

The two men entered the living room. Russell stood to one side of the sofa, leaning against the mantle. Scott walked back and forth before the fireplace. She went through the motions of exchanging used towels for fresh ones as she listened. Rey waived his right to have an attorney present. From the corner of her eye, she noticed he was watching her.

"All right, let's get to it." The sheriff pulled off his hat and tapped it steadily against his thigh. His gaze narrowed at Rey. "Can you explain your role in this murder?"

Rey blinked, but kept his expression composed. "My role?" He paused as if considering an appropriate response, tapping his bottom lip. After a moment, he nodded once. "Victim, I guess."

From her hideaway in the kitchen, she tried to bite back her smile but was too late.

Not only did Rey notice, but Russell did, too. "A comedian. Megan, honey, you didn't mention that when you called." His scowl grew deeper. He tossed his hat onto a chair. "Deputy, take a note: possible hostile witness."

Scott stopped and retrieved a small spiral pad from his shirt pocket and flipped it open. "Will do."

She felt her back stiffen. She'd spoken to Russell many times regarding his use of deprecating endearments. Since there was an audience, he was baiting her again. She could take him on or leave it for now. Scott gave her a level look, as if to warn her. Fine. The interrogation would end sooner if she dropped it.

"Victim. Well, well." The sheriff's tone was mocking as he advanced on Rey. "The boy's the one dead, now isn't he? Looks like you're still alive."

"Yes, I am." Rey matched the sheriff's tone. "No thanks, of course, to the helicopter pilot who tried to bury me."

"Come on, now. Megan told me about that, plus your tales of locked shacks, vicious gunmen and mysterious aircraft. Here in Snagtooth?" Before Rey could speak, Russell continued. "Lack of oxygen at this elevation can cause disorientation. You sure this chopper story of yours isn't a fabrication of some fuzzy imagination?"

"I had neither hypothermia nor disorientation. Other than an old knee injury resurfacing, I'm fine."

Enough with the verbal warfare. Megan interrupted before Russell could fire his next volley. "Carrol, would you like something hot to drink while Rey tells you his version of what happened? After all, you did come here to listen. Right?"

The sheriff bristled, but kept silent. Megan took that for a 'yes' and turned to her brother. "What will you have, Scott? Decaf coffee or herbal tea?"

"Neither."

She entered the kitchen and opened one of the cupboards. "I usually have cocoa on hand for Rachel, but Alison finished that off earlier." She paused, wishing she could take back that last remark.

"Alison? Who's she?" Scott glanced around as if suspicious.

She gritted her teeth. That would keep Russell here for at least another hour. "Another member of Rey's group. Dave Edwards rounds the party to three. They're downstairs."

"Scott, ask them to join us."

"They didn't see the man." Rey tone was firm. "I'd like to leave the others out of it, if possible."

"You would? How nice. Scott, take another note. Attempting to conceal potential witnesses to influence investigation. Mark it as a possible obstruction of justice."

Scott checked the point of his pencil, then nodded. "Got it."

Megan was speechless. Russell was treating her brother like a lackey. He didn't object or even seem to mind.

The sheriff meandered across the room to stand shoulder-to-shoulder with Scott in front of the fireplace. They were nearly the same height. Each stood with feet slightly apart. Great. A united front of wayward male hormones.

"Can we get on with this?" After filling a coffee mug with tap water, she opened the door to the microwave and set it inside. "Time is ticking away."

Russell walked toward the kitchen. "We're trying to hurry, but first let me give your guest a little advice." After pulling a chair away from the table, he turned it backwards and sat facing Rey. "You've fallen into a pretty cozy set-up here, Harrison. You'd be smart not to jeopardize your position, if you know what I mean."

"I don't believe I do."

"Then let me spell it out for you. You can either cooperate or move your ass to the jail-house. Since I won't allow you to leave town until this investigation is concluded, those appear to be your only options."

"No problem. I'll stay."

The timer buzzed, startling Megan. Her heart pounded. Stay? For how long? Although the thought pleased her, it was unfair to Rey. She retrieved the mug and set it on the table, then shoved the jar of instant coffee in the sheriff's direction. "How can you detain him when you haven't asked a single question? I suggest you start or be on your way."

Russell picked up the spoon she slammed down. "I'm getting to it. What's your rush? He's not going anywhere."

"But you are." She smiled sweetly. It was as artificial as the saccharin in the packet he was holding. "Rey's next dose of pain medication is due in twenty minutes. When the big hand hits the twelve, you're out of here. Have I made myself clear?"

Megan turned to Rey. "Go ahead and start. The sheriff will interrupt only if necessary."

Russell scowled but kept silent as Rey told his story. Megan noted with appreciation his pleasing tone and precise re-telling of events. No wasted words, no irrelevant comments, no editorials. No matter how often the sheriff tried to throw him off track, Rey maintained a smooth, consistent story. He didn't lose his head as she seemed to do so easily when Russell was around.

Scott scribbled notes in haphazard manner, sometimes staring off into space. Megan peered over his shoulder at the page. What had happened to his handwriting? This stuff was barely legible.

When he'd finished, Rey sat back and listened to a barrage of questions. Who else did he know who roamed the woods with loaded rifles? Did he make a habit of trespassing? Ever ski on unstable slopes before? Then the clincher: had Rey shot the boy in revenge because of the avalanche?

Russell's tone said it all: he wasn't pleased. He'd have to work for a change. Digging up clues instead of spending his time harassing civilians. The revenge angle was a long-shot. She checked her watch. Almost nine o'clock.

"That's enough for tonight." She stood. "It's bedtime here."

The sheriff peered over at her. His expression was as black as yesterday's storm. She didn't back down. Finally, he stood. "I don't like it. Too many loose ends."

"That's why we have you. To tie them up and report back." Crossing to the chair, she picked up his hat and handed it to him. "Sorry. Bedtime around here is not negotiable. I have to be up and out at first light."

Scott tried stuffing the note pad into his pocket three times before he hit the right spot. His earlier irritability had eroded into drowsiness as the questions wore on. She preferred the latter, frankly. "Scott, would you like to stay over? The couch is taken, but there are still extra bunks downstairs."

That seemed to snap him awake. He straightened. "No, thanks." He grabbed his jacket.

His eyelids were no longer at half mast. He seemed better, but drifting to sleep while on the road was still a possibility. "Okay, but be careful. I'll see you Tuesday."

He gave her a confused look.

She stepped closer and lowered her voice. "Dinner, remember?"

He sighed. "I remember." Zipping his jacket closed, he glanced over to the couch, then at the sheriff, as if to make sure the other men hadn't heard.

Was he embarrassed? They were family, after all. No one should care that they shared this tradition. It was the only one they had left since their parents' death. All the rest had been abandoned over time, leaving gaping holes in her life.

Scott prepared to leave. Her earlier question still dangled in the air. A feeling of isolation filled Megan. Had he chosen not to answer or had the question already slipped his mind? She realized that she was holding her breath. "Scott?"

"Yeah?"

"About dinner?"

His tone was sharp. "I'll be here."

Her expression must have pressured him. Feeling as if she'd begged, Megan crossed to the door. She opened it. The night was cold, raising goose bumps on her neck and arms.

As Scott went out the door, Megan reached out for a hug, a handshake, anything. He kept on walking. She let her hand drop to her side. "See you." Her words fell on deaf ears. Stepping onto the deck, she watched his departure.

She turned, then stopped in surprise. Sheriff Russell was in her face, blocking her movement back inside the cabin.

"You'll be seeing me too, honey. I want a report on Harrison's activities every day. Delivered in town, in person."

"I can't. Maybe by phone."

"No, in person, or I'll be back out here. You can count on it."

❊   ❊   ❊

The driveway leading to Cowboy's private residence was long, narrow and unlit. Mitchell took the curves with great care. Logan had verified the location easily. Arthur F. Turnople's cover as a respectable, though eccentric, land developer made following him child's play. His house was a showcase. And since it had been entered in the Seattle Parade of Homes tour years back, his partner was able to pull the directions from the *Seattle Times* fiche library.

Why would a man with his sordid background put his hideaway on display? Showmanship, of course. Power. Ego. He'd most likely done so simply to spit in someone's eye, as he seemed to enjoy spitting in Mitchell's. At least that was how it felt each time Cowboy slipped through the traps.

He switched on his high beams and set the wipers to double-time as he slowly followed the slight incline toward the house. To his left, the property was thick with aspens; the right was open to Possession Sound several hundred feet below. Not a single tree cut the wind rising off the wide expanse of water. His grip tightened on the wheel of the black Buick to hold it on the road.

He wasn't in a hurry. Figured he had at least twenty minutes. One of his partner's contacts spotted Cowboy in an Everett restaurant less than an hour ago. The only road in and out of this secluded location was blocked off by a two car accident, thanks to Logan and the boys. No one would get through.

A triple car garage came into view. Time for the show to begin. Mitchell parked directly in front of a stone pillar then flipped on his dome light. He fussed with the contents of his briefcase, scanning for previously-missed price tags and stickers. He checked his pencil for lead and flipped through an oversized appointment book. Let the occupants of the house observe him for a while. Maybe they'd more readily lower their guard. He even hit the horn once with his elbow for effect. Finally, with his hair crisply parted and his dark-rimmed bifocals in place, he stepped out. He'd had to trim his beard close for this persona.

The door was answered on his third knock. The woman standing before him was easily in her sixties. He switched his briefcase to his right hand and extended his left. Hopefully that would be memorable and she'd forget his face. Plus, he didn't want to give away the weakness of his grip. "Eric Marshall. King County Medical." He

flashed a smile along with his latest business card, fresh off the printer. "How are you this evening?"

"Fine." She scowled and examined his attire.

"I'm from the Consumer Relations Department. We're checking on the quality of services rendered by our local health care
providers during the last budget period. This shouldn't take long."
He pulled an appointment card from inside his suit jacket. "Are
you Marion Dodge?"

She nodded.

"Is James Dodge at home tonight?' Interesting that little
brother Jimmy had taken his foster mother's name. Even more
interesting, given Cowboy's over-extended ego, that the name had
been retained.

Marion looked back over her shoulder, as if considering her
response. It was a stroke of luck the wind chose to gust that very
moment. She clutched her sweater closer to her chest, nodded and
motioned for him to enter. A trusting soul. He was in.

Eric quickly spread the contents of his briefcase over the surface
of her living room coffee table. Some of the forms were genuine, he'd
leave those behind. Most people simply tossed them out. But if
Cowboy did happen to see them, that would work in Eric's favor. The
more nervous the suspect was, the more mistakes he would make.
Just one and the trap would close.

He rambled on in a constant, non-threatening tone. Words
describing their current focus on excellence, interspersed with
enough medical techno-babble to cause her eyes to glaze over. She'd
cooperate. She'd want him gone before she fell asleep on her feet.

"Is this a good spot to interview Mr. Dodge?" Eric glanced
down the long hallway. "Or would another location be more
comfortable?"

"This is fine. I'll tell him you're here."

Perfect. As soon as she left the room, he stood and slipped on a thin pair of gloves. The living area opened to both the kitchen and the hallway. She could reenter from either direction, but if Jimmy were in a wheelchair as the files indicated, the narrow aisle in the kitchen wouldn't be her first choice.

With a quick glance toward the bay window, he reaffirmed that no one would be able to see inside. That section of house extended over the cliff's edge. He turned and chose the roll-top desk for starters. It was farthest from the entryway. That was good, since the search was illegal. After examining it, he knelt before an end table. Again, nothing.

The search was really secondary. He'd come here to meet the brother. To find out if Jimmy was involved. To ensure that Arthur was Cowboy. To establish how close the two were. Overall, to find the chink in Cowboy's armor.

It was unusual for a room to be so sterile. The bare hooks on either side of the fireplace indicated that pictures used to hang there. Except for a single wall-mounted case displaying brass belt buckles and an assortment of travel books below the coffee table, the rest of the trimmings were gone.

He straightened and returned to the sofa as voices grew louder, stuffing the gloves in his pocket. Eric picked up one of the photo books and thumbed through it as if he'd put his wait-time to good use. A snapshot fell out. Jimmy and Cowboy. Gotcha. He stuffed the photo into his pocket and flipped the book shut to view the cover. Hopefully it was a place he could speak of knowledgeably. Argentina. Strike one.

"Mom said you're here to see me. How can I help?"

Mom? Eric glanced at Marion. She stood behind the young man, as if ready to do battle if necessary. Surely Cowboy didn't think of this woman as Mom. Men like Cowboy didn't have mothers.

Eric picked up his portfolio and opened to a blank page. "I'm here to verify that you're happy with the therapy services being provided by the Outpatient Center."

"I am." Jimmy's smile was warm and open. "They take me in right on time and work me hard. I used to have nightmares about being parked in a corner somewhere, but not anymore." Marion laid her hand on his shoulder. The young man laughed. "And if I keep pace with the machines, my therapist gives me an extra ten minute massage." He winked and lowered his tone. "I try very hard."

Marion slapped his shoulder. "Enough."

"You're wrong. Never enough."

Eric couldn't help but smile. The accident might have damaged his limbs, but there was still plenty of spirit left in the boy. He ran through a few appropriate questions so that the interview would sound official. Time to move to the small talk that would naturally follow as he re-assembled the huge mess spread out on the table. What he'd really like to do was lose Jimmy's keeper for a while, so the man would talk candidly. Eric coughed several times, then asked for a glass of water. Marion reluctantly left Jimmy's side.

"I've been lucky. Mrs. Dodge, that's the name she asks me to use, loves me. That's why I call her 'Mom.' To let her know that her love is returned. And Art." Jimmy sighed. "He's not here, but I wish you could meet him."

So do I. With handcuffs, Eric thought. He kept himself busy shuffling papers.

"My brother seems serious on the exterior, but down deep he's just a jokester waiting to emerge. I think he'll lighten up after our move south."

Eric's movements stopped for a split second before he caught himself. He knew better than reveal himself through nonverbal clues. The book lying beside his briefcase caught his eye. He casually picked it up and tapped it, smiling. "This far south?"

Jimmy nodded. "I'm praying that it's warm there, though I think the place Art chose is in the Andes. I guess we'll be trading some of this rain for snow."

Eric set the picture book down and picked up his notes from earlier. "I should add this to our records. Do you have a forwarding address yet?"

"I never ask. Art likes to make all the arrangements. He wants to surprise me, I think."

Right. "Do you like surprises?"

"Yes." He smiled cheerfully. "Once when I was trying to find out more, I kidded him about wanting to spend part of my trust fund on a built-in swimming pool. He lectured me for days on what that money's for. I dropped the subject after that."

Jimmy was spilling information almost too easily. Was the boy lonely? He shook aside his pangs of guilt and pressed on. "Does Marion know the particulars?'

"I doubt it, though she's going with us." He shook his head. "Art continues to remind me she isn't family. The blood running through our veins is what counts, he says. She'll never be 'Mom' to him, but he knows I love her." He sighed. "I think he's missing out on a lot. He works too hard. It makes him cynical."

Makes him a mean son of a bitch, too. "When are you moving?"

"Any day now, I guess. Marion is already packing. Art says he's wrapping things up, relocating his office."

Shit. Eric looked at the bare walls again, then toward the kitchen. Through the doorway he could see several cardboard boxes stacked in one corner. He'd been searching through drawers while the evidence was smacking him in the face.

His watch alarm went off. Why not just be sharing hors d'oeuvres when Cowboy strolled in? He needed to call Logan. Correction. He needed to get the hell out of here, then call Logan.

Eric looked back at the young man, so full of appreciation for the little that life had handed him. Hoping his brother would relax and lighten up soon. Sorry, Jimmy, and hang on to that trust fund. Things will only go downhill from here for big brother.

❄   ❄   ❄

Rey leaned against the sofa bed cushions. The cabin was quiet except for the ticking of the mantle clock and Megan's movements in the kitchen. She'd wiped down the table, then moved on to the countertops. Now she was washing the single coffee mug, over and over. It was as if she were trying to eliminate all traces of the sheriff, all memory of the interrogation. She hadn't looked his way since her brother and Sheriff Russell left.

He'd been expecting her to bring over the bottle of painkillers soon after closing the door, since that was the reason she'd given to dismiss the two men. She hadn't forgotten, he already knew her too well for that. Only one explanation remained. She was avoiding him.

"Megan?"

She removed one hand from the suds, shook the excess water off and reached for her watch. Setting it back down, she called to him over her shoulder. "It's not time yet. Another five minutes." She remained facing forward.

Was it something he said? Had he been short with her brother? Rey looked again at the photo of Megan, Scott, and Thia on the end table. He'd noticed a second photo on the window sill, earlier today, of just Megan and Scott. Judging from the turkey and trimmings, they'd posed for it at Thanksgiving. But what year? Though Megan looked the same, Scott had aged substantially.

"Megan?"

"Yes?"

His heart ached at the sound of her voice. It wasn't angry or impatient. Instead it was flat. "When was this snapshot taken?"

"A couple of months ago. Thanksgiving." She still didn't turn to face him.

He peered closer, frowning. Scott was at least twenty pounds lighter now. He had dark circles visible beneath his eyes tonight that weren't in the picture, either. The kid was growing old at a break-neck pace. Something was wrong.

Was he sick? Tonight he'd appeared irritable, then distracted. Rey had wanted to shake him, to admonish him for letting the sheriff treat his sister in such a disrespectful way. But he'd kept his mouth shut. He couldn't defend her to her own family.

Not yet, anyway.

His eyes widened. The urge to protect her was unexpected. How absurd. Megan was the most self-sufficient woman he'd ever had the pleasure of meeting. Straightening out her brother would draw a reaction from her that Rey would hate to live with. He'd stake next quarter's profit margin on the fact Megan preferred fighting her own battles.

Rey sank back against the pillows, watching her. Her athleticism showed with her every action. Clean, simple lines. Economy of movement. And though she'd cleared the table with the same overall efficiency he was becoming used to, something was different. What was it?

He watched her again. Within minutes he'd pinpointed it. Her stance. Her shoulders, normally squared, were slumped.

Had tonight taken a harder toll than she'd let on? He hoped it wasn't the added burden of his staying with her. At least Dave and Ali had retired early with Megan's backgammon game in hand. It would be wiser to wait until tomorrow before standing, but he'd do it in an instant if she'd accept his help. His leg would probably hold his weight if he was careful not to twist the knee.

Megan leaned forward, propping herself on her elbows. Since he couldn't hold her and assure her that whatever problem she was facing would blow over, he would do the next best thing. He'd make her withdrawal to her bedroom as easy as possible.

"Megan?"

"Yes?" This time her voice broke. She cleared her throat and responded again. "Yes?"

"I'm going to skip the pills tonight. I'm practically asleep, as is." He faked a yawn and stretched out full length on the mattress. "Good night. See you in the morning."

Turning, she quickly grabbed a towel to dry her hands. "No, you don't." She reached for the familiar bottle near the back of the counter, then filled a glass with water. "These will help you rest, if nothing else." She crossed the room and placed the glass on the end table. Standing by the side of the couch, she shook two tablets into her palm and handed them to him.

Rey accepted the medicine, then looked up. The rims of her eyes were red. Her face was flushed. He maneuvered himself into a sitting position and quickly swallowed both pills. She handed him the water.

He sipped it. "You're upset. Was it something I said?"

She looked at him. "Of course not. It's Scott. What he's doing to himself. How he allows Russell to push him around." She shrugged. "It's hard to put into words."

"Then try these; your brother treats you disrespectfully." He softened his voice. "You deserve better."

"Thank you." She wiped the corner of her eye with her palm. "It's not the first time, of course, but he used to wait until we were alone. Not insult me in front of an audience."

"Sit with me a moment. I'm not as sleepy as I thought." He handed her the empty glass. "Last night you listened to me. I want to return the favor."

She took it from him and set it on the table. She was silent for a moment, then sat on the edge of the mattress. "You want a bed-time story."

"Yes. Tell me about Goldilocks visiting the Okanogan at the wrong place and time. How she made the owners of the forest cabin very unhappy by moving in unannounced and staying indefinitely."

She smiled. "You have a few of your facts confused."

"The truth is that tonight wouldn't have happened if I weren't here. I'll leave tomorrow." He was confident that with a few calls, he could be out of her hair in less than twelve hours. Corporate jets were like that. Nothing, if not convenient.

"Don't be ridiculous. The sheriff just said you're not going anywhere for several days."

"Was he serious?"

She nodded. "Don't second-guess him. I made that mistake once." She looked down at her hands, folded in her lap.

"Want to talk about it?"

"No."

He wouldn't press. First thing in the morning he would contact his lawyers. They were experts at business law, but he was sure they could recommend a good criminal lawyer if needed. He'd find out his options, in case he decided to move quickly.

She looked up and met his eyes. "You can stay here as long as it takes. I have plenty of room."

"You told Ali that you hate company. The extra workload."

"It's not so bad. I'm getting used to having you here." She blushed. "All three of you."

"Even Dave?"

She laughed. "I must admit, Dave took a bit longer to adjust to than the Harrison siblings. I'll extract my revenge by charging him double." She leaned forward. "I'll share a secret with you. My impatience with him stems from the fact I'm used to doing things my own way. I've lived alone for a long time."

He covered her hands with one of his. "You're not alone now." He hadn't meant for his voice to turn raspy. He hurried to cover up the implication of his words. "You have a house full of us. When we're gone, Scott will come around. Family is important."

She looked away.

They had nothing in common. She was as tied to this backwoods world as he was to corporate yuppie-dom. Oil and water. It could lead to nothing.

Releasing her hand, he settled down into the mattress and closed his eyes. "Sweet dreams, Megan."

He didn't know how long she sat by his side. But what he did know was that he felt her presence long after he drifted off to sleep.

❄   ❄   ❄

Sheriff Russell pulled open his desk drawer, tossed in his mechanical pencil, then slid the drawer closed. Enough paperwork for tonight. He should have gone home after the interview at Megan's but he knew sleep would be a long time in coming. She had that effect on him. And roaming around that firetrap of his would merely depress him further.

His olive green living room couch was pre-World War II era. The three-legged end table next to it augmented the ratty decor. The marbled Formica top on the dinette table had chips and cracks large enough to lose chili bowls in. How had his parents coped? He should have given it all away, as he did their clothing. Started over as his sister did by fleeing to Seattle. Yes, Betty was the smart one.

He reached for a cigar, struck a match and inhaled slowly. The tip glowed red in the dim office light. Leaning back in his chair he raised his boots to his desk. He loved this particular vice of his. Who said that being sheriff meant sainthood?

He knew he was far from being anyone's model hero. Megan would be the first to testify to that. She hadn't forgotten. She would never speak of the incident, that would incriminate herself. But he could see in it her eyes. He heard it in her voice tonight as she taunted him with his given name.

There'd been a time when she found him attractive. He'd felt it. Not during his high school jock days, of course. She'd been barely out of diapers at the time. But recently. Three years ago, in fact.

He'd returned to Snagtooth and run for sheriff under the banner of Home Town Boy. She had looked at him from the sidelines with curiosity in her eyes. He could kick himself for choosing her vain sister instead.

Thia, Superstar. He'd hoped some would rub off on him by mere association. Fat chance. She hoarded it and paraded it when it suited her purposes. When it came to using people, she had fewer scruples than he.

Emptiness clawed at his gut. He had loved Thia despite her flaws. Or because of them. Kindred souls recognizing one another, that sort of thing. He grimaced. What did that say about him?

After readjusting his jeans, he inhaled deeply a second time, trying to capture the peacefulness of a few moments ago. He held it, letting the smoke escape in a single ring. It hovered over head, then dissipated as it reached the ceiling. Simply disappeared, as if it had never been, just as Megan's feelings had a year ago.

The phone rang. He glanced at the handset. His private line. It could be only one person this late at night. He grabbed the receiver on the third ring. "Sheriff's office."

"You're up late." The voice on the other end was muffled. "Expecting this call?"

"No." He took another pull on his cigar. "I find that it pays to keep my expectations low and my guard up."

"Smart man. Must be how you rose to such an exalted position."

"Could be." Russell swung his feet to the floor. "It's midnight. You called to discuss my illustrious career?"

"No. There's been trouble out your way."

Another puff. "I'd say that a dead body fits into that category."

"Only one?"

"Yeah. As far as I know."

"Word has it, there was an avalanche, too."

"Correct, but the body was found nearly a mile from there." He drummed his fingers against the desk. "The boy's death and the slide are not related. Coincidental, at best."

Silence.

His pulse began to accelerate as the moments ticked by. The muscles in his neck tensed. "Damn." He stood and ground his cigar into the ash tray.

"That's right."

"It never crossed my mind."

"Then you have shit for brains."

He suppressed the urge to kick his desk. "Now what?"

"You have procedures, don't you?"

"Of course. I've already interviewed the accident victim." Crossing to the window, he leaned against the frame and ran his fingers back through his hair. "I'm detaining him for the sake of appearances. A 'revenge' theory: the boy pulled a gun on Harrison earlier, was also in the chopper when the avalanche was triggered, Harrison went after the boy for revenge. It's thin but it'll work."

"Plan a second visit. A last visit."

"But he knows nothing." Why risk it? The guy was harmless. "Do it."

The caller's tone turned Russell's blood cold. He stared into the night, trying to squelch the nausea rising to his throat. The street lamps cast a sickly yellow glow on the snow-covered boardwalk. A pack of mongrels must have chosen to relieve themselves there all at once.

The small town feel-good facade was beginning to crumble. Ugliness was seeping in through the cracks. Soon it would be exposed. The virtuous people of Snagtooth, how many would be able to start over?

He frowned. Someone was out for a stroll. The man passed the black-curtained windows of the shop adjacent to the General Store without a pause. Good. No one got into that area without an invitation. Checking out the newcomer was imperative, but he had more pressing demands at present.

He turned away. "These things take time." His voice didn't sound like his own. That shouldn't surprise him, though. He was no longer his own person. "Give me a few days."

"You have exactly one. We've already tried for the shipment twice. A parked snowmobile got in our way this morning."

Megan's. He'd seen someone messing with it yesterday morning near Desolation Point. He'd wanted to follow the man but was running behind schedule. Hadn't mentioned it to her, didn't want her asking too many questions, such as why he was there in the first place.

"Keep the ranger out of our way."

The line clicked off; the dial tone buzzed in his ear. Russell slammed down the receiver. He was in deep, and drowning.

FIVE

THE STAIRCASE DOOR creaked as Alison pushed it open and entered the living room. Rey glanced up from the magazine he'd been perusing since first light. "You're up early."

"Dave snores." A smile lit her face. "I can't wait to tell him."

"I bet."

Ali sat on the foot of the mattress and crossed her legs. "What are you reading?"

He showed her the cover, keeping his thumb inside to mark his place. "*Backwoods Habitats*. Before that, *Hunting Today*." He indicated the second publication by his side. "Kind of a naturalist's version of Lifestyles of the Big and Hairy. Hard to say which is my favorite."

"Nice." Rey watched as she struggled to keep a straight face. "Not exactly the business section of the *Seattle Times*."

"You're right. A few more pictures, if nothing else."

Actually, it was the Biathlon News that had really grabbed his attention. He knew next to nothing about the sport. The women's competition was a relative newcomer to the Olympic Games, a sporting extravaganza that had always held his interest. The magazine was a true eye-opener. He especially enjoyed the article describing the rigorous training and precision demanded of the athletes.

One of the bulletin's advertisements had a close up picture of a biathlon rifle. The sights mounted above the stock resembled the rifle leaning against the fireplace.

Ali touched the mattress and grimaced. "Boy, you've had it tough. Quite different than your waveless waterbed. Did you sleep at all?"

He nodded and took a sip of coffee. "I'm fine. How were things below?"

"Great." She leaned back, propping herself on her elbows. "I passed on sleeping in the bunks. So did Dave. We each picked one of the single beds." She yawned. "Megan has a great setup down there. Not too much privacy. By the way, where is our landlady this morning?"

"She's gone for a morning run." Megan had attempted to slip out around five without waking him, but he was a light sleeper. The memory of her tiptoeing across the room in her socks, easing the refrigerator door open and quickly unscrewing the inside light bulb, brought a smile to his face. When she placed a thermos of coffee next to his bedside he thought he was in real trouble. He'd pretended to be asleep, peeking only once or twice at her form-fitting body suit unobserved.

It wasn't until she went outside, bagel in one hand and boots in another, that he'd wanted to call her back. He never meant for her to change her normal routine on his behalf. And stepping into snow on the front porch wearing her ski socks had to be out of the ordinary.

Dave's footsteps on the wooden stairs drew his attention. The decision Rey had made in the pre-dawn hours would thrill Ali and most likely push Dave's patience to the limits.

"Good morning." He signaled for Dave to pull up a chair. "I've revised the trip plan."

"Good. I've been considering a few alternatives, too." Dave sat down. "Right now we're two days behind schedule. On Tuesday evening there's a meeting I can't miss."

"I know. I took that into consideration." Rey set his cup on the end table. "I can't leave, but I want you two to go on ahead. Complete whatever testing you can before you fly home late tomorrow."

Ali grinned, but Dave's face registered shock. "Without you?"

"You can handle it." Rey gave him a half-smile. "I was merely along for the ride, anyway. You're the mountaineering expert."

"But you're the one who desperately needed a vacation."

"I'm having one." Rey waved his hand over the sofa bed. "See?"

"Right."

"Stop arguing, Dave. Rey's onto something here."

He'd guessed that Alison would like the idea. "I know it's not what we had in mind, but still the change of pace is relaxing for me. I'll be back on my feet in a day or so."

"Was Megan open to the idea of your staying longer?"

"I haven't asked her directly. Thought I'd discuss it first with you."

After what appeared to be a split-second deliberation, Ali grinned. "I guess it's settled." She stood and approached Dave. "Spit it out. Do you have a problem with the arrangement, Edwards?"

"No."

"Don't want to spend a couple of days alone with me?" She raised her chin. "Well, maybe you're not the best of company, either."

"I said it was fine."

"Good. Then bring your coffee and let's get packing." She headed toward the connecting door. Her footsteps thumped heavily down the stairs.

Dave exhaled, running his fingers through his hair as he watched Ali depart. Rey adjusted the pillow behind him and tried not to smile. The silence stretched between them.

"There's really no other choice, Dave. You've got commitments you can't miss and she'd only drive herself crazy staying here, getting under Megan's feet. I'm enough of a disruption."

"I said it's not a problem." Dave leaned back against the chair. "I know that Megan rents out her place. Are you sure she has enough room for you to stay indefinitely?"

"First, I should be here no longer than a week. If Sheriff Russell has ideas of detaining me further, I'll get our lawyers involved. Second, I assumed Megan had space available when she volunteered to house us." He reached for a three-ringed notebook on the shelf beneath the end table and opened the first tab. "But since then, I found this."

He showed Dave the computer printout. "No reservations until next weekend." He pointed to the notation on the document's bottom left hand corner. It was yesterday's date.

"I guess you're set, then." Dave stood.

"Not quite." Rey cleared his throat. "Would you say the downstairs sleeps five?"

"Seven. All one room."

"I was curious because I have a favor to ask." He hesitated, remembering the detailed equipment log he'd found in the back tab of Megan's notebook. The bottom line was significantly in the red. The cabin rental revenue appeared to be Megan's primary means for offsetting her biathlon training.

"Jot down this number for the hut-to-hut system." Rey pointed to the top of the empty guest list page. Dave pulled his glasses and a pencil from his pocket. "Make my reservation official. Guarantee it to the company card. Register me as Harrison."

"Sure." Dave noted the number, then glanced up. "Entire cabin?"

"Yes. I have an uneasy feeling about the sheriff. Her brother, too, as bad as that sounds. But there's more to it." Rey frowned. "I want to stay. The man who died was one of the two I saw with the chopper. I want to follow it through until his death is explained."

"It's your decision. But is any part of it related to wanting to protect Megan?"

No one else leveled with him as Dave did. Still, he had to follow his instinct. "Yes."

"Then I would tread lightly. It's my guess that she's used to caring for herself. She might not accept your taking over that task as easily as Ali did."

Rey had never considered the fact that Ali might object. Someday maybe, but right now she needed him. He looked at his partner. "Your advice has been heard and duly noted. If Megan throws me out, you're absolved of all downstream guilt."

"Good." Dave folded the slip of paper and put it into his pocket along with the pencil. "Anything else?"

"Watch my in-basket for me. If there's anything urgent, send it to me via the Internet. Megan transmits her daily reports to the office. I'm hoping she'll let me use her modem."

Dave nodded. "Sounds like a plan. Just don't get too comfortable." He picked up his coffee and moved toward the door. "Ali and I will be on our way within the hour."

Rey shook his hand.

A noise from below caught his attention. He tilted his head toward the staircase. Drawers were being closed and bags were being unzipped. Ali was humming as she packed. Rey's smile widened. "Good luck."

"Thanks." Dave drew a deep breath. "I'll need it."

❋   ❋   ❋

The dual set of ski tracks near the front steps caught Megan's attention as she approached her cabin. Visitors? She wasn't expecting any. If Sheriff Russell were out for some early morning harassment, he would have arrived by snowmobile, not on skis. Unless, perhaps silence was a desired effect.

There went her imagination again. She pulled her vehicle alongside the shed and glanced at the porch. The stack of boots and skis she'd set there last night were gone. Her anxiety increased. She parked, dashed for the house and flung open the door.

While kicking off her boots, she noticed the sleeper sofa was reassembled. The throw pillows had been returned to their original position. He was gone. She walked over to the couch and picked one up, hugging it to her chest.

The curtains were drawn back off the bay window. She looked out, hoping to catch a glimpse of him. There was nothing left but his departing tracks. Soon the wind would sweep them away. She didn't care. Of course not. She reached for the radio, needing to fill the silence. There was a noise downstairs. Water running?

She paused and looked at the coat rack. A single ski jacket remained. All three visitors had worn similar clothing, but this particular teal stripe she remembered. She hoped that Mr. Harrison was feeling better this morning. His own comfort was about to end.

Megan walked toward the connecting door. The downstairs water was no longer running. She descended the stairs quickly, then stopped and took a breath. Rey had emerged from the bathroom in a cloud of steam, towel-drying his hair. What he was wearing or rather, not wearing, was memorable. Black satin boxers. There was bare skin, lots of it, above and below.

Her throat went dry. He wasn't aware of her presence. The damp curly hair on his chest narrowed as it disappeared beneath the elastic waistband. He had biceps an athlete would die for, not to mention thighs. She wanted to touch him.

Swallowing, she reached behind her for the banister, unable to look away. How could she have thought of him as an invalid? Had she really insisted, that first day, on helping him remove his pants? She blushed at the thought.

He turned toward the single bed and began drying his upper body. The silky fabric once again drew her eye. She'd never wished before for static cling. The nurturing instinct faded, replaced by curiosity. Had he lain beneath that quilt all evening in something equally scanty? She was glad she hadn't known.

She stepped back, thankful her feet were encased only in socks. How embarrassing to be caught gawking. The stair creaked. Rey spun around in a karate crouch. She fell back against the steps as he pivoted on his left foot. His eyes were hard. His right leg was about to kick her in the face.

Recognition set in. "Damn." He straightened. "What the hell are you doing here?"

"I live here." This was not the same man she'd tucked into bed the last two nights. Her grip tightened on the hand rail.

He bent and picked up the wet towel. His features softened as he looked at her. "I almost hurt you."

"No kidding. Another moment and there would have been footprints across my nose."

"Sorry." He rubbed his left knee. "I think I overdid it."

"You were supposed to be resting."

"I know." He smiled. "Are you okay?" His expression was once again the warm and inviting one she remembered. Amazing transformation.

She really didn't know anything about this man. He'd been gentle and sympathetic with her, tender and playful with Ali, respectful and engaging with Dave. Now he'd shown her a different side of his personality.

Maybe he was no threat, but she'd been fooled before. She'd only been attracted to one other man and that had been a disaster.

He reached out and covered her hand with his. "Forgive me."

Pulling away, she edged onto the second step. "I thought you'd left. Your equipment was gone." She saw the boots near the door, the skis upright in the corner. A single set.

"Dave moved those inside for me."

"Is he out skiing with Ali?"

"No. They're gone. He had a commitment for tomorrow night. Ali was getting cabin fever. I sent them home."

Alone. She and Rey and his tiny black boxers would be alone. She needed more breathing room.

He looked at her. "You're shaking."

"It's nothing." She backed up the stairs. "Do you want lunch?"

"I'll put some clothes on and be right up."

She nodded and fled.

❋   ❋   ❋

Forget food. She couldn't possibly eat when her system was pumping this much adrenaline. Megan jotted a quick note for Rey, complete with solo lunch instructions, then grabbed her jacket. Hopefully he would accept her explanation. She closed the front door, hurried down the steps and started her snowmobile.

Breathing room was on the top of her list. As she sped along the path, she filled her lungs with the crisp, cold air.

She knocked six times before Rachel's door opened. Normally she would have given up after three, but there was not a chance her friend was out. Rachel's evenings were devoted to clashing with the outside world. The male population of Winthrop, to be exact. It was the latest strategy for dealing with her husband's death. At this hour of the morning, she'd be in.

Rachel peeked out from behind the door, still dressed in a fleece bathrobe. Her dark hair was matted at the crown and the ends were pointing every which way. Snow swirled in, covering her bare toes. She stood there calmly, yawning, not bothering to look down.

Megan glanced at her watch. Nearly noon. "Skipping practice again?"

"I overslept."

"You'll get fired."

Rachel's grin was accompanied by a casual shrug. "So I'll live off Pete's life insurance. No big deal. That's what it was for, right?" She waved her inside and closed the door. "It's the only goddamn thing he left me."

She followed Rachel into the kitchen, hurting for her. After removing her coat, she picked a spot at the table. Rachel leaned sleepily against the counter. Megan folded her hands on the place mat and gentled her tone. Arguing would serve no purpose. "I don't want to sound like a nag."

"You already do, so stop." She covered her yawn.

"It's not as if you hate working with the Rangers. You thrive on it. Rescuing people, saving lives."

"That's you, Megan. Not me." She gripped the counter behind her. "Believe me, my passion for the ice and snow died over a year ago. I can show you the precise spot, in fact."

"No thanks."

"I thought not." Rachel sauntered over to the kitchen table. Pulling out a chair, she dropped into it. "Wake me when the sermon is over." She folded her arms and rested her head on them.

Megan sighed. Her friend had mostly good days, but this wasn't one of them. She talked about Pete often, but nothing of any consequence was ever said. Just pokes and jabs at some reprehensible behavior pattern, a side of him that Megan had never seen.

It wasn't as if Pete had been a stranger to Megan. Sometimes they'd played three-handed Hearts together late into the night. Laughter had been plentiful, no matter who ended up with the most points. Did Rachel blame him for dying young? Did her bitterness stem from that?

She placed her hand on Rachel's elbow. "Time to move on. This is eating you alive."

"Tell me something new." Her voice was muffled against the table.

"Maybe counseling."

"Screw that." She lifted her head. "You're a fine one to talk."

"We're discussing you, not me."

"Let's switch."

Her grip tightened. "Damn it, Rach, what if there were an emergency? You couldn't save anyone in this condition."

"I know my limits. Find another pulpit. This one's closed."

Megan drew back. They'd had this conversation before. Shaking her wouldn't help. Standing on the sidelines and simply watching, though, wasn't an option between friends. "It's got to stop."

Rachel watched her for a moment. When she finally spoke, her words were unsteady, her breathing ragged. "The memories. When do they stop?"

Megan shared her pain. It reflected the chasm in her own soul. "You can't fill the void with drinking and dancing."

"Says who? I'll try harder."

As usual, her friend was trying to divert the conversation with sarcasm. This time, Megan wouldn't let her. "It won't bring him back."

"Back?" Color rushed to Rachel's cheeks. Her eyes widened. "Is that what you said?"

Megan nodded.

Sitting forward, Rachel placed one clenched fist against the table. "After what he did?"

"It wasn't his fault. Accidents happen."

"Some accident."

Megan heard the harshness in her tone. She covered Rachel's white-knuckled fist with hers. "You and I know better than anyone that Pete and Thia loved living on the edge." She lowered her voice. "I am the one most to blame."

Rachel shook her head slowly. "You have no idea, do you?"

"Neither of us were there that day, but I can imagine a dozen scenarios."

"So can I." Rachel cupped her hands around her face, as if to hide from the conversation.

Megan tried again. "What if . . ."

"Case closed." Her voice was muffled. "Lay off, before I say something I shouldn't."

Nodding, she dropped the subject, respecting her friend. She was a private person herself. That's why the gulf in their relationship was so painful. Rachel had been the only one to whom she'd revealed any of her personal life, the first she'd trusted to listen nonjudgmentally.

She'd been right on with her choice and now missed having a confidante, a fact she kept to herself. Rachel was too busy reassembling the pieces of her own life to be concerned about Megan's inability to deal with death.

Rachel lowered her hands, looked across the table and sighed. "I appreciate your caring about me. It's something I count on." Before Megan could respond, her friend switched gears. "What brought you over this morning? Did the hoards of company drive you away?"

More avoidance strategy. She allowed herself to be led in that direction. It was the subject that had originally drawn her here. "Actually, the crowd has dwindled down to one. The others are gone."

"Where?"

"I didn't think to ask."

Rachel set her cup down, laughing. "Well, good for you."

"What do you mean?"

"Simply, that a gift is a gift. No explanation needed. If you're interested in him, go for it. Have fun."

Megan lowered her gaze, staring at the mat. "I came here for the He'll-Be-Too-Much-Trouble lecture." She traced the pattern with her nail. "It would help me considerably if you would stick to your normal script."

"Screw that. I think this guy might actually be good for you."

She looked up. "You're kidding, of course."

"No." Rachel shrugged. "I like him. Not sure why. Maybe it's the way he discussed the accident with us so seriously. Or his gentleness with his sister. The obvious respect of his friend." Her tone turned playful. "It could be the way his gaze never left you. How his expression warmed without needing to smile."

"Stop it."

"He's definitely interested."

Megan diverted her eyes. There was no way to stop her cheeks from flushing.

Rachel leaned back in her chair. "Well, well."

"What?" It was obvious Rachel wasn't through harassing her yet.

"You're also interested."

No use denying it. No way she'd admit it, either. "Maybe."

Megan stood and walked toward the front door. Rachel's voice came from behind her.

"Tell me why it's a problem."

She looked out over the landscape in the direction of her cabin. "He's merely passing through. Will be gone in a matter of days."

"Seattle's not that far."

"I'm saving my heart for a man I know inside and out. Someone guaranteed to be here for years to come. No matter what."

Rachel's chair made a squeaking sound against the floor. Megan braced herself. Rachel could be so damned convincing when on a mission. She felt her friend's hand on her shoulder.

"Great idea. You've just described the sheriff. Unfortunately he's transparent as a sheet of ice and moving at the speed of a glacier."

Megan turned quickly. She could tell by her expression that it had been an idle comment. An attempt at humor. Rachel couldn't know. Megan relaxed and looked out the window again.

Rachel placed her arm around Megan's shoulders. "My recommendation? Enjoy Rey's company while he's here."

Megan leaned against her. "I wasn't asking."

"You should. It's sound advice." Rachel chuckled slightly. "From one psycho to another."

Megan had to smile. They stood silently, gazing at the snow lightly covering her snowmobile tracks. After a moment, Megan reached for her coat. "I'd better go."

"Take care." Rachel opened the door and stepped back.

Megan glanced out across the yard. Her attention focused on the tall, solitary figure snowshoeing through the woods about fifty yards away. Behind him was Granny's garden, a brilliant burst of red today. "That's the new boarder, Eric Mitchell."

Rachel followed her onto the porch. "I heard about him, but this is the first I've seen him."

"He moved in Saturday."

Rachel frowned. "Did she say what he was planning to do here?"

"He's with the university, researching grizzly bear habitats."

"One of Grandma's numerous causes." Rachel pulled her robe tighter. "She probably offered to house him for free."

Megan nodded. "Someone should tell Mr. Mitchell that grizzlies hibernate this time of year."

"That's right." Rachel laughed. "But I think it's easier to study their environment when the bears aren't actively using it. Don't quote me on that."

"It's a bad time for newcomers to be appearing out of nowhere." Megan zipped her parka. "Granny seems to like him, though."

"She likes anyone who can remember to wipe their feet on the front mat."

"You're right." Megan pulled on her hood and tied it. "I thought I'd drop by for a visit tomorrow to find out more. I can't today, I'm headed into town."

"Good luck avoiding Russell."

"Actually, I'm meeting with him."

"You're kidding, of course."

"No. I agreed to update him on Rey's situation every day or so."

"Watch out. Whenever the two of you are within ten feet of each other, he puffs out his chest. It doesn't help that he's full of hot air to begin with."

"That's his problem, not mine." She stepped off the porch and walked toward her snowmobile. "I'll do Granny a favor while I'm there and ask the sheriff to run a check on Mitchell."

"Good idea. You do realize, though, that Grace hates anyone sticking her or his nose into her business."

"Yes, but Interference is her own middle name." Megan smiled. "I'd say that I'm allowed one infraction."

"At least." Rachel smiled. "Remember when she paired you off with the friend of her son? What was he? Sixty?"

Megan smiled in return, then mimicked Grandma's voice. "But he has a nice personality, dear."

Both women laughed.

As Megan climbed onto her snowmobile, her tone turned serious. "Take care of yourself, Rach. If you need someone to talk to, stop by."

"The same to you." A glimmer of mischief shone in her friend's eyes. "And beware. I might just visit sooner than you think."

❅   ❅   ❅

Lute walked unescorted down the hall to the main office, pleased his status must have changed overnight. The fact was, they'd missed yesterday's stash. Cowboy accepted the parked snowmobile news very well. Almost too well.

Since joining the organization, he'd watched his back. Cowboy already knew he was a liar and a cheat. He'd had been caught shortchanging him when they met. Luckily, in this line of work that was a bonus. Cowboy had taken a liking to him. His boss knew Lute would cheat him eventually. He would, but on his way out. He had no loyalty.

After giving the three-knock signal, he entered the room. He'd been waiting for today's orders all morning. Maybe there would be no pickup today. Gripping his ski cap in his hands, he forced himself to relax. "The new rookie's here, Boss. I'll take him out with me today."

"Any problems bringing him in?"

"No hassle at all." He closed the door behind him, grinning at the hall guard as he shut him out of the conversation. Lute turned toward Cowboy's desk. "His name is Billy. Don't let that fool you, though. It sounds much sweeter than the guy is. He's a street punk that knows his stuff."

"Little fools me."

He swallowed hard. If Cowboy did let him go out again, it might set up to be Lute's last run. He needed to calm down. To have another chance at escape was worth whatever subservience it took. He'd swallow his pride, grovel if he had to. His guardian angel was tired, would resign soon, and he'd be on his own.

Cowboy was making notations in a legal-sized ledger book. He wasn't looking at him at all. Lute kept his tone upbeat, accommodating. "The kid's definitely trainable. I'll get to work on him right away."

His boss didn't pause, his head remained bent over the books. "Good. There's a new shipment at dawn. The Needles." He closed the ledger. Shoving it to the side, he reached for the phone and thumbed open a spiral address book. "I want a full report when you return."

"We're still going then?"

"Of course."

Hot damn, what luck. His boss's attention was on dialing. Lute had obviously been dismissed. He turned to go, forcing himself to walk slow. There was no reason to return from the Okanogan at all. Grab the shipment, fly south.

"Take Princess along. She'll watch over the two of you."

Like a hawk. His shoulders slumped. He knew where her loyalties were. So much for an easy retirement.

"Pick up the Desolation stash, too."

Two shipments in one run. Shit.

"And the skier's still alive. The avalanche missed. I've asked Rusty to take care of it. Make sure it happens."

Two shipments and a quick murder. Lute was glad he was facing the door.

Cowboy was speaking low into the phone. Whether a certain place was livable or not. Heating ducts. Flooring contractors. A new building? Lute had never been to Cowboy's, but talk was, it was fabulous.

He'd never seen his boss rattled. What was he up to?

Cowboy slammed down the receiver. Lute flinched. Bad time to be lingering by the door. It could be interpreted as eavesdropping. Maybe he could make it look like he was waiting on purpose.

He turned around. "One last thing. The skier I'm watching, where's he now?"

"Staying at the ranger's house. Ranger Jeffers. The woman who rescued him." Cowboy turned back to his ledger. "Just take care of it."

Lute tried reading the page upside down. At the top was a name. Arthur, somebody. He caught the word construction, too. Nothing else was distinguishable. He couldn't be caught staring. "Will do, boss. Anything else?" Maybe the moon.

"Report to me as soon as you return."

"Sure. You know me."

The brim of Cowboy's hat tilted a fraction of an inch upward. "For your sake, Lute, I'd better."

❊   ❊   ❊

Megan's boots echoed on the wooden planks outside Russell's office. With any luck he would be out on patrol, with one of his deputies manning the place. Possibly Scott. If so, she'd leave a note regarding Rey's condition and be off the hook for the day.

No such luck. When she thrust open the door Russell was stooped near a file cabinet. He shoved the lower drawer closed and slowly stood to his full six foot height. "This is a welcome surprise." His voice was laced with sarcasm. "You don't come down off your icy throne very often to mingle with us common folk."

"My reporting daily was your idea." Megan unzipped her jacket.

"I hear resentment in your voice. If the trip into town is too much trouble, keep in mind that I have a vacant spot for him here." He pointed toward a closed door. "It's free room and board, too."

"I've seen it." She'd been in that damp, musty cell before to retrieve her brother. He'd been picked up at age fourteen for driving their father's car, one of several bad choices he'd made that year. Twin matchbox-sized cells. Yellowed inch-thick windows. Plastic coated mattresses which made slithering sounds whenever the occupant of the bed rolled over. "Tomorrow I'll call in my report. Scott's coming for dinner. I could use the extra time."

"No deal."

Megan held her tongue. She not only wanted his cooperation for Rey's sake, but had a favor to ask, too. The security check on Mitchell. Arguing with Russell wouldn't solve anything. She shoved her hands into her pockets. She would play this one calm and collected.

He was waiting for her response. She would try harder to cooperate. Back-burner her loathing. The current situation would be resolved soon, then she would retreat. Other than Rey's coincidental tie-in to the murder, she usually didn't cross Russell's path.

"Which will it be?" He stepped closer. "Want to move lover boy down here?"

"We're not lovers." She instantly regretted her words. Why give him the satisfaction of hearing her defend herself once again?

"I didn't think so."

Her cheeks burned. No more verbal missteps. She was not only older, but wiser.

"Can we get down to business?" Megan pulled off her coat and tucked it under one arm. Drawing a deep breath she plunged ahead. She added a light touch of formality, nothing heavy-handed. "Rey's been at my place continually since he arrived. I have nothing to report."

"And his sister and ski buddy, Edwards? They're a bit more mobile than your patient. Any suspicious activities? Phone calls?"

Megan hesitated. She bought time by crossing the room to hang her jacket on the coat tree. She didn't meet his eyes.

"You always were a terrible liar." He followed her, standing less than a foot away. "Spill it."

She turned and lifted her chin. "They're gone."

"What?" Russell practically spit the word at her.

"Left this morning." She paced to increase the distance between them, then shrugged. "Not everyone can put their lives on hold at the drop of a hat."

"Shouldn't we say, the drop of a body?"

Megan took a deep, calming breath. "Your instructions were for Rey to stay put. Not the entire group. Either way, I can't be responsible for their actions."

"No. But if I have reason to believe Harrison will also run, it's my duty to have him under lock and key." His gaze seemed to bore into hers. "That would break up your cozy little arrangement, now wouldn't it?"

She stifled the urge to match his tone. He needed to think they were on the same side. "I should have called immediately. Sorry."

"That's better." He nodded and moved toward the receptionist's desk. "Anything else I should know?"

"There was an incident yesterday morning. I forgot to mention it last night."

"Define incident."

"Unexpected tracks near my snowmobile." Megan filled him in on time and location. "I didn't find any tampering, though."

"Would you like for me to check it out, have a mechanic look at it?"

Why was he being so considerate? "That would be great."

"Consider it done." He sat on the edge of the desk. "Can I ask you something?"

He had never bothered with permission before. His tone was different, open and caring. She kept her guard up. "About my snowmobile?"

"No. A personal question." His gaze slowly raked her from head to toe before he spoke. "From one friend to another."

She swallowed.

"What's really between you and Harrison?"

"Nothing."

"Last night you hovered over him like a grizzly with her cubs." He folded his arms across his chest. "Cute, really. Your mothering someone other than Scott."

She wanted to smack him. Instead, she reminded herself she wanted something from him. "It's simple. Nothing more than a leftover reaction to his skiing accident. He still needs quite a bit of assistance to get around. Practically an invalid." She forced images of Rey dressed in his boxers from her mind and tried to keep a straight face. "I'll tone down the Florence Nightingale act."

"I got the impression there was more to it."

"Don't be ridiculous." If there was, she'd make sure he was the last to know. "I just met him two days ago."

He nodded. "I worry about you, alone in those woods." He sounded genuinely concerned.

"I'm perfectly safe."

Russell leaned closer. "How can I put this delicately? Let's just say that you're a bit naive when it comes to men."

She tried not to flinch. How could the bastard bring that up? "Can we get back to business?"

Maybe sitting was a good idea after all. She chose a chair in front of the desk and settled into it. "I'd like you to run a check on someone for me. Rey's not the only newcomer to Snagtooth."

"I know that." He stood and moved behind her. His hands rested on the back of her chair. "Let's discuss it in my office."

Not on her life. She winced at the words she'd almost said. "I'm fine here." She moved away from his hands and retrieved a slip of paper and pencil from the receptionist's desk. "Grandma Grace has taken in a boarder named Eric Mitchell. He moved in a couple of days ago."

"I've heard the name. No problem." Russell let go and walked slowly around in front of her. This time when he perched on the edge of the desk, his legs were slightly spread.

Megan tried to ignore his close proximity. His denim-encased hip brushed the side of the note pad. He raised one foot and rested it against the seat of her chair. The toe of his boot grazed her thigh. She glanced up. His knee was less than a foot from her face.

He nodded toward the paper. "While you're at it, write down a description of Mitchell. Nothing elaborate."

She scooted sideways in her chair, signaling a need for elbow room. As he hovered, she kept her face averted. She could almost feel his breath against her hair.

"Megan." He cleared his throat. "Thia's been dead over a year."

God, she didn't need this. Not now. She continued to write.

"Maybe it's time for us to talk about what happened." He swallowed. "There are things I've never had a chance to say."

There would never be a right time. She handed him the pencil and paper then stood. "I have to run."

"Tomorrow, then."

She stepped further away from his suffocating presence. "Remember, I'll call in. My days will be full until Rey's on his feet."

"When will that be?"

She retrieved her coat from the rack. "I'm not sure. Probably when you give him the green light to return home." Megan added a touch of innocence to her smile. "I should be the one asking you for a schedule. You're keeping him here, not me."

The sheriff stared at her, tapping the pencil absentmindedly against his thumb. On the third tap, it hit the paper. He looked down at the description, as if just remembering it was in his hand. After a moment of silence, he crossed to his private office and closed the door.

Megan let herself out. The confrontation had ended in a draw, better than most.

❊   ❊   ❊

Russell laid Megan's description of the man called Mitchell on his desk and stared at it. He'd seen this guy in town late last night, strolling the boardwalk as if headed somewhere important. The odd thing was, Mitchell passed the only action in town. The poker game next to the General Store.

The game was illegal. No one had been hurt by it, though, in the year or so it had been going on. Just the boys, out for a little fun. Looking the other way seemed such a small concession at the time. He regretted it now, knowing where it had led. Hindsight was always more accurate.

A favor here, a pardon there. Slowly he'd been reeled in, they'd changed his sleepy little town. Sure, there were still Main Street parades and pancake breakfasts at the Grange Hall. But now the events were used as distractions. He should have closed down the game, but the perks they'd offered had been too attractive, at least back then.

His head throbbed. What had he gotten himself into? He reached for the near-empty bottle of aspirin in his desk drawer and swallowed two tablets dry. He'd better restock, there was no end in sight.

He had desperately wanted to be sheriff. Viewed it as a chance to be the big fish in the Snagtooth pond. But the salary was minuscule. Accepting bribes had been the best means to the end. Now his reign was drawing to a close. He could feel it with every breath he drew. A heaviness, that made him ache for another life.

Russell propped his elbows on his desk and let his head fall forward to his hands. He was tired and had been careless. Time to turn things over, begin delegating the requests to someone else; a patsy with a weak personality and greed as strong as his own. He had the perfect person in mind. After shifting the focus off himself, he'd be gone. And if the new gopher was more likable, more malleable, they would probably let him slip away quietly. Peacefully. Alive. But first, there was a murder to deal with.

He lifted his head. The description caught his eye again. He tried visualizing the man from last night, not wanting to overlook a thing. His stance, his body movements. Was it that same man he'd seen tampering with Megan's vehicle? If so, he would answer to Russell personally.

Megan. Why he cared about her, he didn't know. She'd been nothing but trouble. No matter what had passed between them, he wanted to help her. But how? She needed to lay low until he figured this one out. He'd put things right with her somehow, then extract himself from the entire mess. Maybe she'd wise up and leave, too. He could warn her, but words alone never got him very far with any members of the Jeffers family. No, he'd have to try another tack and hope for the best.

SIX

A SHARP KNOCK against the living room bay window interrupted Rey's martial arts routine. Rachel waved to him from the deck. He hadn't realized the porch circled that far around the house, but how could he? He hadn't been outside since his arrival.

Standing, he signaled her toward the door. As he walked over to let her in, he shook out his arm and shoulder muscles. The workout felt good, even though he'd overdone it. There wasn't much else to do. He'd finished reading Megan's wildlife magazines. The only other choices were her low fat cookbooks. Dave was right, the word relax wasn't in his vocabulary.

He slid the bolt back and pulled open the door. "Good to see you again. Megan's out this afternoon."

"I know." She motioned him to move aside, then entered.

She was here to see him. He stood back, somewhat amused and definitely curious. As she passed, she looked him over from toes to shoulders then sighed. "Megan has all the luck." She pulled off her gloves. "Guess I'm shopping in the wrong places. Singles bars, dance clubs. I should be looking under avalanches."

He suddenly felt underdressed. Crossing to the kitchen chair, he retrieved his sweatshirt and pulled it on.

Rachel followed, stuffing her gloves into her pockets. "Though baby-sitting overstates my purpose a bit, I did promise Megan I would stop by. She went into town for the afternoon."

Megan was worried about his being alone? The thought made him smile. Having company, someone to talk to now that Dave and Ali were gone, would be nice. He pushed his sleeves up to just below his elbows. "I'm glad you did. It's been quiet here all day."

"Being bored will speed your recovery." Rachel slipped her arms out of her backpack and unzipped her jacket. She hung both on the coat rack. "Assuming, of course, that you'd like to recover. And return home someday?" She turned, hands on her hips. "That's a big assumption on my part, of course. Correct me if I'm wrong."

"You're not."

"Good, then follow me. I make the world's best hot chocolate, a sure-fire remedy for everything. It will either cure you or make you not care that you're hurting. Want some?"

"Sure."

"Then grab the box." Rachel led the way to the kitchen. "Top shelf, I think."

Boxed hot chocolate. He cleared his throat. "Bad news. We're out of instant."

Rachel smile was closer to a smirk. "Oh, we are, are we?"

Rey hoped he wasn't blushing. The cabin was already feeling like home. Nothing like the family estate of his childhood or his current high rise condo. A real home. He'd better not get used to it. "I meant to say, Megan is out of cocoa. At least that's what she told Sheriff Russell last night."

"Russell." She shivered and crossed to the stove. "One of the worst examples of humanity I've ever run across."

Finally, they found something in common. "Megan doesn't appear to be very fond of him either."

"That's an understatement." After checking the water level in the tea pot she rummaged through the cabinets, frowning as she pulled out a box of herbal tea. "Megan will need something stronger than this after their meeting today."

"Meeting?"

"You heard me." Rachel opened the refrigerator and stared inside. "I have an idea. Let's make it from scratch."

He'd never cooked a day in his life, but was willing to try. Was willing to do just about anything to keep Rachel talking. Megan hadn't mentioned a visit to the Sheriff's office. He was disappointed at finding out this way and not sure why. There was no reason for her to share her plans with him.

Moving to Rachel's side, he peered over her shoulder. "I'm game. Let's see. We need milk and chocolate?"

"Confession Time." She propped her arm over the open door and leaned against it as she scanned the shelves. "There's not a domestic bone in my body."

"Come on, now. It can't be too difficult."

"You wouldn't think so." She reached in and grabbed a container on the top rack. "Here's the milk. See anything that resembles chocolate?"

"Not in here." He had already ransacked the fridge earlier while preparing a sandwich for lunch. Aside from the normal condiments and an array of fruits and vegetables, there wasn't much there.

Rachel stepped away. "Wait. I have something that might work." She crossed to the rack where she'd hung her backpack and unzipped the front pouch. Inside were two chocolate bars. She proudly held them up as if they were first place ribbons in the giant slalom. Within minutes the bottom of an aluminum pan was covered with warm, brown goo.

Rey added a half cup of milk while Rachel stirred. "What were you doing when I arrived?"

"Tae Kwon Do."

"Black belt?"

Instead of answering he stepped back and bowed slightly, hands at his sides.

"Figures." She shook her head and grinned. "You took Megan by surprise, you know. She beat a new path to my house."

"I didn't intend to. She startled me." He picked up the carton and added more milk to the pan. It didn't help. The lumps were still quite sizable. "She didn't say anything about it to me."

Rachel gave him a level look.

Was his last remark naive? "I'll apologize."

"No need. It would only make it worse." Rachel thumped the spatula against the side of the pan, set it on the spoon rest and switched to a wire whisk. "Any other surprises up your sleeve? If so, come clean and I'll advise you on approach."

He had one. His identity. But he wasn't about to reveal it quite yet. He preferred Megan reacting to him without knowing about his money. "I'll keep that in mind."

He switched subjects. "I've always wondered what it would be like to have unlimited free time. Now I know. Never thought about the fact it could be so lonely, though."

"Don't be fooled. You can be lonely even when you're not alone."

He glanced at Rachel. She seemed to be completely absorbed in chasing lumps around the pan. He set down the carton he was still holding. Was she aware of how much her last comment revealed? He left it untouched though it rang true for him, also.

"I have another question for you." She paused, as if awaiting permission.

He knew better. "Go ahead."

"All right. Why are you still here?"

He drew back from her slightly. "The sheriff asked me to stay until the investigation is over. I'm a key witness."

"Suspect would be more like it, if I know Russell." She didn't look away. "His orders aren't worth the breath he uses to issue them. I'm sure you sensed that. Besides, a good lawyer could get you out of here in a flash. So I repeat." She tapped the whisk against the side of the pan. "Why are you really here?"

She was right, he'd told Dave essentially the same thing and he hadn't bought it either. He watched her for a moment, then sighed. "Just between you and me?"

Rachel leaned closer.

He didn't believe for a minute that she'd keep it to herself, but there was no harm in telling her. And she'd asked. "I want to be here. Saturday morning, I saw a young man alive. Hours later, he was dead. Sure the events are coincidental, but I want to see this through. Does that make sense?"

After a moment of silence, Rachel nodded. "Look on the bright side. If Megan arrives back here with cuffs you'll have a lot more time on your hands." She dipped one finger in the pot then licked her fingertip. "You could use it perfecting our recipe."

"Cuffs? As in handcuffs?"

She shrugged. "She had other errands to run, of course."

It was no longer funny. "What are you saying?"

"Let's walk through this together." Setting the whisk down, Rachel folded her arms across her chest. "A martial arts expert is found buried under an avalanche which should never have been triggered in the first place. Ranger rescues him and brings him home, with his entire ski party, of course. The usual background checks are skipped, due in part to the nature of the emergency and in part to the skier's engaging smile."

She tapped her chin with her forefinger. "After questioning by the authorities, two of the three members of the party hightail it out of town. The remaining one is personally acquainted with the area's most current murder victim. Might have had a motive of revenge, for doing the kid in himself. Are you following me yet?"

He stepped forward, astounded. "Megan thinks I killed that innocent looking kid?"

"No. But then she always was the trusting sort. I, on the other hand, would suspect the Pope if he were there that day."

He ran a hand back through his hair. "My intent in staying wasn't to frighten her. I'll make arrangements to leave as soon as possible."

"Don't be silly. You've brought more excitement to Snagtooth than we've had for quite awhile."

"But you just said . . ."

She laid her hand on his shoulder. "I was describing my suspicions and maybe the sheriff's, not Megan's. And I'm no judge. Look at my life. My husband cheated on me until the day he died. In fact, it's what killed him."

He flinched. She'd said it without emotion. Either she truly didn't care or it hurt too much to think about it. "I'm sorry."

"Don't be. He was a big boy. Knew the risks. I give my trust considerably slower these days." She squinted, examining his face. "Megan sees something in you."

Rey tried to hold still for another visual inspection.

"Maybe it's your eyes. Yes, I'm beginning to see it, too." She winked and grabbed a sponge.

"You just might be good for her, Mr. Harrison. You've already shaken her from the post-Thia depression that's held her hostage this past year. For that alone I owe you my thanks."

He wanted her to continue. "Megan has told me a little about her sister."

"If she's said anything at all, it's a step forward." Rachel shrugged. "We all react to death differently. I talk non-stop about Pete and she listens to me. She won't even mention Thia's name."

"But you and Pete were husband and wife. Is that so unusual?"

Rachel snorted. "Considering he and Thia died together, it is."

His heart seemed to stop for a moment. My God. She hadn't mentioned that. He tried to recall specific discussions he'd had with Megan. Maybe she'd avoided telling him.

"Anyway," Rachel waved her hand, brushing further questions aside. "You've given her something new to worry about. Something besides that weak-kneed brother of hers."

"Scott."

Rachel nodded. "Thank goodness she only has the one." She glanced down into the pan. His gaze followed. The milk was at a rolling boil now, scorching the metal sides. She pulled it from the stove, sighed, then dumped the contents down the sink. "Don't worry. I have another idea."

He was afraid of that. His head already was spinning from information-overload. He'd asked for it, though.

She turned on the water and filled the pan. "Granny will make us hot chocolate. That will get you out of here for awhile and reduce your cabin fever. With any luck, she'll fall in love with you, thus keeping you out of the slammer."

"Great plan." He frowned. "How, exactly, will that help?"

"She'll put in a good word for you with Megan. Having Granny on your side carries a lot of weight around here." Rachel raised the whisk in mock salute. "Here's hoping that her endorsement, plus your own boyish charm, will be enough."

He stared at her. Was she serious? Until he could think of something better to do, he'd follow her advice. Besides, he could use the fresh air.

Glancing down, he caught sight of chocolate spots on the front of his sweatshirt. "I'll shower and change first." He headed toward the connecting door.

"Just change."

He turned back toward her. "We're in a hurry?"

"No." She glanced up. "Word is, you strike quite an image after your shower. Let's see. Something about little black shorts." She paused, then shrugged. "Nope, I can't quite remember. But skip the shower, okay?" She went back to scrubbing the pan.

Megan mentioned that? He wanted to hear more, how she'd described him, but Rachel's attention was focused on washing the pan. He turned toward the stairs, smiling.

❄   ❄   ❄

Russell paused in front of Scott's office door. His eyes burned. Memories of last night's phone call had kept him awake until dawn. He felt trapped.

The illusion that Harrison was the prime suspect for the kid's death had to be maintained. If it wasn't then, as sheriff, he'd have to identify another bogus suspect. This case couldn't be closed as quickly as Thia's and Pete's had been, that one had raised too many eyebrows. And if he followed orders, Harrison would be dead, remembered more as a victim than as a suspect.

But what if the skier were to run? That would make him look as guilty as hell. And if he were killed while fleeing, so much the better. That would work, except for one minor flaw: how to do it?

From what he'd seen of the man during the interrogation, he wasn't someone who avoided controversy. Megan's defense of Harrison made him think the two had grown close. If so, he wouldn't leave her.

Wait. What if Harrison were convinced his staying would cause more harm? Yes, that just might work. Now to shift the responsibility.

❄   ❄   ❄

Scott peeled off his jacket and hung it on the back of his office chair. It was noon. His day was going from bad to worse. He sat and patted his pocket. Empty, just like his bank account. He lit his last smoke. He would have to roll more soon. Sheriff Russell said he wanted to see him. His head ached. He had tons of work to do, but reports were impossible to deal with when his hands were shaking. They would have to wait.

The scraps of paper in the back of his desk drawer were piling up. He scooped them together and sorted them by date. He'd begun recording his poker wins and losses on a whim, to make himself feel better. No wonder he was broke. Despite the risk, he'd bet this month's rent on last night's game. He needed cash. Lots of it. Soon.

The sheriff opened the door without knocking. Scott flinched and tried to shove the slips of paper casually back into his drawer. "I've got a DWI report needing your signature."

"Later. Something much bigger has come up." The sheriff glanced down at the notepad in his hand and tapped it with his pencil.

Scott stood. "Like what?"

"Your sister was in here earlier, asking for a rush security check."

"On who?"

"Eric Mitchell."

"Who's he?"

"The man who moved in with Grace Larsen despite my advising against it. I think we should check out Rey Harrison while we're at it."

"Why?"

"Lots of reasons. The dead body, unidentified tracks near Megan's snowmobile, the questionable report of the locked hut, those kind of things." The sheriff looked at him silently for a moment. "He's living with your sister. Aren't you the least bit worried about that?"

Scott wanted to cringe. He hated that tone of voice. "Sorry. I didn't give it much thought."

"Maybe you should. Or doesn't the thought of more dead bodies around here bother you?" The words hung in the air as Russell stared at him.

He shifted from one foot to the other. He'd said the wrong thing. Hell, he had bigger things to worry about. Still, he needed to answer. He couldn't risk losing his boss's respect. "Initially I was concerned, but then I backed off. Harrison can't ski, at least not for awhile. I figured Megan would be safe."

Silence. Was the sheriff buying it or not? He straightened, composing what he hoped was a serious expression. "I was wrong. Leave the background check to me. Anything else?"

Russell moved slowly around the desk and sat in Scott's chair. He really didn't mind his boss moving in on his personal space. In fact, maybe it was an outward sign of camaraderie. He tried to add a touch of authority to his voice. "How about if we haul Harrison in here for questions, alone, then convince him?"

He'd heard secondhand that the sheriff used that technique on occasion. Since he and his boss never discussed it, Scott hoped he was showing his ingenuity. It's not that Harrison would actually get hurt. Not unless the man was too stupid to listen to a little friendly advice.

His comment seemed to grab the sheriff's attention. Was he pleased or just surprised? Scott waited.

"That would certainly take care of it, nice and neat."

Scott puffed out his chest and preened.

Russell leaned forward. "One problem. We haven't caught Harrison at anything yet. We'll need to be more subtle, Deputy."

Scott nodded as if seriously reconsidering. He hadn't a clue as to what his boss really wanted. Looking good was high on Scott's list, though. Someday he hoped to be sheriff himself. That would mean giving up a few of his newer habits, but if the goal was clearly in sight he could do it. "How subtle?"

"Very. What other ideas do you have?" Russell reclined Scott's chair. He seemed content to wait.

The sheriff was leaving it up to him? It would be his show? Scott pursed his lips. "We could go a number of ways." He was sure they could, if only he knew what they were. The clock ticked overhead. Scott thought harder.

The sheriff snapped his fingers. "Maybe we could motivate Harrison into leaving your sister's on his own."

Thank God for the jump start, his own mind had been a blank. "Yeah. Megan might be able to convince him." Scott frowned. "But, wait. Weren't we the ones who ordered him to stay?"

"We did, but think about this." Russell leaned forward. "If Harrison were to run, it would look bad for him, wouldn't it?"

Scott nodded sagely.

"We'd have the perfect right, then, to drag him back anytime we wanted. And in the meantime, he'd be out of our hair. We would be saving the taxpayers the cost of the security report, too."

"Right." It was becoming clearer and he liked being on the same team. "Why don't we just release him, then?"

"Because our investigation into the death below Devil's Elbow isn't complete. It's only been two days. It wouldn't seem right to wrap up the paperwork so soon, now would it?"

"I guess not."

"Think about it from this angle." Russell continued. "Harrison most likely didn't commit the murder, their meeting was simply coincidental, right? And you know he must be a burden to your sister."

Scott made a sound of agreement, though he didn't know exactly where the conversation was headed.

"Then his fleeing is actually doing us all a favor." Russell's words became more enthusiastic. "Think of it. Additional taxpayer dollars saved by not housing him here in our jail. Money could be spent on, let's say, other programs. Ones you could manage."

Scott swallowed. "Damned straight."

The sheriff stood and laid a hand on Scott's shoulder. "Handle this one right and maybe some of the extra funds could be funneled into a raise for you. I'll see what I can arrange."

This was more than he hoped for. And the money couldn't come at a better time. Getting Harrison to leave should be a cake walk. "Thanks, boss."

"No." Russell slowly shook his head as he headed for the door. "Thank you."

❄   ❄   ❄

Rey was having second thoughts. They began immediately after Rachel patted the snowmobile seat and issued the instruction to 'climb on, big boy.'

Though her dry sense of humor amused him, she had a rough edge to her personality. In contrast, Megan's exterior was smooth, like water flowing over stone. Touchable, approachable, even yielding perhaps.

Together the women made a formidable pair, as independent and forceful as their chosen environment but in different ways. Megan's determination and attention to detail would see her past any hurdles. Rachel would blast her way through like dynamite.

Rachel drove the snowmobile around fallen logs and past low-lying bushes, making the ride to Grandma Grace's both short and harrowing. The cabin lay less than a half mile from Megan's in a direct line, but Hardscrabble Lake was in-between and they had to contend with it. Rachel exhibited good judgment by skirting the frozen pond.

As they approached the house, Rey stared in amazement. The field next to it was filled with varying shades of red. He tapped Rachel on the shoulder and leaned forward to speak near her ear. "How does Grandma Grace do that?"

"Do what?"

"Grow fuzzy red flowers in the dead of winter?"

"She'd skin you alive if she heard you say that." Rachel turned slightly and gave him a mocking grin. "Those are Cambridge Scarlet Bee Balms."

Bee Bombs? He didn't dare ask.

"It would help your position immensely if you would remember that, Mr. Harrison."

What position? He didn't dare ask that either.

When Rachel guided her vehicle to a halt and climbed down, Rey noticed she was still grinning. "What's so funny?"

She pulled off her helmet. "Go ahead. Get it out of your system."

"All right. What are Bee Bombs?"

"I said Bee Balms. Don't drop the L. You were right the first time, they're fuzzy red flowers. Every last one of them is artificial."

"But why?"

"They use less fertilizer?" She shrugged. "Lord only knows. Just don't ask Granny. Remember, you want to be on her good side."

"And why is that, again?"

"So Megan won't throw you out. And if she does, don't assume you can stay with me." She winked.

He'd rather fight for a cot at the nearest shelter. He wasn't sure he wanted her to know that, though, while she was helping him walk through the drifts.

The snow was deeper than boot-height on this side of the lake. Though his knee was firmly wrapped and the pain only a dull ache, a fall at this point would set him back. So far, nothing Rachel had done could be labeled as predictable. He held on tighter.

When they reached the concrete walk, he managed on his own. Though snow-covered, the surface was firm and even. When they stood before the heavy wooden door, Rachel turned to face him.

They were nose-to-nose. He quickly stepped back.

"Listen." She put her hand on his arm. "I should explain something before you feel compelled to stand clear across the room from me each time we're together. I enjoy being outrageous. It's a new persona for me. I'm still trying it on to see how it fits, but so far it feels good. It beats being a door mat." She removed her hand and pulled off her knit cap.

"What happened to the old one?"

"I buried it along with Pete." She tucked her hair behind her ears. "I'm building a new life for myself. Trying new things is part of that process for me. I'm keeping a list of which ones work and which don't."

"Isn't that confusing?"

She shrugged. "Overall I think I'm moving forward. But at the same time I'm gaining quite a reputation."

He tried not to smile, but failed.

She laughed. "All right. Out with it."

"No."

"Say it."

Though he was still shaking his head, he gave in. "A reputation of being unstable?"

"No. As someone available, if you know what I mean. It doesn't seem to matter there hasn't been any action to back up my words. And I'm not bothered by what people say." Her voice lowered. "There's no one around for me to answer to. Not anymore."

Rey simply listened, amazed at her directness and sorry for the misery he heard in her words. Even if she were asking for advice, he didn't have any to share. He hadn't answered to anyone but himself for twenty years.

Rachel knocked on the door then brushed the snowflakes from his jacket. "Since I can't seem to guarantee which direction I'm headed on any given day, I go with the mood of the moment. Don't take my flirtatious behavior to heart. Down deep, I could be mistaken for Mother Teresa."

The latch on the door rattled, interrupting his opportunity to ask how deep. Rey switched his attention to Grandma Grace, Queen of the Fake Flowers. Which of his many mental images would prove true? The front-running caricature was a short, cookie-dough figure with a beehive hairdo.

The woman answering the door didn't fit at all. Grandma Grace was long and lean, with a hint of fire and mischief in her eyes. Another determined woman. He was surrounded. He braced himself for more confrontations to come. Maybe that was a requirement to live this far off the beaten track. The crochet hook tucked behind her ear, though, was somewhat expected.

"I heard you drive up." She motioned for them to enter. Following Rachel's lead, Rey stomped the extra snow from his boots. He did better with his right than his left, not wanting to jolt his knee. As soon as the door was latched again, the older woman pulled off her glasses and gave Rey a slow once-over.

"Hello." He'd hoped to distract her from the inspection but failed. He glanced at Rachel. She seemed to enjoy his discomfort.

When through, Grandma returned her glasses to the bridge of her nose and met his eyes. "You're either a Rescue Ranger or Rachel's new beau. Maybe both." She sniffled and pulled a tissue from her sleeve to dab at her nose. "Either way, I expect you'll do."

"Thank you. I think." He bowed slightly at the compliment, not bothering to hide his smile. "Sorry to say, though, I'm neither. I'm simply staying at Ms. Jeffers' cabin while my leg mends. I jammed my knee during a fall."

"Jammed a tree? That must have hurt something terrible. It's a wonder that you didn't break something while you were at it. Here, let's find you a seat." She motioned him to follow her down the hall.

"Thank you, but it wasn't a tree. I said knee."

Grandma Grace didn't turn back. He was about to raise his voice and try again when Rachel nudged him. "Don't argue. If she heard tree, then that's what you said. Go with it."

"Why?"

"We love her dearly, even if she does let the batteries in her hearing aid overrun their useful life."

"Is that safe?"

"It's nothing to worry about. She doesn't live alone anymore. I'll fill you in on that later." Rachel shrugged. "When conversation becomes truly unbearable, we just drop by replacement batteries. We leave them on the counter. Grace throws out the old ones when she's good and ready."

Grace stopped under an arched doorway that led to a combination television room, dining room and sewing closet. Amid stacks of purple fabric squares there were countless skeins of yarn in coordinating shades. She tossed those residing on the chair to the couch and motioned for him to sit. "Take the load off, young man."

He did. Grace sat across from him, behind her sewing machine. She leaned her forearms on the extended cutting surface. "You're staying with Megan? How nice for you both. For how long?"

"Through next weekend. Unless my knee recovers sooner."

"Well, don't try to hurry Mother Nature." She smiled at him warmly. "Healing takes time. Enjoy yourself."

"He has to go back eventually, Granny." Rachel glanced around, looking for a clear space to sit down. "A job. Maybe a family. Isn't that right, Rey?"

"Yes."

Grace lowered her glasses. "A wife?"

"No."

She nodded and leaned back against her chair. Rachel moved a stack of clutter from one couch cushion to another.

He felt guilty. Rachel had been left to find her own seat while he was being fussed over. He started to stand, but Grace pointed her finger at him. "Stay put. Rachel was just about to fix us some afternoon tea. Weren't you, dear?"

She was in the process of lowering herself onto the couch. Instead, she straightened. "Sure. Can we make that three hot chocolates instead?"

"If you want." Grace crooked a finger in Rachel's direction, signaling her to come closer. She did, bending close to the older woman. Grace lowered her tone to a raspy whisper. "It's not like you to miss out on the action, Rachel, with such a handsome man. What happened? Did Megan beat you to the punch?"

"Sad, but true. I'm slipping." Rachel's tone was laced with regret. "Maybe when she's through, I can have a turn."

She nodded and patted Rachel's hand, then began sewing.

Rey watched as Rachel bit her lower lip to keep from laughing. She was right about her reputation, it had obviously preceded her.

"Well then. Where were we?" Grace readjusted her glasses on the bridge of her nose, then picked up a piece of purple material.

Rachel headed for the kitchen. Grace snipped at the fabric. "Since you're nicely settled in at Megan's, there's no real need to hurry back to the city." Her warm, hazel eyes glanced up at his. "Is there?"

It wasn't really a question, more a request for agreement. He cleared his throat. "Actually . . ." he began.

"And there's no better place than right here to recover in total peace and quiet." Her gaze continued to hold his. "Is there?"

Another non-negotiable point. Other than the discovery of a dead body, Grace was right. He remembered looking out Megan's bay window, and the feeling of serenity the view had evoked. He'd indulged his urge to recline against the pillows with coffee mug in hand. The fir trees, branches heavy with snow, stood tall and solitary against the rich colors of the pre-dawn sky. Black and white against deep, endless blue.

"I can see why Megan loves it." He settled further into his chair. "It's not what I'm used to."

"Get used to it then."

He sat up straight.

"You're never too old to learn new things. Look at me, for example. I'm in my mid-seventies and I'm still learning."

Rachel reentered the room. "Grace, where do you keep the mix?"

"Heavens no, it's not fixed. Darn faucet has been dripping since yesterday. Just leave it. I have a call in to the plumber already. Thanks anyway." She turned back toward Rey then winked. "Last time Rachel helped, it cost me twice as much to have it done over."

Rachel circled around Grace and knelt on one knee, position-ing herself so they were at the same level. "All right, but don't say I didn't offer." She touched the older woman's hand and waited until their eyes met. "One other thing, though, while I'm in here. The cocoa mix. Which cabinet?"

"On the top . . . oh, dear. I forgot. I lent the last of it to Megan. How about tea?"

Rachel glanced over her shoulder at Rey. He tried not to smile. "Tea would be great."

"I thought you'd say that." Rachel quickly stood. "Tea it is. Grace, the pot of water is already started, but I've got to run. Knowing how you love company, I mainly wanted you to have the opportunity to meet Rey. If there's time, maybe you could answer some of his questions regarding Eric."

"My new boarder?" Grandma Grace looked across at Rey. "Whatever about, dear?"

He hadn't a clue. Where was Rachel leading him? He tried to be supportive, yet vague at the same time. "Several things, actually. Rachel, maybe you could explain for me. You're much closer to the subject than I." That much, at least, was true.

"Sure." She pulled a chair out from beneath the dining room table and scooped the fabric squares from the seat. "Grizzly bear research is only one of a number of environmental projects that Rey champions. The current government proposal to re-populate the North Cascades is of particular interest. He hopes it will come before the voters soon, and wants to know how he can help."

Rey continued to smile and nodded as if in agreement. Bears? Maybe he should question his own hearing. Why was Rachel leading Grace on a wild goose chase? There must be a point to all this.

"Gotta go." Rachel stood then gave the older woman a warm hug. "Take care of him for me or Megan will have both our hides."

"I certainly will." Grandma Grace patted her on the back.

Rachel released the older woman. "By the way, do you think Eric would mind bringing him back to Megan's later?"

"I'm sure he wouldn't. He's a nice man. Works hard and has good manners, too. Other than being late for meals, that is." Grace glanced at Rachel and lowered her glasses. "I think he's available. Maybe you should drop by sometime when he's home. Come for dinner."

Rachel reached for her coat. She mumbled something.

"What, dear?"

Rachel smiled brightly. "I would love to." She turned to Rey. He stood and extended his hand. She ignored it, bestowing a hug on him equal to the one Grace had received.

His shock vanished when he heard her whispered message. "Find out everything you can. Her boarder is as odd as a three-legged skier."

"All right."

She let him go. "Until later, then."

He smiled absently, his mind still replaying what she'd just said. Another transient, in addition to himself? Someone exhibiting strange behavior? Even to him, grizzly bear research in the dead of winter sounded suspicious.

Rachel quickly zipped her jacket. He wished they had more time to talk. She called out to Grace. "One more thing. I'm planning a trip to the General Store. Make your weekly list. I'll call for it in the morning. Your hot chocolate is at the top of mine."

"Nine it is. See you then."

Rachel winked at him, then headed down the hall. He turned back toward Grandma Grace. She signaled for him to sit. When he did, she positioned his hands. Within moments, she'd slipped the skein of yarn over them and started winding a loose purple ball. "Now let's see. Where were we. Ah, yes. Megan."

❊   ❊   ❊

If only Alison could see him now. She would call one of the news magazines and offer to furnish an exposé into the lives of the rich and loony. Here he sat, Reynold Harrison Moore III, surrounded by quilting squares, pattern pieces and yarn skeins. Both his hands were upright and stationary, like goal posts. He was enjoying himself immensely.

Across from him, Grandma Grace wound up the strand of purple yarn. With each new dye lot, she spun tales of Megan's childhood. They started with kindergarten, where the stories were amusing. But as the afternoon wore on, Rey pieced together a picture of a middle child's struggle to find her place in the family.

Basketball honors for baby brother. Megan coming to cheer him on at his games, but selling popcorn instead because they were short-handed. Skiing ribbons honoring Thia which wallpapered their shared room, crowding out Megan's achievements. Rey's life at boarding school had been quite different, but equally unsatisfying in a family sense.

"And the fire. Almost nine years ago now, I guess." Grace shook her head and made a sympathetic sound. "It was Scott's fault. He was smoking and trying to hide it. The back side of the house was destroyed. Her mother couldn't get out. And Megan couldn't reach her. Tried, until the firemen pulled her out of the house."

Only the rhythmic creak of Grace's chair broke the silence.

Sorrow pulled at his heart. Megan loved Scott. Didn't seem to harbor any resentment toward him. Would he have been that forgiving in the same situation? Though the circumstances were quite different, Rey had no intention of ever forgetting the face of his father's murderer.

He could identify with the sense of helplessness she must have felt. He'd stood by and watched the life flow from his dad. Actually that was a glorified accounting. He'd hid behind bushes on his knees, trembling, unable to change the course of events and unwilling to let the same thing happen to himself.

The last of the yarn slipped from his fingers. Granny tucked the end under a loose strand and placed the ball into her wicker basket. Another skein, a lighter shade of purple, took its place. Rey swallowed to relieve the tightness in his throat. "How did Megan's father take the news?"

"He handled it in the typical Jeffers' way. By ignoring the pain and pretending everything was fine." Her tone was disapproving. "No crying, no chance to come to terms with their grief by packing up her things. He handled the entire situation very badly."

Rey wasn't sure what he'd been expecting. Courage? Strength? Not denial.

Grace continued. "Megan's new prom dress had been hanging in her mother's room. Her father insisted she go to the dance despite the funeral. He wanted their lives to go on as planned. She didn't want to upset him further, so she went." Grace wrapped the yarn vigorously. "Megan wore Thia's gown though it was inches too short. Not only that, but it had been featured on the front page of the Snagtooth paper just the year before."

"Let me guess. The older sister was prom queen."

Grandma paused in her winding efforts. "How did you know?"

He sighed. "Either that or Senior Class president." Megan hadn't mentioned her mother's death the other night. Hadn't originally included Thia in her accounting of brothers and sisters. Seemed to need a great deal of Scott's attention last night. Her father wasn't the only Jeffers handling death badly. "How's her father coping now?"

"He only lived a year longer than her mother. He died of lung cancer, or so the newspaper said. I think he died from a broken heart." Grandma Grace readjusted her glasses. "Megan used her college fund to fix the house so she and Scott could continue to live there. That meant no four year university after her junior college stint. Thia could continue her studies because of her involvement with the biathlon team. She'd won an athletic scholarship the year before."

"Couldn't Megan do the same?"

"Sure she could, but wouldn't. She didn't want to leave Scott. I read that situation differently. She never believed she stood a chance, so she didn't pursue it."

"Didn't even try out?"

Grace shook her head. "Megan always stayed close to home. She used to look forward to Thia's visits, so they could sprint through the mountains together. Megan always had the same dream, you know, just not the means."

"She wanted to race competitively?"

"Not just race, but also shoot. The biathlon is a preposterous sport, if you ask me. Imagine trying to decrease your heart rate in the middle of a run, just so you can shoot in between beats."

Rey didn't answer. His own conditioning in the martial arts was geared more toward building personal strength than heart rate. He knew, though, after an evening run his pulse took awhile to resume its normal pattern.

Grace turned the yarn ball ninety degrees in her hand and went back to work. Her rocking increased. "Thia was faster, but Megan had the home turf advantage. The race course was imprinted in her mind. They would let their timed results tell all."

Rey's discomfort increased. He should stop now, before asking the next question, but he didn't. "How did Thia die?"

Grandma Grace put the ball of yarn aside. "Skiing accident. She was out that afternoon with Rachel's husband. Pete must not have known the area well enough. He should have, if you ask me. He was a Ranger, after all."

Grace leaned back and looked at the ceiling, speaking absently, as if he weren't there. "Pete and Thia were too close to the ledge at Devil's Elbow, as the story goes. They weren't paying attention, or maybe something distracted them. Anyway, an avalanche at Last Chance swept them clear over. A terrible shame."

Rey sat forward, trying to sort through what he'd heard. Rachel mentioned her husband had been having an affair. If it had been with Thia, how had Rachel and Megan's friendship survived? Another case of ignoring the past? "Sometimes slopes can be misleading. My partner Dave has warned me several times that a slide can surprise almost anyone, depending on conditions."

"Not Megan. She's one of the best there is around these parts."

"Then she was there, too?"

"No, not at the exact time. Earlier. She had just checked out the slope. In fact, she had pronounced it moderately safe." Grace shook her head.

Enough. Megan would have to be the one to tell him more. Maybe she would speak of it. They could swap stories about the way they handled self-guilt. He'd been battling his own for twenty years.

"It's getting late." Rey attempted to stand. His knee had stiffened after resting on a foot stool for nearly an hour. It was time to go home. He corrected himself for the second time that day. To Megan's.

"My goodness. You're right. I need to start dinner." She stood, collected their teacups and headed into the kitchen. "And not one word discussed about the grizzlies, either. My apologies."

"No problem." He stopped. Walking back to Megan's on his injured knee was impossible. No sign of Eric Mitchell, either. And at this moment, he wanted to return to the cabin more than he'd wanted anything for a long time.

Rey followed Grace into the kitchen. "If I could use your phone, I'll ask Megan to pick me up."

His hostess drew the kitchen curtains aside and glanced out the window. "If she's there. I don't see her vehicle in the yard. No way to tell how long she'll be in town." She let the lace fall back into place. "Don't worry. If Eric doesn't appear shortly, I can always lend you my snow scooter."

If he stayed a bit longer, he could pursue the line of questioning Rachel had wanted. Wouldn't have to admit he'd spent the time dissecting Megan's background instead. "Have you always taken in boarders?"

"Eric's my first. It's a favor, really, to my son's school, the University of Washington. Eric is here on a UW research grant and needed a place to stay for six months or so. A bed and breakfast would have run him quite a bill, not to mention people always coming and going. Or the lack of privacy."

Grace ran water in the sink then reached beneath the cupboard for the soap. "He'd have to deal with all those guests. Too disturbing for someone trying to concentrate, that's for sure. When he made his case to me, I took him in. Not everyone is as pleased about it as I am."

He could easily believe that. Had she checked his credentials? He picked up an embroidered tea towel and began to dry the few dishes already in the rack. "How long has he been with you?"

"A little over two days. He moved in Saturday and has been no trouble at all. He's barely here, except to eat and sleep. That young man is gone from dawn to dark. He keeps his space neat as a pin, though, and brings his dishes down without being told. He plans to do his own laundry, too. I won't need to step foot in his room. I think he'd make a fine husband, once he's ready to settle down."

That comment brought back thoughts of Rachel. He had no idea what information Rachel had wanted. He wished she would have elaborated.

"How about you?"

Rey looked at his gray-haired companion washing imaginary stains off one of the teacups. Since she was pretending to scrub, he could pretend to misunderstand. In fact, now that he thought about it, she hadn't misheard a single word since Rachel left. He looked out the window as he dried a plate. "I don't know if he's the marrying kind or not, Grace. I haven't met him."

She raised her head. "Squirming, are we?"

He waited a moment before turning away from the window to meet her eyes. "Guilty."

"Why aren't you married?" She rinsed the cup and handed it to him. "I figure it could be only one of two things."

He refrained from laughing. "What are my choices?"

"Either you haven't met the right girl yet or you're simply a coward." Grace took his towel from him and hung it over the stove handle to dry. She turned back to face him. It appeared she had no trouble hearing when they stood face-to-face. "Speak up, now. Which is it?"

"Still looking for the right partner." There had been plenty of volunteers through the years. For marriage and other less permanent arrangements. But the cost was high, they all wanted something from him. It varied, but it never seemed to be love. Ending unsatisfactory relationships took too much of a toll on him. He'd learned it was easier not to start one.

"Well, don't worry." She put her hand on his arm and winked. "Maybe you've been looking in the wrong places. Up until now, that is."

❄   ❄   ❄

Before Grandma Grace could return with the keys to her snowmobile, the back door opened. A tall man pushed his way in, head bent against the blast of a cold cross wind. Rey watched him from across the room. After shutting the door and pulling back the hood of his parka he stopped, as if startled to find company.

Rey stepped forward. "Rey Harrison. You must be Eric Mitchell. Grace told me all about you."

"She did?" His expression transformed from surprise to wary congeniality. "And just what did she say? Anything of interest?"

"That you arrived Saturday, same as I, except I'm on vacation, and you're here for research on behalf of the university. How long is your project expected to run?"

"Why do you want to know?"

The man's expression had changed again. Intense. Unyielding. Rey continued to meet his gaze head-on, choosing not to back away as the man seemed to want.

His complexion was weathered. A trimmed beard and mustache covered most of the lower half of his face, but left an uneven scar showing. Why had a sweet pushover like Grace agreed to share her home with such a seedy character?

His hostess entered the room and glanced at both men. "Watch your manners, young man. That is if you want to continue staying beneath my roof." Her tongue clucked a warning. "Mr. Harrison is an invited guest of mine."

"Sorry."

Grace raised her chin. "Don't tell me, Eric. Tell Rey."

Mitchell turned to him and nodded. "Please excuse my manners."

Rey suppressed the urge to smile as he mentally amended his earlier "pushover" thought. He could see exactly who was in charge.

"That's better. Now we can all be friends." Grandma exhaled. Chapter closed. She crossed the kitchen to stand next to Mitchell touching his sleeve. He drew back slightly, obviously not wanting her too close.

She ignored his feint to the side and patted his arm. "You're much too late to share tea with us, but you can make up for your lapse by taking Rey home." Her voice didn't sound as if there were any options. "His leg was injured a couple of days ago. He needs a ride."

"Sure." Mitchell frowned.

"He's staying with Megan Jeffers." Granny pointed out the window. "Do you remember my telling you about her? She lives directly across the lake."

"Yes." Mitchell hesitated. Rey noticed the awkward way the man held his coat closed. Curious. He was obviously hiding something.

Granny was relentless. Her voice turned sharper. "You can take my scooter if you're conserving gasoline."

Eric glanced again at Rey, then nodded. "I'll be ready to go in just a minute." His smile seemed forced. "What I meant to say is, if that's all right with you."

Granny beamed at her protégé. Rey cleared his throat in an attempt to cover a laugh. "That's just fine. Thank you."

Mitchell hurried from the room.

Rey walked with Grace into the front hallway to retrieve his coat. He wanted to caution her about her boarder, but he didn't have a definite reason. He'd find out more, after speaking to Rachel. Might ask Megan's advice, too, unless she had a lot on her mind. He hadn't a clue as to what her meeting with Russell had been about today.

Grandma held out his parka, squeezing the fabric between her fingers as if checking the insulation. "Kind of thin, don't you think? Couldn't you find anything heavier for this January weather?"

He slipped the jacket on. "It's made with a new kind of insulation, called Thermex."

"Never heard of it."

"You will." At least he hoped so, hoped everyone would in fact. "It works great. Seems to really cut the wind."

Granny made a sound in her throat, communicating her disapproval. She adjusted her glasses farther down her nose and peered over them at his logo. "What is this little picture?"

"A purple mountain range."

There went that sound again. He tried zipping his jacket before she noted that the logo matched the one on his sweater, but he was too late. She reached out and tapped at the woven material.

"This is fine for afternoon visiting, but make sure you have something heavier on if Megan invites you out on one of her runs."

"But this one's fine."

"Don't tell me it's another new-fangled invention. I've been knitting since you were knee-high to a grizzly." She lifted her chin to look at him down the length of her nose. "One thing I know better than anyone else around is sweaters. Next time you come, I'll measure you for one. Knitted with real wool. Not a store-bought imitation." She lowered her voice to a whisper. "In a real man's color."

"Not teal?"

Granny shook her head sternly. "Not teal."

The remainder of his marketing program was saved by the sound of boots on the wooden staircase behind him. Hard to believe he felt relieved to see Mitchell, but he was. Within moments, and after giving a promise to return, Rey left with him.

❄   ❄   ❄

The return trip seated on the back of Grandma Grace's snowmobile was short, with no time for discussion. He would never be heard over the racing engine, anyway. Rey waited until he and Mitchell arrived at Megan's cabin. When Mitchell stepped off the vehicle instead of leaving immediately, Rey saw it as the perfect opening for questions. "So what area of the Okanogan are you researching?"

Mitchell's gaze shifted to the open shed. "Pretty much where you and your buddies were traveling."

His voice didn't sound speculative. How did he know where Rey had been? Granny must have mentioned it to the man earlier. "Did Megan tell you about that?"

"Actually I haven't met Ms. Jeffers yet." Mitchell's shrug was casual. "But news travels fast around here. How's the leg?"

"Improving."

"Can you ski on it yet?" Mitchell fiddled with the wrist straps on his gloves instead of meeting Rey's eyes.

"Not yet." Rey was surprised the other man wanted to prolong their conversation. "Coincidence, don't you think, that my injury was one of two mishaps in the same area Saturday?"

Mitchell nodded. "I heard about the second accident, too."

Smooth movements, cool tone. Maybe Rey could shock him into revealing something. "Of course, the murder was more cause for alarm."

Mitchell lifted his eyes slowly to meet Rey's. "Did you know the boy?"

Rey drew back. The murder label hadn't surprised the man. Mitchell certainly was up on the local news for a newcomer. The victim's age. His gender. He couldn't have read it in the paper. Megan had said the *Gazette* only came out on Fridays.

"Yes, I did meet him. Only once, though. How about you?"

"No."

If Mitchell knew anything substantial about the boy's death, then he was good at hiding it. Rey had expected him to take off in a cloud of exhaust fumes. It was almost if he wanted to be questioned.

Rachel had said, find out everything you can. Odd as a three-legged skier. "I wonder how many deaths happen in this part of the forest each year. I just heard about two others that occurred twelve months ago. A lot of unexplained problems for one stretch of woods, don't you think?"

"Very coincidental, I agree." Mitchell pushed back his hood. His face was more relaxed, transformed into one of a close neighbor settling in for a lengthy chat. "You used the word 'murder' earlier. Is that the official verdict or was that your assessment?"

Rey casually shrugged. "You'll have to ask Sheriff Russell."

Mitchell changed subjects. "You said you knew the boy. How?"

"Met him that morning at Desolation Hut."

"Due east of here, right?"

"That's correct."

"And hours later he was dead."

"You've got it."

The smile disappeared from Mitchell's face. "Then I guess I wouldn't want to be in your shoes, Harrison." He climbed back on Grace's vehicle, turned the key and the engine roared to life.

Rey watched him leave, feeling drained. Who had actually questioned whom? Was he a suspect?

SEVEN

MEGAN CHOSE TO take the long way home. It gave her some time to clear her head. The path wound its way through a narrow switchback, coming in above her cabin. She paused and let the engine idle. Coincidences made her skeptical. The scene below looked like a rendezvous. A prickling feeling raced up the back of her neck and into her scalp.

How did Rey know Eric Mitchell? Though she hadn't met him yet personally, his identity was no longer a guess. She would recognize Granny's Devil Red snowmobile anywhere. The custom paint job, red with black racing stripes, had been a gift from Grace's son who lived back east. If his mother was going to be cruising around these hills alone he wanted to be sure she'd be seen.

Megan turned off her engine and watched the meeting below. The men stood several feet apart. No handshakes, no shoulder-punches, no other male rituals in sight. Maybe they'd just met. Had Mitchell come calling or had Rey met him somewhere? If the latter, did Rey think he had field trip privileges? If he couldn't provide a verifiable excuse for entertaining guests maybe it was time for him to leave.

She felt a tinge of guilt. Why was she suddenly suspicious of him? The strange occurrences over the last few days were making her irritable. He'd been straightforward with her so far. If Rey told her about the meeting, it would confirm her trust was well-placed. If not? She didn't want to consider that scenario.

The same benefit-of-the-doubt courtesy wouldn't be extended to Mr. Mitchell. She'd keep an eye on him in the days to come. His arrival in Snagtooth was poorly timed, even if he were innocent. Granny might have bought his grizzly research story, but Megan hadn't. Not yet.

She waited until Mitchell fired up the engine to start hers again, certain that Granny's 598cc twin cylinder engine would muffle the sound of her own. Rey went inside. She sped down from the ridge as if nothing were out of order.

After pulling up to the shed, she removed her helmet and climbed off. The sun was nearly down, making it hard to see in the gray tones of dusk. Rey stepped back out onto the deck.

"You should be off that knee."

"It's feeling much better."

She would set the stage. Make it easy for him to tell her about Mitchell, then wait and see. They could work on a project such as re-waxing her skis. His, too. Spending time together, that should do it.

Drawing a fortifying breath she climbed the steps into the cabin. She nodded a thank you as Rey stood aside and let her pass.

❋　　❋　　❋

Other than the kitchen light being on, the cabin was dark, as if no one had been home for hours. Maybe her first instinct had been right: Rey met Mitchell somewhere else and just returned. She crossed to the living room to switch on a light. Halfway to the fireplace she stopped. Something was wrong. Chills raced down her arms.

An unusual odor permeated the air. She glanced back at the kitchen. No one had been cooking. Everything seemed in order. What was it? Moments passed before she spotted the problem. A scarf lay on the couch.

Not any scarf. The one she'd searched for after Thia's funeral. It was neatly folded and sitting innocently atop one of the sofa cushions.

"Where . . . ?" Her heart pounded. She couldn't breathe.

Rey stood. "Where what?"

His voice sounded muffled, as if he were emerging from a tunnel. She turned to him, unable to speak. She pulled her turtleneck away from her throat.

Rey moved to her side and placed a hand under her forearm. "You look faint." He urged her to sit. She followed his lead willingly until it became apparent he selected the couch. She jerked away.

"Megan, tell me what's wrong."

She couldn't force words past the lump in her throat. She simply pointed.

"You mean, this?" He lifted the purple and red scarf from the cushion and brought it closer. "I don't understand. It's just a scarf."

"Where did you find it?"

"I've just seen it now for the first time, with you."

She kept her distance, staring. It couldn't be the same one. One end of the knitted garment slipped from his hand and unfolded. Megan peered down at the small, white tag near the tassels and read the familiar label. She hadn't been wrong. Grandma Grace's handiwork.

"It's Thia's." Her voice shook.

Rey nodded and reached for the trailing end. He began refolding the scarf.

Megan swallowed. "I'll do it."

He glanced at her. "It's upsetting you. I'll put it away. Somewhere out of sight."

"Holding it will help me believe it's real." Reaching for the scarf, she gingerly touched it and eventually accepted it into her hand.

She stared down at the intricate pattern. After assuring herself it was real, she lifted the scarf to her face and inhaled.

What had she been expecting, for the yarn to smell like Thia? Certainly she wasn't prepared for the pungent scent of tobacco. She lifted her head. It was the same odor that lingered in the air. Faint, but nevertheless there.

"There could be a simple explanation, Megan." The carefree expression she was growing used to seeing was replaced by a determined set of his jaw. "Maybe it fell from a closet shelf. If Ali saw it and didn't know where to put it . . ."

"Impossible." If it had been stored at her cabin for the time it had been missing, it wouldn't smell of cigarette smoke. She stared down at the pattern again. "We looked for it after Thia's death, but couldn't find it anywhere."

"It appeared from somewhere."

"I haven't seen this in almost a year." She raised her gaze to his. "Actually, that's wrong. I saw it yesterday. We all saw it."

He raised an eyebrow.

Megan knew she wasn't making sense. It didn't make sense to her either. She continued anyway. "In the photo. The one Rachel brought by." She drew an unsteady breath. "The dead boy at the bottom of Devil's Elbow was wearing it."

❄   ❄   ❄

Russell stopped in front of Scott's office door. The kid had done good, even if he didn't check the idea out first. The intent had been right. He was to be congratulated on his imagination, too.

After knocking, Russell waited to be invited in, then opened the door. "Good work, Deputy."

"Huh?" Scott rubbed his eyes. "Oh, Sheriff. Come in."

Russell frowned. Had the kid been napping? His hair was flat on one side. The tight yellow curls had separated, forming a vertical part above his ear where no one would want one.

Okay, so Scott was tired. It was forgivable. Jeffers had accomplished his task in record time. Without further direction being required at all. Now they'd sit back and hope for the best.

The deputy stood and quickly looked around for his holster. He tugged it on. "I was just about to . . ."

"Whatever it is, it can wait."

He stepped further inside the office, closed the door and dropped into the guest chair. "Have a seat. I'm impressed with your solution. I assume you somehow planted it on Harrison. Any results yet?"

Scott's expression seemed confused. He glanced nervously toward the door.

"Don't worry. Everyone's out right now. We can talk." Stretching, Russell raised his arms overhead then linked his fingers behind his head. He inhaled deeply and arched back, letting the vertebrae between his shoulder blades contract, then relax.

Jeffers was staring at him, looking as dumb as a rock. Was the kid just overwhelmed? He tried again with a friendlier tone. "Tell me straight out. Where did you leave it?"

"Sorry? I'm not sure what you mean."

"The scarf."

"What scarf?"

He didn't want to hear it. Blood pounded in his ears. His jaw muscles were locked. He stood. Had to force his mouth to move, to form the words. "The one our murder victim was wearing." His hands clenched. "It was secured in our evidence box until now. I was logging the items and I noticed it missing."

"I don't know anything about it."

Drawing a deep breath he held it, afraid of what he might say. Even more worried about what he might do. But sparing the kid from bodily harm wasn't the most weighing problem on his mind.

If his deputy hadn't taken it then someone else had.

❄   ❄   ❄

Irritation replaced the shock Megan initially experienced. Sitting at her computer desk, she gripped the receiver tightly and swung her feet onto the bed. She crossed one ankle over the other. Russell droned on, ignoring her concerns about Thia's scarf.

Her hands were shaking. She'd called him a dozen times before getting through. And now Carrol was fully engrossed in being his usual son of a bitch self.

She interrupted him. "It's my turn now, so take notes. Someone entered my house. Someone with a key."

Sheriff Russell raised his voice. "I heard you the first time. Harrison might have left the door unlocked. You don't know for sure. Don't take it out on me."

"So forget the key. Where did the scarf come from?"

"I told you, I don't know. It was locked in my evidence box." She heard him curse then kick something, probably a trash can. "It pisses me off that someone was in there. It was right under my nose and I don't know when or how."

She interrupted. "What I want to know is why."

"I don't know that either."

"Call me when you do." She slammed down the phone. It was a childish gesture, but still, it felt good.

She left the bedroom and joined Rey in the kitchen. He stood in front of the stove, a lit match in hand. With the other, he adjusted the stove top control. "Did Russell provide any leads?"

"No." She fixed her gaze on the fire. It was easier that way.

As he lowered the match stick to the front burner, flames jumped six inches high. The towel draped over his arm caught fire.

Megan flinched. Rey tossed the towel in the sink. In a series of quick movements he'd shut off the burner and turned on the faucet. He was saying something, but she couldn't hear.

"Megan?"

"I'm fine."

"Sorry about the towel." He wrung it out and hung it on the oven door to dry. "I'm still getting used to your stove."

"I overreacted. It's been a long afternoon." She withdrew. After crossing to the table she sat, folded her arms and let her head rest against them, trying not to remember the other fire. The one that had changed everything. She closed her eyes.

Mother, I'm coming! The sweat pants Megan wore to sleep had caught fire, scorching her legs. She'd beat on them with a throw pillow. Finally she'd torn them off before continuing her trek to her mother's room. Despite the burns. Wearing only a T-shirt. But it was too late. A fireman pulled her away shouting. She's gone. No . . . Mother.

Rey's fingers skimmed her neck. He brushed the hair at her nape aside tenderly and stroked the skin beneath. His touch was cool and gentle. His thumbs pressed and circled in rhythmic patterns on opposite sides of her spine.

She focused on the strength of his hands. The memories of burning, crackling bedroom walls, her mother screaming, the firemen shouting, were replaced by other sounds. Deep, murmuring sounds. And eventually words. Words of comfort. Similar to those he'd used the night before, to ease her nerves after Russell left. She could grow used to this. The image of the home she'd loved, ablaze, faded.

She lifted her head and glanced around the kitchen. A stack of her cookbooks still sat at the other end of the table. Rey was making himself right at home. She realized that she didn't mind.

"Would you like something to drink?"

His voice was close to her ear. Not sensual. Soothing. Caring. "It might help you relax."

She nodded. "Chamomile tea. Top cabinet."

He released his grip on her shoulders. She followed his unhurried movements around her kitchen as he set the kettle to boil again. Earlier, this same man had been practicing high kicks in her basement wearing sexy, black boxers. She'd just caught him conversing with the most dubious character on this side of the mountains.

Rey set two mugs on the table along with tea bags, spoons and saucers. He took a seat at right angles to her. As he arranged the items before her, she rejected her earlier, distrustful thoughts. He was serving her, Grandma Grace style. Either he was a professional butler back home in Seattle or his late afternoon field trip had been merely across the lake.

"Did you spend the afternoon at Granny's by any chance?" She made her selection and tore open the package.

"Yes. How did you know?"

"Wild guess."

"Rachel stopped by and invited me to visit. Delightful lady."

She set the bag in her empty cup. "I assume you're referring to Grandma Grace."

He smiled. "Correct."

Rachel must have had a purpose. Her friend did nothing without an agenda. Megan reached for a spoon, casually introducing the subject that had been bothering her. "Did you meet Grandma's houseguest?"

Rey nodded. "Eric Mitchell." He stood to retrieve the whistling kettle. "Rachel and I went to Granny's specifically to find out more about him. Unfortunately Rachel left without telling me what she wanted to know." He poured water for them both.

He didn't appear to be trying to hide anything but he still hadn't revealed much. Megan rolled her shoulders, relieving the last traces of tension. Then she leveled with him. "In the short time since he arrived, a murder has taken place, my snowmobile might have been tampered with, and Thia's scarf reappeared twice. First on the victim, then in my living room. That makes Mitchell a rather suspicious character. Why were you with him?"

"He brought me home, at Grace's request. As I said, Rachel left early."

She watched him, digesting the information.

"Megan, Mitchell and I arrived the same day."

She nodded then looked away. They sat quietly for several moments. Finally, she leaned back against her chair and sighed. "To be honest, that timing crossed my mind." She squeezed the tea bag with her spoon then set it aside.

He did the same. "Painfully honest. I understand, though. You hardly know me."

"True." She raised her eyes to his. Her voice was soft, barely audible even to her own ears. "But I think I know enough."

Her heart pounded against her chest as she waited for his response. When he answered, it was in his usual, straightforward manner. "Thank you."

Standing, she crossed to the counter and stacked cookbooks. "Did Rachel give a reason for coming over?"

"No. Didn't say." Rey set his cup down. "Maybe I didn't make the right impression the first time we met. She seemed as if she were checking me out further."

Her conversation with Rachel this morning probably started those gears turning. "She's nosy. Just say it."

"You won't get those words out of me. These walls may have ears." He picked up the stray wrappers and wadded them into a ball. "It was nice to have company. And I must have passed the test, since she deposited me at Grace's."

Megan turned and smiled at him, but said nothing.

"I assume she wouldn't have done so if she thought I was a serial killer."

"She set you up. Inquisition, Part Two. The Sequel."

"Now that you mention it, Grace did have a few questions for me."

"I'll bet." Megan opened a cabinet and shoved a handful of books inside. "By the way, why are these out?"

He stood and walked toward her. "You won't laugh?"

"I'll try not to." She watched him. Though he was still favoring one leg, his movements were definitely less awkward than before.

He leaned against the counter. "Rachel and I attempted to make hot chocolate from scratch this afternoon."

"Rachel was cooking?"

He nodded. "We both were." He handed her a second set of books. "I thought, in case the situation arose again in the future, a recipe might help."

Their hands met. She looked up at him, the urge to laugh fading. She was tall at five foot nine. He was taller. Suddenly her kitchen seemed very small and Rey, very close.

His fingers were long, the nails clipped short and straight. She wanted to turn her hands over, meeting his palm-to-palm. Hers were rough from her work outside. She pulled away from his touch. "It's getting late. Put those on the top shelf. After starting dinner, I need to dial into the system. I want to file an official report regarding Thia's scarf; one that even Russell can't ignore." She was rambling but couldn't stop. She picked up the mugs and carried them to the sink.

He laid his hand on her shoulder. "I'll fix dinner."

She looked at him, disbelief mirrored in her expression.

"Start your report. If we keep the meal plan simple, I'm sure I could pull together tonight's menu."

She focused on the we part of his comment. Not only would this give her more time to file her statement, but it would provide distance, too. She'd save the ski waxing project. She'd had enough closeness for one night. "All right. Let me see what we have."

Crossing to the freezer, she opened it and took out a package wrapped in white paper. "Hope you like fish. It's frozen, not fresh. I get to the store only once every few days."

Without stopping for confirmation, Megan pulled out a few other accompaniments and set them on the counter. Her instructions were quick and concise. All the while, Rey nodded. Twice he glanced at the cookbooks on the top shelf.

"Did you get all that?"

"Yes."

He didn't sound very confident, but his eyes met hers straight on. Her own private chef. She liked the way that sounded. He'd picked up tea-serving quickly enough. He'd do fine. If not, there seem no shortage of her friends around, including Rachel, apparently willing to provide private lessons.

Smiling, Megan headed down toward her combination bedroom and office. "Call me if you need something." She left her door open and tonight's nourishment in his hands.

❄   ❄   ❄

Dinner was interesting, to say the least. Rubberized halibut and petrified carrots. But he'd fixed it for her. She doubted he'd ever been in a kitchen before. And the conversation had been good. Entertaining stories, some real, some embellished. He'd kept a distance between them as if he'd sensed her reticence. He'd been right. What was she afraid of, anyway?

Megan secured the door to the shed, wondering why she'd bothered. The wooden structure was old and flimsy, a padlock wasn't really necessary. A solid punch could knock over any one of the four walls. But habits were hard to break. She gave in, spinning the tumbler one more time to ensure that it caught.

The stars were out in full tonight. Inhaling deeply, she turned and stared at Snagtooth Ridge. It stood tall and dark against the night sky like a fortress wall separating her from the Devil's Elbow. On clear, crisp evenings such as this, thoughts of sleeping outdoors always came to mind. The fact that she would develop frostbite by midnight, though, kept her sensibly indoors.

Her compromise was as simple as it was frequent. She'd sleep with the bedroom windows open a crack. Not far enough as to invite furry, four-legged company inside, or the two-footed variety for that matter, but wide enough to be able to imagine that she was still outdoors. Maybe one day she'd indulge herself by investing in an expedition-style tent and polar sleeping bag. Or put it on next year's Christmas list.

As teenagers, she and her sister Thia traded secret cross-your-heart wish lists each year at holiday time. There was always an unspoken promise between them: each would hint to their parents of the other's special wishes before the shopping was over and the money spent. When Thia moved away to college, Megan thought the tradition would die. It hadn't. Thia had called the first year; Megan had denied wanting anything special. How could she admit such silliness to an older sister who already had everything? Besides, what she had secretly wished for, money couldn't buy.

She bit her bottom lip. Time to quit feeling sorry for herself. Didn't she already have more than she'd ever thought possible right here? She vowed to focus on her home, her job, and her close friends. Not on her family for a change.

A movement in the kitchen window drew her gaze. Rey was finishing their dinner dishes. He'd insisted on doing that task, nudging her away from the sink. Something he could easily do despite his bum knee, he'd said, accompanied by one of his heart-stopping smiles. Foolish though it was, she enjoyed his company; sharing her table, thumbing though her magazines, asking her opinion.

He'd be gone soon. Now there was something to think about.

She walked around to the right side of the shed, toward the wood pile located near a stand of fir trees. There was a second, larger stack of wood inside the structure, but those logs were freshly cut, still green. Pulling back the tarp, she spotted three medium sized logs on top. Perfect. She shouldn't need more than that. One quick trip and she'd be done.

After loading her arms with wood, she turned toward the cabin. The door opened as she reached the bottom of the stairs. Rey came out on the deck, zipping his coat. "Can I help?"

"It's too icy." She ran her boot along the step in front of her. "Especially the stairs."

"Compromise, then. Hand me those. I'll take them inside and come back for more."

She stared at his outstretched arms, not at all irritated that he'd interrupted her communion with the night air. She imagined him reaching for her instead. Ridiculous.

He kept his distance. She wasn't sure if he was respecting her space or trying to avoid her. What did she want from him? Her intimate relationships with men had been brief and lousy.

She climbed the stairs and stood in front of him, but didn't drop the logs into his waiting hands. She wanted him to come to her, if only in this small way. He did.

He curled his hands around the load of wood she held, one above and one below. His fingertips brushed the front of her jacket.

She stepped back, thankful it was dark. "A few more trips, maybe a dozen logs, should do it."

"Fine. I'll stash these and be right back."

She wanted to kick herself, but instead moved on with the task. As she leaned over to collect a second load of wood, a shot rang out. She ducked and released the logs, snagging the tarp with her boot as she fell to the ground. A bullet clipped the side of the tree next to her, spraying shards of bark across the sleeve of her jacket. One fragment scraped her cheek. The second shot had her scrambling onto the plastic tarp, headed for the trees beyond. She grabbed for her pistol.

She never reached it. The body-slam from behind was less expected than the gunfire. It bruised her hip and propelled her forward. The plastic acted as a sled and she coasted on her stomach toward the far end of the woodpile.

It was Rey on top of her. He yelled into her ear. "Get down!"

"I am down."

"Someone's shooting at you."

She wanted to confirm her awareness of that fact, sprinkled with as many four-letter words as she could remember. Her arms were buried beneath her, trapping her securely in a face-down position. Without her gun, she was defenseless.

In the distance, an engine started. The snowmobile had to be somewhere near the ridge. "Get off me. They're getting away."

"Good."

She tried to shrug him by rolling over. No luck, he outweighed her. "I need to know who shot at me."

"The bad guys did, what else do you need to know? What's important here is that you're safe."

His voice was calm and controlled. He was speaking to her as if she were a child. Her anger soared as the engine faded in the distance. Now she'd never know. Exhaling slowly, she counted to three. It didn't help. "I'm a good marksman. I could have stopped them."

Rey turned to one side. Though she was able to roll face-up, his arm still held her trapped. "It's too risky."

Adrenaline continued to race through her, causing all rational thought to flee. "My risk, not yours."

He frowned. "Is that right?"

"Yes. Are you getting the picture?" She studied his expression, hoping to see comprehension. Instead he watched her watch him.

"Wrong, Megan. You're not alone in this." He moved closer. His gaze lowered to her lips. "Now get this picture."

He kissed her. So unexpected. So unfair, for him to do so when she least expected it. She shoved at his shoulders. There were more important things right now, such as chasing her attacker.

But his mouth was gentle, convincing. Coaxing her to respond. He didn't say a word except for her name, and that he whispered against her lips. In response she tightened her hold on him. Thoughts of gunmen vanished as the pleasure of his kiss swept though her. Other sensations, too: his thighs resting heavily against hers, his warm palm cradling her cold skin. It didn't matter that the temperatures were below zero. She wanted this to go on and on, here and now.

The gun inside her jacket dug into her ribs. She wiggled her trapped hands out from between their bodies, moving her pocket aside with her elbow. Her actions must have caught him off-guard. He paused and raised his head, as if puzzled about something.

God, did he want to discuss this? She didn't. Simply wanted to feel. The scent of his heated skin melted her defenses. She wanted him to kiss her again.

Something landed inches from her head. She flinched. So did Rey. Her training kicked in. She rolled over, out from under him. In a split second her glove was off, her pocket emptied and her pistol in hand. Perfect firing position.

Squinting, she saw that a fir cone had dropped, nothing more. A small one at that. After setting the safety again, Megan pointed at the culprit with the tip of her barrel. Glancing over her shoulder at Rey, she shrugged. "Sorry."

He was motionless, staring at her .38. If he'd been looking into the distance with that same expression, she'd have thought someone was behind her with a high-powered rifle.

"What's wrong?"

His words sounded forced. "You have a gun."

"I have several."

He stood.

"You saw my rifle the day I rescued you." No response. She frowned and rolled to her feet. "Target practice is a hobby of mine. I know what I'm doing."

"A rifle is different. This is a handgun."

How observant. "A Colt Mustang to be exact. The safety is on." She held it out to him so that the porch light would illuminate the metal. He frowned and stepped back.

Not only was she insulted, but she wasn't through being kissed yet either. "What's the matter?"

"Just put it away."

"Can't we talk about it?"

"No." He stared at her for several seconds then cleared his throat. "Actually, yes, but not now." He took a deep breath. "I was once a pawn in a game of Russian Roulette. I have an aversion to handguns."

He walked toward the cabin, then stopped and turned back. He was waiting for her. He wanted his space, but wouldn't leave her alone. Damn but he made life hard on himself. And her. Her muscles tensed.

She slowly followed him up the slick steps. By the time her coat was unzipped and hung on the rack, Rey was downstairs. The connecting door at the top of the staircase was closed.

❄   ❄   ❄

He'd acted like such a fool. When would the nightmare of his kidnapping fade? It had been over twenty years ago and yet it seemed like yesterday. The sight of a handgun, any gun, always brought it back full force.

The timing had been very poor. Her response to his kiss had been extraordinary. He'd like to continue where they left off.

The phone on the end table rang. Rey grabbed the receiver and sat down on the edge of the bed. "Moore, here." He grimaced at the slip. Not only had he answered Megan's phone, he'd used his real name.

"Don't you mean Harrison, big brother?"

"You're right." His tone softened. "How are you?"

"Surviving. You sent me off with Dave, remember? What a fun guy."

The sound of Alison's sigh made him smile. "Take it easy on him. I need him to be back in Seattle tomorrow. In one piece. Rested."

Alison snorted before changing subjects. "How's the knee?"

"Fine. I'm exercising it daily." Other than entertaining Rachel, visiting Granny, cross-examining Mitchell, and trying to protect Megan from a sniper, he hadn't done a thing all day. "It's good to hear your voice. Is Dave nearby?"

"Oh, I see. The here's-your-hat-what's-your-hurry routine. Great. Yeah, I'll get him."

"Say hello to Mildred for me when you get back to the condo. Tell her I'm learning to cook. The kitchen will no longer be off-limits."

167

"I can't wait to tell her." Another snort of laughter. "She'll be drafting her resume faster than you can say ham-and-cheese-omelet. Just a minute."

She shouted Dave's name. Rey pulled the receiver away from his ear too late.

"Here's my old man now. See you soon, I hope."

After a series of heated whispers, Dave came on the line. "Rey. How are you?"

"Fine. What was the 'old man' in reference to? Did you have trouble keeping up today?"

"No." He hesitated for a moment, as if polishing his word choice. "We pretended to be husband and wife earlier. It was quite innocent, but she hasn't stopped ribbing me since."

Rey smiled but didn't comment.

Dave cleared his throat. "I owe you an explanation, I guess."

"No need."

"Indulge me, then. We ran across a group of heli-skiers this afternoon and engaged them in conversation. It was a foursome that has vacationed here for years. They've never heard of Mountain High Adventures." Silence reigned for nearly a minute before Dave dropped the next bomb. "Neither has Lilly, the B&B owner."

"Megan saw them."

"But the real question is, had she ever seen them before? Or only on the day of the murder?"

"I don't know. I'll have to ask."

"Do. Meanwhile, I'll have someone check it out from Seattle."

"Good. I have another item for your list. A man named Mitchell. Eric Mitchell. He just moved in next door, and is renting a room from Megan's neighbor, Grace. His cover is that he's a researcher from the University of Washington."

"My alma mater."

"Exactly. Maybe you could find out something from the graduate office. He's supposedly studying the habits of grizzly bears."

"In the winter?"

"Doesn't make sense to me either."

"I'll see what I can find out. Anything else?"

"Those two items, plus running the business while I'm away, should keep you busy. I'll try dialing into our e-mail system. If I'm successful you can send documents to me regarding Mountain High Adventures."

"Will Megan let you use her computer?"

"I haven't broached the subject yet." He paused. "The PC is in her room."

"Close quarters, right? Just keep me posted. And remember, stay off your feet."

The only time he'd been truly prone today had been while tackling Megan in the snow. And immediately afterwards, of course. The latter part was very memorable. Next time, he'd expect the gun. Wouldn't run. Hopefully there would be a next time. "I'll see what I can do."

❄   ❄   ❄

"Fucking cool." Billy unhooked his lap belt to get a better look out one of the copter's windows. "A cake walk, Lute. No sweat."

Lute scowled at the kid. This punk wouldn't last long. Too full of himself. Probably had his ride to the top of the cocaine pyramid mapped out in his mind, with loose women and fast cars sprinkled into the picture along the way. He wasn't even old enough to go to the prom yet. Lute felt his jaw tighten.

He hated flying after dark, but Cowboy's orders had been clear. The Desolation Point stash was to be retrieved tonight. And the Needles drop. No more excuses. Tomorrow the deliveries would resume.

Cowboy was antsy. His Canadian partners must be turning the screws, livid that their product was backing up. Lute couldn't think of any other reason for Cowboy's recent behavior, except for maybe that phone call today. Builders. What was his boss building, anyway? It was even causing him to growl at Princess.

The chopper had taken off from the airstrip so fast this evening, they hadn't stocked their regular supplies. No food, no water. He didn't have time to grab his backpack, either. If the copter went down, they'd be stuck in the forest without emergency provisions. But Cowboy had made his point. The time for errors was past.

Lute pulled a note pad from his pocket and scanned the last entries: dates and corresponding bag counts. He thought about adding tonight's pickup to the list. When they were back in town, Princess would recheck the count before anyone else was let on board, then countersign Lute's arithmetic. Crude, but it was Cowboy's method of inventory control. There were other, less obvious ways to skim off product if so inclined. He didn't have the stomach for it, thank God.

The kid across from him wasn't belted in. Reminiscent of the last rookie. From the way his fists were clenching and unclenching, adrenaline must really be pumping. He was grinning as if this were an amusement park ride and making some kind of noise. A combination of humming and singing. Tossing his head back and forth. Next, he'd start playing air guitar.

"Shut up and sit still." Lute didn't try to mask his disgust.

The kid stopped and stared for a moment, as if he didn't have a clue. Then, in an instant stroke of genius, he clipped himself in and grabbed for his headset. "Sorry. This is just so fucking cool."

"You said that already. About a dozen times."

The kid shrugged and strummed the air in front of him. Shit. This gofer would be dead within a week.

"Next stop, Needles. Coming up on your right." Lute focused his attention as Princess' voice crackled through his headset. "ETA five minutes."

He pushed the transmit button. "Ready back here." He drew a deep breath and glanced out the window.

The night was clear, the sky thick with stars. The hut came into view as the chopper began its descent. He ignored the kid behind him. There was a creepiness about this, almost as if they were being watched. The same feeling had crawled up the back of his neck last time he was here.

Princess's voice brought him back to the present. "One hundred feet. Now fifty. Get ready."

He grabbed one of the empty backpacks and tossed it to Billy. Lute would finish this pickup, then make tracks for Mexico. Better to be poor than dead. He turned to the window. Soft landings took too long. He braced himself.

A glint of light flashed from among the small stand of trees. Was it the moon's reflection or the copter's landing lights? He didn't know and didn't care. For an instant, the profile of a snowmobile was visible. Damn.

"Abort. Abort." Thank God he hadn't unclipped his mike yet. "Princess. Get us the hell out of here."

"Cowboy's not going to like this."

"We have company."

"I read you." He heard her sigh. "Over."

The chopper lifted. His heart was beating so fast he thought his chest might explode. Why, this time? A leak in the network?

Cowboy would be pissed, but this one wasn't his fault. He would explain. Make the risk clear.

He didn't know if that would be good enough.

❄   ❄   ❄

Eric lowered his night goggles and cursed. Mountain High Adventures finally makes an appearance, and he tips them off. Parking this close to the Needles had been a fool's mistake, especially on a starry evening. He should have known better. It didn't matter that his right hand gripping the steering had lost all sensation, he should have followed procedures. What the hell was he doing up here anyway, at less than one hundred percent efficiency? Damn his drive for revenge.

Cowboy's chopper was flying outside their normal morning pattern again. Logan's man stationed at the Lost River Airstrip had earned his pay today. The chopper had been pegged at the Needles. If his snow scooter, as Grace called it, had started he would have arrived in plenty of time. He suppressed the urge to kick something. Instead he glanced at his illuminated watch. Eleven P.M.

The ride back to Grace's dragged on. Logan would be pissed and he had every right to be.

This was a sorry way to end his career as a field agent. He dreaded turning in his trench coat for a tie and parking pass. It would be hell to sit behind a desk, just as sure as dealers made bail. He squeezed the handlebars tighter, willing his right hand to perform. It wouldn't.

As he topped the last crest, Megan's cabin appeared below him. Then Grace's and Rachel's, forming a distant triangle around the frozen lake. The warm glow of their living room lamps disrupted the blackness of the night. Such a cozy little wilderness community. They should begin to feel the tension in the air. Soon, they should be scared.

Two dead bodies last year; one so far this week. That would scare most people. He didn't know Rachel, but she had the reputation of being as tough as a street-wise cop.

On the other end of the spectrum was Grace, his landlord. Her turn-of-the-century hospitality made her vulnerable. If Cowboy himself appeared on her doorstep, she would invite him to dinner, provided he didn't track snow in on the floor. He shook his head at the memory of her warning him not to stay out too long after dark.

Of the three, Megan Jeffers was the one who should be scared. He'd meant the appearance of Thia's scarf in her cabin to be a warning. She was getting too close. Cowboy was on to her, checking her out and looking for her weak spot. Both hers and her houseguest's.

Cowboy's list of killings was lengthy. Topping Logan's report was a recent slaying at an Everett truck stop. The victims were two innocent kids who'd picked an unfortunate time to walk past one of Cowboy's delivery trucks during a redistribution of goods. They were probably on their way to get potato chips and soda pop. Cowboy wouldn't hesitate to add Jeffers' name to the list. Or Harrison's either. Mitchell's own name was on the roster of near-misses. He squeezed the right hand grip on the snowmobile, just to make sure he still could.

As he neared the homes he eased up on the gas. The residents would be asleep by now. Logan had confirmed that local residents were being questioned. Some private investigator back in Seattle was already poking into records. He'd expected that, but not so soon.

Harrison's picture was being circulated on the streets, too. And not by Logan. Luckily for Mr. Moore, Cowboy was looking under the wrong name. Good thing for his sister, too, wherever she was. Their shared Seattle condo was still empty.

Eric pulled in front of Grace's rear door, turned off the engine and pocketed the key. Cowboy wanted that stash, wanted it bad enough to try for it a third time. At night. There had to be a way to keep Jeffers and Harrison out of his hair until he and Logan could close in. He refused to accept any other scenario.

He climbed off his snowmobile, trudged up the stairs and pushed open the door, suddenly wishing for company. He'd even welcome another inane conversation with Grace. This time maybe she'd choose a dissertation on how runny noses were good for cleansing the mind. He would listen attentively. Anything to delay his call to Logan.

All was quiet. Damn. He climbed the steps one at a time.

EIGHT

EGAN PARKED ALONGSIDE Granny's century-old Mountain Hemlock. No one had actually verified its age but since Granny had declared it to be nearly one hundred, no one argued. She sat silently beneath the array of homemade bird feeders, staring at the garden near the lake. Granny had selected Apricot Parrot Tulips as her *frauds du jour*. Megan shook her head and climbed off her snowmobile.

She needed a subtle way to gain information about the new boarder without putting her friend on edge. Did Mitchell have an alibi for the time of last night's shooting? If she could obtain proof he was here for legitimate reasons, she'd back off. If not, then he'd better get out of her neck of the woods. No one was going to take advantage of Snagtooth's number one senior citizen while she had anything to say about it.

She walked around to the back of her vehicle and stood in the foot-deep snow while she unpacked her decoy; a fresh cinnamon loaf, the supposed reason for her visit. The charade had been Rey's idea. He'd baked the loaf while she was out on her morning ski run. Some vacation. She wasn't sure what she'd call being cooped up in a twelve hundred square foot cabin with an absent host and a stack of cookbooks, but it wasn't vacation.

When she'd found the bread on the kitchen counter, she wanted to thank him but the door to the staircase had been closed. He might have been napping, but that wasn't the real reason she hadn't gone downstairs. Neither was the fact that he might emerge half-dressed from the shower again. Her imagination was still racing from the first time.

The snow pack crunched beneath her boots as she high-stepped over to the walkway. Looking down, she stared at the bare slate which fitted together like an ancient jigsaw puzzle. The walk was newly shoveled. She raised an eyebrow.

The door opened on her fourth knock. Granny's eyes lit with surprise. She removed the sewing pins from her mouth before speaking. "Come in. It's cold enough today to send Eric's grizzlies packing for Florida." She stepped aside so Megan could enter. After closing the door, Granny led her toward the parlor.

Megan called after her, holding the brown paper sack aloft. "I thought you might like a snack."

"Oh, heaven's no. I'm not at all tired. Got plenty of sleep last night." The older woman waved a handful of fabric at her, signaling her to follow. "And I have too much to do to take a midday break now. Nice of you to think of me, though."

Megan glanced at the bag in her hand, shrugged, then laid it on the entryway table. Time enough for that later. If nothing else, she could use the same loaf as an excuse tomorrow. Following Granny's invitation she proceeded down the hall, straightening the hooked rug with the heel of her foot as she went.

The official guest chair was already in the position of honor, directly in front of the antique sewing machine. Megan usually moved it there whenever she came to visit so Granny could hold a conversation while continuing with her work. It was the heavy, high-backed wooden variety, one that shouldn't be lifted by a woman in her seventies. She'd have to speak to her friend about that. Maybe it was time for something on rollers.

Taking her seat, she scanned the project underway. Megan tallied at least five coordinating shades of purple fabric. That included the yardage around Grandma's shoulders, the one under the needle and the others on the back of the sofa.

"These are lovely." Megan ran her hand over the closest strip of lavender calico. "Another home economics project for the high school?"

Granny shook her head regretfully. She removed the pins from her mouth one by one and stuck them into her wrist cushion. "No, dear. Ever since Christmas break, the little darlings haven't been able to manage a single seam." She pumped the pedal. "They're back on pot holders, hand-sewn, until they settle down."

Megan stifled the urge to grin. Her friend had been assisting with Home Economics classes ever since indoor electricity had come to Snagtooth, maybe earlier. And no one graduated from Hades High, as the kids called it, unless Granny said so.

As the machine began to hum once again, Megan scanned the parlor and the kitchen beyond. Every window was primly covered with ruffled curtains. Each piece of furniture was already decorated with homespun trimming. There was nowhere in this house for anything new. Must be another quilt, but purple? It wouldn't match anything. "What are you making?"

Granny looked up, repositioned her glasses and sniffed. "Why, nothing. Did I leave that oven on again?" She turned toward the stove, shaking her head. "Be a dear and check it for me, will you?" The needle started moving once again.

Megan stood and crossed to the kitchen. Rachel had already laid claim to the task of shopping for new batteries. Hopefully she'd go today. This would be a good chance to look around unobserved. Maybe she'd find some clue that would pin down the elusive Mr. Mitchell.

She strolled over to the refrigerator. On it were class photos from the last decade of students, autographed by the seamstresses themselves. Mementos such as these were the only payments Granny would accept. Her gaze stopped midway down the fridge. Covering the lower left corner of The Class of '94 was a small Polaroid of Mitchell. The cross-hatched appearance made her guess that it had been taken through the window screen.

She kept her voice low. "Grace, you sneak." What luck. Removing the magnet, she cradled the snapshot in her palm and studied it. The man's lips were parted, his expression startled. Suspicious individual if she'd ever seen one. Maybe if the sheriff faxed a copy of it to the police they would identify him quickly.

Granny's chair squeaked as she scooted across the floor. Megan shoved the picture into her shirt pocket.

"What's your opinion about the recent happenings concerning Cutthroat Pass?"

Megan moved closer toward the kitchen doorway, frowning. "I guess I haven't heard."

"One of the local heli-skiing groups is reopening service up there. Starting Saturday." Granny removed a fabric marking stick from behind her ear and drew a notation in chalk. "I think it's just terrible."

"I agree. Those runs haven't been popular since the hut closed two years ago for repairs. I'm surprised they're bothering. The terrain is rocky and hard on skis. Seems like a waste of money to me."

"I was referring to opening the hut in its unadorned state, my dear." Granny looked at her as if explaining that snow was cold. "Not a stitch of happiness anywhere." The older woman scooted the material back into position under the foot. "Can't have that. It reflects on the entire area."

Granny resumed her pressure on the pedal. The calico fed through the machine, inch by needle-hammering inch. The noise was beginning to give Megan a headache. She joined Granny by the sewing machine. "I hope you don't take this wrong, but the Cutthroat Hut is too far for you to go alone. You'll have to wait to decorate it until I have time. It'll be at least a week until I can . . ."

"Thanks for caring." The aging eyes seemed to warm as they looked at her. Granny patted her hand. "But I won't be alone."

"You won't?"

"No. Eric's offered to take me there. He suggested it while we were working on these curtains last night."

"We?"

She nodded. "He pinned, while I sewed."

That explained the guest chair. Megan scowled at her friend. "I don't think that's a very good idea."

"He doesn't know how to sew."

Megan sighed. "I meant, don't go anywhere with him. Not until we know him better."

"He's a nice young man. Did you see the walk outside?"

Megan nodded.

"Not as solid and friendly as your young man, of course." Granny's eyes twinkled. "But he'll make some lucky girl a good husband someday. After I finish training him, that is."

"My young man?" Megan words almost stuck in her throat. "You mean Rey?"

"Of course." She pushed her glasses down the bridge of her nose and looked over them. "Unless there are others."

Megan was speechless.

"No need to blush. Are there several gentlemen calling on you these days?"

"Rey didn't come calling. He's living in my basement. That's all."

"Times are different now, aren't they?" She heard the clucking sound again as Granny frowned.

The older woman set down her sewing. "Maybe we should talk about that for awhile." She pointed to the seat in front of her, indicating she was in the mood for a nice long chat.

Megan needed to get her back on the right conversation track. Time to forget subtlety and dive in head first. "Maybe another day on that subject. I need you to listen to me." Megan moved the chair from the far side of the machine until she could sit next to her friend. "Please don't go anywhere with Mitchell until I've had a chance to check him out."

"I can assure you, he knows all about snow travel. We'll be perfectly safe. I've lent him my little Red Devil on several occasions." Granny shook her head slowly. "That snow scooter of his is ready for the junk pile, you know."

Megan leaned closer and spoke slowly, making direct eye contact. "I'm not convinced he's here for legitimate reasons."

The older woman's gaze widened for an instant before she began shaking her head, chuckling slightly to herself. "Rey was concerned about the same thing." She leaned forward. Her tone was conspiratorial. "I advised him to find another way."

Megan frowned. "To do what?"

"Go courting, of course." Granny pulled the measuring tape from around her neck. "I believe a bit of jealousy is fine, as long at it isn't taken to the extreme. And telling tales out of school just isn't right."

"Tales?" She sighed. It couldn't have been the shooting, he'd visited Granny before that had occurred. Rachel's photo of the murder victim? That was it. "Did he mention the excitement we had Sunday night?"

Granny stared at her. "Of course not. He's too much the gentleman for that, I would expect." She continued before Megan could get in another word. "Envy isn't necessarily bad, in fact sometimes can help speed things along." She checked the fabric's width then nodded, satisfied. "But Eric is eons away from being ready to settle down. My money's on Rey. I told him to simply relax. Let nature take its course."

Megan's temples throbbed. How had he reacted to these remarks? Her face flushed at the thought. She stood. "I've got to be going. I have a few things to straighten out at home."

"Don't blame you a bit. If I were younger, I'd hurry home, too." Granny chuckled before turning back toward her machine. "Give my regards to your young man."

"Believe me, your name will be mentioned."

❄   ❄   ❄

Eric focused his binoculars on the departing helicopter. High Mountain Adventures, the drop-off crew, was buzzing around Snowy Lakes. Would they be back on pattern today: one side in, wait two hours, other side out? Their start time was already off. Early morning was more their style, when the legitimate charters flew.

He'd retrieved the message from Logan's spotter just in time. Instead of waiting in his room for the call, he choose to inhale fresh-baked cinnamon rolls and suck down Grace's tea in the kitchen. The treat was his reward for shoveling her walk. He'd agreed, but asked for them to go. She'd clucked at him disapprovingly, mumbled about poor digestion before completely ignoring his request and setting him a place at the table.

He hated tea, but Grace reminded him he'd had coffee yesterday. Too much of a good thing makes it a bad thing, she'd said, capping it off with a smile as she shoved the tea bags toward him. He'd had no choice but to accept.

Rising from behind the snowdrift where he'd crouched for the last half hour, he didn't bother to brush off his jacket. Though his perch was less than a mile due east of Desolation Point, it was well away from Jeffers' training route. A perfect location, since the stash was still at the first hut. At the Needles, too. But they'd attempted neither this run. Maybe he'd missed a successful pickup. He flicked the ashes from his thin cigar, twisted and tore the end, then stored it in his pocket.

As he scrambled down the icy hillside, he shifted his binoculars to his right hand. If he fell, he wanted to be ready to brace himself with his left. His next stop was home; he'd report in to Logan then wait for the spotter to call again for the pickup.

Home. Grandma Grace's. Eric shook his head. His gray-haired warden had gotten to him in a mere three days. Hell, it was better than living on the streets. Would anyone fault him for enjoying the fuss she made? Not unless the distraction screwed up his mission, of course.

When he reached flat ground, he fumbled for his keys. He had flipped open the storage compartment on Grace's snowmobile before realizing his right hand was empty. He turned. The binoculars were behind him in the snow, halfway down the hill. He'd dropped them even though he hadn't fallen. He'd dropped them without realizing it.

Shit. His hand again. He rubbed his jacket sleeve, where it covered the scar on his forearm. Guilt made his head pound. Logan should be out here, not him. He wanted to be the one who brought Cowboy down. But if he failed, he'd have a hard time living with himself. His pride just might lose him the battle. Damn it. Backtracking, he retrieved the glasses. He wouldn't consider the possibility of defeat. Not yet.

After climbing onto Grace's snowmobile, he gunned the engine. He gripped the steering hard, willing life back into his right hand. There was some sensation; enough to drive but not enough to shoot. He knew what his course of action would be as clearly as he knew it was wrong. He'd be damned if he'd miss this chance. Revenge was a bitch.

He headed toward home.

※　　　※　　　※

Megan pulled into her side yard and switched off the engine. The smell of soup cooking caught her by surprise. What next? She climbed the steps and pulled open the door. Rachel was curled up on her couch, Rey was executing another of his martial arts routines. When through, he turned.

She stood still, taking in the scene. He was performing for Rachel. Was he merely doing so while waiting for lunch to simmer or was there some other agenda? At least he'd emerged from his downstairs sanctuary. Guess she had Rachel to thank for that.

"Don't let me interrupt." She pulled the tab on her coat with unnecessary force, nearly jamming the fabric in the zipper. Today was not going well. She expelled a slow breath and calmly shrugged out of her jacket. "Continue. I insist." She walked into the kitchen, chin up, a forced smile on her face.

Rachel stood. "We're making soup. Rey thought you'd enjoy having lunch ready when you returned from your morning rounds. Didn't you, Rey?"

He nodded. "Yes."

Megan turned. The two were standing side by side. Conspirators. She felt like a third thumb but kept her tone even. "I'll take over in here. Please continue with your exercises. It will help speed your recovery."

She glanced around the kitchen. A soup pot full of vegetables, cookbooks scattered everywhere again. Her long forgotten recipe box, chocked full of dog-eared index cards, was also out and had been rifled through. Where had he found that old thing?

Rachel came forward, joining her in the kitchen. "Megan, he was halfway through his routine when I came in. I asked for a demo." Her voice was a near-whisper. "I'm sorry."

"There's nothing to be sorry for." She flipped one of the books closed and returned it to the top shelf.

"I was curious. And I thought it would pass the time." Rachel put a hand on her sleeve. "Don't be ..." She swallowed the last word.

Megan finished for her. "What, jealous?"

"Angry."

"I'm neither." She kept her voice low. "In fact, I'm curious, too."

She spoke to Rey over her friend's shoulder. Her tone was cool, distant, and professional. "I'd love to watch you perform. I've always thought that the many martial arts disciplines were dramatic and beautiful." Keeping her expression noncommittal, she made her way to the couch and sat. "Please continue. That is, if you haven't overworked your knee yet."

Her gaze had not met his yet. She kept her eyes focused downward, pretending to remove lint from her ski pants. He was motionless. She felt rather than saw him watching her, waiting for an acknowledgment.

She didn't know how long she could remain still. For God's sake, even Rachel was quiet. She would strangle her friend when this was over. When he refused to move, her gaze traveled slowly upward, from bare feet, past fleece-covered thighs, over his muscular sweaty torso until she was looking straight at him.

Rey bowed, never losing eye contact with her, then began his routine. He executed a graceful maneuver, revealing his profile. Effortlessly he turned the other way. She liked that view just as well.

His exercise gained speed, interspersed with rapid explosive movements. Each time he leapt and spun, she cringed, thinking that he'd land on his injured leg and sink to the floor. But he never did.

The patterns were repeated, then varied. Only his left leg went airborne, not both. Each time she held her breath. He was using caution. She must be the only one feeling reckless at this instant.

Though there was no radio on, no stereo, she swore she heard background music. At times she wanted to sway with it, at other times her heart raced on ahead.

The phone rang and Rey stopped. Megan couldn't move. She glanced at Rey. He was breathing hard. Picking up a hand towel, he dried his neck and watched her. It rang again.

Rachel cleared her throat. "How about if I get it?" She stood and crossed to the kitchen.

With Rachel gone, the living room suddenly seemed smaller. Megan tried to think of something, anything, to say. "Thank you for the demonstration. I . . ." She swallowed. "We enjoyed that."

"Any time."

He moved closer. "I'd like to talk about last night."

His upper torso was glistening with perspiration. She glanced down. In all the confusion, she hadn't bothered to remove her boots. The snow had melted from them, leaving behind a puddle on the hardwood floor.

"Yes, well." She cleared the lump from her throat. "I would, too. But I'm not thinking clearly just now. Could it wait?" She stood. "I have a mess on the floor to clean up."

"We can postpone it, not ignore it or pretend it didn't happen. All right?"

She nodded.

He lingered for a moment longer then went downstairs.

Rachel caught the phone on the fourth ring.

"Russell. Greetings, big guy. What can I do for you?" She paused. "Of course I'm not Megan. How kind of you to notice." Another pause. "Well silly you, calling my number instead. Better luck next time. Bye." She pressed the switch hook then dropped the receiver into a drawer and shut it. "That takes care of that. Let's have lunch."

Megan entered the kitchen and nodded her approval at the phone. "Thanks. If you set the table, I'll get some towels." Rachel began slinging plates, bowls and utensils around, pausing to give the soup an occasional stir.

After removing her boots, Megan attacked the job of sponging water from the living room floor. When Rachel began humming the theme song to a famous love story, she stopped her with a single glare.

"Well, I think things are heating up nicely."

Megan gave the floorboards another pat, then stood. "You'd better be referring to the soup."

"You've got it bad, my friend."

"This discussion is off-limits." Megan quietly closed the door to the room below. "I mean it."

"All right. I'll respect your wishes, against my better judgment. But only after I go on record as saying, go for it."

"That's your recommendation for every situation, Rach. You have no self-restraint at all these days." She walked over to the hall bath and tossed the towels into the hamper then stopped to wash her hands. When she entered the kitchen, Rachel was ready for her.

"That's because I believe holding back is a waste of time. It won't earn you brownie points in anyone's book. You'll come out the loser. Look at me, I'm living proof."

"I'm not trying to rack up points." She straightened the napkin and silverware next to the nearest plate. "I'm just trying to get through the next week with my heart intact. Got that?"

"Ah ha. Now we're getting somewhere." Rachel looked smug.

Megan backpedaled. "All right. So I'm attracted to him. That doesn't mean I plan to do anything about it."

"Why not?"

She sighed. "Because he's not interested, okay? There. I've said it."

"Your vast experience led you to this conclusion?"

Megan glared at her.

"Then, how do you know? Have you asked him?"

"Of course not."

"You should."

A second glare.

"All right. I'll ask Rey for you."

"Don't even joke about that."

"Ask me what?" The door to the stairwell was once again open.

Megan turned and said the first thing that came to mind. "Your theory on the scarf that reappeared yesterday."

"That's right." Rachel turned, so that her back was to Rey then lowered her voice. "What scarf?"

"Thia's."

Color drained from Rachel's face. "My God."

"It just appeared." Megan put her hand on her friend's shoulder. "I don't know why. A sick joke of some kind."

"Where could it have come from?"

"Again, I don't know."

Rey stood closer to Megan. "I feel as if I have a personal stake in this. Tell me again about the history of the scarf." He looked at her directly. "It would help clear things in my mind."

"All right." She put her fingers to her temple and pressed to relieve the sudden pounding. "That would help me too."

Rey pulled out a chair for her, one for Rachel and a third for himself. "So where do we start?"

"With the last time we saw it." Megan picked up a spoon and fidgeted with it. "Thia was wearing the scarf the morning she died. She always did, for good luck. I didn't find it later with her things, so I simply assumed it was lost in the aftermath of the accident."

"Some of Pete's personal effects were also missing." Rachel shrugged. "We both figured there must be a reasonable explanation and didn't question it. Since it now seems that we really need to know, I guess I'll look for the pictures."

"What pictures?"

"Of the accident. I believe they're packed away in a box I gave to Pete's mother."

"If you can find them, we'll verify she's wearing it. We can also match it to the one the boy was wearing the morning I arrived."

"I'll send for the box. His mom lives out of town."

"Good." Rey pushed back the plate in front of him then made a bridge with his fingers. "The fact that he died later that day, in a manner similar to Thia and Pete, can't be ignored."

Megan nodded. "And now the scarf reappears in my living room. Full circle. Why?"

"And how? We can't overlook that, either." Rachel stood. "No broken windows? Unlocked doors?"

"Not that we're aware of."

Megan sensed heat rising to her face. She liked the way he said we.

Rachel leaned against the kitchen counter. "Well I'd like to get the son of a bitch who's playing these games. I hate reexamining who was wearing what, when. Especially when it involves my ex-husband. That's my stake in this. Rather uncomplicated really."

"Your former husband, Rach. Not your ex."

"A slight technicality." She crossed her arms over her chest. "And your stake, Rey? I assume you could arrange bail if you needed to."

"Correct." He straightened in his chair. "I was the last to see the boy before he died. That connects me to this situation. But that's not the total story. Not anymore. There have been too many accidents and unexplained events."

His fist was clenched. It rested not far from her own tightly gripped hands. "The shots someone took at Megan last night, the tracks by the snowmobile, the intruder, I feel as if they're all tied together somehow. The incidents started when I arrived." His shifted his attention to Megan. "I intend to see this through."

His gaze locked with hers. She wouldn't be the first to look away this time. He would be there for her, had said as much right here. In front of a witness who could later pinch her if she thought she'd been dreaming; Rachel, who would never let her forget it. No one had ever offered that kind of support before. Maybe she should reach out, take his hand and cradle it in hers.

Rey looked away, toward Rachel. Megan noticed a pink flush near his ears. So he'd felt the same intensity. The unspoken connection both pleased her and scared her.

He stood. "Try to locate the photos, Rachel. We'll go from there."

"Sounds good." Rachel walked over to the coat rack. "Forget lunch. I just lost my appetite." She shoved one arm in her jacket. "I'll call later if anything comes up."

"We'll be out this afternoon." Megan joined her friend by the door. "Call tonight, after dinner."

"Sure. Where are you two headed?"

"I thought I'd take Rey with me to the range." She turned to him. "That is, if you'd like to go."

"I'd love to. What range?"

Megan looked back at Rachel. She was grinning, not so slyly, her eyebrows raised. Her friend wouldn't be so cruel as to mention that she always went alone. Please no, Rach.

Panic must have shown on her face. Rachel's expression was one of pure innocence. "That would be the rifle range. You know, target practice? Bang, bang?" After a brief mimicking of the procedure, Rachel left with a final wink and a smile.

❄   ❄   ❄

Megan leaned right and pulled hard on her poles as she turned the final corner. She didn't slow until she was within the one hundred foot mark. Gliding toward the flag, she transferred both poles to one hand. She tossed them onto the ground when she was in position at her makeshift firing range. "Now." She signaled to Rey, who held the stop watch.

His only response was a slight nod. Nice that he knew not to engage her in conversation.

Her UV Polaroid sunglasses cut the afternoon glare. They'd taken a healthy bite out of her monthly salary, but were worth it. She could afford them more easily than the snow blindness that would result from sub-standard lenses. Plus it was nice to have something that wasn't a hand-me-down.

She aimed at the biathlon target. It was also secondhand. She'd found it tucked into one of Thia's boxes that were sent home from college. The old steel frame was pock-ridden and rusty in places, and one of the legs was slightly bent, but still Megan felt lucky to own this piece of semi-official equipment. Before the discovery, she shot at twenty-five centimeter circles taped onto sand-filled pop cans.

This item of Thia's was the only one Megan had actually put to use. The other throwaways she'd simply re-boxed. Even Thia's rifle, much newer than Megan's, was still in the basement of her cabin.

Dad had given it to her with a grand flourish after the funeral, but she'd never used it. Had stuffed it under one of the beds with her sister's skis and boots, not wanting the gun and glass case he'd mounted it in to be daily reminders of her own lack of achievement.

No doubt Thia's rifle would outshine the one she currently used, but at least the older model was all hers. She would triumph on her own or do without, not borrow part of her sister's glory. No more distractions. She drew one arm, then the other, through the rifle's shoulder harness strap, ready for the next step.

Her heart rate was not slowing as quickly as she'd hoped. There would be time later to worry about that, now she needed to concentrate on breathing steadily. Shifting her Anschütz 1827 into her left hand, she loaded a magazine clip and closed the bolt. She dropped to a prone firing position.

Thia had made this part appear so easy, but it wasn't. Sometimes Megan's skis popped off. Thia had customized hers not to release, no matter how hard she jarred them. She'd lost a ribbon once by such a mishap.

If Megan's left elbow wasn't directly under the rifle, her balance would be off and her aim forced. She tried to visualize the cardboard mock-up she and Thia had made for practice sessions. It had seemed silly at the time, but Thia had reminded her that all biathletes used them at first. She scooted backwards, letting her center of gravity correct both grip and orientation until they felt comfortable.

The right elbow's position was even more crucial than the left. There were three points, her forearm, the stock and the ground, that needed to form a triangle of a certain dimension. She realigned her hips so that her body line was thirty degrees off from the rifle line. Better. She'd been assured that eventually this position would be as natural as breathing.

The rear and front sights now were lined up on the target. Megan breathed deeply and relaxed, making sure that her torso rested on the ground at the base of her rib cage. Any higher and her heartbeat would interfere with her aim, any lower and her own breathing would throw off her shot. Good. She closed her eyes for a split second, then blinked and rechecked her target.

She squeezed off five rounds, moving smoothly and horizontally across the target. In competition, there was no time to adjust between shots. She would be either on or off. Today, since she had an audience, she certainly hoped she was on.

Leaving the bolt open, she stood and swung the rifle onto her back. In the beginning, she used to have trouble regaining her footing from the spread eagle position. She used to trip constantly, sometimes landing face down in the snow. But not anymore. And thank goodness not today. Megan leaned over to grab her poles and pushed off with her left ski.

"Stop the clock."

"Got it."

It wasn't until after the second turn that Megan let up on her pace. Reinstating the racing heartbeat quickly after firing was important. She checked her watch. Back up to 160. Good.

She placed her hands on her knees and glided over to her snowmobile and passenger. Her discomfort increased. Rey stared at her from his spot in the driver's seat. He didn't look away, didn't even seem to blink, as she approached.

He made her nervous. This was her private passion. She'd never intended to share it. Sharing meant opening herself to criticism.

She allowed herself a moment to catch her breath before speaking, hoping to keep the emotion from her voice. "What was my time?"

"A minute twenty."

She slipped out of the harness. "Not bad."

"It was fabulous."

The tone of his voice stopped her flat. Admiration. There had been no one, except Rachel, who had ever encouraged her. She let the rifle rest against the side of her vehicle then glanced at him. "Sixty seconds would be fabulous. This was okay."

"I've never seen anything like it."

Megan laughed. "You know, that's one of the sad things about this sport, hardly anyone knows it even exists. When I say biathlon, most people around here think of summer Olympics track and field."

"How did you get involved?"

"Involved is a strong word. Thia was involved, I'm merely an amateur. She went to school out east. It was easier to get to the Lake Placid National Training Center." Megan tucked her gloves into her pocket. "She was on her way to making the National Team before her accident last year. Snagtooth's local celebrity." She let the last words fade softly as she dug in her pack for her water bottle. Leaning back against her Vmax she took a long drink.

"Do you have the same dream?"

Do pigs fly? She shrugged. "The conditioning is fun and fits well into my lifestyle. That's all." Megan wiped her mouth against her hand, glancing at him in warning not to pursue the subject further.

He was frowning, as if holding back his next question. Her pulse beat faster. Please don't probe further, she wanted to say. He was already too close to understanding her broken dreams.

Megan looked away, out across snow field, tracing the rugged outline formed by Desolation Peak. Clouds dotted the blue sky. She heard the hum of yet another helicopter. At least it wasn't blue, like the one was she saw this morning near Snowy Lakes. High Mountain Adventures.

His voice broke the silence. "Why not go for it?"

"What?"

"You're good. I know commitment when I see it. Why don't you try out as Thia did?"

She laughed, but it rang hollow. "Only a few dozen reasons. First, I've never been to an official clinic or a single training session. Lake Placid is a long way from here. It costs money. Money I don't have. Athletes need training. I have no idea how much I would need."

Stepping away from the snowmobile, Megan kicked at a snow drift. "I've never even been in a race. You can't earn national points without competing." She pointed to her rifle. "My equipment is out of date and barely fits me. They wouldn't let me in the starting gate with this one. The newer rifles weigh much less and have gizmos that you and I could never imagine. Thia's was in the shop being customized for over a month before she could use it. So were her bindings. Anyway, I don't want to bore you with all that."

"You're talking about material goods, Megan, not the things that really count."

"Such as?"

"Natural ability."

"Statistics from across the nation are published in the Biathlon Bulletin. I'm nowhere close."

Rey stepped down from the vehicle. Most likely he was simply stretching his leg, but Megan moved back anyway. He was getting too close, causing her to examine her own motivations in the light of day. They weren't coming up very rosy, either.

"Even more important than natural talent is the desire to succeed. You have that, Megan. I could see it when I watched your workout. That's something that can't be learned."

Pipe dream. The two words that usually pounded through her head were becoming a faint whisper. No. She had to remember her skiing was only a fantasy. If she didn't, she'd fall victim to the sugar-coated world his words were painting. She would wish for things that could never come true. And once the dam was open, how could she control what flowed through? Wants and desires such as Thia's return or her family's respect. Dead and gone. Over.

No, she couldn't start now. Slowly, Megan removed her sunglasses and tucked them into her pocket. She was having trouble not balling her hands into tight fists. "What about your desires? Are there things you want that you can never have?"

Rey opened his mouth to speak, then closed it. His gaze shifted from Megan to her rifle. After studying it for a moment, he reached for the gun, curled his fingers around the stock and picked it up. He cradled it in one arm. His free hand traced the sleek lines of the wood.

"I grew up in the east. When I was a kid, The Wild West was my favorite game. There were no other kids to play cowboys and indians with, no woods to hide in, no snow fields to run through. That didn't stop me, though. I still devoted a part of each day to being Davy Crockett. My make-believe rifle might have been a discarded broom handle, but to me it was a Winchester."

He raised her Anschütz, fingered the open bolt and safety, then placed the butt plate against his shoulder. He took aim down range, just as she had earlier. His words flowed smoothly. "In college, the weekend sport of duck hunting was popular. Whether or not I wanted to sit in a blind in the pouring down rain was irrelevant. All of the hunters had rifles and I wanted to be there with them. But I wasn't."

After his pretense at firing was over, he lowered the gun and leaned it against the snowmobile. "I've never owned a firearm, only dreamed about it."

"Why didn't you?"

"Someone aimed a loaded gun at me once. He was playing a game, amusing himself." He met her gaze directly. "I didn't see the humor and never got over it."

She laid a hand on his forearm. "I'm sorry."

"Don't be. I was a lot luckier than Dad was. They aimed at him too, after I escaped."

"That's how he died? You said . . ."

"They killed him. Either to cover their actions or in retribution, I don't know. There was no way to find out."

So he'd also lost a family member. Knew the hurt of being left behind and the feeling of guilt for his part in it all. Though it sounded as if some of his remorse had subsided over the years, she knew that there must have been a time when it racked his soul.

"Bottom line, there was no duck hunting for me. No military service, either. I studied martial arts instead, for self-defense as much as for show. I've never touched a loaded weapon before. You handle them daily." He raised his hand and stroked her cheek. "Never that is, until today."

Her throat was tight; her words whispered. "Why now?"

"Your grace and skill erased the other thoughts, I guess." He ran his thumb back and forth against her jaw line. "Thank you."

She leaned into his palm. He was so close she could hear him breathing, imagined she could feel a soft whisper of wind move across her face. If she leaned toward him would he kiss her again? Would he, if she raised herself onto her toes? And if he didn't, would she live through the embarrassment?

She'd never know. The mood was shattered by the sound of a helicopter just over the next ridge near Snowy Lakes. Rey moved back. She did the same. Though she didn't look up, she imagined an aircraft with blue and white lettering. She was beginning to hate High Mountain Adventures.

NINE

DAVE SCANNED THE dingy meeting room allocated to the program called A Step Toward the Future. It hadn't changed much since his own passage from despair to newly recovered addict. The florescent lighting gave the room an artificial brightness, the aluminum folding chairs a very real coldness. Soon those chairs would be filled with adolescents of both sexes, waiting for tonight's message. And most, if not all, would be hoping that the message was strong enough to motivate them into fighting their addiction for one more week.

The walls were covered with crayon drawings, courtesy of the nearby Sunday School class who had adopted this group as their mission project. The pictures had a poignant, comical effect. Lopsided houses with green-haired occupants. The children's artistic talents were still being formed. So were the drug-fighting skills of tonight's impending audience.

The teens filing in were still fragile. Sure, most had graduated from a treatment program of some sort, but this stage was recovery and control. He knew that controlling an addiction to a substance such as cocaine was a lifetime commitment. He hoped these kids had family members and non-using friends to support them.

Many of the weekly speakers were former addicts. Someone who had struggled first hand with addiction was best equipped to reach a drug user. That was why he was here, doing his thing, week after week. He was still trying to give something back.

His subject for tonight was centered around Step Eight: Choosing Replacement Activities. He brought slides from some of last year's ski outings. His film wasn't yet developed from the Okanogan trip, since he and Alison had only returned hours earlier by corporate jet. Canceling his attendance was never an option, whether he was on the docket to speak or not. He saw his ongoing participation as a requirement for his own health and well-being. After all, Helping Others was Step Fourteen.

The group leader came forward to the podium and shook his hand. "Did the projector decide to cooperate tonight?" He nodded. The man looked skyward, offering a private thank you. After a brief introduction to benefit new members, Dave had the floor. As the lights dimmed, he scanned the audience once more. EJ wasn't there.

He clicked through the slides, narrating each one with bits and pieces of his own experiences. He kept his message upbeat though sprinkled liberally with reality. Recovery was hard. He'd been there. He could help them if they'd let him.

The members split into smaller discussion groups, dragging their chairs behind them across the linoleum floor. Dave took his time putting his materials away. He glanced up occasionally. But EJ wasn't there.

He'd made a promise to himself when he first started mentoring this group, no one kid would mean more to him than another. In fact, in the two years since his wife Joan died, he hadn't let anyone become too close. It didn't matter that her overdose was accidental. The fact remained that she was gone before their life together had really begun. Dave had sold the suburban home they'd planned to raise their future family in. He'd purchased a condo and never looked back.

It didn't really matter why EJ was so important to him. The boy never attended with a family member or dragged along a sober friend. Despite his flip attitude, Dave knew the young man was hurting, tottering on the brink of failure. He knew, because the teen reminded him of his younger self.

He put the projector away, grabbed his jacket then braced himself against the night wind. With the slide tray under one arm and his briefcase in the other hand, he pushed outward against the door and into the night.

❊   ❊   ❊

Lute moved the newspaper aside to get a better look at the dark-haired youth sitting across from Billy at the highway truck stop. The twenty-four hour restaurant was so nondescript it could have been located in Anywhere, USA: plastic menus with tattered paper inserts, sleepy-eyed staff serving stale coffee, pay phones with more inbound traffic than outbound. Lute wished he were home in bed reveling in today's success at Snowy Lakes.

He sipped at his cup of sludge, checking out the latest customer. He had chosen the table near the door in case he wanted to make a quick exit. Billy was in a separate booth less than ten feet away, near the window.

Billy's punk friend had arrived on time. The kid didn't have a name, only initials. But he was smart enough. Lute had been prepared for worse, since Billy had gotten on his nerves in record time. He sighed and accepted a refill from the waitress. Poor thing. A rat's nest for hair, blue eye shadow an inch thick, and she was making eyes at him.

He would drink this cup slowly, not wanting her to return and block the sound. The sooner they were out of here, the better.

Billy's tone became agitated and dangerously loud. "This new position is great, EJ. I've been on two pickup flights already. The money's great and the benefits—well let's just say they're out of this world."

EJ appeared nervous. "Why did you want me here? You said it was urgent." The kid went up another notch in Lute's estimation.

"It is, man. It's your future we're here to discuss." Billy leaned forward and lowered his voice. Lute shifted sideways and opened his *Seattle Times* to a new page as Billy motioned his friend forward. "Since I've moved up, I need someone to take my place. In distribution, you know."

"I'm off that stuff now."

"You don't have to smoke the proceeds. Now shut up and listen."

EJ folded his arms across his chest and slumped back against the booth.

"Some gratitude." Billy slammed a hand against the table. "I'm here with the deal of the century and you're acting like I'm holding a gun to your head. What's wrong?"

"Nothing. Just not interested."

"Afraid to disappoint that fancy ass corporate friend of yours?" Billy snorted. "Well, don't be. He's not your father. Your daddy is in jail or have you forgotten?"

EJ sat forward, one hand clenched around a fork. "Leave my father out of it."

"You'd like that, wouldn't you? You'd like for me and him and all your other buddies to disappear. You think that jerk in his striped suit could take our places. Well, I've got news for you, buddy, you're too old to be adopted." Billy grabbed the fork from EJ's hand and tossed it toward the wire rack at the end of the table. Sugar packs went flying.

Lute considered leaving, stranding Billy there and then. EJ started to rise, but Billy pulled him back down. "Listen, I'm the best friend you've got. Maybe the only one. I've looked out for you, haven't I? Gave you a place to crash when you were high and puking in the gutters?"

"Maybe."

"I'm telling you, this is a good deal. You don't have to start using unless you want to, though you'd be a fool not to. I've tried it and this shit is good."

"I'm not gonna start again."

"Then just take my place peddling. Use it as kind of a testing ground. The big boys will take notice if you really hustle. Look where it's gotten me." Billy made eye contact with his friend. "And when I can bring you further in, I will. Trust me."

EJ shrugged. Lute was impressed. Despite the fact he had orders to find a new gofer, he was glad the kid was on the road to being clean. Time to walk out, call off the deal, before the kid wavered.

"I'll think about it."

"Think about it? Shit, man." Billy wadded his napkin. "Don't think too long. As they say, it don't get much better than this." Billy stood and tossed down the mangled mess of paper. "I'm out of here."

"How can I find you? You're never at your place anymore."

"I'll find you." As Billy strode out, he bumped his hip against Lute's arm. The *Times* rattled. Lute snarled at him.

Lute tossed down some change and picked up his paper, chancing a full-faced peek at the corner booth. EJ still sat there, his forehead resting on cupped hands. It's a tough world, kid, he wanted to say. And not everyone makes it through.

Lute turned and left.

❄   ❄   ❄

Scott leaned right as he shaved a new corner on the turn near Desolation Point. That trail had been too narrow anyway. He steered his snowmobile down off the bank.

Harrison was still living with his sister, despite the gunshots. Of course if he'd been shooting at Harrison, instead of Megan by mistake, maybe the outcome would have been different. Next time, he'd do so in better light. Or try something different.

Scott gunned the engine of his snowmobile and felt the surge of power. It was exhilarating, flying over bumps and veering around turns. Russell hadn't been pissed when he heard the news, had merely said try again. Would his boss have been so forgiving if the missing scarf wasn't on his mind? Whatever, Scott had been given a second chance. He only hoped he wouldn't screw up again.

The wind slapped his face. Snowflakes burned in his eyes before melting. Life was good. Time for him to make the most of it. Being the third child in the Jeffers household had been a tough draw. To compound the bad luck, he'd been forced to follow behind two female over-achievers.

Megan hadn't been as bad as Thia, but what a waste. She worked hard for something that would never pay off. He'd tried to tell her so once but Megan hadn't been willing to take his advice. Sure, she paid a lot of attention to him but he always felt like the know-nothing little brother. She treated him that way constantly, Miss Perfect always trying to look out for him. She called it being supportive. He called it interference. One would think his umbilical cord had been attached to her instead of to their mother.

He'd never mentioned her training again after she'd brushed him off. Now he didn't have the time. Had his own career to concentrate on, which was finally paying off. Megan would have to take care of herself.

Why couldn't she leave town as Thia had? He'd be top dog then and wouldn't have to worry about her sneering at his post-work activities. She wasn't aware of his new entertainment. Only a couple of people were; Jeri being one. She'd dumped him for it. And if Megan ever found out, there would be no keeping her out of it either.

Maybe he could convince her to go at the same time he persuaded Harrison to beat it. The sheriff would surely be proud of him then. Scott hadn't missed the animosity between Megan and his boss. It had the potential to solve two problems at once.

Enough with the worrying. He crested the ridge. No more. Tonight, everything would go his way. Adrenaline raced through his veins. He was on a non-stop trip to the top. God, how he loved being invincible.

Letting his vehicle idle, he looked at the surrounding area. A wonderland of white powder, nearly unmarred by trails or track marks. The few tracks present were most likely his sister's. Just one more thing that she'd ruined.

He was up here because the sheriff had asked for him to check out Megan's training course. As a personal favor to him, he'd stressed. He wanted her to be safe while practicing. After all Desolation Point was as godforsaken as its name. It could be dangerous for an independent woman with a predictable routine. Russell had said so. Alone up here day after day, no telling just what might happen. He'd would sleep easier if Scott could confirm that Megan's makeshift firing range was at least out of sight from the nearby hut.

Well, it wasn't. And though his sister had caused him tons of grief, he didn't want her hurt, just wanted her gone. He'd report back, then let Russell tell her to move it. The sheriff's plan was really quite transparent. Russell actually didn't care about Megan, he was playing up his concern merely to get on Scott's good side. Totally unnecessary. He would do anything to keep his hard-earned position as Number One Deputy. Sometimes you had to . . . to do . . . things . . . in order to get the result you wanted.

His euphoria turned sour. That was the most difficult part of his job, a fine point that many people didn't understand. Not everything in this world was black or white. In fact, there was more gray than he could deal with at times. Sheriff Russell faced the same concern. The struggle was written all over his face. Scott liked having that bond between them.

He followed the ridge a little further, shouting as he flew over a bump in the trail. He should come up here more often. It was a kick. He was soaring high. Later, when he was off-duty, he'd soar even higher. From now on, he'd partake of the good life. No restrictions.

The evening air was crisp and cold. He breathed deeply, then winced. His nose was still bothering him. The edges of his nostrils were raw. Maybe there was something at the General Store that would help. He couldn't ask Megan. She would give him another damn cold tablet. A lot of good that would do. Maybe he could sneak a quick hit before arriving for dinner.

He'd seen enough. It wasn't the report the sheriff wanted, but Scott would let Russell know that extra concern for Megan wasn't necessary for his loyalty. Time to get on with it. His next warning would be stronger. Then the guy would be gone.

What if he could get Harrison to act like a jerk during dinner tonight? Would Megan send him on his way? Maybe. It couldn't hurt. And if not, he'd try something else tomorrow. He'd mull over a few ideas at the poker game later. Brainstorm with the boys. Hypothetically, of course. Yeah, it sounded good. He bounced on his seat. He could do it.

The poker game. God, he needed to win tonight. The coke was draining his bank account. He wouldn't focus on that now. He'd send Harrison packing first.

❄   ❄   ❄

Megan paused at the sound of a snowmobile topping the crest above her meadow. She set down the paring knife and tomato. On tiptoes, she peered out through the small window above the sink and waved. Scott pushed his cap back and gave her a two-fingered salute. That was a good sign. Tension slipped away from her neck and shoulders. She signaled for him to park next to her vehicle inside the wood shed. The snow was falling hard tonight.

She rinsed her hands then turned to where Rey was setting the table. "The towel, please?"

He grabbed it from his shoulder and tossed it to her basketball-style. It cleared the ceiling fan by inches.

She caught it. "Thanks."

"Sure thing. What else can I help with?"

"You've done enough. Besides, Scott's here." She folded and hung the towel in its proper place. After crossing to the door she looked out. He was still wiping down his snowmobile.

"He'll be a few more minutes. Rey?" She shoved her hands into the pockets of her fleece pants. "Scott's been on edge lately. I don't think he's been sleeping well. Please go easy on him tonight."

He walked around the dining table and stood before her. "People say I'm an easygoing guy."

"His irritability is due to a run of bad luck lately. His girlfriend Jeri moved out before Christmas. He's run up some gambling debts, too."

"Don't worry. If I said something inappropriate when he was here the first night, I'm sorry."

"At times he needs to let out his frustration." She shrugged. "I'm the closest."

He took her hand in his. "I was defending you. It wasn't right for him to say what he did."

"He didn't mean anything by it." She squeezed his hand. "He's still young."

"Not that young. He's what? Twenty-three?"

She withdrew her hand. "Twenty-five."

"Old enough to tote a gun on city streets."

"He's feeling alone. I want to be there for him. He never got much support from Mom or Dad." No one related to her brother's pain as deeply as she did. How could she describe to an outsider the residue left from parental rejection?

He reached out and cupped her chin. "Tell me this, Megan. Who's there for you when times get tough?"

She pulled away.

He paused for a moment. "You need to know what devil is driving Scott before you can help him."

"I know that."

His tone gentled. "I'll be good. But no one should be another person's verbal punching bag. Not for any reason."

Scott's footsteps thumped against her porch steps. Rey released her and opened the door, his disarming smile back in place. Scott stood before him, arm raised as if to knock. Rey extended his hand in welcome. "Come in. And before you ask, yes I'm still here."

❄   ❄   ❄

Scott entered the cabin and pulled his ski cap off. Rey stepped back, not surprised that his words had been ignored. So that's how it would be? For Megan's sake he'd allow her brother a wide berth, but disrespect toward her he wouldn't tolerate.

After shaking the snow loose from his hair, Scott bent and gave Megan a quick kiss. "Smells good. I'm not too hungry, though. Sorry." He scowled at Rey. "I'm surprised to see that you're still here."

Megan placed her hand on her brother's chest. "Don't be rude."

"Why isn't he gone by now?"

"Russell insisted that he stay, remember?"

"Yeah, but does it have to be here?"

"That's really none of your business."

Scott shrugged and turned toward the mirror. He ran his fingers through his hair.

Rey studied him. He'd had plenty of practice reading people. He was a good judge of character. From what he had seen so far, Scott was weak and his attitude adolescent. No doubt the kid took his lead from the sheriff instead of deciding things for himself. Hard to believe that he and Megan came from the same parents.

The circles under Scott's eyes were hard to miss. So was his grayish complexion. She hadn't been exaggerating. Her brother must have been losing sleep for quite awhile. He appeared worse, in fact, than he had just two nights before.

Scott looked away from the mirror and pulled his jacket off. He hung it on a peg, letting the snow hit the wood floors. "So when are you leaving, Harrison? Friday?"

"No." Rey moved closer. "Does it matter?"

The younger man shrugged. He cleared his throat but the hoarse, raspy sound remained. "Not really. Just wondering."

Scott didn't want to meet his eyes. Interesting. "Is someone keeping track?" Rey tried to remove the edge from his tone. Megan was being threatened, Scott was losing sleep. Were the events related?

Megan put her hand on his shoulder. "Dinner's ready."

Her tone was quiet, as though their hostility bothered her. Rey backed away from the younger man immediately. He regretted the attack. In the business world, he was expert at being subtle. His normal instincts weren't working.

He moved toward the table and waited for a clue as to where to sit. For all he knew, her brother had a favorite seat. And, if being in Scott's good graces meant that he would relieve some of Megan's anxiety, it was worth it.

They consumed dinner in silence, except for her brother's sniffling and occasional coughs. Megan was obviously trying to draw Scott into conversation, since he wasn't in the mood to eat. He only seemed to respond, though, when asked a question directly.

"How's work?"

"Fine." He glanced sharply at her. "Why?"

"No reason." She shrugged. "I was just hoping that you were involved in an interesting project or two."

"They're called cases."

"Interesting cases, then."

She paused, but Scott didn't pick up the conversation. Megan swallowed and looked over at Rey. He didn't know quite how to help. Everything he did or said seem to infuriate her brother. He figured that keeping quiet was best.

Megan tried again. "Are you involved in the murder case?"

Scott stared at her, as if trying to decipher her words. Within seconds, he exploded in anger. "Are you interrogating me, Megan? If you are, forget it."

"I'm not."

He slammed down his glass. "I don't have to answer to you. I'm on my way to the top now. I won't let anything, or anyone, stop me. Especially not him." He tilted his head in Rey's direction.

Rey calmly set his own glass down on the table. He'd never witnessed such a change in mood, except in the drug rehab program he and Dave supported. He wanted to say something to ease the tension, but instead waited for Megan's lead. After a brief look around the table, Scott pushed his chair away and grabbed his jacket. But instead of leaving, he headed toward the bathroom.

The silence that followed was painful. Megan breathed deeply. He reached for her hand. She glanced at him, then quickly away, withdrawing from his touch. After folding her napkin she stood and began carrying dishes to the sink. He assisted her.

Why was she trying so hard to include herself in this kid's life? Scott alternated between ignoring her and deliberately shutting her out. But even if Rey could help her, she wouldn't appreciate it. For all of her independence, she obviously needed Scott.

When her brother returned, his sour mood was gone. He walked swiftly to the coat rack again, hanging his jacket. As he turned toward Megan, he smiled.

Energized, animated and loving. Rey frowned. Had Scott been attacked by remorse while he was gone? If so, maybe there was hope for the kid yet. As he ran a sponge over the table, Scott playfully sauntered over to his sister.

After untying her apron, he teased her with the loose ends until she tried swatting him away. Using that opportunity, he caught her by the upper arms and danced her into the living room. Megan's laughter filled the kitchen.

Rey paused by the counter. Something wasn't right. He was having trouble viewing this objectively. The thoughts racing through his mind seemed almost disloyal to Megan. He didn't want to believe that beloved brother was in over his head. But he guessed that Scott's jacket pocket contained more than keys to his snowmobile.

At each rotation, she smiled over Scott's shoulder as if to convey the message that she'd been right all along. Scott loved her. Scott was family. Rey used the gaps between their turns around the living room to position himself closer to the coat rack.

He leaned casually against the wall. When the dancers looked away, he knocked several jackets to the floor. He shook his head, deriding himself for his clumsiness, then knelt. As he sorted through the coats, he put his hand inside her brother's pocket. He was right. Scott was using.

Concealing the items in his own pocket he replaced the jackets on the rack. "I'll be right back." Megan nodded to him before Scott spun her away.

He headed downstairs. There was a small mirror, probably a simple dime store variety. Next came the Ziplock and razor blade. The blade was uncovered, but Rey had been expecting that. Carelessness was typical of users. He couldn't stay away long. After finding a secure hiding place for the evidence, he flushed the toilet and ran water for his hands.

Scott used Rey's reappearance as a cue to end the evening. Rey feigned disappointment for Megan's sake. Predictably, as soon as her brother slipped on his jacket, he felt inside the pockets.

At first his expression was one of disbelief, but quickly his actions turned frantic. He glanced at the floor, shoving the neat line of snow boots aside with his foot. He searched among the other coats, knocking one to the floor and stepping on it in his rush.

Megan moved forward, putting a hand on his arm to quiet him. "What's wrong? Did you lose something?"

"Yeah. Have you seen . . ." He stopped and glared at Rey. His eyes narrowed.

"What's missing?" Rey kept his tone flat. "I'll help you look."

"You've helped enough." Scott pressed his hands to his temples. Glancing up, he caught his sister staring. "Just forget it. Gotta go." He yanked open the front door and tripped over the threshold.

Megan followed him, gripping the door frame. "Would you like to spend the night?"

Scott started down the stairs, saying nothing.

She tried again. "I'll see you in town. We can have lunch."

"Yeah, right." He walked backwards, scowling at Rey. "Alone."

"Well . . ."

"Come alone or don't bother." He stumbled into a drift, fell to his knees and braced himself with his hands. Megan started forward, but Rey touched her shoulder, urging her to stay by his side. She'd had enough for one night.

Scott didn't miss Rey's interference. He straightened and smacked his gloves together to eliminate the snow. "Just come alone." His voice sounded more like a whine than a command.

Rey released Megan and moved to face her. He didn't want her to see what was really happening to her brother. If she knew, it would break her heart. "Let me help. Maybe I can talk to him." Talk some sense into him, he wanted to say.

Megan hesitated briefly then agreed. "Okay, but be careful. He can be overly-sensitive sometimes."

Aggressive was a better word. He'd be fearless while high. "I will." He gave her shoulder a squeeze. Megan nodded and turned back toward the cabin.

❄   ❄   ❄

Rey followed him to the snowmobile. Scott must have sensed his presence and backed away. "You stole something from me."

"Unless you want your sister to know what you're up to, lower your voice."

Scott glanced over Rey's shoulder, then raised his eyebrows. "Why are you protecting me?"

"I'm not. I just don't want Megan hurt by your stupidity."

"Megan this, Megan that." The deputy's tone was sing-song. "Why is everyone so concerned about her? What about me?"

Rey felt as if he were doing everything wrong. He called on his prior training, forcing it to return. "You're not the first person to get hooked on cocaine." He reached toward Scott. "I know a treatment program . . ."

"Leave me alone." Scott pulled away. "The stuff is mine. You had no right."

"You can't do it by yourself. You need help."

"I do? That's funny." His laugh was harsh. "Really funny. You'll be needing a hell of a lot more help than I do if you don't get out of here. And Seattle might not be far enough. I'd choose another state, if I were you."

Rey grabbed Scott's arm. "What are you implying?"

Scott tried to jerk away, but Rey held him. Even so, he didn't let up on the taunting. "Let me put it to you in plain Snagtooth English, City Boy. Beat it, or else."

"Or else, what?" When Scott didn't answer, Rey loosened his grip.

Scott climbed onto his snowmobile, switched on the engine, then leaned close to deliver his final shot. "Or else you just might be making things a lot worse around here. For yourself and for Megan. Ever think about that?"

Rey shouldn't have let the boy drive. Shouldn't have, but did. He suddenly had more important things to worry about.

❆   ❆   ❆

Rey sat on the bed to unwrap his knee bandage. He'd handled Scott badly. Messed up and felt like a jerk for not telling Megan about the drugs. He needed time to plan a new approach. Maybe Dave would have some information that would help. He dialed, pleased when Dave answered the phone.

"How was your flight back?"

"Fine. Only one trouble spot; getting Alison to leave."

"After all her skepticism about the great outdoors?" He smiled, remembering her outrage when they started the trip. It had only been four days ago. Seemed as if he'd known Megan a lot longer. "Ali's idea of roughing it is camping at the Hyatt Regency, Dave. What changed her mind?"

"The pajama party in the loft at Lilly's Bed and Breakfast last night. Your sister now plans to return and open her own B&B on the banks of the Methow River."

Rey stretched out on the bed, propping a pillow against the headboard, another under his left knee. "Well, she might meet a nice ski bum, settle down and leave you alone. At last."

"She's given up on me. She made it clear that her place would be for party types, not bores like myself. She might make an exception for family, though, and let you visit."

Dave made a noise that sounded suspiciously like a laugh. It had been a long time since Rey had heard his right-hand man laugh. Ali was good for him. Dave had the tendency to carry the world's weight on his shoulders. Guilt and self-imposed punishment had done that to him. Rey had always hoped he would find a way to forgive himself someday.

Rey switched subjects. "How was your presentation tonight?"

Dave hesitated before responding. "Fine. Excellent turnout."

"Any new faces?"

"Three or four. Two brought parents with them. The others brought friends as their support partners."

"Good. Everyone needs at least one person in their personal cheering section." Rey stopped after hearing his own words. He shouldn't have withheld Scott's drug usage from Megan. He'd wanted to spare her the hurt that would follow. But Scott needed someone on his side if he was to have a fighting chance. Rey would sleep on it tonight and figure out what to do.

He turned the conversation toward a more personal subject. "How did EJ do this week?"

No answer.

"He didn't show?"

Silence reigned for several moments before Dave cleared his throat. "That's right. He didn't make it."

"He's only missed once before."

"I . . ." More silence.

Rey waited, giving him plenty of time.

"If EJ chooses to drop out, then the kid's missing his chance. I can't go looking for him each week. It has to be his choice."

Just as it had been Dave Edward's choice eighteen months ago. And Ali's, two years back. And in the nine months since Rey had brought them on board with Moore Comfort, neither had ever faltered. Not once. One more thing that Alison and Dave had in common.

"You're right, it has to be his choice." He heard Dave exhale. "I have a favor to ask."

"Name it."

"As you research Eric Mitchell and the helicopter service, would you add another name to your list?"

"Sure. Who?"

Rey hated what he was about to do. He sat upright and lowered his voice. "Scott Jeffers."

"Why?"

"He's using cocaine. Maybe his record shows some sign of slacking off on the job. See what you can find."

"Megan's brother? How is she taking it?"

"She doesn't know. Not yet anyway."

"She'll need to."

"I know. Have your inside contact handle this one carefully. We don't want to alert anyone that we're investigating him."

"Especially not anyone who's related."

Rey grimaced. "Exactly."

"Hope you know what you're doing."

"So do I, Dave. So do I."

❄   ❄   ❄

Lute gripped his beer with one hand and turned his back on the men seated at the bar. The stress of the last few days was really getting to him. Cowboy had been pleased about the pickup at Snowy Lakes. The fact that Cowboy had given him a new task was a good sign.

Poker. Lute was good at the game. Good enough to cheat without being caught. It didn't hurt his odds, either, that the other players were stoned. He'd simply passed out a few samples, let the fog settle in and scooped up the dough. The boys boasted, bragged and basically spilled the beans about whatever subjects Lute chose.

Assignments of this type were easy. And Deputy Jeffers had been the loudest lip-flapper of them all.

He walked over to the pay phone and cradled the receiver. Cowboy picked up on the third ring. "Yes?"

Lute forged ahead. "The interview went as planned. The gofer seems to be okay. He has his orders and is prepared to follow them. I gave him a few ideas. The setup will be tomorrow."

"Tell me more."

"It'll be at noon. Fewer witnesses that way. The skier, Harrison, should be out by evening."

"It's a go, then?"

Lute allowed himself a slight chuckle, remembering the age-old joke. "Nothing's for sure but death and taxes, Boss." He hoped to thaw the tone he heard in Cowboy's voice.

There was a long pause on the other end of the line. The juke-box droned on the background, interrupted by the hum of voices and the clink of billiard balls hitting one another before falling into the pockets. "Sorry. Bad joke." Lute rushed to continue. "What I meant was that everyone here appears to be properly motivated."

"Good. Keep it that way. Help him, if he needs it."

"Will do. I'll get a room here overnight and follow up tomorrow." Lute forced the authoritative note from his voice. "If that's all right with you, that is."

"Fine."

"Have Princess pick me up at midnight. The air strip."

"There's been a slight change in plans."

Lute heard a long draw, then a heavy exhale, over the receiver. Though a cloud of common cigarette smoke lingered around him, he could almost imagine that it was Cowboy's unique blend of cigar poisoning the air.

"Make sure the event takes place. Meet at tomorrow's pickup site after that. Princess will bring you in."

"The Needles again, right?"

Cowboy's tone turned harsh. "Lute."

He cringed when he heard his name being spoken openly. Cowboy's point had been clear. Phone lines were not secure. "Sorry, again. I'll look for the sign."

"Good. We'll give the original destination a rest until our visitor's gone."

"All right. And don't worry about a thing. I'm right here."

"I'm counting on that."

❄   ❄   ❄

Scott threw back the blackout curtain separating the poker room from the rest of the bar. He was getting the hell out. How could he have been so stupid? He'd known his limit. It was essential for him to win or at least break even. Now he was even further in the hole.

As he crossed the smoky room, he looked around. No one following, so far. Not even their newest player, the burly red-haired man. When the newcomer had abruptly left the game, supposedly to pee, Scott thought he might be setting him up. Planning to follow him. Instead, the guy was merely using the phone. Calling home to his wife, no doubt.

Why in the hell did he feel so suspicious? Maybe because the man was always watching him; hanging on his every word. He'd probably heard Scott was the top-ranking deputy. At least in the sheriff's eyes he was. His status probably put the guy on edge. That was all. He tried to shrug the feeling of paranoia aside. At the poker table, everyone was equal, until their chips ran out.

He pushed through the back door and braced himself against the wind. His luck was bad tonight. First his adoring sister interrogated him, then her new boyfriend swiped his stash. Now he was so far in the hole he'd never be able to pay the rent. Thank goodness Big Red had given him a sack of freebies to tide him over. Maybe the man would come around more often.

Back in the old days, four months ago to be exact, Scott had been content to play an occasional hand of stud or draw poker with some of the other regulars; men who were stuck in Snagtooth. He kicked at a lump of ice which had formed on the wooden walkway. Lifer's, he called them. Simple guys on a road to nowhere.

Then the new card-players started visiting town, bringing with them high stake pots and free samples of pure heaven. Whether they came from Winthrop or Mazama, he didn't know and didn't care to keep track. He'd simply wanted them to keep coming. As they moved in, they had included him in their circle. His old poker buddies who played weekly above the Grange Hall had kicked him out.

He'd started small and that's where he should have stayed. The occasional smoke. A snort or two. Jeri had tolerated that, though she didn't know for sure why he was always low on cash and even lower on patience. When she'd found out, she'd fought him tooth and nail for exactly one month then had moved out. Shape up and I might come back, she'd said. Right. As if he would be interested in someone who would desert him like that.

He didn't need her any more than he needed Megan's hovering. What he did need was another hit and a chance at a big pot. The next game wasn't until Friday. Lucky for him the sheriff was beginning to talk about giving him his own budget and special errands to prove himself. A chance to reline his pockets until he became flush.

Until then, he didn't have many choices. He could advertise for a roommate or live with Megan. God forbid. It was too crowded out there, anyway, at least until Harrison left. If Megan left with Harrison, maybe she'd give Scott the cabin. That was a nice thought.

He'd run a few of his ideas past the guys for flushing the two-some out. They applauded his imagination. Gave him encouragement. Big Red had even provided a few more suggestions. Some were illegal, some weren't. But even if they weren't exactly wrong, it didn't mean they were right.

Shit. There was that gray area again. But after the run-in with Megan and her protector tonight, it would give him pleasure to encourage them to leave.

He shuffled down Main Street, heading for the office, not able to shake the feeling of being watched. A single light still burned above Russell's desk. Hard to believe that the sheriff of a town Snagtooth's size would have to work late, but he did. His boss was typically there until midnight, on poker nights at least. Scott didn't question it, simply hoped to be as successful some day.

After another glance over his shoulder, he ducked his head and crossed the street against the frigid wind. He'd run his ideas by Russell. Just talking about it would rebolster his spirits.

❆   ❆   ❆

Eric moved further into the shadows near the saloon as Scott hurried by. He hadn't expected the poker game to break up so early and had nearly been caught off-guard. The kid must be further down on his luck which, according to Logan, was already running pretty bad.

When the deputy disappeared into his office, Eric emerged from the alley and walked down the snow-covered boardwalk, carefully avoiding any planks that might creak. He'd worked hard at creating a viable cover on short notice. He couldn't afford to blow it now.

He paused by the front bay window of the deserted store. Though blackout curtains hid the game inside, the players voices could still be easily heard. The electronic bug he planted along the pane would record discussions. Simple.

Why would Cowboy resort to mixing with the locals; showing Lute's face in plain view? It wasn't like Cowboy to resort to such amateurism. He must view the red-haired giant as disposable.

Maybe Eric was expecting more since the operation had eluded him for so long. Hard to say. But over-estimating his adversaries was much preferred to selling them short.

He casually strolled further down the boardwalk and picked another hiding place. Time to tune in to the bug he'd planted a half hour earlier in the sheriff's office. He inserted the ear piece and turned on the remote unit in his pocket. Good, the device was operational. He'd replay the full tape later. Russell was relaying pieces of his phone conversation to the kid. Insignificant portions. Small mountain-town stuff such as tomorrow's avalanche forecast.

Eric was getting closer. The operation was firmly in motion. Now if he could just maintain his cover for another week, he'd be home free. But the size of that "if" depended on a lot of things. Some were under control and some were uncontrollable.

❄   ❄   ❄

Rey heard her footsteps upstairs, moving around the kitchen. It was late. The ache in his knee was reminding him he'd over-exercised it today. The martial arts performance for Megan had been the main contributor.

There was no reason to hide. They were both single and free to pursue whatever they might choose. One big difference, though. He knew what to do about the mutual attraction. She didn't seem to be very experienced.

The way she responded to his kiss last night was confirmation. She'd surprised herself. They needed to talk or he would never get to sleep. His attraction to her was too new, too uncertain. He pulled on his sweats and climbed the steps slowly.

Time to set a direction for the days ahead. His guess was she'd had a boyfriend or two. Maybe an intimate relationship gone sour. No, the word relationship wasn't right. Encounter, perhaps. Technically not a virgin but not experienced either.

He opened the door. She was in the kitchen, facing away from him. He loved watching her, especially when she was unaware of it. So graceful. Athletic, feminine curves that aroused him, yet she didn't seem to know it.

He hesitated at the top of the stairs. Until he knew her better, he would let her set the pace. Be candid about his own interest yet not push. It would be her decision. That was key. It was a lousy time to start a relationship. She was being threatened physically and was still struggling emotionally. But he'd let her know he was open to the possibility. Then wait for her invitation.

❄   ❄   ❄

Rey stepped on a squeaky floorboard. Megan instantly turned. "You surprised me. I expected you to be asleep by now."

"I thought the same about you." He walked toward her. "It's past eleven. You're usually out the door before first light."

"You're right. But I had to file a report on the avalanche near Eagle's Crest before turning in. I want it posted on the Internet before first light. It took longer to compose than expected." She picked up the kettle on the stove. "I'm having some chamomile tea. Are you interested?"

"Sounds good."

She placed an assortment of bags on the table then grabbed a second mug.

"Megan, I'd like to finish the conversation we started earlier." He paused. "If you're willing, that is."

She was opening drawers, retrieving spoons and napkins, anything but looking at him. "We started many, Rey. This place has been like Grand Central. I can't seem to finish anything these days."

When she set a mug of hot water in front of him, he placed his hand over her wrist. "The discussion I had in mind involved last night. Out in the snow." He gave her wrist a slight tug forward. "Sit with me. For just awhile."

Her gaze lifted to his. After a moment, she nodded. "All right."

He released her and pulled out a chair. After retrieving her cup from the counter, she sat. So did he, next to her. So simple, yet it caused his pulse to quicken. She quietly stirred her drink, waiting for him to start. He did.

"I enjoyed our kiss."

She started to stand. He placed a hand on her arm, encouraging her to stay. After a brief hesitation, she complied. He waited for her to look at him again.

"Something is happening between us, Megan. I don't want to ignore it or hide from it." He moved sideways and laid his arm along the back of her chair. "We both have baggage we carry with us from our pasts. It's impossible to change that. We'll each deal with it in our own way."

"That sounds bad." She stirred faster. "Like the thirteen plagues are following me."

"It's worse, actually."

She glanced at him curiously. He grinned. "I heard plagues are generally treatable. This affliction might not be."

He saw a tinge of red color her cheeks as she turned away to stare across the kitchen. She hadn't stopped him, though.

"My first reaction when the gunfire began last night was to protect you. But afterwards, when the threat passed and we were laying side by side, my thoughts changed." He raised his hand from the back of her chair and let his fingers toy with the small elastic band which formed her ponytail.

The room was so quiet he could almost hear her breathing. But there was still no objection, no pulling away. "The kiss was important to me. I would enjoy exploring a relationship with you, but realize the timing is bad." He tugged the elastic band free. Her hair fell gracefully down the nape of her neck, spilling over the back of her sweater. "Let me know when it feels right for you. I'd like to see where it might lead."

She turned fully toward him. Her cheeks were flushed. There was an intensity in her gaze that made him catch his breath. But there was confusion, too. Reaching out, he cupped her face and ran his fingers through her hair, starting at the temples. When his hands met at the nape of her neck he leaned forward and kissed her forehead. She rested against him.

For several moments they sat quietly, then he eased away from her and stood. He walked toward the staircase.

"Rey?"

He looked back over his shoulder. She was standing. One of her hands rested on the table, the other gripped the back of the chair. He waited.

"I would like that, too."

Her words contradicted her expression which still conveyed bewilderment. He nodded slowly and smiled. "Then we have something to look forward to." This time on the way to the staircase, he didn't stop.

TEN

REY OPENED THE connecting door to the stairway and listened for a moment. The house was quiet, the kitchen dark. Megan's bedroom door stood open. There was no keyboard clicking, though, no soft humming. He was disappointed.

It was six A.M. He'd hoped to catch her before she left. Crossing to the entryway, he glanced out the window. Her Vmax was no longer parked in the shed. Instead it sat at the foot of the steps. Maybe she wasn't gone after all.

He turned. A florescent message pad had been left on the kitchen table, propped against the sugar bowl. He picked it up. "Rey, have fun. I'll be back this afternoon." Next to the note were the keys to the snowmobile. Beneath, her owner's manual. On the nearest chair cushion was her spare helmet. He clutched the key ring. It wasn't having the means to escape for a few hours that brought the grin to his face.

The knee was better this morning. He flexed it without pain. Twisting it might set him back a day or two, so skiing was out. Megan had obviously known that and had rightly guessed that sitting around was driving him batty.

Which direction should he explore? Avoiding an accident was his first concern. That eliminated the ridge and most of the forest. Second priority was not getting lost, thus preventing a repeat rescue mission. He'd stay close by. Grace might like company again. Another opportunity to investigate Mitchell.

Since it was too early to go visiting, he lit a burner for the tea pot. He tuned the radio to the weather station and sliced a banana for his cereal. Thoughts of missed business meetings and his over-stuffed in-basket were soon replaced with updates to the grocery list and mental notes of other much-needed errands. And as he went downstairs to retrieve his coat, boots and long johns, he whistled a tune from Megan's favorite CD.

✻ ✻ ✻

Rey stepped onto the running board, swung his right leg over the side and settled onto the Vmax's front seat. He felt like a kid with a new toy. Not caring who might be watching, he bounced on the cushion a few times.

The sky was clear and blue, the temperature hovered near zero. The breeze blowing from the west made the day feel even colder. Several inches of white powdery snow had fallen overnight. Rey squinted as he reached for his sunglasses. After putting them on and fitting the helmet over them, he scanned the horizon.

Grandma Grace was outdoors near the lake pulling up flowers. To one side of her lay a bright red pile of flowers. Garden replacements. He smiled. Her favorites, no doubts. Even in the short time he'd been here, those particular flowers were a repeat. What had Rachel called them? Bee Balms. This little mountain neighborhood had obviously wormed its way into his heart if he was starting to keep track of Grace's garden.

He switched on the engine. He had to stifle the urge to head out into the wide open spaces. This time, he'd take it easy. After examining the instruments, he headed in Grace's direction. The ride was smooth, once he became familiar with the hand controls.

Grandma Grace looked up as he approached. Rey climbed down and pulled off his helmet.

"For goodness sakes." She tossed the handful of peach-colored flowers to the side and inserted red ones into the holes. "I thought you were Megan."

"Good to see you, Grace. Hope I'm not interrupting." He peered closer. Each bunch sat in its own small tube embedded in the ground. That made him feel much better. He'd hate to think this elderly woman was spearing artificial stems directly into the frozen snow pack.

"Where's Megan?" Grace started to rise. Rey lent her his arm. "She's not hurt, is she?"

"No. She's using her Forest Service vehicle this morning."

"And left this one for you, did she?" Grace tucked her gloved hand into the crook of his elbow. She made her familiar clucking sound. He knew by now that it signified approval. "Well, well. That's a new one for my book." She smiled up at him.

Rey was glad she'd read the same significance into the situation as he had, but felt a bit awkward. As if he'd constructed a billboard announcing his interest in Megan. He switched subjects. "Can I help?"

She patted him. "I'd say you already have. Megan's been alone too long. It's about time, that's all I have to say."

"I was referring to the garden."

She sighed and released his arm. "But I find the other subject much more interesting." After adjusting her glasses she walked over to the larger of the stacks. She shook off the snow that had drifted onto them. "Beautiful, aren't they?"

"Yes. I'm curious as to why you're replacing them. Isn't it a lot of work?" He accepted the bouquet she offered him and, without thinking, sniffed them.

She frowned, then leaned toward him, lowering her voice. "They're dead, Raymond."

"I know. Habit, I guess."

She snatched the bunch from him. "I'm replacing them because of the avalanche near the Needles yesterday."

Batty, but lovable. Megan said the slide was at Eagle's Crest, but he saw no point in trying to correct her.

"Do you change colors each day?"

She looked at aghast. "No, that would be silly. I do so only when necessary."

This was going nowhere fast. He changed subjects, mimicking her conspiratorial tone. "It's Reynold, by the way."

Grace straightened. "What is?"

"My name. Reynold Harrison Moore," He stopped.

"I didn't quite catch that." Grace pulled off one glove and adjusted her hearing aid with the nail of her index finger.

"Reynold Harrison." He cleared his throat. "Do you have other flowers? Other colors?"

"Yes. Let's see. Pink baby's breath. Golden ranunculus. Double bloom peonies. Grape hyacinths." Grandma Grace wiggled her finger at him. "Don't let that last name fool you, though. The hyacinths are blue."

"I won't." Rey kept a straight face. He was amused and relieved to have diverted her attention.

She wandered over to the flower pile and resumed her position on the foam kneeling pad. Rey stood next to her. He wanted to help but wasn't sure how.

Grace glanced up at him "Don't even think about kneeling, young man." She pulled a handful of flowers from the ground and shoved them toward him. "Here, take these."

He did.

"When your arms are full, toss the parrot tulips on the first pile and bring me another stack of bee balms."

He could handle that, although the overall mission of the project had him baffled. But that was her business, and it seemed to make sense to her. They worked in harmony as he tried to question her subtly about Mitchell.

"Where's your boarder this morning? Out chasing grizzlies?"

She handed him a double bunch of flowers and peered at him over her glasses. "You're from the city, right?"

"Correct." He smiled. "Seattle."

She shook her head. "Bears hibernate this time of year, Reynold." She resumed her task. "I'm afraid Mr. Mitchell is doing the same this morning. Stayed out too late at the local poker game." Grace made a disapproving noise with her teeth. "I don't believe that researchers make very much in this day and age. Hope he didn't lose all of last week's paycheck."

"And not be able to pay the rent?"

"It's not that. These local boys play for keeps. Their games can get rough." She lowered her voice. "Between you and me, they might have pegged Eric as an easy mark. I'm afraid he's rather a spendthrift."

The one time Rey had seen the man, he'd been dressed in Goodwill cast-offs. "Why do you think that, Grace?" He swapped a bundle of apricot for a red one.

"He collects expensive toys. I wasn't surprised by the computer when he moved in. Nor the high powered binoculars. Even the pocket recorder, for making notes in the field." She motioned for Rey's arm. He helped her stand and move to a new spot. She resumed her pulling and probing without missing a beat. "His portable phone is what really raised my eyebrows. I ask you, what's wrong with using my telephone?"

Rey thought of his own cell phone. "That's really not so unusual, Grace."

"And the telescope. Why, you'd think the man was a Peeping Tom the way he sets that thing up each night."

A chill worked its way down Rey's spine. He wanted to run this news by Megan and Rachel, but pangs of guilt spread through him for prying this information out of sweet Grandma Grace. She was being rather cooperative, though. He decided to feel guilty later. "Have you asked him about it?"

She shook her head. "I'd only embarrass the man, I'm sure. Everyone needs a nasty habit or two. But still, it has me worried."

"You've actually seen him use it, then?"

"No. He keeps it hidden behind the curtains in the evenings and in the closet during the day." She sighed. "It's the fact he's hiding it that bothers me. Must think I'm going senile. I know when things belong and when they don't, after living in this house for thirty years."

Telescope. High powered binoculars. Cell phone. Not unusual all alone, but together? What was the man really watching in these woods?

He stood. So did Grace, smacking her gloved hands together. "I guess that's it. The only way I can think of saying thanks is to offer you lunch."

"That's kind of you, but I think I'll head back to Megan's. I'll help you carry the tulips inside first, though."

"You'd turn down homemade vegetable soup and fresh baked bread?"

He paused. It was really no decision at all.

She smiled at him and patted his cheek. "I didn't think so."

❄   ❄   ❄

Though Megan's pulse was well above her training zone, she couldn't force herself to stop. One foot slid ahead of the other, propelling her forward, her skis slicing tracks through the new snow. With each swing of her arms, she planted her pole and pulled hard. Was it adrenaline or anger pushing her on?

Scott's behavior had sunk well below what she expected from him, which was saying a lot. Her expectations these days were rock bottom. Short temper. Surly attitude. If he truly hadn't wanted to be there last night, he should have said so. She'd never cajole him into dinner again. The weekly tradition just brought her heartache. She'd rather eat alone than put up with his moods. What had Rey thought? It was embarrassing.

She raced by her last marker. She wasn't ready to loop back through the trees as usual. This direction would lead her to the Desolation Point turnoff, then on to Devil's Elbow. Her mind was no longer calling the shots. Her thighs strained, her heels lifted. Every stroke caused her biceps to tense and her forearms to tighten.

All right, she thought, her breath coming fast. She'd heed the Devil's call today. This stretch of the Okanogan was her home. This particular square mile section couldn't be avoided forever. But she would face the cliff from below, not from above, as Thia had. Time to put her demons to rest.

She slowed to a stop beneath the rock outcropping and looked up. Though the base was a relatively easy climb, above it the landmark was vertical, looming three hundred feet over her. It formed a stark, rugged V against the blue January sky. Sunlight reflected off the icy surface, causing her to squint despite the sunglasses she wore. She shook out her arms to relieve her fatigue but knew it was as much mental as physical.

Pulling off her glove, Megan touched the thick layer of ice that hid the bleakness of the stone. She curled her fingers and let her nails slowly scrape down the side of the outcropping. They didn't penetrate even a fraction of an inch. She flicked away the frost embedded beneath her fingertips. One nail was broken near the quick.

She and Thia used to ski here and it had been her mother and father's favorite run when they were alive. All three were gone and now in many ways Scott was lost to her. She lowered her head until her cheek rested against the ice and let the memories come.

The weather hadn't been as perfect the morning of Thia's death. Instead of the crisp zero degrees she was enjoying today, a warm front held the temperature near thirty. The skies had been cloudy and the air heavy with moisture. She'd rushed her work that morning, including the slope above Devil's Elbow.

The entire ridge west of Snagtooth should have been closed, but she hadn't been able to provide the data to support her claim. There hadn't been time to go back and dig again. How ironic. She'd argued and lost. Thia and Pete had been the real losers.

If only Thia had waited for her at the motel, she could have warned her sister about this section. But no, she'd canceled both her breakfast with Megan and her day trip with Russell at the last minute. Thia had only skied once before with Peter Aldridge, why the sudden urgency that morning? Megan pulled back away from the sheet of ice and welcomed the dull throb in her cheek. One more bit of proof that she was still alive. Could still feel pain. Anything to distract her from the memories.

Glancing again at the rock, she took note of the snow patches blemishing the gently sloping surface. She released her skis and stepped out of them. It was foolish, but she wanted to see what they had seen, feel for herself some of the terror they'd felt. Adrenaline pumped through her system. Now was as good a time as any for a little recklessness. Choosing her first handhold, she pulled herself up.

The snow in the crevices chilled her fingers but she kept climbing. The newly broken nail burned as wetness seeped in. The toe of her ski boot made her movements awkward, but she kept her gaze fixed on the small ledge five feet above her. She could make it. Her foot slipped; she chose her next spot more carefully.

She mantled onto the ledge, scraping her leg in the process. Her upper thigh would be bruised. Cold seeped in through the thin fabric of her training suit. She blew on her fingers to warm them.

She'd tried to close the slope; the office ignored her recommendation. In either case, Pete's experience should have alerted him to the avalanche danger. Her professionalism wasn't really on trial here. She was using that as an excuse. It had been hard following in Thia's shadow but it was even harder carrying the shadowy weight of her sister's death. Closing her eyes, she leaned back against the rock. The rough surface pulled at the woolen strands of her ski cap.

Thia'd had it all: looks, talent, and a brashness men loved. And not merely as it related to sports. Thia's gifts were natural. Megan's one stab at imitation had ended in disaster. She could barely face Russell, even to this day.

Squeezing her eyelids shut, she vowed not to cry. She hadn't then and wouldn't give in now. She was used to being second best. The late bloomer. The little sister. The one people settled for when they couldn't get close to Thia, the star. But meeting Rey had caused her to reevaluate. He liked her without any pretense or effort on her part. Would he still, if he knew?

Why? All the other questions surrounding the accident had been answered by the officials, but that one puzzle still remained. No one asked anymore, but she posed that question to herself daily. And every time she did, she remembered where she'd been that morning. Could she ever forgive herself?

❄   ❄   ❄

That should do it. Scott backed out of the shed then closed and re-locked the door. Damn, he'd been lucky, picking a time when no one was at home. The fact that Megan was with Harrison, though, didn't sit well with him. He could see her Vmax sitting in front of Granny's front door. Well, at least they hadn't gone far.

He turned his palms over and saw black smudges where the marker had rubbed off on his skin. Wiping his hands against his jeans didn't help. His sniffed his fingers. Damn, even he could smell the gasoline, despite the recent problems with his nose. His gloves would provide some of the needed cover, but where else had he spilled it? He glanced down at his boots. The bottom of one pant leg had splotches. He'd have to get back into town without anyone seeing him.

That sounded easier than it was on some days. The fine citizens of Snagtooth seemed to think that his being a public official also meant he was public property. He didn't mind waving to them or exchanging greetings while passing on the sidewalk, but they expected him to stop and chat. As if he had time for that. No, it would be safer if he arrived sight unseen.

He switched on his vehicle and left as quickly and casually as possible. As if his visit had all been in a day's work. Would the warning be enough to drive Harrison away? He certainly hoped so.

Scott inhaled the fresh noon time air. He could almost feel the well-deserved pat on the back from Russell. He was banking on more, though. Much more. Extra assignments, followed by tangible rewards such as hard cold cash. And after last night's losing streak, the more the better.

❊   ❊   ❊

Megan returned from her morning field work to find Rey executing a series of strikes and kicks, blocks and attacks in her living room, in the same set pattern as yesterday. She was exhausted. Seeing Rey was a welcome relief.

Instead of continuing he stopped, waved a greeting then picked up a towel from the arm of the sofa. "Hi. Have a good training run this morning?" His voice sounded breathless.

"Great." If only he knew how big that lie was. "The snow conditions are better than expected. I only had to close one section of the mountain. Eagle's Crest."

"Why?" He shook out the towel and rubbed it over his face and neck as he took several steps toward her. "Another avalanche?" When he moved the terry cloth to his chest, her eyes moved with it. She could get used to this.

She quickly looked up. "Not yet, but there's a moderate possibility for the second day running. Better to be safe, you know how the saying goes." It would be nice to put her job behind her for awhile and focus on him. She was thankful, at least, they were discussing a subject she could speak coherently on. Less thought required.

"That makes two areas closed, then."

She frowned. "What's the other?"

"The Needles. Grace said there was an avalanche there yesterday."

"I wonder why she said that?" She dismissed it with a shrug. "Maybe Granny was forecasting again."

"I could have misunderstood her."

She unzipped her coat and tossed it onto the nearest chair back. When her brother had done the same the night before, she'd gotten on his case about it. However this was her house and she had no intention of moving from this spot, not while Rey was so close. "How was your morning? Did you have a chance to get out?"

"I certainly did. Went to visit Grace." He draped the towel around his neck and walked toward her. "Thank you for lending me your Vmax. I must admit, I wasn't expecting that."

"I thought you'd enjoy escaping for awhile."

"I did, very much." His hands were mid-chest, gripping both ends of the towel. "It's rather confining indoors."

"Very." Megan nodded, trying to not to let her voice give away her nervousness. What had he meant last night by relationship? This felt more like a full sensory attack.

His gaze had drifted down her body, away from her face to linger on her racing suit. She knew what he must be seeing, form fitting Lycra mixed with nylon. No insulation anywhere.

The mental imaging was working both ways. His breathing had slowed, hers had increased. He'd also mentioned something about timing. They had some available right now. Their eyes met; she was determined not to look away.

Rey reached out and touched Megan's forearm. His fingers trailed lightly downward to her wrist. When they reached her watch, he turned her hand over. "What is this?"

How could he speak so calmly? "My heart rate monitor."

He examined the digital read-out. "How does it work?"

She was happy for the excuse to keep him talking. To keep him touching her. "The sensor is here, around my chest." She drew an imaginary line parallel to the edge of her sports bra.

He watched her movement. "Here?"

He trailed his fingers where she'd indicated. His touch didn't stray upward a single centimeter. She wished to God it would. He paused when he reached her ribs then met her eyes.

Megan ignored the tightening in her throat. "The transmitter picks up my heart rate, the watch displays the count. I use it to pace myself. Throughout the run, I mean." She was babbling.

"What is your goal?"

"When I'm executing a basic training pass, I try to keep my pulse below one sixty. When I'm working on endurance, one eighty."

His fingers strayed toward the center of her midriff but never higher. "And when you're not training?"

"Sixty."

Rey turned her wrist over again and glanced at the watch. "It's at ninety now."

"Yes." She swallowed. "Well you see, I'm not resting."

He moved forward, narrowing the gap between them. His palm relinquished its position on her stomach and took up residency on her hip. His fingers were splayed across the smooth nylon. She felt the heat from his hand through the fabric. She considered touching him the same way but didn't know whether to go over or under his arm.

Rey pulled her forward until she stood against him. When he spoke, his breath stirred the hair at her temple. "And now?"

He was still holding her left wrist. Together they read the display. One hundred ten.

His grasp on her left hand shifted until they were palm-to-palm, fingers interlocked. With their joined hands, he touched her cheek. His mouth was only a fraction of an inch away. What was he waiting for?

She didn't think twice. Helicopters and gunshots, be damned. This was what she wanted. She leaned forward. His mouth was warm and firm. Where she was impatient he was gently reassuring, almost hesitant. His lips brushed softly against hers, exploring. Testing. As if there were a lifetime of hours stretched before them instead of this one stolen moment in time.

She tightened her grip on his shoulder, wanting more. To feel the pressure of his mouth hard, not gentle, against her. Feel him nip at the tender edges and then kiss away the pain. Instead he drew back. Just a fraction. Watching her. Did he want her to say something? And, if so, what?

After a moment, he removed his hand from her hip and stepped away. Her fingers slipped from around his neck. He exhaled slowly. "I need a shower. I'll see you in a little while."

She nodded. What the hell had just happened?

❄   ❄   ❄

Lute leaned against the seat. The day's haul was secured in the cargo compartment. He exhaled as the copter lifted off. At least this task had gone right. He hadn't seen a soul on his approach to the Needles hut this afternoon and Princess had arrived exactly on schedule. He'd check the status of the other assignment, then beat it out of here.

He fastened his headset and keyed in his mike. "Princess, patch me into Snagtooth."

"Will do."

After only a few moment's pause, Lute had his man on the phone. "So far, so good. The snowmobile's hidden where we agreed. Thanks for the loaner."

"Don't call me during the day." Though muffled, the voice was still harsh. "I thought I'd made that clear."

"You did. But I made myself clear, too." Lute tried Cowboy's infamous, no-screw-ups-allowed, manner on for size. "We want the visitor gone. Today, not tomorrow. Are you ready to confirm that for us?"

"No. It will be today, though. Someone's working on it. Call back tonight. You'll have your results then."

Despite the news, Lute smiled at the subservience he heard. The tough guy on the other end of the line was gone. It was good being the hard-ass for a change. "Tonight then. You accepted payment already."

"I remember."

He could almost hear the guy swallow. Lute broke the connection and let his head rest against the door's interior.

Princess's voice came over his headset. "Good work."

"Thanks."

Yeah, it had felt good. He tried not to let the fact his pilot had monitored the call sour his mood. Nor would he fool himself about whose butt was really on the line. He was the one who would have to stand in front of Cowboy tonight and offer excuses, not the in-town patsy.

His temples throbbed. He stifled the urge to rip off the headset. That and other luxuries, such as peeling off his jacket after his long drive to rendezvous with Princess, would have to wait. He couldn't risk leaving the Okanogan without finishing the job. If his presence was needed later on, the reappearance of Mountain High Adventures would be too conspicuous.

"Let's play hide-and-go-seek for awhile. Okay with you, Princess? We're not finished yet."

"Good idea. I'll find us a spot."

"Great."

He closed his eyes as she banked left. Nothing was simple anymore.

ELEVEN

THE DOOR TO her bedroom was partially ajar. Through the opening Rey could see Megan still working at her computer. He'd offered to make dinner over an hour ago, which she gratefully accepted. The meal preparation he could easily handle alone, but he'd been hoping she would venture from her room to keep him company.

She seemed to be withdrawing from him. Hiding. When he'd said this was a confusing time for them to start a physical relationship, his intent hadn't been to cut-off contact.

He viewed it as a promise to each other to wait until they could more clearly identify the emotion they were feeling. Fear was no way to begin a future together. Maybe she didn't see it that way.

After turning the stove to simmer he walked toward her room. He knocked on the door. "Megan?"

She glanced at him over her shoulder. "It's time already?"

"This is the official five minute warning."

"Good." She raised her arms and stretched over head. "I'll transfer this document to the main office, then I'm through with business for the day."

"Great."

She resumed her task at the keyboard. It would help immensely if he could use her computer to access his office files. That would not only ease his conscience about being gone for so long, but would relieve some of Dave and Ali's workload, too. And if Dave could send the investigator's reports to him over the Internet, Rey could read them first hand.

The only problem was the machine was located in her bedroom. Awkward. Intimate. He smiled. He'd ask.

Megan turned toward him, her eyebrow raised. He released the doorknob and stepped forward. There was no time like the present. "Dinner's ready. Are you?"

"Yes." She glanced away, waving at him to enter. "Come in if you like." Her attention was already back on the screen.

He crossed the room, choosing to stand by the side of her desk, farthest from the bed.

Megan pressed the send key. "Is your home computer similar to this?"

"No. The one at the office is, though."

"Funny. I didn't peg you as an office type." She shrugged. "I don't know why, it's not as if we ever talked about it." She picked up a file folder and began sorting its contents. "What sort of work do you do?"

He refrained from saying, any sort I want. He wasn't ready to discuss his life back in Seattle. He tried to be vague. "I'm in retail. Ski wear, primarily."

Megan looked up from her paperwork, sympathy etched in her expression. "Sales? Sounds a bit boring. Do you work in a mall specialty shop or in a large department store?"

"Neither. The corporate offices." That much was true. "What were you writing?"

"A recap of the afternoon mountain conditions, plus a forecast for tomorrow." She picked up the printout, tapped the pages against the desk to square the edges, then stapled them together. "I love working outdoors. That's the best part of this job. I even like writing about it. I'm sure my reports seem boring to someone else."

"No. In fact, I'd like to read one."

She met his eyes for a moment. "Sure. But don't think for a moment that you successfully changed the subject. We're talking about you." She slipped the stack into a folder. "Ever get involved with the marketing end of the business?"

"Sometimes." Other than establishing budget limits and approving new seasonal lines, he mainly let Dave run that department solo.

"Well, stay clear." Megan dropped the file folder into the bottom drawer and pushed it closed with her knee. "The publicity hounds used to track Thia through rain and snow, simply to wave contracts in her face. Infuriating."

"She could have refused."

"I should have been more specific. It infuriated me, not her. She loved it. The attention. The pursuit." Megan frowned. "The under-the-table money put her through college."

She shook her head then stood. "I'm through here." She waved her hand toward the desk. "Feel free to use the computer, if you wish."

"Thank you. I'll dial in tomorrow." He waited until her attention was elsewhere, then glanced around her room. The furnishings were so unlike the rest of her cabin. Except for her actual work area, the room was frilly and romantic. Lacy pillow shams, a rosebud quilt. It showed a whole new side of her personality. One that he'd never expected.

Megan crossed to her four-poster bed, picked up her shoes from the floor and sat down of the mattress's edge. "Rey?"

Had she observed him studying her surroundings?

"I know how tight the job market is. Are you putting your employment at risk by being here so long?"

He felt a strong need to bring the truth closer in. "I'm not in danger of losing my job."

"But if you can conduct some of your work from here, it might help keep your position secure. Feel free."

"You're sure?"

"Yes. I have everything backed up. You can't do much damage." She glanced up from tying her sneaker and pointed to her swivel chair. "Have a seat."

She ran through a few basics about her individual set-up. He listened enjoying the sound of her voice. It wasn't until he successfully connected and his corporate logo appeared on the screen that he realized his mistake.

"That's the design on your coat." She moved from behind him, to stand at his side. "Yours, Dave's and Ali's."

"Yes."

"That explains quite a bit, you know." She glanced down at her hands, played with her thumbnail, hesitating.

He waited. Was now the time to tell her?

After a moment, she met his eyes again. "I must admit, I did think that the three of you dressing like triplets was a bit silly. I'm sorry. I didn't know it was a show of employee pride. You probably get an attractive discount too."

He drew a deep breath. "Actually, Megan, it's more than that."

She held one hand up. "No need to explain. I take back what I said earlier regarding flamboyant marketing practices. My feelings are still the same, but I should have kept them to myself." She glanced toward the kitchen. "Smells good. Should we check on dinner?"

He'd be here for several more days at least. There would be other opportunities. "Sure." He stood. "And thanks. Are you sure I won't be intruding in here?"

She was watching him closely. Her cheeks were a bit flushed. He hoped she was imagining the same bedroom images that were running rampant in his own mind. When she spoke though, her voice was quiet, her words were sincere. "I'm sure. After all, the cabin itself is close quarters."

He smiled at her. That was an understatement.

❄   ❄   ❄

Megan sank further down into the bath water, allowing the bubbles to tickle her chin. Her Victorian claw-footed tub was her second major indulgence, though not quite as expensive as her tricked-out snowmobile.

The water temperature was perfect, just a degree or two below skin-scorching level. She spent a full five minutes submerging, one appreciative inch at a time.

The tub and accompanying raised tile platform were in a small alcove off her main bedroom, behind the door and to the left. Had Rey seen it? Probably not. The door had been open. She hadn't missed the way he paused when looking around the room, taking in the rocking chair with the crocheted afghan thrown over the back rails, her antique foot locker draped in doilies, the hand-sewn comforter. Grace's creations. She loved them dearly. She'd never considered how frilly they might look to someone else.

A thin mist of perspiration formed on her upper lip and forehead. She reclined against the inflated pillow and let the image of Rey working at her desk come to mind. What did he mean by, dealing with the baggage from her past? She was supposed to do this in her own way, but didn't know which way that was. And the way he said relationship made her think of some foreign object. How did two people develop one? She would need time to figure these things out. Probably more time than they had left together.

Her washcloth hung on the hook above her left shoulder. She reached for it then for the bar of unscented soap in the porcelain holder. The rectangular lump of ivory in her palm made her feel as sexy as a spinster. Placing the bar back in the dish on the rim, she stood and opened the mirrored-oak cabinet above the tub. Water ran in rivulets down her body as she scrounged through the cabinet. Behind the razors, adhesive strips and aspirin was a small sample-sized round of honeysuckle soap. Yes, much better.

There was a knock on the front door. Who would be visiting this late? She was about to reach for her towel when the floor boards in the living room creaked. Rey must have had heard the knock, too. Rachel? Megan had forgotten to call her after dinner.

The conversation drifting into her bedroom proved her right. Rachel and Rey, laughing. Here she was, covered only in suds, while they conversed freely in her kitchen. Only one room away. One thin wall between them.

She sank back against the heated enamel tub and listened to their voices. Rachel's: quick, pointed and filled with outrageous digs. His: rich and deep, almost musical when he laughed. He did often. When had she ever laughed so easily?

It was scary, admitting how much she'd grown used to him living with her. Hearing his voice each morning. Watching him roam her cabin, taking care of things. Sensing him taking care of her. Wishing he didn't have to eventually go.

The voices in her kitchen grew softer. Good-byes were being exchanged. Within moments her front door opened and closed. The pressure change caused her bedroom door to become unlatched. She raised an eyebrow.

Interesting predicament. Maybe he would poke his head in and say something clever before securing the door. Did she want him to? She listened, not daring to breathe, sinking farther beneath the layer of suds for modesty's sake. There was no sound except for his footsteps moving about her kitchen.

Her towel was across the room, on her bed. She couldn't fetch it. Too risqué. She'd let it go for now and enjoy the song he was humming. She rubbed the soap against the cloth, working up a lather.

Starting with her shoulder, she ran the wash rag across her chest, then down the length of arm. Memories of him touching her earlier through her racing suit, came to mind. Enjoyable. Curious. So different than her prior run-ins with sex. Her gaze moved toward the door. What would it be like with him?

She dunked the wash cloth with too much force. A wave splashed over the edge of the tub. Leaning forward she peered over the side. The spillage had missed the platform and run onto the wooden floor. It was her fault for not paying more attention. She'd have to mop soon or the water would leave marks.

Maybe if she stretched far enough, she could use her hand towel to sop up the mess. She grabbed it, leaned forward and attempted to toss it on top of the spill. Her elbow knocked the soap holder off the tub's rim. The porcelain shattered as it hit the floor. The bar skidded across the puddle.

"Megan? Are you all right?"

His footsteps grew louder as he approached her room. He called her name again with more emphasis than before. She should answer him. Say something. If not, he would come in. She slid beneath the bubbles and kept quiet. The door opened.

"Megan?" He entered and stood staring at her blank computer screen, hands on his hips. He was such an expert on relationships. How was this for timing?

"I'm fine. I knocked the soap dish over by accident."

He turned. After a brief glance at her face, his gaze followed the direction of her hand. He stared at the broken object by the tub's footings for several moments before his eyes slowly met hers again.

His waist was at eye level, inches from the tub. Had fleece sweat pants ever been so sexy before? She looked upward, past the neckline of his shirt, past the day's growth of beard on his chin. Her heart beat increased. He said that he found her attractive. His eyes were repeating the message now. Why didn't he say something?

He moved forward.

She broke the silence. "The floor is wet. Be careful."

Leaning over, he picked up the soap.

She cringed, imagining what it must feel like to his fingers. "I'll take that." She held out her hand.

He cupped his free hand below hers and let the bar slide into her palm. His touch remained for a moment longer than necessary. He stepped back. No straying glances below her collarbone. No attempt at kissing her. His hand was covered with a slick, soapy residue.

She could invite him to rinse it in her bath water. Lean back on her inflatable pillow, lower her lashes to half-mast then bat them. Ridiculous. He must see she was interested. Why reach for her towel instead of for her?

"Anything else?" His tone was huskier than normal, but she hated that he'd recovered first. He was injecting normalcy back into the situation. "I could grab a mop."

"No. I'll do it later."

"All right."

Three feet away. The waiting game, again. Her one fist clenched the lathered cloth, the other the bar of soap. She wanted to understand him better. Were all relationships this physically intense? Maybe that meant they already had one. If so, then damn the timing. Come closer, she wanted to say. The words seemed too much. Blunt and obvious.

"I should go."

The word "stay" stuck in her throat.

"I have one piece of advice before I do." He shifted his gaze toward the water. "Hand soap and bath bubbles don't mix." After a brief smile he left.

She glanced down, too. She'd never know, nor would she dare ask, how long the suds had been gone.

Rey's hand remained on the outside doorknob. Megan. She'd wanted him to look at her. Her eyes held an invitation, but did she know what she was asking? If she could say what she wanted, his doubt would disappear. That was the invitation he needed: not only action but the right words to back it up. Would she ever trust herself enough? Trust him?

He released the handle and walked slowly across the living room. Toward the door to the downstairs. The distance between them increased, making each footstep a bit easier than the last. It would be a long night.

Lute's flash light picked out the piece of white note paper lying on a tarp in the dark woodshed. That was the warning? A few gasoline fumes and a comic book style threat, written in black marker? Harrison was no pansy-ass, that would never drive him out of town. Shit.

He was tired, wanted this over. No more missions. If he'd known what the organization demanded at the start he'd have said no thanks. Found some other way to chase the golden buck. He folded the note and shoved it into his pocket.

The kid was stupid. So was Russell, for not doing the job himself. Cowboy would be pissed. And he, Lute Ferraty, was the one who would pay. He'd better take care of this little job right now.

Picking up the metal container, he splashed the contents in a wide arc around the shed, careful to leave a dry patch near the door. Time to split.

He pulled the note with the childish scribbling from his pocket then opened the door to the shed. He peered out. No movement near the house. Good. Maybe he could find a way to still pin it on the deputy. He bent and flicked his lighter, setting the paper aflame. After tossing it inside he ran.

❊   ❊   ❊

"Where in hell have you been? It's the middle of the night." Eric paced the length of his bedroom, cell phone gripped firmly in his left hand. "I shouldn't have to call your home phone."

Logan returned the attack. "Relax, Mom. I investigated Cowboy's spread in the Andes today, per plan. Watched baby brother and his warden pack more boxes, as we agreed. Did every other goddamned thing you asked." His partner sighed and dropped the defensiveness from his tone. "My cell phone must be dead. Dropped my pager in the toilet this morning, too. Sorry, Mitchell. I blew it."

"Forget it." Eric ran his hand over his eyes, glad Logan was alive. That had been his fear. He was a damned good partner. "They completed another pickup this morning. The Needles hut." He refrained from kicking the side of the bed.

"And the other?"

"The original package is still there. Too hot. Maybe they're on to me."

"You suspect a leak?"

"I suspect everything. Makes it simpler." Eric peeled off his jacket then unhooked his shoulder harness, letting it slip to the bed. He flexed his shoulders. "There was activity at the ranger's shed tonight."

"Go on."

"Her brother was sneaking around. Left a note. *Harrison go home*. Can you believe it?"

Logan snorted. "If the place is still standing, then he wasn't taking his direction from Cowboy."

He picked up his hand exerciser, then crossed to the window. His goal for tonight was two hundred repetitions. "I can't say. I'll keep an eye on it."

"Take care. If they blow you away, I'll have to start over."

Eric frowned and kept quiet. He didn't deserve the respect he thought he'd heard. He was lying by omission. He swept back the curtains, then bent one of the metal blinds downward with his finger. Shit. "Fire. Gotta go."

"What?"

"The damned shed. Later." He hung up then grabbed his holster and coat. It was going to be a long night.

❄   ❄   ❄

Rey sighed and rolled over, burying his head beneath his pillow. Daylight was beginning to sneak in beneath the curtains. The orange glow of the morning sun. How could it be daylight already? His eyes burned as though he'd just climbed into bed.

Megan had probably been up for hours, doing her stretching routine on the living room floor. Or maybe she was already preparing a brown bag snack to take along on her field work. He remembered watching her move about the kitchen yesterday while making lunch. No indecision, no foot-tapping. Her every movement was economical and purposeful. Her only frivolity was her bedroom furnishings.

He smiled as he remembered the delicate rosebud comforter and lace dust ruffle. They were charming and provocative when he first saw them. Much more when the decor had included Megan, wearing only suds. And not many at that.

If he'd known, he would have stayed out. Once he was in, why had he left? Waiting for the danger to pass may not be the right thing to do. It was the most sensible but that meant only his mind was engaged in the decision. What about his heart?

He tossed his pillow aside and rolled onto his back. He should rise, dress and start the day. Guilt would set in if he stayed in bed, knowing she was already outdoors training. It didn't matter that his own agenda was empty. He sat on the side of the bed and tested his knee movements. Much better. Bending his leg was fine; twisting motions still had him worried. The exercises were helping.

He stood and glanced toward the window again. Strange. Now that he was fully awake, he noticed the color was wrong. Plus, Megan's cabin faced west. It couldn't be daylight. He heard a popping sound, similar to a child's cap gun going off. He rushed to the window, his heart beating faster. Good God. One corner of the woodshed's roof was engulfed in flames.

He reached for his boots and jammed his bare feet inside. "Megan!" She wouldn't hear him through the closed door. Rey straightened, cleared his throat and yelled again. Louder this time. "Megan, get up."

His long johns would have to be clothes enough. He'd designed the fabric to sustain sub-zero temperatures. Some field test this was.

Grabbing his parka he wrenched it on as he ran to the stairs. He raced upward taking them two at a time. At the top, he threw open the door.

"Megan!"

She emerged from the bedroom. "What's wrong?" Sleep fuzzed the edges of her voice but her tone was alert. The bedroom light silhouetted the calf-length nightdress she wore.

He crossed to the coat rack. "The shed's on fire." She stopped yawning. Her eyes were wide. He tossed her jacket to her. "Any chance that your outside faucet works this time of year?"

"It might." Megan pushed her hair back from her face then shoved her arm into the coat sleeve. "The hose is dried and coiled, near the stairwell. I shut off the outside water, late October." She rushed to the kitchen, stared out the window. "My God. If the spigot is frozen, could we hook it up to the kitchen faucet?"

"We can try."

Her fingers gripped the sink's edge. "How could this happen?"

"Later. Turn the main control valve back on, then meet me outside."

She knelt and opened the cabinet door beneath the sink. By the time Rey reached the front door, Megan had cleaners, sponges and scrubbers flying. Her nightdress had ridden up her thigh, revealing a long length of leg. "Before you come out, throw on a pair of pants. You'll freeze if you don't."

She nodded and continued tossing items out from under the sink.

The night air was like a cold slap against his face. The fiery outline against the frozen landscape, was out of place. The flames spread, quickly devouring the brittle wood. The crackling sound made him want to flinch. Smoke curled a path into the star-lit sky. By the time he had the hose connected and running, the right front quarter of the shed was beyond hope.

The blaze moved down the roof line to the left with a loud swoosh. Toward the woodpile, closer to the house. He adjusted the nozzle so that the stream of water hit the fire's leading edge. A loud hiss sounded as water met flame.

Megan emerged, stuffed into boots, nightshirt trailing out behind her parka. Her hair spilled disheveled from under her hat. She was beautiful.

One hose was useless against the inferno. He yelled above noise. "We probably can't save the building itself. Where's your snowmobile parked?"

"In the back."

He grimaced. The entrance was demolished. Crumbling. An idea came to mind. "Is it near an outer wall?"

"Yes. Close to the left side."

"Good."

"What are you talking about?" She turned, raising her voice. "You're not going in there."

"Here. Take this." He handed Megan the hose, then signaled with his hand. "Follow that fire line, back and forth across the crest. Got it?"

She nodded. Her eyes were wide with questions.

"Your keys?"

She dropped them into his hand. "You're not going in."

"I don't intend to." He touched her cheek. "Not in the traditional way, at least. I'm going to cut a new door for you." He hurried toward the flaming shed. The roar was deafening. The heat scorched his cheeks. When he reached the side of the building, he bent and retrieved the ax.

Signaling to her, he shouted. "Keep the hose moving." Debris fell, singeing his hair. He brushed away the embers without slowing his pace.

She said something he couldn't hear but her face was a mask of concern. He nodded at her then turned the corner. He heard the spray of water hit a new section of roof and offered a silent prayer. He didn't doubt for a moment that this accident was linked to the others. The kid's murder, the gunshots aimed at Megan. Why? Next time, it could be the house.

❄   ❄   ❄

She coiled the hose and stared at the remains of the wood pile. Dozens of thoroughly soaked logs were strewn across her front yard. They would be frozen solid by morning. That was the least of her worries.

The fire had burned itself out, leaving behind a pile of blackened rubble. Tomorrow was soon enough to take care of the mess, after the sheriff came out to investigate. Great. Another visit from Russell, on top of everything else.

Megan climbed the steps to the deck, flung open the door and hung her parka on the coat tree. She headed for the kitchen and retrieved her bottle of cognac. Forget the usual cup of tea. She poured a shot into two glasses, sure that Rey would join her shortly. Next, the phone.

She dialed. The recorder clicked on. Was he home, and not answering? If so, she hoped the machine's volume was turned to maximum. Her voice certainly was. "Russell. If you can hear me, pick up. It's Megan." She waited. No response. Where would he be at midnight?

"Someone torched my shed tonight. Stop hiding behind your paperwork and do something." Her voice broke. She had more to say but hung up instead.

Rey walked toward her, his coat still on but unzipped. It was almost as cold indoors as it was out. She just hadn't noticed until now. She shivered. He wrapped his arms tightly around her. Her tears started instantly.

"It's all right." His warm breath brushed against her ear. "The cabin is safe. I got your vehicle out of the shed. Everything else can be replaced."

She shook her head. "That's not it. Those things don't matter. What if . . ." she drew a ragged breath. Crying was such an ugly venture and she was so damned good at it today. Just a few hours earlier she'd been clinging to the rock face below Devil's Elbow, grieving over Thia. Now she was clinging to Rey.

"If what?" His hand cupped the back of her head. "Tell me."

"If you hadn't wakened. If the house had caught fire and you were trapped downstairs." She buried her forehead against his chest. "My mother didn't make it. I couldn't reach her in time. I tried. Her bedroom . . ." She couldn't finish.

"I know. Grace told me."

His arms enfolded her. She let him simply hold her, gently comforting her. Rey. His hands rubbed her back. He rocked her slowly. She let the tears fall until she swore his chest would be soaked. She had never felt so safe.

His voice was slow and gentle. "You were courageous tonight. You never flinched. Never backed off."

"I hated it. And I resented the hell out of having to do it."

"You did what was necessary." He continued the rocking motion. "The fire didn't win. You did. We did."

We was the most beautiful word on earth at that moment. She let it echo in her ears until the ring of the phone obliterated the sound.

Without releasing her entirely, Rey picked up the receiver. "Jeffers' residence." A pause. "Sheriff. How nice of you to call." He paused. She leaned more fully against him, enjoying the way his chest rumbled when he spoke. "Yes, there's been a fire. Luckily no one was hurt."

He leaned back slightly as if nudging her to look up at him. She did. He silently questioned whether she was interested in taking the phone at all. She nodded and reached out her hand.

"Here's Megan." After handing her the receiver, he stepped away and brought her a tissue.

"Russell, just a minute." She blew her nose. "No, I'm fine. Just peachy, considering." Her tone turned business-like. "I want a full investigation. I want this bastard caught."

"Of course. I'll look into it right away. Tomorrow." He cleared his throat. "Megan, I missed your call because I was down at the office. I've been considering all the events of late and, well, I'm not going to sugar-coat this. These little accidents started happening right after Harrison arrived."

She turned her back to Rey, walked several steps away and lowered her voice. "That's a coincidence and you know it."

"Now calm down. I'm not saying he caused them. The point I'm trying to make is that maybe these attacks are aimed at him. He shouldn't stay with you anymore." He paused. "I'm moving him out of your place tomorrow."

"Rey's leaving?" Her voice was nearly a whisper. Her chest felt like lead.

"Yes. Now hear me out. I'll move Harrison into the jail, for his own protection, of course. It won't be as cozy as your place, but it's not bad. If the attacks against you stop, then we'll know."

A shiver ran down her spine. She missed Rey's arms around her. Already she had grown use to him standing by her.

Turning, she looked at him. He was frowning, had obviously deduced what the conversation was about. Him. All she could do was stare.

He signaled for the phone. "May I?"

She handed it over.

"Sheriff Russell." His voice was softly controlled, each word carefully articulated. "I'm not leaving. Unless you're ready to play Bet your Badge with evidence you think will hold up in a court of law, then let it rest. Concentrate your energies on the investigation instead." He paused, placing his hand on her shoulder. His fingers slowly traced a path down her arm until they interlinked with hers. "It's late. We'll see you here tomorrow."

Rey replaced the receiver, then held his arms wide. She walked straight into them. "He said it's not safe here. For you."

"Then we're both leaving." He smiled down at her. "Any place in particular you'd like to go?"

"Russell's coming out to inspect the damage in the morning. We have to be here."

"Technically we don't." He kissed her forehead. "But we might choose to be." He shrugged. "So we don't go far. Have any ideas?"

She thought for a moment. "Yeah. In fact, I do." She smiled at him, then ran her hand across his chest, beneath his open coat. "You know, I love these silk long johns you're wearing, especially the racing stripes, but I'm afraid they won't do for what I have in mind. Put on the warmest clothes you brought and meet me back here in fifteen minutes."

"We're going out at this hour?"

"Yes."

He captured her hand in his and kissed her palm. "I'll be right back."

❆　　　❆　　　❆

The twin bed was narrow for the two of them. Megan sat next to him. Their backs were against the wall, their knees bent and legs tucked. Three out of four knees, anyway. His left was extended straight out in front of him. Fighting the fire had not done his injury any good.

Leaving her cabin had been more symbolic than anything else. They were no safer hiding out at Desolation Hut, which was emphasized by the rifle she'd propped by the foot of the bed.

It was ironic that she'd chosen this particular place. If he hadn't stopped here the first day, they might never have met. That morning, someone else had carried a rifle. For the last time. He pushed that thought to the back burner.

The sun would be up in a few hours. The adrenaline surge had worn off, leaving him exhausted. She was relaxed beneath his arm, her head resting against his chest. Grandma Grace's yellow quilt was wrapped around the two of them. He enjoyed holding her. Trading stories, small bits and pieces of their lives, passed the time and kept other dangerous thoughts at bay.

"Tell me about your father."

He frowned. Not so simple. "I already told you he died. Twenty years ago."

"You did." She snuggled closer. "Now tell me how you coped with feeling responsible. How you went on without him."

He nodded. Memories of Thia must be driving these questions. Pain and guilt that Megan faced everyday. "It was tough. Life changed permanently for all of us. We adjusted, but it took a long time."

She lifted her head. "Elaborate. That is, unless it's too personal."

"All right." He nudged her head back down to his shoulder. He could concentrate better when not meeting her eye-to-eye. It was easier to hold a coherent thought.

"I was sent away to boarding school after the kidnapping media blitz was over. Ali was only a baby. Mom had a new husband within five years. From a distance, I viewed her remarriage as disloyal to Dad's memory. I coped the best way I could. I stayed away and tried to forget about the home front."

"You grew up alone?"

"If you can define being with thousands of students as alone."

"I can."

"Then, yes. But I gained strength from it, I think. The problem was I'd deserted Ali. Forced her to also grow up alone."

"But you were so many years apart in age."

"Fourteen. A lifetime it seems. We never would have been buddies, but I could have protected her."

"From what?"

He focused for a moment on the wood stove, inhaling the
smoky scent, enjoying the warmth. "Sure you want to hear about
my run of bad judgment?"

"Only if you want to tell me."

He tightened his arm around her. She settled closer against
him. "I returned home after graduate school, lived and worked
nearby. Ali was twelve. By the time she turned sixteen, I didn't like
the relationship I was convinced had formed between her and our
step-father. I confronted him directly. He chose to be silent on the
matter, offered no defense, no excuse. Ali however, verbally
attacked me. Said I never cared about her in the first place. Asked
me to butt out. I packed and left town within a week. Chose the
farthest place possible."

"Seattle."

"Right. Once again I forgot the home front, drove it from my
mind. I was fairly successful at it, too, for about three years. Until
an acquaintance at the King County Jail gave me a courtesy call at
work. Ali had followed me to Seattle, made friends with the wrong
people and had ended up involved with drugs."

"You felt responsible?"

He shrugged. She lifted her head and he turned to face her.
"Don't try to convince me it wasn't my fault. I know it wasn't.
Even so, I was glad when Ali moved into a spare bedroom at my
place. We've been there for each other ever since."

She lifted his hand and kissed it. "You're filling the gap left by
your father. She never knew him."

"I'm trying. I hope I'm not off base with this remark, but I see
you following in my same footsteps."

"You mean, with Scott?"

He nodded and ran his fingertips along her jaw. "Look at it this way." He cupped her chin. "We've just found something in common."

Her smile was a touch bittersweet. "There's a key difference. You made it through."

"And so will you." He leaned forward and gently kissed her. Demanding nothing. Asking for the pleasure of her touch, enjoying the feel of her lips against his, her breath against his cheek. She was innocent, but not inexperienced. Experimenting. Then she opened her mouth. Her tongue sought his.

Did she realize the passion she'd just invoked? Most likely not. Her movements were tentative, curious. He followed, mimicking her actions. She seemed to be assessing his every response, poised to flee if the situation were to take a wrong turn.

He wanted to teach her to trust him. And to desire him. One might naturally follow the other. He ran his fingers along her ribs. She reacted by shifting her arm upward, encircling his neck tighter. The movement pressed one breast more directly against his chest. The other was very close to his fingers.

He wanted to touch her there, to see where the passion might lead. To lift her shirt and cup the sweetness in his palm. To lay her back against the bed and taste her. One simple turn and she would be in his hand. She would be his.

He let his hand linger to see if she would take that step. It would be a sign. Combined with the right words, it was the invitation he was looking for.

But she didn't. The kisses must be enough for her for now. He tried to forget about next steps, to enjoy the part she did want to share.

Eventually her breathing slowed. Her forehead came to rest against his neck. The even rise and fall of her chest confirmed that she was asleep.

Trust was one thing but he'd hoped his kisses were a little more stimulating. He shifted uncomfortably, then laid her against the mattress. When they were prone, side-by-side, he drew the quilt over them. She curled against him.

Merely holding her while she dozed was surprisingly enjoyable. But sleep was the farthest thing from his mind.

TWELVE

M EGAN STOOD BY the sink and glanced out the kitchen window. Sunlight filtered through the branches of the fir trees and bounced off the snowy landscape. Grace's pink double bloom peonies blew back and forth in the breeze. Rey was right. Ignore the charred shed. No reason to ruin a perfect day by staying home, waiting for Sheriff Russell.

Investigating the fire was Russell's job not hers. She merely wanted the results. And after last night's snuggle-fest, she wouldn't waste another minute away from Rey's side. Time was too precious.

Breakfast at noon, not her usual routine. Rachel would applaud her lack of dedication. The office hadn't given her a bit of grief when she'd called at six A.M. Word of the fire had preceded her. Her back-up would cover her duties for today. She'd thanked the crew without a tinge of guilt and climbed into bed for a nap.

Rey had slipped quietly downstairs while she'd been on the phone. No good night, not even his usual see you. Odd, considering their closeness at the hut.

She wanted a physical relationship with him. No maybes. No more hesitation. She didn't give a damn whether the time was right or not, or what a relationship actually was. When they were close, she felt alive. She trusted him and was ready to take the next step. But how?

"I want you." She winced. No, she could never say that. "Make love to me." Too bold. Too embarrassing.

Their future may be uncertain, but the present was as clear as a mountain stream: it was time to move forward. That was it. The perfect place. She would share her sanctuary, then ask to share more. It would be dark. All the better.

She walked swiftly to the connecting door, pulled it open and called to him downstairs. "Rey? Breakfast."

"Thanks. Be right up."

She pulled several cereal boxes from the shelf and set them on the counter, her palms sweating. No time for cooking today. She had an outing to plan. She'd set the stage then ask for what she wanted.

Today.

❄   ❄   ❄

Lute re-fitted the floorboards and straightened the rug. Though the hot pink strands were woven together with lighter, more boring colors of the same material, the overall effect was still jarring. Who would have thought you could buy colors like this? Maybe the old lady dyed her own. Must have time on her hands.

"Beneath the floor. So fucking simple." Billy, at Lute's side, stared at the rug. "Who stashed it here?"

"None of your business, kid."

"Bet I could figure it out. Bet I could help you in lots of ways. I could think of new ideas, new locations."

Wouldn't Cowboy love it? Advice, from a snotty kid. One who couldn't keep his hands off the product, for God's sake. He should encourage the kid. Then he wouldn't have to deal with him anymore.

Billy was looking up at him, beaming with coke-induced arrogance. Nearly bouncing with untapped, though misguided, enthusiasm. Two pickups today. Christ. He didn't need the extra pressure of this kid harassing him. "Follow orders and keep your nose clean."

Billy thrust his chin forward. "That might be enough for you, but I want more. Look at the upside here. You could start your own organization. Kiss Cowboy's crap good-bye."

Lute bristled for a moment, then ignored him. He wanted out, not more. The kid should, too. Idiot. The punk was a goner, just didn't know it yet. Time to move on. He glanced around the room.

He'd never been to Smuggler's Peak hut before and didn't want to return. But he needed to make sure that nothing had been disturbed. No more screw ups.

Billy rambled on. Pushing. Bragging how he could do better. Lute shoved the kid's words to the back of his mind. He gritted his teeth. The cocaine had been beneath the floor for three hours, but cross-country ski traffic through the hut was unpredictable. Someone was on to them, Lute could feel it in his gut. Someone other than the injured skier and his forest ranger sidekick.

If Harrison had actually discovered the stash at Desolation Hut last Saturday, the narcs could be tipped off and lying in wait for Lute's arrival. It was only a matter of time.

The recent deliveries had been larger than usual. As if Cowboy also knew that the end of their fortune was near. His boss was more abrupt, yelled more often. He had to get out. The stakes were too high.

Billy's voice reached a loud pitch. Lute tuned in.

"You could bring part of the stash back. He'd never know. Start building your own little nest egg. Then when you're ready . . ."

He advanced on the smart-mouthed kid. "Listen to me, punk. You and me are never going to be partners. Get out of my face."

Start his own operation, right. With someone who snorts more often than he pees.

"You gotta do something. Everyone knows he's going to bump you off when the time is right."

Lute grabbed the kid by the neckline. "And how did you get so fucking smart all of a sudden?"

Billy swallowed. "I heard him."

"You heard what?"

"Cowboy. Talking to that woman pilot."

Lute released the kid, shoving him backward. Why was this punk getting to him? He already knew Cowboy would do him in. Loyalty wasn't worth shit. He was banking on being long gone. Billy could stay and climb the white powder pyramid if he wanted, until it collapsed.

Princess burst through the door. "The ranger's on her way. Let's go."

Shit. He handed a burlap sack to Billy and a second to Princess. Grabbing a third he straightened the rug once more. He left the hut without looking back. No stopping at Desolation Point today.

❄   ❄   ❄

Eric was barely into position behind a large rock outcropping when Mountain High Adventures flew overhead. Due west. Going home, he hoped. The day had been a real bitch and it was only a little past noon.

After watching the Canadians leave Smuggler's Peak, he'd located their stash and wired it. Hard evidence. No matter that it wasn't in his possession. The noose was tightening. Nailing down Cowboy's exact distribution chain would ensure he didn't walk.

When the wiring was done, he'd rushed back to check out the fire damage before Jeffers returned. But she'd never left. Her snowmobile was still cold. He wasted three hours waiting for her and Harrison to leave the cabin. Why the hell was she changing patterns now? Couldn't anything stay the same for two days in a row?

The copter was gone, just a speck in the cloudless sky. Time to find out where the Vmax was. He focused his binoculars and scanned the slopes and hills. It didn't take long. The vehicle was parked south of Smuggler's Peak. Nowhere near her regular trails. And where was Harrison, skiing with her? That was a fast recovery.

He'd go down there. Check it out. Damn but he was tired of surprises.

❄   ❄   ❄

The small vertical opening in the rock wall beneath Smuggler's Peak was easy for most passers-by to miss. Now she would share it with Rey.

She switched off the snowmobile's engine. His hand lingered on her waist, as he stepped from the vehicle. "This is it?" His expression was skeptical.

"Yes. My private hot springs. Before I moved into the cabin, it was the one place I had to call my own. No one knows of its existence except for Scott and Rachel. I love spending time here alone, replenishing mind, soul and body." Her voice was trembling. "I've used it often these past twelve months."

He turned away from examining the hillside to look at her, to pull her closer. "And now?"

"I want to share it with you."

His gaze met hers briefly before he leaned forward and kissed her.

It was just a brief touching of lips then a sigh. She let her cheek rest against his for a moment, reluctant to draw away. When she finally did, she lightened her tone. "Take a closer look. I'll unload the towels."

"Look where?"

She put a hand on his shoulder and turned him in the right direction. "See the steam rising from the foot of that drift?" As she pointed, her arm extended over his shoulder. He leaned back, turning slightly. She loved feeling his weight against her. "To the left of that stump."

His eyes were fixed on the embankment ahead. His hand shielded his gaze from the glare of the afternoon sun on the pristine snow. After a moment, he glanced at her. "I still don't see it."

"Such little faith." She gave him a small push. "Go on. I'll meet you inside."

As Rey headed toward the opening, Megan let out the breath she'd been holding. Her pulse pounded. Her palms sweated inside her gloves.

She walked around to the rear of her vehicle and flipped open the storage compartment. There were towels, water bottles and assorted snacks within, everything he would need to be comfortable on his own for awhile. After a quick practice run, she'd return when he was already in the pool.

Music would be a nice touch. She retrieved her cassette player and several tapes. Soft rock, light jazz. Music left behind by previous skiing twosomes. Lovers who had passed long, romantic evenings in her rented room downstairs.

She closed the trunk and took a deep breath. She could do it. The alternative was wasting precious days that could be spent as lovers, in addition to being friends. She would let him know what she wanted, then let him decide. Whatever happened, at least after this she would know.

❄   ❄   ❄

The stream was narrow enough for Rey to step over without leaping. He climbed the short incline cautiously. The opening to the cave faced west. The enclosure was the size of an average room, with the steaming pool off to the left. The scent of minerals permeated the air, but not the harsh smell of sulfur he'd expected.

Water splashed from a crack in the far wall. It cascaded across the granite boulder, polishing the rock to a gleaming brilliance. He could see a small ledge beneath the water, running the length of one side. The hot springs was more than large enough for two. Romantic. Did she have that in mind when she suggested this place? If so, he would make it an afternoon to remember. No snoozing in his arms today. He would wait and see.

Rey slipped off his boots then both layers of socks. The smooth floor was covered with a smattering of moss, a sharp contrast to the snow outside. The surface beneath his toes felt like green velvet. Cold, but incredibly soft. He dipped his foot into the pool. The temperature was perfect.

"So what's the verdict?"

Rey glanced over his shoulder at Megan. "I'm staying forever. Send the rest of my things up tomorrow."

"No problem."

He crossed to where she was standing and took the cassettes and player from her. While he placed them by the water's edge, Megan set the towels on top of a rock. She turned and looked at him hesitantly. "They'll stay drier up there. Out of the way."

"Good idea."

She walked toward the edge of the pool. Had she put distance between them on purpose? She hadn't been nervous with him last night. Today's setting was different, though. Intimate. He let several moments pass before he joined her by the swirling water. Something was on her mind. "Is there a more serene place anywhere on earth?"

A bittersweet smile curved her mouth. Wordlessly, she shook her head.

He waited until she raised her eyes to his. "Thank you for bringing me here."

She looked at him, her face only inches from his.

Breathing deeply, he let her familiar scent draw him closer. He wanted to kiss her, to hold her. To feel her eyelashes against his cheek and her breath against his chin.

"Why did you bring me here?"

She stared at him for several moments. Her face was flushed. It was as if she wanted to say something but couldn't put it into words. He didn't dare touch her. If he did he might lure her into something she wasn't ready for, through the urgency of his own need. He would wait. Until her trust convinced her this was right between them. Christ it was difficult.

Suddenly she stepped away and regained her voice. "You're supposed to soak, of course. A change of pace. It must be terribly boring for you in the cabin each day."

"It is. I miss you when you're gone."

She breathed deeply then backed toward the entrance. Away from him. "Climb in. I'll return after my training run."

"All right. Good luck."

"Thank you." She pulled her gloves from her pocket and secured the wrist bands. "Enjoy your time alone. I'll be back before you know it."

"Will do." He would know it, all right. Would wait for her, hoping she'd join him after all. "Hurry, okay?"

When she finally raised her eyes to his, she nodded slightly. Even though she still left, he interpreted her expression as a very good sign.

No use wasting time. He stripped down to his skin and stepped into the pool. The few stones he felt on the bottom were small enough to be pushed away with his foot. The surface was as smooth as a chalkboard. The ledge was wide enough for sitting and long enough for two. The water embraced his skin with heated, swirling strokes as he submerged inch-by-inch. He reclined against the edge until his shoulders were covered.

Time seemed non-existent as the steam rose around him. His scalp tingled. He ran one hand back through his hair. At the moment, he didn't care if it stood on end.

He exercised his leg. His fire fighting efforts last night had taken their toll. The pool was idyllic for working out sore muscles. His knee wasn't the only part of his body that ached. Visiting the springs should be part of their daily routine. If she were with him, it would be perfect.

The warmth of the water seeped into his senses. It swirled and stroked his bare skin. He closed his eyes, envisioning her return. Her coming to him, asking for what she wanted. What they both needed. Images of other types of caresses consumed his thoughts.

❄   ❄   ❄

Eric barely made it back upstairs when his phone rang again. "Logan. You're six hours early."

"I know."

"Good timing, anyway." He closed the door to his room and began peeling off his jacket. "The load at Smuggler's Peak is now in transit. West."

"I know that, too. It's not why I called. There are moving vans in Everett. Three of them."

"At Cowboy's?"

"Guessed it in one."

"Shit." He clenched his fist, wanting to break something. Anything. He tossed his shoulder holster on the bed. "Have you checked the airlines?"

"Someone's on it. If Smuggler is his final load, I hope it's enough to nail him."

"There's still a stash at Desolation Point. Would he walk away from it?"

"He might, if he had enough."

"Do these bastards ever have enough?" If Cowboy's game was to skip town, he could forget it. Eric wouldn't let two years of surveillance go down the toilet that easily. "I'll continue to watch. Until there's zero activity in the area, my job is here."

"Agreed. My team will do the rest."

Eric hesitated for a moment, remembering Jimmy. A brave man with wasted admiration for his scum-bag big brother. "Do me a favor."

"Yeah?"

"Cowboy's younger brother." How could he phrase this? "Let me know if the boy and his guardian leave with the trucks today."

"Why?"

"I was hoping he would make it out early. Before the rest of the family."

"Now's a bad time to develop a weak spot."

"Believe me, I know." Eric reached for his hand exerciser and started pumping. "Just keep me posted."

"Sure, partner."

Megan stared at the hillside, toward the hot springs. If only she could come up with something witty to say. A clever remark to diffuse the silence that would greet her when she stepped inside the cave. Her run through Devil's Gulch and around Smuggler's Peak had taken twenty minutes. She took a slow, steadying breath. She could do this. She wanted to do this. Hyperventilating would not help.

She hurried through her normal routine: wiping down her rifle, storing it in its case, securing her harness. Anticipation made her heart pound. Her fingers fumbled the chamois drying cloth.

After crossing the stream, she climbed the hill and walked toward the enclosure. Gentle saxophone melodies emanated from the cassette player. No humming, no water splashing in the background. Was he asleep? She peered inside. Definitely napping. His head was pillowed on a folded shirt against the pool's edge.

She entered and walked past him, kicking a few rocks along the way for good measure. They bounced off the side wall, sounding like hail against her roof. When that didn't wake him, she took off one boot then dropped it from shoulder height. Success. He startled forward then quickly reached behind his head for his shirt, catching it before it touched the water.

"You're awake."

He turned and stared at her for several moments, as if emerging from a dream. "Yes. Welcome back." He started to stand then changed his mind. "What time is it?"

"Two thirty. Have you been enjoying the spring?"

"Yes."

She slipped her arms through her suspenders then pulled the sweater over her head. After folding it, she set it on the same rock as the stack of towels. Next she reached for the zipper tab on her overalls. After unfastening them, she casually scooted the snow-pants down, exposing her long johns. "And how is the water?"

"Soothing. Enticing." His words seemed to slow. "Shallow."

His voice had a husky edge to it. The sound reminded her of when she woke by his side this morning at Desolation Hut. Sleepy. Intimate. She'd like to hear it more often.

Crossing her arms, she grabbed the hem of her thermal undershirt. She heard his quick indrawn breath as she pulled the garment off. He seemed to start breathing again when her swim suit was revealed. Teasing him was fun. The possibility had never crossed her mind before.

Turning away, she stepped out of her thermal pants. It was probably too dark for him to see her blushing, but she didn't want to take the chance. After folding them, she placed them on the rock next to her other clothing.

"You're coming in?"

"Of course. Scoot over." She walked toward the shallow end of the pool. "I've been looking forward to this."

"I'm not wearing a suit."

She glanced down at the water. "I know."

His gaze intensified, became more curious and inviting.

Sitting, she dangled her legs casually in the water. "So you think this is unfair." She nodded seriously. "I only see one solution." Sliding from her seat she crossed to where he was. Ripples on the pool's surface widened around her.

The water was at chest level. Rey remained seated, watching her come closer. When she was a couple of feet away, she pulled down a single strap on her suit and slipped one arm free. Then the second strap. The water, and the swimsuit, barely covered her breasts.

She looked up. He was waiting. Her actions weren't enough. Did she have to say it? "Help me with this."

He stood and narrowed the gap between them. "With the suit?" His hand cupped her shoulder.

"No, more than that. I want to make love with you. I'm not sure how to say it." Her heart pounded.

He seemed to look into her soul. "You just did." His thumb traced a line over her collarbone then moved upward toward her neck. Then he smiled.

Relief threatened to buckle her knees. She swallowed. "Waiting seems such a waste."

"Shhh." He kissed her ear, her temple. His words grazed against her skin. "Your timing is perfect."

Her hand covered his. She brought it down to the free-floating neckline. He needed no more convincing.

He kissed her, then slowly drew the suit down her body. She stepped out of it. He tossed it onto the edge then took her hand and led her to the side of the pool.

Sitting, she was submerged up to her chin. The water was soothing, a stark contrast to the anticipation clenching her stomach. He reached out and touched her breast.

"Sometimes I can barely breathe when you're close by." He drew lazy circles with his fingertip.

"I haven't been able to concentrate on a single, coherent thought in days." Was that her voice? "I can't unravel the mystery that's happening around us if all I can think about is you."

He massaged her skin gently and thoroughly. "I want more between us than just one afternoon."

She leaned into his palms. "So do I."

His lips met hers. Her skin tingled as his hands moved across her body. She encircled his neck and pulled him close.

His touch slid downward to her waist. He turned and lifted her to him until she was straddling his thighs. The strength of his hands, firm yet gentle, thrilled her. Gave her a sense of courage she'd never known in an intimate situation. She rested her knees on the ledge. His hardness pressed against her and a shiver ran down her spine.

He kissed her neck, her collarbone, the hollow near her shoulder, lower. When he exhaled, it warmed the damp skin. She leaned slightly away yet still held on, encouraging him. His tongue caressed her with slow, deliberate movements. This was what she'd wanted.

Perspiration beaded her forehead. Water running down rock was all she heard save the thundering of her heart. The solid feel of his body felt good. She wanted more.

She reached between their bodies. When she touched him his own explorations stopped. He lifted his head then slowly closed his eyes. The sigh he uttered resembled her name. It was his turn to hold on tight as her hand glided smoothly over him, surrounding him. He moved. It was still not enough.

She scooted forward, rising upward on her knees. He opened his eyes. His hand at her waist stopped her. "Wait."

"For what?"

"There are some risks we can't take." His breathing was unsteady.

She withdrew, feeling awkward. "I thought you wanted this."

"I do. But I can't protect you here. I brought nothing with me."

Her heart raced. She'd been stupid. No, naive was a better word. Her brain had been disengaged this morning when she planned this. "I wasn't thinking. Only feeling." She looked away, mortified.

He touched her cheek, bringing her gaze back to his. "I have another idea." He helped her to her feet.

"I don't understand."

He kissed her lips then moved downward to nuzzle her throat. "There are other ways. Let me show you."

"Other ways?" Was he asking what she thought he was? God, she certainly hoped so. He was gently molding her again with his palms, massaging her until she fell against him in sheer pleasure.

"Do you trust me, Megan?"

"Yes."

He ran his fingertips slowly across her back and down her spine. The cool air on her shoulders was a stark contrast to the warmth building within her. When he trailed his fingertips lower, lingering at the top of her thighs, she shivered.

He nudged her legs apart with his knee then captured her mouth once again. As his tongue stroked hers, his hand glided upward along her inner thigh until he found her passion awaiting him. She gripped his shoulders, steadying herself.

So this was what the magic was about. An exhilarating non-stop spiral. Upward. She tightened her hold, not wanting to fall or sink. Shock waves wove their way through her limbs, sensitizing each nerve ending.

Their kiss ended too soon. He drew back. She wanted him to continue, never wanted the sensations to stop. Disappointment settled over her. She let her forehead rest on his chest.

"Let's move closer to the wall."

She moved backward until her heels touched the rock bench.

"Hold on to the edge of the pool." He slid his hands over her hips. She suddenly felt more than naked. Exposed. In a way that had nothing to do with clothing. He must have felt the tension running through her. "You said you trusted me."

"I do. But I also want to bring you pleasure." As true as that was, her words were also an evasion tactic. She blushed at the way she'd blurted them out.

He smiled. "We have all afternoon. For now, just hold on." He lifted her lower half slowly from the water, his leg beneath her hips for support. Then, as if asking her one more time, he paused.

She looked into his eyes as she composed her answer. This was what she wanted. But it did require trust. She took a deep breath and slowly leaned back, abandoning herself to him. She steadied herself by gripping the rim. Cold granite beneath shaky fingers.

He leaned forward. The feel of his shaven cheek against her thigh caused her breath to catch. She laid her head back into the water and closed her eyes. Cool air caressed the heated skin at her waist. Her scalp tingled. Her breathing quickened.

Ripples of water caressed her chin and neck. Each stroke of his tongue was more intense than the last. Each sensation more electrifying. When his hands tightened on her thighs, she opened more fully to his touch. Stars formed behind her eyelids. She stopped trying to think.

In a position such as this, she could drown from pure pleasure. She didn't care if that happened, but later. She didn't want it to end too soon.

THIRTEEN

T HE RIDE BACK to the cabin seemed to take forever. Rey wanted to see her face, to make sure she wasn't having second thoughts. Memories of her skin, smooth and firm beneath his touch, were still foremost in his mind, as were the echoing sounds of her pleasure. Being seated spoon-style behind her on the Vmax seat was a nice concept in general, despite the amount of clothing they were wearing. But hugging her this way, holding on for dear life, was clearly different from their earlier embrace.

When they pulled in front of the charred remains of the shed, Rey was the first to step down. Megan merely turned in her seat and stared at the blackened embers. His gaze followed hers. For a short while they had escaped reality. This destruction was a shocking welcome back.

She swung her leg over and off the vehicle, and walked into his arms. He pulled off her helmet and stroked her hair. "We'll get to the bottom of this."

"I know." She leaned back and looked into his eyes. "Thank you for being here."

"You're stuck with me now." He smiled and after a quick kiss, released her.

She glanced at her watch. "I hope Russell made it here today to investigate. Or sent Scott in his place. It's getting dark. Tonight's forecast calls for more snow. That might obliterate the evidence." She shrugged. "If there is any."

He didn't think there was much left to see. He'd examined the site earlier and found nothing. The thought of Scott examining the arson didn't bring him comfort. Surely the deputy wouldn't arrive in a coke-induced state, though. He dismissed the degrading thought. It was unfair to expect the worst. The guilt lingered on.

Tonight, he would tell her about Scott. Would find some way to address the subject. Then together they would help her brother help himself. "Let's go in."

She nodded, then glanced again at the damage. "First I want to take care of a few things out here."

"I'll help."

"No." She looked back at him, barely meeting his eyes. "Go on. Light the fireplace. See what we might have for dinner."

"All right." He heard unsteadiness in her voice. Was it embarrassment over their lovemaking or did she want to be alone with her memories of the fire? Either way, he would give her the peace and quiet she was asking for. Placing a finger under her chin, he brought her gaze up to his.

"The last few days have been difficult. For me, too, watching you go through this." The words stuck in his throat. "And as for our relationship, it's a new feeling for me also. We'll work through it, until it's as natural as breathing."

"I'm looking forward to that." Her voice was so low, it was barely distinguishable.

She tried looking away again. He didn't let her escape that easily. "You're not alone." He kept his tone soft, comforting. "I'll be with you. We'll figure this out together."

"But you can't stay forever."

He could, he wanted to say. It would take some doing, but he could. If it was right for both of them. "Let's take it one day at a time." He wrapped his arm about her shoulders and pulled her close until they were nose-to-nose. "Have I thanked you yet for sharing your hideaway with me?"

Her eyes met his. She opened her mouth to speak but no words came forth.

"Being there with you was fantastic. More than I imagined it would be." He leaned forward to place a kiss on her nose. "So were the hot springs, by the way."

He watched the color rise to her cheeks. This woman, who excelled at almost everything, was vulnerable here. He wanted to hold her in his arms all evening if that's what it took for the awkwardness to pass.

Though she'd initiated their physical relationship, he was the one who wanted to prolong the emotional closeness. There was something building between them that he hadn't experienced before. Something he'd always dreamed of. He never knew that the sharing of feelings afterwards could be as intimate as the act itself. With the right person.

She smiled at him and snuggled close against his chest. He stroked her hair, feeling the dampness at the ends.

The sound of an approaching vehicle broke the mood. He released her. Megan stepped away, putting her hands to her face as if she could drive the flush from her cheeks. Her efforts were wasted. When the snowmobile rounded the last curve in the trail, he recognized Scott.

Their newfound relationship might not withstand another run-in with little brother quite so soon. Rey tilted his head toward the cabin. "I'll start a fire. Come in when you're ready."

She was already looking past him. She'd assumed a straight-backed stance with chin uplifted, as if physically preparing for verbal combat. He wanted to kiss her again. Instead he unhooked the bungee cords on the back of her Vmax and picked up the stack of semi-frozen towels. One less thing for her to explain.

❊   ❊   ❊

Scott steered toward Megan. She was standing near her shed. He was still in shock from Russell's news: her shed had gone up in flames last night. When he heard, he'd wanted to shout *I didn't do it!* but instead took the credit. Sheriff Russell was pleased, so he didn't want to deny involvement. After all, he'd sprinkled around some of the contents of her gas can. Had left a warning note. It was his idea, even if fate had played a hand in it.

Someone needed to be blamed for the fire, and Harrison was the perfect choice. That would get him booted back to the city, even if nothing else worked. Extra insurance, so to speak. Could he stage that, too?

He definitely could. Smiling at his own cleverness, he patted his pocket then pulled alongside her. He cut the engine. Earlier today, he'd set up part one. When he was through with part two, no one would question the identity of the guilty party.

❊   ❊   ❊

Megan sensed her brother's mood the moment he stopped his snowmobile. He unsnapped his chin strap and pulled off his helmet, glaring at Rey retreating through the cabin's front door.

"I see Harrison is still here."

Megan's mood quickly changed. "I'm tired of hearing you say that every time you arrive. It insults both of us."

"Does not." His smirk accentuated the lines stress was carving around his red, tired eyes. "In fact, I feel fine."

"I was referring to Rey." She looked at him critically. Scott was lying about his health. He looked like an advertisement for cold medicine. Maybe lying was too harsh of a word; exaggerating was better. She hated to think that his rudeness was deliberate.

Scott's life seemed to be a series of bad days lately. Her heart went out to him. She wished there was more she could do to help. But not only did she have her own share of troubles at present, he didn't want her assistance. Not really. She softened her tone. "I like him being here."

"I would think after a catastrophe like this fire, he'd pack his bag."

"Why?"

"Maybe he had something to do with it." Scott got off his vehicle. His first step was wobbly. He held the handle grip to steady himself.

Megan observed his movements and frowned. Was he drunk? He frequently consumed beer when playing poker with the boys, but it was daytime, not evening. She didn't smell alcohol on his breath. Were his cold tablets making him dizzy?

She touched his shoulder. He pulled away. Then, as if realizing it was her, he apologized. "Sore muscle. Let's get back to the distasteful subject of your freeloading houseguest."

"That subject's closed."

"Just tell me when's he leaving. Then I'll back off."

Removing her hand she let it fall to her side, stifling the urge to clench it. She reminded herself that Scott wasn't feeling well, that he needed her support. He cared about her, that was all. She relaxed her jaw and said the first thing that came to mind. "Rey is planning to stay through the coming weekend. No need to ask again."

Scott ran his fingertips through his flattened curls. "Let's be honest with each other, Megan. Has it ever occurred to you that

Harrison might be behind all this?" He made a grand sweep of the wreckage with his free hand.

Megan crossed her arms over her chest. "Don't be ridiculous."

"He knew the dead skier, didn't he?" Scott leaned closer. "You remember, the one with the bullet hole where most people have brains?"

She wasn't about to let her brother intimidate her. "That morning was the first and only time Rey ever saw the boy."

Scott gave her a level look. "So he says. Does he have proof?"

An insult like that didn't deserve a response. She stared at him; he paused for what appeared to be a dramatic moment. At times his behavior was so odd it seemed he was putting on a performance. Why couldn't they just level with one another as they did when they were kids?

His face was becoming more flushed as she returned his stare. Beads of perspiration dotted his brow, despite the falling evening temperatures. She broke the silence by addressing him sharply. "Rey couldn't have shot the boy. He has a strong aversion to guns. Besides, the medical report said the murder victim was higher than a kite. Maybe he was playing around and shot himself."

"With a rifle? One was found, not too far from the body."

"Did the bullets match?"

"I haven't heard yet. However it turns out, there's a lot of circumstantial evidence surrounding Harrison." Scott sniffed. "Too much for you to be safe."

He scrounged for a handkerchief. The first pocket that he tried was zipped shut. Instead of opening it, he glanced at her quickly, then checked the other. "I'd lose him, fast, if I were you. He's bad news."

Although her brother's voice was losing its raspy edge, his eyes were still watering. More so now than when he first arrived. He was one sorry sight indeed. Megan sighed. The tip of his nose, cracked and raw from his cold, hadn't healed yet either. When she moved toward him, he backed away. "Don't mother me."

She flinched. Hurting her was becoming a regular past time with him. Rey's advice replayed in her mind. Don't be anyone's punching bag. Would her brother stop if she didn't forgive him so readily each time? She glared at him, not speaking. That approach appeared to work. Scott's expression turned contrite.

"I'm a little on edge." He blew his nose, then refolded the handkerchief. "Just don't rule Harrison out as a suspect. A prime suspect. And keep a close eye on him until he's gone. I plan to."

Megan crossed her arms over her chest. "Don't be ridiculous."

"You said that already. Having a closed mind won't help." He kicked a snow drift with his heel then braced one boot against it. "It's my job to look for clues. To spot anything out of place. Harrison can't be ignored."

After meeting her eyes for a few moments longer, he crossed to the shed. He swung back the charred door and stepped inside.

There was no way to win this round with Scott. Megan dropped the subject and followed him inside the ruined shed. Streams of late afternoon sunlight filtered through the ceiling where the roof had given way. Time to start her own search.

The worst of the damage was near the entrance. She remembered standing in front, battling the flames with the meager hose, feeling so insignificant. The hole ripped in the back of the shed caught her eye. Rey had risked his life to save her vehicle. It could have been replaced eventually. The shed could be rebuilt. She'd been so scared for him.

Stepping over a fallen timber, she reached for an overturned bucket. When she tried to hang it on a hook, it fell from her hands and clanged against the remains of the snow shovel.

Scott turned sharply. "Jesus! Don't surprise me like that." He motioned toward the door. "Wait for me inside the house."

"I'm helping."

"It will go quicker without you."

"It's my shed. Who could better identify something unusual?"

He frowned and pressed his fingertips to his temple. "All right. But stay over there. No more sneaking up on me."

They resumed their independent searches in silence. Scott glanced her way often, as if checking on her. Megan was on her knees behind the center post when Scott called out to her. "Over here." His tone was laced with satisfaction. "Just as I thought."

Scrambling to her feet, she maneuvered her way through the debris. He pointed at a small crate near the wall. On top sat a piece of broken glass. She peered closer. The object was actually a small, jagged-edged mirror covered with bold lettering. There were words scribbled in black marker.

Noting the uneven edges, Megan picked up the mirror with caution. It was singed around the edges. She adjusted the angle in the fading light until she could read the words. *Go Home*. A shiver ran down her spine. She was home. The message must be directed at Rey.

Megan quickly flipped the mirror over. No further markings.

Scott peered over her shoulder, nodding in agreement. "Matches my sentiment exactly." He turned and looked at her. "That makes two of us, at least. Maybe more that want Harrison out of here."

She glanced at her brother, not comprehending. Her throat was suddenly parched. Words wouldn't come.

Scott raised one side of his mouth in a lopsided smirk. "You know. Another charter member of the Reynold Harrison Un-Fan Club. A small but elite group of people refusing to knuckle under to his charm."

She ignored the sarcasm, swallowing hard. Her voice was low. "There must be a mistake." She moved away from the scene, toward the cabin, dropping the mirror in her hurry to get away from the hate-filled shed.

"Hold on a sec." Scott grabbed her arm. "The only mistake around here is yours. For trusting a guy like that."

She swung around to face him in the fading light. "A guy like what?" Unchecked, her voice rose along with her mounting anger. She wrenched away from his grasp. "Stop with the insinuations and just tell me."

Scott bent and retrieved the mirror. He ran a finger along its surface. The words didn't smudge, was that what he was trying to prove? She waited. When he was through, he handed it to her. A small amount of light-colored dust was piled to one side of the glass.

Megan shook her head. "What? Ashes?"

"No, too grainy. More like small crystals." He moistened his fingertip so that a bit of the white powder would stick. Bringing the sample to his tongue, he tasted it then grimaced. "Just what I thought. It's nose candy. You know, the Big C." He wiped the remainder on his pant leg.

She continued to stare at him.

"Let me put it to you in more simple terms, Megan. Cocaine. Harrison's a user." He exhaled as if totally disgusted. "Maybe he shortchanged his supplier, I don't know. But somebody's pissed off and they're after him." He pointed at the shed again. "This was just a warning."

❄   ❄   ❄

Hurrying inside, Megan looked around the living room for Rey. The fireplace was cold. Dinner wasn't started. The connecting door was open. She called him. He answered immediately, his tone brusque. "I'm down here. Join me. There's something you need to see."

She crossed to the stairs, talking only to herself. "It can't be anything remotely close to what I have for you." Tucking the mirror into her jacket pocket, she hurried down the steps. Scott followed. Rey was sitting on the edge of his bed.

Someone had taken an egg beater to the contents of his drawer. Briefs and handkerchiefs were half-in, half-out. His silken long johns were strewn across the floor, racing stripes pointing every which way. He was re-matching his socks.

"What happened?" Megan stepped over the mess to be nearer to him. Her stomach clenched. This was turning into an afternoon from hell. She sank onto the mattress.

"I don't know who did this. No clues yet." He reached out and covered her hand with his. "It's not a robbery. The contents of the nightstand are untouched. My wallet, my cell phone are still there."

She glanced toward the small table and lamp. The shade wasn't even the slightest bit crooked.

"All cash and credit cards are accounted for. The closet wasn't searched either."

Scott cleared his throat loudly, causing Megan to flinch. Her brother's gaze moved from her face, slowly downward, shooting daggers at their interlinked hands.

By God, this was her house. She'd be the one to decide what she did and didn't do. She gritted her teeth, not wanting to speak while her emotions were so close to the surface. Dangerous combination, fear and anger.

Scott bent down and retrieved the silken material by his feet, letting it dangle from one index finger. "Let me get this straight, Harrison. Someone broke in to my sister's place just to fondle your fancy underwear."

"Check the doors, Deputy." Rey released Megan's hand, set the pile of newly folded socks aside and stood. He snatched the garments from the younger man, shoving them into the drawer. "I never said anyone broke in."

"You left the cellar door unlocked?" Scott stood next to him by the chest of drawers, observing the scrambled contents. Reaching inside, he felt around the inside edge with one hand.

"You have a search warrant?" Rey tried to shut the drawer.

"I could get one." Scott held up his free hand, warning Rey to back off. "You trying to hide something from me?" His smirk had returned. "Or from Megan."

"That's enough, Scott." She stood. "Put your testosterone on hold while you're in my house."

He ignored her. "I think there's something in here you don't want us to see." His free hand continued to search beneath the clothing still in the drawer.

Rey stared at him. "This is an invasion of privacy."

"It's my job, now stay clear."

Megan felt sick to her stomach. She wanted Scott gone. Needed time to think. She stood and touched Rey's shoulder. "Let him look." The sooner Scott investigated, the sooner they'd be alone. She could then discuss with him the warning she found in the shed.

"What? I'm the victim here."

"I know, but . . ."

"Well, lookee here." Scott dangled a plastic bag in front of their eyes. "Your little private stash, Harrison?"

Rey eyes narrowed as he stared at the baggie, then at the younger man. "You should know, Jeffers. It has your fingerprints all over it."

"That's a brilliant comment, considering I'm holding it."

Rey stood silent, his jaw visibly clenched.

Megan reached for the bag. Opening it, she walked to the bed and spilled the contents for a closer look. A razor blade, a small lump of white chalky crystal, a second broken mirror and an aluminum teaspoon. The kind found in any kitchen.

Reaching into her pocket she carefully extracted the first mirror. After glancing at Rey, she laid it alongside the second. The jagged edges matched.

A knot formed in her throat. She swallowed hard. "I don't understand."

"It's not too difficult." Scott stepped forward and wrapped his arm about her shoulder, drawing her away from the evidence. Away from Rey. "That's crack. Your houseguest is a user."

Her mouth dropped open. Scott merely shrugged. "It's worth, let's say, no more than fifty bucks. Only a fraction of what his silk underwear costs. My guess is that his drug-pushing friends paid your shed a house call and left their business card behind."

"How dare you." Rey advanced toward him.

Scott instantly went on the attack. "How dare you put my sister in danger? I'm hauling your fancy ass down to jail."

Megan stepped in between the two men. "You're not hauling anything, anywhere, until I've had a chance to think this through." She looked at Rey, who was now watching her.

He was quietly calm, wasn't defending himself. Why? This couldn't be true. He seemed miles away. If he needed help, he could have asked. She'd be the first to stand by him if he would let her. "There must be some explanation."

"There is." His gaze never wavered from hers. "One that's a bit late in coming, I'm sorry to say."

Her eyes widened. "Tell me now."

Rey tilted his head toward the paraphernalia. "I took this stuff from your brother's pocket two nights ago." He paused. "I should have told you then."

"You're accusing Scott?" Megan's head was pounding.

Rey nodded. "I was wrong not to tell you right away." He reached out his hand.

She stepped back. This couldn't be happening.

"Nice try." Scott laughed harshly. "But she's not buying it, Harrison." He sauntered over to the bed, quickly reassembled the paraphenalia and stashed it back inside the plastic sack.

Her feet were riveted to the floor. She was unable to quite comprehend what was going on around her. Rey lying? By omission, at the very least. Scott using? Cocaine was a big city problem, along with murder, arson and illegal search and seizure. When did these evils make their way to Snagtooth?

Scott zipped the plastic bag shut then crossed to stand next to her. He draped an arm about her shoulders. "I'm taking this evidence into town. I'll be back with the cuffs."

Megan looked up at her brother's face. More smirking. More grinning. She was ready to explode. "Leave it."

"What?"

"I said leave it. Get out."

"Me?" He thumped an index finger against his chest. The bag, held firmly by its edge within the same hand, swung back and forth with each movement. "Harrison would say anything to worm his way out right now. Don't listen to him."

Megan ducked from beneath her brother's embrace, putting herself an equal distance from the two men. She looked back and forth in quick succession, then let her gaze come back to Rey.

It was several moments before she trusted herself to speak. "He's not a user, Scott. He'll explain this to me when we're alone."

"And I'm a coke-head? Just like that?"

Her attention swung back to Scott. Her baby brother. Someone she would go out on any limb for. She'd failed him by her ignorance. Megan swallowed hard but didn't look away. "You could be. It's quite obvious now. Your perpetual cold. Your irritability." Tears blurred her vision.

Scott clenched his fists and took a menacing step forward. "You're choosing him over me? Over family?"

She flinched. The seriousness of the situation was beginning to sink in. She hadn't caught onto the signs. Was ignorant. Naive. She'd remedy that, though. She'd get to the bottom of this, one way or another.

"Scott, forget what I said earlier. Stay here. I'll call the doctor. Ask him to meet us at the hospital." She started toward the nightstand and picked up the phone.

"The hell you will." Scott shoved the bag into his pocket and moved quickly. He wrenched the receiver from her hand and threw it. The heavy base fell and crashed to the floor. He drew his arm back. She instinctively ducked.

"Stop it." Rey gripped her brother's arm, not letting him strike her. Scott turned on him.

"This is your fault." They went tumbling onto the mattress, Scott on top. His hands curled around Rey's neck. A growl came from deep in his throat. "I'll kill you for this, Harrison."

Megan cringed. Reaching into her jacket, she searched for the horizontal opening in the liner. There it was, her hidden pocket. She withdrew her Colt Mustang and released the safety.

Scott heard the distinctive click and stopped. He levered himself off the bed and stared wide-eyed at her. "What the hell? Now you're planning to shoot me?" He laughed harshly, then looked with disgust at his opponent.

Rey sat up, staring white-faced at Megan. She lowered the gun. Scott towered over him. "You're such a pansy-ass." He leaned closer, his tone mocking. "She was pointing the pistol at me and you're the one freaking."

Rey's tone remained steady. "You need help. Listen to Megan."

How could he stay calm in the midst of such hatred? He probably knew, better than she, how to approach someone who was high. She looked at her .38. Not on the preferred list of self-help tools, no doubt.

Scott made a loathing sound deep in his throat, shifting his eyes back and forth. "You two make me sick." He moved toward the door.

"Don't leave, Scott." She let the gun rest at her side.

"Oh, but I am." Yanking the door open, he took a step outside. "You want to shoot me? Well, go right ahead." He pulled his own weapon from the holster. "We'll go one-on-one."

Scott stood before her, motionless, not five yards away. Her typical target range from a standing position was one hundred times this distance and only twice as big as his fist. She exhaled. How could she draw a comparison, even for a moment? She stared a moment longer, more from shock than from indecision. That, plus the barrel of his gun was four times the size of hers. She reset the safety.

Scott laughed again. It was more like a cross between a snarl and a spit. "Well, well. Once again you don't have quite what it takes."

She looked away, ashamed. "I don't know what I was thinking."

"Of course you don't. This jerk's screwing with your head." He leaned heavily on the door frame, sneering. "Think about this. When he's gone, I'll be all you've got." He stepped away into the flat gray light of early evening. The door slammed behind him.

Silence followed. Megan could feel the blood pounding through her veins. She ran a hand over her eyes, squeezing them shut. She needed to convince herself that what she'd just seen, what she'd just done, had been a dream. Not her own life. She opened her eyes to find Rey watching her. He was probably wondering what asinine thing she would do next.

She didn't know either. So far her entire day had been a disjointed string of unusual events. Maybe she was the one who should be carted off to the hospital.

"Say something." Was that raspy sound her own voice? She tried to steady it, to force out more air. "Rey, say anything."

"Put the gun away."

Lifting her right hand back up, she turned her palm over. The Colt was nestled easily within her grasp. She'd forgotten it was there.

"This?" Sure the safety was in place, she tossed the weapon onto the bed. He flinched. She didn't know why she was deliberately taunting him. He'd never mocked her fears.

Because she was mad. But that was really no excuse. "Sorry. It's not loaded."

"You pulled an unloaded gun on someone. Are you nuts?"

"He's my brother. I wasn't going to shoot him."

Rey exhaled loudly and let his shoulders slump. "As far as the gun is concerned, I guess I'm relieved it's empty. I'd hate to think that you run around these woods each day with a loaded weapon."

She shrugged. "I'm out of bullets."

"And just what would you shoot with this? Grizzlies? Bambi, maybe?" He stood.

"Anything I damn well please." She lifted her chin. "Not that's it's any of your business, but I carry it for protection. I'm often in the backwoods alone."

"There are arsonists and drug users out there, Megan. And God only knows who else."

"That's why I carry it."

"They'd kill you if you pulled a gun on them. In a shoot-out they'd blow a hole right through you." He tilted his head toward her weapon. "This would leave a mark like a tattoo."

"Stop." She held her palms over her ears. "We're different. Too different for this to ever work." Her mind knew that, even though her heart was blind. "You can't change who I am."

He nodded and shoved his hands into his pockets.

She lowered hers to her side. Her voice was unsteady. "Why didn't you tell me about Scott?"

"I was wrong to keep it from you." He swallowed hard. "It's difficult for me to admit why."

She waited silently.

"Your love for him made you blind to his symptoms. He's not at all the same man you described him to be, or showed me in your family photographs." Rey reached for her hand. She didn't resist. "I developed a foolish notion that maybe I could help him without you ever having to know."

"You didn't want me to be hurt."

He nodded.

"You can't protect me from things like this. I don't live in a gilded cage. Never have and never will." Pulling away, she crossed to the steps. "He's my brother. I'd do anything for him."

"He would have denied it, Megan. I didn't want you to have to choose which one of us to believe." He held her gaze. "I thought I would lose."

Megan squeezed the banister, hating that her eyes were filling with tears. "Well, maybe you lost anyway." Turning, she took the stairs one at a time, never looking back.

❄   ❄   ❄

Dave briskly gathered his papers and shoved them into his brief-case. The meeting had gone well. Attendance had exceeded eighty percent. Any self-help group leader would have been proud to report those kind of statistics. He wasn't. A key participant had been missing for the second time. EJ. He took it personally.

Pushing back his wire-framed glasses, Dave scanned the dingy ill-lighted room. People were shuffling out, ready to merge back into their separate lives with high hopes of defeating the devil. One day at a time. Some of the members were surrounding him, being careful not to nudge the brick beneath the table leg that kept the surface level. He had to shake off his anger. Be supportive to the ones who thought enough of themselves to be here. Not for one cowardly drop-out.

When had the kid become so special to him? When had he anointed himself as EJ's guardian angel? He wasn't God. Not everyone made it through hell. He would forget the boy. Concentrate on those who continued to try.

He looked at them. Their faces showed the fatigue of their personal victories. Joan, Andy, Mike, even the reluctant Mr. John Doe who still hid behind his mask of anonymity. They would make it. And he, Dave Edwards, ex-drug user, would help them, paying back a small token of the priceless gift given to him two years ago. He shook their hands, wished them well and sent them on their way.

When he was finally alone in the room, he sat at the head table. Let his head drop forward into his hands. Dammit, EJ, where are you?

❊   ❊   ❊

Dave trudged along the dark streets. The storm sewers were gurgling noisily. The lamp posts that were still functional cast yellowed circles on the wet pavement. Ever since the city pay phones stopped accepting inbound calls after eight at night, more people hung around in alleys than on the sidewalks. There was still the foot traffic, though. And no one strolled by this part of town to walk off an expensive salmon dinner or to stretch their legs after a night at the theater. Especially not in the rain. They were here on business.

Dave headed for the bus tunnel. Metro was his preferred method of travel unless his trip was over to the suburban Eastside. The environment and all. When had he begun adopting so many of Rey's various bleeding-heart causes? Hard to say.

His boss never lectured, never bragged, never grandstanded even once. Instead he led by example, letting Dave make his own choices. Well, Rey hadn't been wrong yet.

As he reached the Pioneer Square entrance to the tunnel, he noticed a youth of medium build, shoulder against the wall, looking away. Even if the Mohawk haircut wasn't enough to identify him, the familiar red high-top shoes glowing under the street lamp would have been a sure giveaway.

"EJ?"

The boy rolled back, until both shoulders were flat against the wall. "Yeah?" He crossed one sneakered foot over the other. "What do you want?"

"We missed you tonight."

"Tough. I was busy." He brought a hand-crafted cigarette to his lips and drew heavily. Pursing his mouth, he exhaled skyward. "I got better things to do now."

"Something more important than investing in your future?"

"Investing. I like the sound of that word." EJ laughed and flicked the cigarette toward the alley. It sizzled as it hit a puddle. "That's exactly what I'm doing. I've landed me a primo job, counselor. Someday I'll have a fancy skyline condo and scores of high-priced women." He grinned. "Maybe I'll even buy your place."

Dave's stomach clenched. Money, drugs. The two were synonymous. He was losing this kid. "Did you inherit a larger piece of sidewalk? This is no life."

"Don't lecture me. I never should have . . ." EJ looked away.

"Go on."

"I shouldn't have hung out here tonight." EJ glanced back. His features hardened into a grimace. "I was going to tell you, man, that I'm going away." He shrugged. "You're the worrying type. I just thought you should know."

"You can't quit now. You're on the road back. All of your hard work, don't throw it away."

"Shit. I've made it now. I'm going inside. With Billy."

Dave didn't know this Billy character, had just seen him once clasping EJ's shoulder. He'd assumed, due to the timing and the fierce expression on the friend's face, that he wasn't very happy with EJ attending the recovery meetings. He was an important member of EJ's circle, a peer. Unfortunately he was entrenched on the wrong side of success. "What do you mean, inside?"

"You know. Distribution. I won't be a small time pusher anymore."

"No, you'll be a mule."

His features hardened. "Screw you, man." He stood straight. "I don't need this."

"If you don't need me, then pick another mentor. A leader you see more eye-to-eye with. I could recommend someone."

EJ leaned forward and squinted at Dave. "You don't get it. I'm blowing this place." Straightening, the boy started backing away.

"Where can I reach you?"

"Forget it. I'm on my way up. So high, you won't be able to kiss my ass." He turned, then walked away, leaving Dave standing there holding on to the bus tunnel sign.

FOURTEEN

REY STEPPED OUT of the bathroom. His skin was still a little damp from his shower, making his sweat pants cling. Toweling dry his hair, he saw the blinking light on his cell phone. He called to check voice mail.

Dave's message was terse, just the number of his private office line. Rey sat on the bed and dialed the phone. He checked his watch. Seven-thirty. Megan wouldn't be back from her morning run until after nine. He had until then to think of what to say.

The line connected. "Dave Edwards."

"You're in early. Didn't anyone tell you the boss is still out of town?"

"A fax just came in from the private investigator. He's found nothing on Russell so far. Maybe the guy's clean."

"How about bank records?"

"Not clear, yet. Seems he has accounts at several banks. The P.I. is checking for aliases. He'll get back with me tomorrow."

"We've had a few developments here." Rey stood and crossed to the window. He pulled back the curtains. "Someone set fire to Megan's woodshed the night before last. We don't know who yet."

"No one was hurt?"

"No." He leaned his shoulder against the glass. "There's more."

"Go on."

Through the window he spotted Grandma Grace emerging from her cabin. She was hurrying out to her flower garden next to the lake, bundled snugly against the crispness of early morning air. Was she waving at him? He narrowed his gaze. No. What at first he'd thought were mittens, were actually bundles of flowers. Out with the pink. Today's color was blue.

"Are you going to tell me or not?"

"Sorry." He turned from the window. "There were drugs involved, too. Cocaine. The usual paraphenalia was left behind."

"Not Scott."

"Yes and no. It was definitely his stash. He tried to pin it on me." Rey gave him a condensed version of the story. "I can't accept that he'd torch his own sister's shed. What would be his motivation?"

"Revenge. You took his supply from his pocket few nights back. "

"Then his anger should have been directed at me, not at her. It doesn't make sense." He sighed. "Dave, I really blew this one. Handled it all wrong."

"How?"

"I never made the time to level with Megan about Scott's habit. It came out in the heat of battle, let's say. Bad timing."

"I'm sorry, buddy."

Rey smiled half-heartedly. No I-told-you-so. No condemnation. Just empathy. "I explained why, but it sounded lame even to me."

"We all make mistakes. I made a bad decision myself."

"But that's long past."

"I'm not talking about my own coke habit. More recent. The finale took place last night." Rey heard Dave's chair creak. He could easily imagine his partner slouched deep into his swivel chair, feet on the desk. "EJ's gone. Dropped out of the recovery program. Some judge of character I am."

"My turn to say I'm sorry."

"I let him get to me. We had a special bond." His voice was louder, agitated. "I must have seen myself in him. It was as if I were failing, all over again."

"Of course you took it personally. It's hard not to. Once in a while, someone comes along who strikes just the right cord in your gut. And you give it all you've got."

"That's it. You hit it head on."

He smiled. "I've been there, my friend."

There was a long silence. They said their good-byes. Rey turned to watch Grandma Grace fuss with her garden. Bending over, she pulled up flowers and tossed them aside. If Megan wouldn't forgive him, maybe there was an opening at Grace's, as gardener.

❊   ❊   ❊

Megan heard the snowmobile approach but didn't pause in her digging. With her luck, it would be Rey. She wasn't ready to face him yet. Not after yesterday's scene with Scott.

"Hello, down there."

Rachel. They were best friends, but Rachel would figure out some way of taking Rey's side over hers. Rach didn't care for Scott, either, so there was no way Megan would open that subject. Maybe she could convince her to go bother someone else.

Rachel pulled next to Megan's vehicle, cut the engine and walked over to the edge of the snow pit. "Look's good. A bit deep, isn't it?"

"This is my job. I suggest you go do yours."

"Oh, we're having one of those days, are we?" Rachel crossed her arms. "What happened?"

Megan stuck her shovel into the snow, then leaned against the handle. "Let's just say that yesterday was rather eventful."

"I heard about the shed." Picking a spot to sit along the edge of the waist-high hole, Rachel dangled her legs over the side. "Taking a day of vacation yesterday was an excellent decision. I hope you used it well."

Megan pulled off one glove and shoved her bangs back beneath her hat. "In case you think I want to talk about it, I don't." She jammed her hand back into her glove.

"Trouble in Houseguest Heaven?" Rachel put her hand on Megan's shoulder.

"Be serious." She shrugged away from her friend's grip and climbed out of the hole. She crossed to her vehicle and flipped open the storage compartment.

"Don't leave." Rachel stood. "I was only trying to snap you out of this mood."

Megan turned to her friend, a thermos in one hand and two granola bars in the other. No sense in putting this off. Rachel would hound it out of her sooner or later. "Take a seat." She extended her hand with the bars in it. "One of these is for you. Do you have an extra cup?"

"Of course." Rachel popped open her own storage compartment and pulled the cap from her thermos.

Megan poured two cups of tea then sat crossways on the cushioned seat facing her friend. "Let me simply give you the bottom line. I pulled a gun on Scott last night."

"What? You're kidding."

"He slapped the phone from my hand. I thought he was going for my face next. Rey restrained him. It ended in a brief wrestling match, with Scott's hands around Rey's throat."

"Brief, due to your gun?"

"Yes." She shrugged. "I didn't know what else to do."

"What started your brother's attack?" Rachel took a sip.

"The news will be out soon enough." Megan studied her friend for a moment, then sighed. "It took Rey only one meeting with Scott to recognize something I would never have seen."

"Go on." Rachel peeled back the paper wrapper on her granola bar.

Megan's shoulders slumped forward. She looked away. "Scott is using cocaine." Rachel kept silent. "All the symptoms were right there in plain view. The weight loss, ashen complexion, surly attitude, chaotic mood swings. The headaches." Megan met her friend's eyes. "I never saw it. Never suspected."

Rachel put her hand on Megan's arm. "Don't be so hard on yourself."

"You don't understand. The perpetual runny nose alone should have been enough to clue me in."

"Just where would you have gained enough experience to spot a problem such as that? Not here in Snagtooth."

"Rey recognized it immediately."

"He lives in the big bad city."

"I should have known."

"That's guilt talking. The train of thought goes like this: If you would have known, you could have helped sooner. Thus you should have known. I might not be knowledgeable about drugs but I'm an expert on guilt." Rachel gave Megan's arm a quick squeeze. "Now that you do know, you can do something about it. Did Scott admit to it?"

"Not in so many words, but it's true." Megan shivered. "And until he wants help, I'm not sure what I can do."

There was a long pause before Rachel spoke again. "I wonder if Russell's aware of the problem?"

"I didn't think of that." Megan laughed bitterly. "He'll have a field day, won't he? He'll turn it around. Somehow, I'll end up responsible."

"You already feel responsible, so you're one up on him." Rachel slid her hand down Megan's arm until it reached her tightly gripped fists. She covered them with her palm. "It's not your fault. Believe that."

Megan nodded. They both sat in silence for several moments.

Finally, Rachel stood. "You can't take on the problems of the entire world."

"I don't. It's just that . . ."

"Bullshit."

Megan glanced at her friend. "I didn't say anything yet."

"You were about to rationalize your part of the blame again. Look at the way you view Thia's death, for example."

Megan moved away and stood to one side. "That subject's off-limits."

"I'm reopening it. You've said a million times that you should have been there for Thia. Should have been with her that day."

The grueling task of digging snow pits seemed eminently better than this. She walked back toward the pit-in-progress. Rachel grabbed her sleeve and turned her around. "Did it ever occur to you that she and Pete arranged to be alone?"

"What are you implying?" Megan realized she was shouting. "How dare you resurrect that when I'm trying to deal with Scott."

Rachel shook her. "Because it's all the same thing, Megan. Different pieces of the same martyr pie. Being blind to everything around you. Around us." She lowered her voice. "I was blind, too."

Megan pulled her sleeve from her friend's grasp. She stared at the snow pit, wishing she could climb in and have Rachel go away.

Instead, she kicked at a clump of ice by her foot. "I have no idea what you're talking about."

"That's because you don't want to hear. I've been trying to tell you this for months. Actually, I've only had enough nerve to face it myself the last few weeks."

Megan's heart beat faster. She glanced at Rachel. Her cheeks were flushed despite the freezing temperature. "Rach, I don't think I want to know."

"Tough. You need to know. I wouldn't be your friend if I kept silent any longer." Rachel faced her directly once more. "My husband and your sister were lovers."

"You're crazy." She put her hands on her hips. "How can you say that?"

"It's true."

She didn't believe any of it, but obviously Rachel did. Her heart ached for her friend. No wonder she'd been so reluctant to speak of Pete. Such a terrible, hurtful thing to have attached to her last memory of him.

Megan's tone softened. "Why dwell on this now? They're dead. They can't explain, defend themselves, or clear up any confusion."

"You're a fine one to talk. I'm bringing it up so you'll stop blaming yourself for their deaths, not so you'll feel sorry for me." Rachel straightened. "They didn't want you along. They were racing off to be alone. Nothing you could have said or done would have stopped them."

Snow was falling all around them now, landing on caps, jackets and eyelashes. Megan didn't care. The silence between them was deafening. She was the first to break away.

"You're wrong." Her tone was unnaturally calm. "I was the one who checked out the slope above Devil's Elbow that morning. I couldn't convince the office to close the run. I can feel as guilty as I damn well please, for as long as I please." She picked up the shovel she'd left laying by the snow pit.

"Megan . . ."

She held up her hand. "Just stop. You've told me, now your conscience can stop working overtime." Megan slid back into the hole and resumed digging. "The report that said 'Warning' instead of 'Closed' had my electronic signature at the bottom, not yours. No matter what Thia and Pete's purpose in being there was, the responsibility was mine."

❈   ❈   ❈

Rey sat down on one of the living room couches, deciding to get comfortable. It was nearly ten A.M. Almost time for Megan to complete her morning work and training run. He would wait right here until she reappeared then stand in her path until he drew her attention. They needed to talk, to put yesterday behind them.

He discovered another bookshelf behind an old packing trunk in Megan's living room, one he hadn't explored yet. He scanned the titles while sipping his morning coffee. Avalanche Accidents, 1980 Case Histories. Weather and Snowpack Guidelines. A Guide to Firearms. He sighed. He was running out of reading material fast.

Between *Surviving the Western Cascades* and *Backcountry Mountaineering* were two operating manuals for her computer and a repair guide for her Vmax. He'd fallen for one heck of an exciting woman. Not a novel to be found: adventure, romance or mystery. Maybe she had those tucked beneath the bed, not wanting to spoil her image.

He was determined to resolve their differences head-on instead of retreating downstairs. He was falling in love with this woman who needed no one. Was it because she put no demands on him? Not only expected nothing, but wanted nothing from him.

She was vastly different from the women he'd dated. Most women, after finding out who he was, made their demands known up front. That was his key reason for avoiding relationships, casual or not.

It was the contrast that he found so appealing. Megan still didn't know who he was. That was yet another thing he'd hidden from her. There had been an opportunity to tell her the night of the fire, but they'd had more important things to discuss. Yesterday didn't seem to be the right time either. Congratulations, you've just made love with a millionaire.

She would probably behave differently toward him if she knew who he was. Would have reserved him a spot at the nearest Hilton. Never would have invited him to stay here. Instead she'd coddled him, due to his city boy status, against the realities of wilderness living.

He sat upright. She was protecting him. In spite of all her protests over his behavior, she was doing the same to him. He laughed. She must care for him.

Yesterday's lovemaking should have settled that question. She seemed to feel safe with him. He would never have accepted her offer if he didn't think there was a chance at a future between them. But what sort of future?

Even with the evidence in her hand she had never considered him a drug user. He would fight to keep her trust, despite the error he'd made with her brother.

He glanced back at the bookshelf again. Merging worlds would be difficult, but not impossible. Not if they both wanted it badly enough. Reaching over he made his selection. Opening the *Guide to Firearms* he began to read.

❄   ❄   ❄

The front door swung open, letting in the freezing winter wind. Megan entered, slid the rifle harness from her shoulder and hung it on one of the coat rack pegs. After brushing the snow from her hat, she pulled it off and unzipped her fleece jacket. Not until all her snow gear was put neatly away did she look at him.

Rey set down the book he was reading and stood. "How was your run?"

"Fair." Megan untied her boots. "I was distracted. My tempo was off and my pulse rate never left the Basic Endurance Zone. It's difficult to improve without exceeding one fifty." She glanced at him, as if checking his interest level, then swiftly looked away. Shoeless, she crossed to the kitchen without another word. She lifted the lid on the soup pot.

He followed. "Let's see. After Basic is the Racing Zone. Did I remember that correctly?"

She glanced over her shoulder, as if checking his distance from her. "Yes."

"Hard to reach, but the best pace for hitting the target."

"Yes."

"And would that be with your rifle or with the pistol from last night?"

She turned quickly, as if ready to let loose an angry retort. She was only inches away, holding up the lid and wooden spoon as if they were shield and sword. Condensation from the lid dripped to the floor.

He pointed to the items held in mid-air. "Put down your weapons. I'm unarmed." She continued to stare at him. He extended his hand. "I'm sorry, Megan. I was wrong to keep your brother's cocaine usage a secret."

She closed her eyes and inhaled deeply. Her mouth trembled. He gently slid the spoon from her hand and retrieved the lid, too. After returning them to the stove he drew her into his arms. She moved into his embrace without hesitation. "Thank you."

Her voice was muffled against his sweater. "For what? For not beating you with the spoon or for not spilling the soup?"

"For believing in me after my own lack of trust." He smoothed her hair with his hand. "I didn't tell you what I knew. I was less than honest. Can you forgive me?"

She drew a deep, unsteady breath then nodded. The tears came, dampening his sweater. He held her tighter.

"We'll help him, Megan. Together."

"How?" Her voice was raspy.

"I know how. The first thing he needs is an informed and supportive cheering section. That's why what I did was so wrong." He loosened his hold so he could meet her eyes. "You'll be prime cheerleader. You're the closest to him. I'll just be waiting in the stands."

She blinked away tears.

Reaching over to the table he grabbed one of the napkins. "Scott will resist, but eventually he'll listen. He loves you."

Megan blew her nose, then crumpled the napkin. "You seem to have forgotten something. I pulled a gun on him."

"He pulled a gun on you, too." Rey smiled. "Interesting relationship the two of you have. One I'll have to get used to I guess."

"You're sure you want to?"

"Absolutely."

They sat at the table. He served lunch. They shared more childhood stories, bits and pieces that alone seemed trivial but woven together was the fabric of their lives. When through, Megan grabbed a magnetized pad of paper from the front of the refrigerator.

"I need to make a grocery list for my trip into town this afternoon." She began jotting down milk and other essentials. "Help me think of what we need."

"I'll go with you."

"No." Her response was quick and forceful. "I mean, after the last few days you should stay off your knee as much as possible. No needless running around." She adverted her eyes and continued to write.

Rey frowned. "Megan?" He waited. Eventually she lifted her head. "My knee is fine. I'm going with you."

"No."

"But it might not be safe for you to go alone." He drew an unsteady breath. He was trying to change. And he'd keep trying until he got it right. "I would prefer you not to go alone. Not until we know more about the fire. About who caused it."

"It's not safe."

He sat back in his chair. "That's exactly what I'm talking about. Someone could be waiting for you. To find you alone."

She swallowed hard. "Has it ever occurred to you that maybe it's not me they're after?"

He opened his mouth to speak, but the words wouldn't come.

"Forget I said that." She shoved the pencil and paper toward him. "I'm merely going to the Snagtooth General Store, not into Winthrop. I know everybody in town. They know me. I'll be fine. Just put what you need on this list."

Looking at Megan a moment longer, he leaned forward and picked up the pencil. He wrote a single word, then paused again before turning the page toward her.

Condoms.

She blushed, glanced at him then stood. "Get your coat."

❊   ❊   ❊

Megan stomped her boots on the faded welcome mat outside the general store, loosening the snow. Rey did the same. She was smiling at him, but it seemed somewhat forced.

"Are you nervous?"

"No. It's just that the shop owner, Hazel Cooper, is the biggest blabbermouth in town. She would print our grocery list in the *Snagtooth Gazette* if she thought it would sell more papers in her store. Let's hope Jeri is behind the register today."

She squeezed the latch and pushed against the heavy wooden door. It wouldn't budge. He motioned her aside, braced a shoulder against the door and shoved. They were in.

He let her precede him. She was scowling, taking in their surroundings as if for the first time. He scanned the room, too. Wood framed windows desperately in need of paint. Walls that needed patching. Shelves that were overstocked in some areas, bare in others. Merchandise in total disarray. He loved it.

"Are the words 'one-horse town' coming to mind?"

"No, 'charming' is more like it."

"Rey, they sell fish bait next to cleaning supplies." She sighed. "Say it. Tacky."

"Colorful."

"It's not what you're used to."

"I'd hate to describe what I'm used to, Megan." A housekeeper who managed his condo. Daily menus created by someone else. A kitchen he'd never cooked in. He put his arm around her shoulder and drew her to his side. "It's charming."

"Hi, there."

Megan stepped away. "Jeri. Hello."

Rey turned toward the young clerk. He liked her smile.

"Jeri, this is Rey Harrison. I mentioned to you, over lunch, that he's staying with me."

"You did. Days ago."

Megan blushed. "Rey, meet Jeri Hurst. Snagtooth native and my long time friend."

"Nice to meet you." He extended his hand.

She accepted. "Looks as if your knee is recovering nicely, Mr. Harrison."

"Call me Rey. And yes, my knee is just fine." Jeri glanced quickly at Megan with a conspiratorial grin. He quickly amended his statement. "I have to take care not to overdo it, though. I would hate to cause a relapse."

"Of course. May I help you find something?"

Megan answered for him. "No. I think we can manage."

He slipped the grocery list into his pocket and seconded her statement. "I'll just take a look around while the two of you catch up on news." He heard them discussing Scott as he walked away.

Now where would condoms be in a store such as this? No bright, gleaming signs advertising Health and Beauty Aids. No signs at all. This section wasn't right. It was mainly the fish bait Megan had referred to earlier.

The women's voices dropped to a soft, indistinguishable level. Were they discussing Scott's drug addiction? Maybe Jeri already knew. From what little Megan had told him about the breakup, the events may have been related.

He was getting closer. Aspirin, cough drops, feminine hygiene products. Bingo. He glanced in Megan's direction. She was keeping steady eye contact with him, over Jeri's shoulder. He waved, signaling success.

Megan ended her conversation and caught up with him near the ice cream freezer. "Well?"

By way of response, he dropped the box into her cart, next to the pork chops she'd chosen. Megan stared at the package. "The family-econo-size box?"

"Well, I thought . . ."

"Rachel has every brand known to man, but I've never seen this one. Are they any good?"

She was gripping the push bar tightly. He covered her hands with his. "Would you prefer to return home and read *Consumer Reports* first? That would take an extra trip, but I'm game."

"Of course not."

"Then let's check out. Remember, this is nobody's business but ours." Taking the cart from her, he rolled it toward the cash register.

Jeri was there. "Find everything okay?"

They responded in unison. "Yes." Megan began stacking their groceries on the counter. He noticed that she hid the box in question amid the tissues and paper towels.

"One of these. Three of these." Jeri began punching numbers.

The canned goods disappeared first into the brown paper bag, followed by fresh fruits and vegetables. An older woman, presumably the shop owner appeared from behind the back curtain. "Megan. How good to see you. It's been ages."

Hazel.

Megan's eyes met Jeri's. In what must have been silent understanding between the two women, Jeri glanced down. She quickly picked up a sack of chocolate kisses and covered the box.

Jeri took over. "Hazel, Megan was just asking about your plans for the Spring Bazaar. She was thinking about starting a quilt to donate to the raffle, under Granny's tutelage, of course. I told her about the catalogs you have stored in the back."

The shop owner preened. "It's a wonderful collection of old time classics. Would you like to borrow a few issues, Megan?"

"I'd love to."

"Then come with me."

As the two women left, Rey gave Jeri a smile of thanks. She simply winked at him. "If you run out, Mr. Harrison, be sure to come back. At Snagtooth General, we aim to please."

FIFTEEN

S COTT STRODE ALONG the snowy sidewalk toward the General Store, part of his daily rounds. The bright green awning provided a protected place for neighbors to visit with each other. The huge picture window offered those inside a view of all the happenings in downtown Snagtooth.

The window of the adjoining store was not so homey, it was covered with black-out sheeting. Deserted. Permanently and fictitiously for lease. He was one of the few privy to what really went on back there.

He slowed outside the store. Not to see Jeri. He liked to think of it as a chance for her to see him. To see what she was missing. Megan had told him many times that he looked impressive in his deputy's uniform. One of these days, Jeri would come crawling her way back to him.

His chest deflated at the thought of his sister. Memories of her shouting at him. Holding a gun on him. Taking Harrison's side against him.

Her truck was parked across from the store, down the street from the Sheriff's office. Had she come to see him, hoping to apologize? It had better be a good one, after her neglecting to call him this morning. He'd pretend to consider her peace offering, let her stew for awhile before accepting. Finally he'd agree to forget what happened, as long as she sent Harrison packing.

Personally he didn't care if the guy was there. But the sheriff was so insistent. He didn't know or care why. Scott merely wanted to stay on his good side.

How would Russell react if Megan told him about Scott's drug habit? He had a pretty good idea that his boss already knew. He wasn't so bleached white himself. Word-of-mouth among the deputies was that the sheriff was famous for looking the other way. If he did good work, maybe one small, nasty habit wouldn't really matter.

Scott glanced inside the shop, suddenly feeling generous. He'd say hello to Jeri for a change today, before dropping in on Megan at his office. Treat her to a few kind, though undeserved, words of greeting. As he reached for the knob, a woman with twins in her shopping cart moved to one side, giving him a clear view of the delicatessen. Jeri was there behind the cash register laughing and smiling with Harrison. Megan was following Hazel, the old bat, toward the back room.

Towards the connecting door? Not many people knew where the door behind the curtains led. Shit. Had his sister spilled the beans about the coke? Was Jeri in on this?

He was pissed. Backing away, he bumped into the man behind him. "Sorry." A tattered hat landed on Scott's boot. He retrieved it, then looked at the man as he handed the item to him. There was no mistaking the red hair and bushy eyebrows. It was his card-playing buddy, Lute.

"Slow down." The older man gripped Scott's shoulder as if to steady him, then acknowledged him with a neighborly nod. "Nice afternoon, isn't it?"

"What are you doing here?" Scott's voice was a notch above a whisper. "It's broad daylight."

"What most folks are doing." Lute tilted his head toward the door. "Shopping."

"The game's not till tomorrow night."

"I know. I'm looking around, getting to know people." He grinned as two ladies passed by. "There's nothing wrong with me coming a little early, is there? Keeping an eye on things?"

Lute's hold on him switched to an around-the-shoulder position. For the benefit of the townspeople, no doubt. Scott pulled away, glanced both ways down the street then spoke out of the corner of his mouth. "I can't be seen with you."

"And why not?" Lute shoved his hands into the pockets of his overcoat, looking disappointed.

"I'm an officer of the law." Scott stood straighter. "I'd be obligated to arrest you if you had . . ." He wet his dry lips and slouched slightly forward again. "If you had in your possession . . ."

"Don't worry." Lute removed one hand from his pocket and crammed something into Scott's, then drew back. "Now I'm clean." He smiled, spreading the fingers of his empty hand wide.

Scott pulled off his glove and felt inside his pocket. A plastic zippered baggie. His knees felt weak. He stepped away, chanced another glance inside the store, then with his most official sounding voice, wished Lute a good day.

❄   ❄   ❄

Lute angled his way between the pool tables, nodding at the new acquaintances he'd acquired since joining the poker game. Nice how the boys accepted him at face-value after he'd flashed his bank roll and established that his sole purpose was poker.

Trusting lot. Especially Deputy Jeffers. That kid was in sorry shape. Standing in front of the grocery, troubled by his sister.

Lute had seen her. Harrison, too. The shed being torched must have shattered the kid's nerves, he was practically begging for the few crystals slipped to him. A little arson didn't bother Harrison, though. He and the lady ranger were out shopping. Not a care in the world.

The pay phone by the men's room was unoccupied, as usual. He dialed the unlisted number, hung up and waited for the call back. He didn't have to wait long before his boss was on the line.

"Eagle's Crest was a touchdown today. Safe and secure."

"And Desolation Point?"

Why was Cowboy asking about that? He hadn't directed Lute to make a two-for-one stop. "Just the single pickup. Sorry if I didn't understand something in your directions." He winced, then chose to make the best of it. It was always simpler to apologize. "Didn't see any activity in that area though."

"You were to ignore it only if the houseguest was still there."

A deadly pause. Lute's palms started sweating. He could swear he'd heard differently. Now he had two problems. Cowboy hadn't heard about Harrison yet. Lute hated to be the one to break the bad news.

"Tell me the boyfriend left town, Lute."

He hated his name spoken over the open line. The fact Cowboy let it roll off his tongue so easily indicated his days of usefulness were numbered. What Billy overheard had been right on. He swallowed nervously.

"He hasn't left yet, boss. The accident happened all right, just as planned. It just didn't faze him." Lute switched the receiver to his other hand and added a faint-hearted chuckle. "Harrison's just one stubborn son of a bitch, I guess."

"Lute?"

He hated the sound of that. Just his name, clear and simple, followed by nothing. As if Cowboy was struggling for patience and losing. "Yeah?"

"The kid didn't set the fire."

"Sure he did." Lute layered on the bullshit. He spoke louder to be heard over the ruckus on the table behind him. One drunk was accusing another of cheating. "Alarms were ringing here at the station. There was commotion everywhere. I heard them firsthand."

"Lute."

Shit. That voice. As smooth as melted butter being spread on a burn. Somehow, his boss knew. "Yeah?"

"The kid set it up but didn't do it. You had to finish it for him. Not very effective."

"All right. So the deputy's a screw-up. He'll learn." Lute wiped the sweat forming on his brow. He tried to minimize the significance of the botched attempt. "No matter who did it, though, the results were the same. The boyfriend's not gone. Having the hots for the ranger seems to be ample motivation for him to stick around."

"The choice is simple, then." There was a moment of silence as Cowboy puffed heavily on his cigar. "Scaring him isn't working. Time to unmotivate him or silence him. Maybe both."

Killing incompetent kids was bad enough. But to seek out his victim and end the man's life . . . for what reason? He couldn't do it. "He'll leave sooner or later, Boss." Lute winced. He shouldn't have said that out loud.

"I wasn't asking your opinion. But since you're my right hand man, I'll tell you why. He and I have a grudge to settle. Interesting that our paths have crossed. Even more intriguing is the fact he's hiding his identity. I never thought we'd meet again." His voice grew cold. "He's to be eliminated. Have I made myself clear?"

"Yes, sir." Lute scanned the tavern for eavesdroppers. It was now or never. He had to impress his boss or face the barrel-end of Cowboy's .45 for questioning him. "I have an idea. One that won't miss."

"You've had enough ideas." Another drag and puff. "Rusty will take care of the happy couple. You stick with the pickups. You're doing a fairly good job with those as of late."

The rest of his work must be shit. Lute tried dislodging the lump that had formed in his throat. In the baggie he'd passed to Jeffers was a note, suggesting that an accident inside his sister's home might be more effective in driving Harrison away. If the boy was smart, he'd already be on his way. Lute couldn't call off the job. If the deputy was successful, maybe Cowboy would notice Lute had arranged it.

He moved on to the next piece of business. "I'm staying here in town like you asked. What's the plan for tomorrow?"

"Meet Princess at the pickup, then return to town."

"Two nights? But you said . . ."

"I want you on site until this is over."

"Oh."

"Is that clear?"

"Of course." Lute paused. He hated to press, but had no choice. "You'll contact me when tomorrow's location is set?"

"Do what the Canadians do. Watch the flags."

God, he felt stupid. Another mistake.

His boss's voice turned sharp. "I've always rewarded top performers, Lute."

"Yes, sir."

"And punished the ones who weren't."

Cowboy reading his mind? Scary, considering Lute's thoughts of Matzalan were occurring more and more frequently. "You referring to anyone in particular, Boss?"

"Yes." Lute's knees went weak until he heard the rest. "The deputy is a liability. Prepare a farewell gift."

Thank God, it wasn't him. The deputy was a goner, though. If he performed well today, maybe Lute could intercede. Maybe not.

The deputy wasn't his problem. He had to forget about lost souls like Scott Jeffers, Rookie and Billy. Time to concentrate on keeping his own body and soul intact. After the next pickup, he would head his cold, weary bones south. "Any suggestions on gifts?"

"It's always a pleasure when they do themselves in."

Lute's blood ran cold at the sound of Cowboy's chuckle. Beer mugs clinking together behind him provided a rather bizarre accompaniment.

Cowboy exhaled again. It sounded as if he'd blown the smoke directly into the receiver. "Poetic justice, I call it, when it's by their own hand."

"I'll cut some coke, then."

"Good man. Set up a big game for tomorrow night. Make sure he's in the mood to celebrate when it's over."

❄   ❄   ❄

Mitchell turned his back as Lute left the bar, then quickly dialed Logan on his cell phone. "Did you get it?"

"Yeah."

He listened as Logan began relaying the highlights. Partially through the recap, Mitchell interrupted. "The deputy's in on it? It's his sister, for God's sake."

"Sure as shit, partner. I'm more worried about what they said later." Logan rattled the tape unit on the other end. "They referred to another idea. Sounds as if the real fireworks are about to start."

He frowned. "Who's the unknown flag-waver?"

"That's why you're there. What's your take?"

"Don't have one yet." He paused as a waitress sopped up a mess on the table behind him. When she left, he dropped his voice lower. "Maybe a few aerial shots would help. That, and another tap."

"Who this time?"

"Sheriff's office."

"Got it."

Time to return to the woods. Jeffer's cabin would be the center of the action. The fireworks could start any minute. "Over and out."

"Wait. Just one more thing, buddy." Logan cleared his throat. "Take care. And call for god-damned reinforcements when the shooting starts this time, okay?"

Mitchell attempted to clench his right fist and failed. Memories of the surgery returned. The depression that followed when he thought he'd lost the ability to do his job any longer. The deception he maintained ever since.

He'd insisted on keeping the bullet they'd dug out of him. He wanted to remember.

❄   ❄   ❄

Vandalism surrounded them. Rey swallowed hard as he stepped through the debris. Overturned chairs, slashed curtains, cranberry juice as dark as blood, seeping between the boards of Megan's wooden floor. The worst by far was the book of matches, lying open atop of the gas stove. The note scrawled inside the cardboard jacket was simple. *Next time, there will be nothing left. Send your boyfriend home.* Whose handwriting?

Would this have occurred if they'd stayed home tonight instead of going to Grace's for dinner? They'd accepted hoping Mitchell would join them. If they'd left earlier, would they have surprised the intruder? The man, or woman for that matter, had a key. Could enter anytime. The possibility sent a chill down his back.

Rey tightened his arms around Megan once more and pulled her against his chest. She was trembling. He had to get her away from all this.

"I'll secure the basement door with two by fours, then grab a few personal things. I won't be long." He looked into her eyes. "I'll be right back."

She stared up at him, unmoving. Her silence worried him.

"Megan?" He reached out and cradled her chin. "I'll be gone fifteen minutes. Maybe less. Will you be all right?"

"They have keys to my house." Her voice was low, almost a whisper.

"I know, I know." He brought her head close again, against his chest. Her hair, brushing against his lips, was still cool from the night air. "We'll go somewhere."

"We can't leave every night." Her clenched palms rested against the front of his coat. "This is my home."

"I'll take you to mine." He felt her shake her head. He softened his tone. "We have to leave. You can't fight this with a pistol and a rifle, Megan."

She wrenched herself out of his arms. Though surprised, he let her go. "What's wrong?"

"I can take care of myself."

"I know."

"You hate the fact I'm competent with firearms."

Her anger must from be coming from pure stress. "The issue regarding your handgun was with myself, Megan. We discussed that."

"Then why did you hide my bullets and spare pistol? Did you think I wouldn't notice?"

"I didn't hide them, simply moved them to the living room. Having a gun mixed in with the office supplies wasn't safe." He stepped closer, tried to touch her shoulder. "Think of it this way.

What if you reached for a stapler and shot yourself in the foot through the flimsy wood?"

She walked away, hands on hips, as far as the kitchen before turning back to face him. "Particleboard and veneer is all I can afford, Rey." Her voice trembled. "And as for handling firearms, I'm a professional. I have to be, out here alone in the wilderness." Her last few words seemed to catch in her throat.

Watching the muscles of her neck tighten, he swallowed reflexively. "You're not alone."

"At the moment, no. I will be though. Soon."

"Is that what this is about? You don't believe I'll be here for you until this is over?"

She hugged her arms across her chest and rocked slightly. "Trust is for the foolish."

Exhaustion. Terror. Those emotions and more crossed her face as he watched her. Whoever vandalized the cabin was within her inner circle. A friend. No wonder she was teetering on the edge. And he, or she, could be after either one of them.

They would rely on each other. He would board up the downstairs, let her regain her composure. She was pushing him away. Maybe she would be more willing to listen in a few minutes.

"I'll be back." He moved toward the stairs.

She lifted her chin. "Stay downstairs. I'm going to bed."

He turned slowly and met her gaze. "I'm joining you."

"No."

"We can negotiate private space later. Tonight, I'm staying with you." His footsteps on the stairs shattered the piercing silence.

❄   ❄   ❄

Megan was already in bed, nightgown buttoned to the throat, by the time Rey returned upstairs. She could hear him knocking

chairs around her kitchen, squeezing water from the sponge, cart-
ing lumber up the stairs and pounding nails into the front door
frame. He was trying make them safe amid the vandalism, but with
each strike of the hammer she flinched. She wanted to escape as
they had before, but how many nights could they run?

No way was he staying in her bedroom tonight, especially
under the pretense of protecting her. She'd been alone ever since
she could remember, including the time spent living at home. She
had gotten by without any of them. He would be leaving soon. She
would get by without Rey, too.

He knocked on her door. She pulled the comforter higher
around her neck. "Go away."

He opened the door and stepped inside. His gaze lingered on
her for a moment before moving to the far wall. She saw him try
to stifle a grin as he walked across her room. Retracting the shade,
he checked the locking mechanism on the window frame then
measured for a board to brace the frame.

Megan glanced at him impatiently. "If they really wanted in,
they would simply break the glass."

"I know." He moved to the next window.

"Then why check the locks?"

"Broken glass would tell us, at least, that they didn't have a
key."

The third and final window was near her headboard, to one
side. She focused her eyes straight ahead. Anywhere but on him.
Well, not on the tub, either. Memories of him standing before her
as her bubbles dissipated were too vivid. Not on her desk either.
Rey sitting in her chair, typing away on God-knows-what was also
a rather pleasant sight.

She could almost feel his body heat radiate from where he
stood behind her. The latch rattled. The shade slid back into place.

Silence followed. What could possibly be taking him so long? She didn't dare look behind her. "What are you doing now?"

"Peeking down your nightdress."

Megan turned quickly, clutching the flannel neckline. Rey stood with arms crossed, the hammer still in one hand, grinning down at her.

"You are not." She faced front again. Damn, but he was making her smile. She hated that.

Laying his hand on her shoulder, he circled around and sat by her side on the mattress. He tossed the hammer onto the braided throw rug, next to her slippers. The bed springs creaked beneath his weight. "Do you know how ridiculous you sound?" He trailed his fingertip down her arm until it reached her wrist. "I won't be able to sleep if I'm worried about you being alone up here."

"Then don't."

"Despite what you might think, I don't spend time evaluating whether or not you can protect yourself. That's not it at all." He turned her hand over and interlocked their fingers. "You see, I simply want to be by your side. Fighting these demons with you."

She bit her lower lip and kept her eyes averted, not wanting him to see that they were quickly filling with tears. Her voice was unsteady. "My life is changing. In some ways it's out of control. I don't know at times where it's headed."

"Ah, yes. The complications we spoke of earlier. They're already settling in." He nodded. "Are you regretting our time together?"

"No." She gripped his hand tightly. "I wouldn't go back, I mean undo, what happened." She looked up at him. "I'm not exactly sure what I'm trying to say."

"I think I might." He stroked the skin along her wrist. "You've survived on your own for a long time. So have I. Having someone else in my life is a fantastic, though very off-balanced, feeling."

"I don't know what's happening anymore. It's an out-of-control sensation."

After raising both of their hands, he kissed the backside of hers. "Being together shouldn't require either of us to feel as if we're giving up something. If it feels like a sacrifice, then it's not right."

He moved their hands again until hers rested against his cheek. It was rough, bristly. "We're both independent people. There's nothing wrong with admitting that. It's kind of nice, isn't it, to choose something different? Even at the risk of losing your heart?"

His breath was hot and moist on her skin. Hers was caught in her throat. She simply nodded.

"I'm not asking that we make love tonight, Megan. Only that you let me stay with you." His fingers touched her mouth, shutting off an imaginary objection. "Please let me." His touch moved slowly over her lower lip, drawing a line along her jaw before moving upward to stroke an earlobe.

His words made their way to her heart. Sentiments about wanting each other rather than needing each other. She loved him. All that he said and did led her to believe he felt the same way, though it was much too early to speak of it in plain terms. Letting go of the comforter's edge, she touched his shoulder, encircled his neck and drew him closer. Danger was still all around them. But it would be there when she was through making love with him, too.

Their pulses beat in unison. His lips brushed softly against her cheeck before coming to rest against her temple. Each time he exhaled, she felt his breath against her earlobe. Instead of tightening her arms around him she withdrew and brought her hand to his chest.

Capturing the top button of his shirt between her forefinger and thumb, she twisted. It released instantly from the buttonhole. She moved to the next one.

He held her gaze. "We don't have to do this. I simply want to be with you. That's enough."

"For you, maybe." She twisted the second button. It also surrendered. "But not for me."

"What about the old adage, one step at a time?"

"I agree, wholeheartedly." She smiled. "And I'll go first." She brought his hand, palm-side down to her breast. The warmth of his fingers could be felt through her nightdress. His thumb gently traced the silhouette beneath the thin cotton.

"As I recall, you initiated the first step last time."

"Someone had to." She leaned against the headboard, inhaling deeply, enjoying his touch.

He followed her down, kissing one side of her neck, then the other, just above the lace edging of her gown. "Are you sure?"

She nodded then resumed the task she'd started earlier. The rest of his buttons gave way easily.

He cleared his throat. "Then I'd say our trip to the General Store was just in time."

❄   ❄   ❄

Rey stood and removed his shirt, hanging it over one of the bed posts. When he reached for his belt, Megan covered his hand with hers. "Let me."

His hand dropped to his side. She wanted to orchestrate this? He relinquished the lead role with pleasure.

She slid from beneath the covers and sat before him on the side of the mattress. His buckle unlatched easily under her touch, as did the snap. She slowly lowered his zipper tab. The pressure of her hand was wonderful. He couldn't breathe.

Her fingers slid further into and around the sides of his opened jeans. With her nails lightly skimming his waist and hips, she eased the fabric to the floor. He gripped her shoulders and stared unseeing at the ceiling.

How similar this was to their time together at the hot springs. This time, their roles were reversed though. She was extracting such sweet revenge. Thank God he'd removed his boots. How unromantic to hobble to a seat.

He stepped out of the pile of denim. His jockeys were next. She knelt on the floor before him. He kept silent. It was as if speaking would break the fantasy she was winding around them.

Her cheek rested against him. Her skin was so soft. The contrast with his own flesh was overwhelming. His pulse raced. He closed his eyes and buried his fingers in her hair, running his nails slowly along her scalp. She shivered, but didn't move away. Instead, she kissed him.

How long would he last? He focused on remembering how to breathe. Her hands trailed slowly up the back of his thighs. Electrifying. Nerve endings throbbed in anticipation. It would be over before he'd even undressed her. Before he'd given her pleasure. "Megan, stop. It's too much."

He drew her to her feet and wrapped his arms around her. She snuggled against his chest. "Together, this time. All right?"

"Yes."

He trailed kisses from her forehead to throat. Encountering the lace of her neckline, he reached for the buttons. When the third was undone, she stepped back and drew the garment off and tossed it on the growing discard pile.

He glanced at the bed, then paused. His hand grazed her hip. "I would love to romance you with dim lights, music, flowers."

She turned to him and looped her arms around his neck. "The first two are definite possibilities. The flowers you'd have to steal from Grace's garden."

"I should have bought some at the store. I wasn't thinking."

"Flowers aren't in our budget."

He kissed her eyebrows which were now scrunched in disagreement. "I can afford them, Megan."

"But we agreed to split things fifty-fifty, remember?"

"When did I agree to that?"

"I don't need flowers." She nibbled on his ear, sending goose bumps down his arms. "I have everything I want right here."

"Then wait no longer." He scooped her into his arms.

The sheets were cool and crisp against his skin. Laying next to her, he ran his forefinger down her length. As he explored, their mouths met and tongues intertwined. Her breath became ragged as he traveled lower. Megan was right. Music and flowers could wait. Romance was a state of the heart, not the setting.

She reached for him, cupping his head within her hands, drawing him upward to meet her mouth again. Her words were whispered against lips. "Now, Rey."

He reached across the mattress toward the nightstand. Where most people kept a nightstand. In this case, though, it was her PC table. And the box wasn't there. She'd unpacked the groceries. Where had she put them? In the drawer? He lowered his forehead to hers. "Tell me the condoms aren't with your gun, Megan."

"Now there's a nice idea." She laughed. "All my protection in one place." Smiling, she lifted his head until they met eye-to-eye. "I never finished unpacking the last bag. Sorry. They're still in the kitchen."

Rey sighed, brushed a quick kiss on the tip of her nose. "I'll be right back."

"You said that before."

"I meant it, didn't I?"

"You most certainly did." She ran her fingernails down his spine and across his hips.

"Hold that thought." After another kiss, he rolled off the mattress and stumbled over their pile of clothes. Hopping on one leg, he tried to unhook the garments that were tangled between his toes. Thankfully, Megan didn't so much as smirk. Normally he would have seen the humor in the situation. Maybe they would laugh together, later.

The box he wanted was wedged between others. He grabbed it quickly and turned, but one corner caught the edge of the grocery sack. The bag and all its assorted contents dropped to the floor. He stared at it a moment, then shrugged. With the mess from the evening's vandalism still everywhere, no one would notice a few stray cans on the floor. He turned towards the bedroom.

"Hurry." Her voice reached him through the open doorway. "We can put them away later."

He raised an eyebrow. She thought he was doing KP? Now? Not likely. He returned to the bedroom. She was smiling at him. He tried being stern as he crossed to the bed. "You wouldn't think this was funny if I told you the ice cream melted all over the counter."

"I put the ice cream back. We couldn't afford that either. Not after purchasing a box this size."

He slid into bed and kissed her. "Lucky we did."

"Lucky is right." She grabbed for it, opened the top, slipped out a single package and dropped the rest to the floor. He looked down, staring at the foil packets littering the rug.

"Pay attention." She tugged at his arm.

"I am."

"Then, come here."

He did. Their laughter soon was replaced by other, sweeter sounds.

SIXTEEN

R EY SAT ON the edge of the queen-sized bed and glanced at Megan. She stood before the mirror, brushing her hair. When she tried to capture the strands smoothly beneath a flat, silver clip they refused to cooperate. He silently cheered. Already the tousled, sleepy-eyed look was gone. He missed it. Didn't want a single part of their togetherness to end. But reality slowly eased its way between them with each stroke of her brush.

The evening had been a first for him. He'd broken his personal rule of leaving before dawn. It was an unoriginal, but successful, method of avoiding morning-after confrontations. He'd never questioned the fact he would spend the night with Megan wrapped in his arms. It was as natural as the winter frost on her windows. The feeling of intimacy was exciting, but at the same time, unsettling. Moving their relationship forward meant exploring new territory and finding common ground.

She continued brushing, glancing briefly at him in the mirror before looking away. Did she feel as awkward and confused with their new relationship as he did? He placed one foot on the bed rail and bent to tie his boot. Not having to meet his eye might lessen the intensity. "I'm almost through; I'll start breakfast."

"Great."

"Omelets okay?"

"Sure."

Another one-word response. Her upbeat tone sounded forced. He tied the other boot. "Granola with yogurt?"

"Whatever." The clip was back out again, banished to her dressing table drawer. She worked on a knot she'd discovered near the nape of her neck.

"Chocolate chip pancakes, whip cream and hot fudge?"

"Sounds good."

Right. As if her cabinets contained such items. Enough with the evasion tactics. Their future was at risk here. Rising, he walked toward the vanity. Her hand movements slowed as he approached. "Frog legs with snake oil syrup?" He stood behind her. They were framed together in the mirror.

She set the brush down. He slipped his arms around her waist. "Any new relationship is bound to be nerve-wracking."

"Try terrifying." He felt her exhale and sink back against his chest.

"We'll get through this. It's important to me." He rested his chin on the top of her head. "You are important to me."

She turned within his embrace. "Look at this logically. Last night's break-in set this up. I was selfish, needy and childlike. Being threatened does that to me." She placed her hands on his chest. "You were feeling protective. One thing led to another."

He kissed her to halt the excuses. He'd wanted to make love to her, it was that simple. "You're wrong."

"I'm serious. That could be all this is."

"Not for me, it isn't." He kissed her again, slowly this time, until he felt her arms slip upward and wrap around his neck. "Don't doubt that this relationship is headed somewhere, Megan.

I can feel it. I believe you can too, or last night never would have happened between us."

He felt her relax against him, her head coming to rest against the hollow of his shoulder. After a moment, she nodded. Words seemed unnecessary. He ran his fingers through her hair to remove all traces of the brush. He loved the way it slid over his fingers.

The sound of a knock at the front door stole the quiet moment. Rachel called to them through the heavy wood and glass. She raised her head; he kissed her nose. "I guess there are a few other things that need our attention first."

"Unfortunately, you're right. I'll call the sheriff. He needs to know about the break-in." She paused and smiled somewhat shyly. "I don't want the magic to end. Reality has a way of doing that."

"This is just the beginning." He hugged her once more then released her. A good start. They would be fine. He picked up the hammer. "I'll let Rachel in."

Traces of vandalism were still evident in the kitchen and the living room. It needed to stay that way until Russell or one of his deputies arrived to check for evidence. Rey crossed to the entry-way, pried off several boards and pulled open the door. "Good morning, Rachel."

"Same to you." She raised an eyebrow at the hammer in his hand. "Is Megan getting tired of company already?"

Before he could respond, the destruction in the kitchen caught her eye. "My God, what the hell happened?" She walked over and righted a chair. "Where is Megan?"

"Someone broke in while we were gone last night."

Her eyes were wide. "How? Through a window?" She glanced around the room.

"No. The doors weren't forced either. I suspect it was the same person who dropped off the scarf."

"Could something have been left unlocked?"

"That would be better than the alternative, but I don't think so." He signaled toward the table and brushed aside a piece of broken glass. "Megan's calling the sheriff right now, arranging a time to take photos. Have a seat."

"Thanks. I will." Rachel followed his lead. She dropped into one of the chairs.

For the first time he noticed her face was flushed, despite the bitter cold outdoors. "Do you feel okay?"

"Yes, I ran over here instead of bringing the snowmobile." She flashed him a half grin. "Guess it will take me awhile to rebuild my endurance. It's embarrassing that I let myself get this much out of shape."

He waved away her comment. "Just keep working at it."

"I will. By the way, I haven't had a drink in several days. Was back home in bed before midnight, too."

"Great."

"Sure, you say that now. But think about the bars in Winthrop that will go out of business."

He laughed. Her hard-as-nails exterior was beginning to soften. "Now stop confessing. Remember, you don't need to explain yourself to anyone."

"Who's explaining what?"

Megan had emerged from the bedroom. He stared at her, the toppled furniture vanishing from view. He wanted to hold her close. To kiss her. She seemed to share the feeling and looked away.

Rachel scooted her chair back and stood. "Congratulations."

For a moment, he'd forgotten she was there. Rachel was watching him, her eyebrows raised. Had his expression given away his thought?

Megan stepped forward, her face redder than before. "Rachel,"

"Don't even think about making excuses. I couldn't be happier." She stood and wrapped Megan in a bear hug. "You deserve the best. I'm not sure he's it, but he appears trainable." Rachel's eyes sought his over Megan's shoulder and she winked. He smiled in return.

Sighing deeply, Rachel released Megan and resumed her place at the table. "Back to business." She tapped the pocket of the jacket she still wore. "Here are the photos I told you about."

"Of Pete and Thia?"

"Yes. Their last day. I decided to drive down to retrieve them, instead of hitting the bars last night."

Megan's gaze was still on Rachel. "A wonderful choice."

"Yes, well . . . let's just say it was time." Rachel reached inside her coat and pulled an envelope free. She wiped her hand across the table, clearing a spot amid the debris, then slid the small pile of photos from the envelope. "Fresh from the storage box. Most of the roll features Granny and her high schoolers. They were taken at The Silver Needles Awards Ceremony the night before Pete and Thia died."

He heard Rachel's voice catch. Megan linked her fingers with his and stood uncommonly still. He felt helpless. After a long silent moment, Rachel took a photo from the bottom of the pile. "This is the final one on the roll."

Megan didn't reach for the picture. Rey's chest tightened. He accepted the photo on her behalf and placed it in front of her. "Look with me."

She nodded.

It was an odd scene. A dark-haired man in his early forties, sitting next to an unsmiling woman on a quilt covered bed. No posing for the camera. No outward sign that their being in the hut together was an event worth remembering. Why had they snapped the picture if not for a souvenir?

Megan pointed, her finger trembling. "The scarf. Look, she's wearing it." She traced the lines on the glossy paper.

"Just as you remembered." He stared down at the familiar pattern and at the initials woven onto both ends. "It matches the one in the closet exactly."

Rachel rummaged in her pocket again. "Now look at this second set." She waved another envelope toward him.

This time Megan reached for the package. "Pete took two rolls?"

"No, these are the official ones. From Russell's investigation."

Megan lifted the flap and slid the five-by-seven enlargements onto another cleared spot on the table. The same twosome. His heart beat faster. This time, however, they were sprawled in the snow near the foot of a large rock slab, their bodies at odd angles. Pete was face down, his head turned to the side. Thia was face up, her upper torso sideways across Pete's legs.

He felt Megan lean against him. He released her hand and placed his arm around her shoulders. Unraveling this strange chain of events might be the key to her peace of mind. He addressed Rachel. "So the scarf's not pictured. Maybe there's a simple explanation."

"Such as?"

"Thia could have left it behind in the cabin, or dropped it in the snow somewhere before her fall."

"Yes, that's possible." Rachel pursed her lips for a moment. "But then why did it resurface after a full year? And not only why, but how?"

The image of the kid from the chopper nagged at his memory. He turned to Megan. "Do you still have the photo of the boy who was killed?"

"Yes, in the cabinet."

"Let's look at it again."

Both women stared at him for a split second. Rachel recovered first. She stepped over a pile of strewn papers and retrieved the photo. She handed it to him.

No mistake. Though the initials weren't visible, the patterns were identical.

"What does it mean?" Megan's voice was a near-whisper.

"I don't know." He placed the snapshot next to Russell's enlargements. "It's fortunate that you took these at the accident site. The fact Thia wasn't wearing the scarf when she fell might be the key we're looking for."

"Actually, I didn't take the pictures. I arrived after the bodies were removed."

"Then, how?"

"When Russell dismissed the case so quickly, I was pissed. He called me into the office to collect Pete's things." She waved her hand over the snapshots. "These were out on his desk. They were private. I wanted them destroyed, not filed, so I slipped them into the box I was holding."

Megan stood. "They're police evidence, then."

"Were, I believe, is the appropriate term. Frankly, I didn't care what rules I broke. The investigation shouldn't have been closed so quickly."

She leaned against the counter and crossed her arms. "After I returned home, I had crazy thoughts of needing them to one day reopen the case. Or of framing them, so I wouldn't forget."

"Forget Pete? Impossible."

"No." Her shoulders slumped. "Like a fool, I used to think that love as strong as ours would last forever. It didn't. It was temporary. These would remind me of his affair with Thia, of our great love gone sour." She paused, reaching for a tissue. "Stupid. I know." She dabbed at her eyes. "Anyway, I couldn't bear to get rid of them, so I sent them to Pete's mother."

She crumpled the tissue then shoved it into her pocket. "I didn't want to soften as the years passed. I hoped the mere existence of the photos would hold my resolve firm, as Thia's rifle and trophies hold you to yours." Her words came more slowly, sounded forced. "He did love me, though. I don't question that anymore. But how or when it changed, I don't have a clue." Her voice finally broke.

Rey winced. Senseless deaths. Lives placed on hold. He could barely swallow, watching as tears formed again in the corners of Rachel's eyes. "Enough's been said."

Megan negotiated the mess on the floor to stand next to her friend. "Rachel."

She shook her head, signaling for them to wait as she drew another breath. "Keep the photos. Use them however you can, then burn them. I refuse to hold on to the bitterness anymore." Her eyes met Megan's. "You're also on the verge of moving on. Do it. You and Rey could really have something here. Don't short-change yourself."

Rachel shifted her gaze toward him. "Don't let her run and hide, Harrison. Stick with this, and with her. See it through." She smiled through the tears. "You've both given me a gift for my own future: hope."

Megan returned to the table and watched as Rachel moved about the kitchen. She was picking things up, making noise, and searching the cabinets for snacks. Keeping busy was her way of dealing with the pain. Megan had asked her to let things be until the police arrived, but to no avail. She gave up and let her roam.

Rey's hands on her shoulders tightened. She indulged herself in his nearness. Rachel had been right. It was time to move forward. To take her life off hold. Their love might not last forever, but for now he was here. Megan leaned against him. God, it felt good simply to be touched.

Sighing, she focused her attention again on the enlargements in front of her. Twisted bodies, deathly still. She grimaced, flipping to the second picture. Thia and Pete's bodies were now aligned in a parallel position. Matching canvass bags and stretchers lay to one side. Such a waste. The third photo showed a bird's eye view of the area.

She squinted, scanning the expanse of white snow, hoping that the scarf was laying on the ground somewhere. But even if it were, how had last week's murdered teenager acquired it? What was the connection? She set the enlargements aside then picked up the snapshots from Pete's camera.

He and Thia were sitting expressionless, side-by-side on the rustic twin bed. The gold quilt firmly pegged the location as the Desolation Point hut. The infamous scarf was draped around Thia's neck, the initialed ends hanging straight toward the floor.

She tapped on the photo. "Do you know what bothers me most? Thia's acting out of character."

"How so?"

"She always hogged the show. Refused to share the spotlight with anyone." Megan turned toward him, frowning. "So why did she agree to pose with Pete, then merely sit there unsmiling?"

"I don't know. She doesn't appear to be forced into it, though." He stopped, peering closer. "I wonder what she's pointing at."

"What?"

He pointed at Thia's left hand. "Right there."

She'd missed that bit of subtlety. "Maybe her boot? The rug? Rach, what do you think?"

Rachel replaced the lid on the cookie jar and moved toward the table. Standing by Megan's side, she glanced down at the picture. "I didn't notice that before, but he's right. She's definitely pointing at something." She took a bite of a chocolate chip cookie and paused while she chewed and swallowed. "Any guesses?"

Goose bumps rose on Megan's arm. "It might be nothing. I don't want to overlook a single detail, though."

Rey pulled out a chair and sat beside her. "I'll ask questions, play devil's advocate. What do you remember about Thia and Pete's last few days?"

"I'll start." Rachel began pacing amid the broken dishes on the floor. "Pete was gone from the house earlier than expected that day. He usually left me a note as to what time he would return. Would leave it propped against the salt shaker." She took another bite of a chocolate cookie, then swallowed. "On that particular day, there was nothing. At the time, I thought it odd."

"Maybe he didn't want you to come looking for him."

"But why would I? I had no idea he was with Thia. I didn't suspect anything at the time." Her voice grew louder. "And even if I had, following him would be a bit pathetic, don't you think?"

Rey interrupted the outburst. Megan was grateful for his slow, steady tone. "Rachel, there's something I don't understand." He seemed to wait until Rachel's attention was firmly on him. "If you had no reason for concern when Pete left home and if he didn't leave a note behind, then why are you so certain now that they were having an affair?" He waved his hands over the photos. "These prove nothing other than they skied together that last day."

Rachel pulled out a chair, brushed the dust off and sat down. She sighed, scooting down in her seat and letting her head tilt back. "I didn't find out about their affair until it was all over. Until Russell told me."

"Russell?" Megan's throat tightened. A shiver ran down her spine. She had to force her words out. "And you believed him?"

Rachel shrugged. "He had nothing to gain by lying. He thoroughly enjoyed telling me, too, if you want my opinion. Every nasty little detail."

Megan felt Rey's eyes on her. She couldn't look his way. Rachel continued in a calm, monotone voice. Megan could hardly make out her friend's words because of the buzzing in her ears.

"Thia must have confided in Russell. Why? I'll never understand. He certainly wouldn't be my first choice." Rachel crossed her arms over her chest. "Anyway, he told me that they'd been sneaking off together for quite some time. What I can't figure out is, where in the hell was I? Why didn't I know he was in love with someone else? We'd been married three years, for God's sake."

Megan's eyes burned as she held off the tears. It was all so unnecessary. Rachel's pain could have eased by only a few simple words. Words Megan hadn't known to say. Words she almost couldn't say now. She drew a deep breath and forced them out. "He was lying."

"What?" Rachel turned to stare at her.

"Not only was Russell lying, but he did so deliberately." Though her voice sounded raw to her, she didn't stop. "Pete wasn't Thia's lover, Russell was."

Rachel sat upright in her chair. "What are you talking about?"

Megan rushed to finish, while she still could. "Thia wanted to keep her affair with the sheriff quiet. She didn't want Scott's position as Deputy to become awkward." She exhaled slowly. "I'm so sorry, Rachel."

Rey reached out and covered Megan's hand. "Maybe this isn't the right time."

"Rachel needs to know this. All of it." She turned to him. "And so do you." She felt his grip tighten. How could he understand when she still didn't?

Rachel interrupted. "Megan, I appreciate what you're trying to do."

Holding up one hand, she silently asked for her friend's attention. No more putting it off. She wouldn't hold back this knowledge another day. They deserved to know, both of them, but it was hard.

She looked directly at Rachel, not wanting to meet Rey's eyes yet. "Russell couldn't rendezvous with Thia that day. He was detained." Silence. She turned sideways until her gaze met his. "Russell was with me."

❄   ❄   ❄

Rey sat on the edge of Megan's bed and ran his hand over the top of the frilly comforter. In many ways, their relationship had traveled far. In other ways, they were just beginning. She'd trusted him enough to be honest about her involvement with the sheriff the morning of Thia's death. That in itself was significant. But there were so many unanswered questions.

He wouldn't ask and didn't need to know. It was her business, not his. He'd told her as much. But from the look on her face he had a pretty good idea of what their involvement had been. He would listen if she needed to talk, if it would help drive the guilt of Thia's death from her mind.

Megan had left with Rachel shortly after the admission, mumbling something about going to town. He didn't ask to go with her. She hadn't invited him, either, and hadn't mentioned a specific destination. His gut told him where, though. Russell's. Her personal day of reckoning.

He sighed, then picked up the phone on her PC table and dialed his corporate office. Hopefully Dave would be back from lunch by now. His cell phone was dead, he'd forgotten to recharge it after dealing with the vandalism last night. He hadn't made it downstairs until morning. That thought made him smile.

"Edwards here."

Rey forced his thoughts back to the present. "Dave, it's Rey."

"Hey. Good timing. I just received the report on the heli-skiing service. The search took an extra day. We had the wrong name. The firm is actually called Mountain High Adventures. Not High Mountain Adventures."

"That was what I had originally jotted down. But Megan had the other in her notes. She seemed so sure." He paused. "Never mind. Let's move forward."

"Right. I'll scan in the report and e-mail a copy to you. Encrypted. You can read it yourself."

"I believe you." Rey frowned. "It sounds unimportant, I know, but right now every detail is relevant."

"Well, either way, the report is in. The phony charter service has regular, posted schedules, a fancy brochure and a list of customer references." Dave paused for a moment. "By the way, how is Megan?"

"Fine. She's in town at present, probably meeting with Sheriff Russell. Thia's death might not be the open-and-shut case it was first reported to be a year ago. There might have been a third person with them, right before the accident."

"What led to that conclusion?"

"Two things. Pete and Thia had their picture taken together."

"So?"

"Who held the camera? Also, Thia was wearing a scarf that disappeared sometime between the two sets of pictures being taken. The first photos were shot mid-morning inside the Desolation Point hut, the second at Devil's Elbow."

"She could have merely dropped it."

"We discussed that, however the scarf reappeared a few days ago. The day you left, in fact. We found it neatly folded on Megan's sofa. So far I've ruled out black magic, so someone else must have picked it up and returned it a year later as a sick joke."

"You didn't mention this before."

"It's just dawning on me how significant that was." A sick joke. The words replayed in his head. Why did Scott's face immediately come to mind?

Dave interrupted his thoughts. "I don't mean to be a broken record, but any idea yet of when you're heading back to Seattle?"

"Soon, but no date in mind." He paused for a moment, trying to sort out how much to say. "A lot has happened this week. I'm not quite ready to leave."

"I assume you're referring to Megan."

"Yes."

"Then that's good, right?" Dave's voice sounded tentative.

"Of course. Yes, it's very good."

"Then congratulations. But remember, you have a business to run. If you're gone too long, Ali just might take your name off the stationery."

"And add hers as CEO?"

"You've got it."

He paused. "You're a good friend, Dave. Thanks for listening." He heard his partner try twice to respond. In between there was silence. When he could finally answer, it was simple and to the point.

"Thank you."

Rey smiled. Did Ali have a role in Dave's new, relaxed personality? Maybe he was finally ready to put his wife's death behind him and stop blaming himself. Rey returned to business. "Send me the report. I'll dial in within the half hour."

Dave voice was crisp, blunt and back to normal. "Sure thing."

❋   ❋   ❋

Megan pushed open the heavy outer door to the Sheriff's office. Her hand trembled on the worn brass knob. Cold winter air blew in behind her as she entered. Each time her boots hit the hardwood floor she gained strength from the harsh sound. She tried not to let her voice waver as she walked into the main office area. "Russell?"

Silence. His door was closed, but the other two stood open. She looked inside. Empty. Just as well. She crossed to Russell's and knocked loudly. Scott opened the door a mere inch. "The sheriff and I are in a conference. Come back later."

"What I have to say, can't wait." Megan walked past him into the room.

Russell was making notations on a piece of paper. He glanced up as she entered. "Megan. What can I do for you?" His tone was calm, his expression guarded.

"You're a son of a bitch."

He stared at her intently and turned the note paper over. He rested his hand on top of it. She moved closer toward Russell's desk.

Scott followed her. "Now, just a minute."

She turned on her younger brother. "We have long overdue business to settle."

"I'm his right hand man. I'm staying." Folding his arms across his chest, he glanced toward his boss.

Russell was still seated, tapping his pencil against the wooden desk. The sound continued several moments longer. It was the only break in the silence, save the ticking of the wall clock. Megan didn't lower her chin even a fraction while she waited. Finally, Russell stood. "No. I'll handle this alone."

Scott uncrossed his arms. "But . . ."

"We'll continue later, Deputy." Russell's smile appeared forced as he walked Scott to the door, one arm around his shoulder.

"Follow up on the items we've already covered. I'll need a report later tonight." He patted the younger man's back, as if urging him from the room. Eliminating the chance for argument. He firmly closed the door. Then, as if on second thought, he locked it.

Megan watched him slowly make his way back to his desk, taking the long route. First he twisted the horizontal blinds shut. Good. She preferred that, also. The fewer witnesses, the better. Next, he switched the ringer on his phone off. With his foot, he pushed his chair farther out from the desk and dropped into it. "Take a seat."

"I'd rather stand."

He ran his hand over his eyes. "Depending on what you want to talk about, this could take awhile."

"You lied to Rachel."

He exhaled slowly. "Megan, I've barely seen Rachel this week."

"After Pete died. You convinced her that he was having an affair with Thia."

"I might have planted the seed of an idea."

"She believed you." Her voice caught. "She carried that pain needlessly for the last year."

"You have no proof that he wasn't." He slouched into his chair, one ankle resting on the opposite knee. "And based on the evidence I saw . . ."

"Cut the crap. When Thia was in Snagtooth, it was one hundred percent you. Always." Megan leaned forward, her fingers fanned out on his desk. "Her in-town lover, she used to call you. Her old stand by."

"I resent that."

"Resent it all you want. Don't deny it."

Russell unfolded his long legs and slowly stood. Heat burned her cheeks. Her heart raced. She stood firm. His tone was cutting. "So it's finally time for the truth."

She nodded, unable to speak.

"Then, let's start with this simple fact. If you knew Thia and I were in love . . ."

"I didn't say, in love. My sister didn't know the meaning of the word." She put her hands on her hips and stood straighter. "Let's just call it what it was. Lust, plain and simple." Her voice had risen to a sharp, angry level. She bit her bottom lip to stop herself from going further.

He was silent, save for grinding his teeth back and forth. The way he clenched them caused his face muscles to form definitive shadows along his jaw line. Finally he moved toward her, leaning forward across the desk until their noses were inches apart. "It was more than that."

"For you, maybe. Thia used to laugh about your naiveté behind your back."

"You enjoyed that part, didn't you?" His smile was cynical. "Your favorite hobby used to be getting in our way. And then in the end . . ."

Megan flinched and drew back.

"Oh, no you don't. We're having this discussion. Here and now. You've forced it and, as you said, it's long overdue." He came around the side of the desk toward her. "If you knew how deeply involved we were, then what the hell were you doing in the motel room that morning?"

She forced the words out. Her voice was barely audible. "Waiting for you."

"That much was obvious. Why?"

"Thia asked me to."

"Bullshit." He laughed sharply. "Imagine my surprise, finding you there instead of her. A willing substitute. You knew that room thirteen was our usual meeting place, didn't you?"

"No."

He raised his eyebrows. "Thia forgot to mention that?"

"All I knew was that the two of you had plans to meet for breakfast. She had to cancel but was afraid to leave you a note." Megan tried to keep her hands from shaking. "Thia didn't think you'd understand. She called me, begged me to wait with her as she broke the bad news to you."

"When I arrived, you were alone."

She shrugged. "My sister couldn't wait any longer."

"If I had such a hot, uncontrollable temper, why did you stay?"

"When I got there, she was gone. The door was left open just a fraction. I was reading her note when you knocked. I had only been there a few minutes."

"You never mentioned the note, or any of this, at the time. In fact, I don't recall much talking at all." He moved forward.

"Don't." Megan stepped away until she felt a chair seat brush the back of her knees. She sat quickly.

"It's time to settle this between us." He followed her. "You were willing, Megan, at least at first. Why so agreeable, knowing I was your sister's lover?"

How could she say this? She swallowed. "Thia told me stories. Not specifics, just wonderful tales of romance. Of passion." Could she go on? Admit that her first sexual experience had been fueled second-hand? "She built you up in my mind until I . . ."

Russell leaned over her, grasping the arm rests of her chair. He was very close now, she could see his strained features. "Until you, what?" There was controlled tension in his carefully spoken words. "Wanted a piece of the action, too?"

She drew back. "I wanted to know what it was all about."

He watched her. She feared for a moment he might laugh. But he didn't. Didn't look at her with pity, either. His thoughts seemed suddenly elsewhere, his eyes might have held a tinge of regret. For that one small gift of kindness, she'd be forever grateful.

She'd said too much to stop now. Time to get it all out and off her conscience. "There's more, Carrol." Instead of riling him as she typically did with his given name, she chose a gentler tone. One she hoped would indicate her wanting to end the past twelve months of animosity.

He must have heard it. His expression softened. "Go on."

"When Thia's stories turned to recounting different escapades, using you as a convenient escort, I thought you deserved better. Had delusions of how I would treat you, if you were mine." Her voice broke.

He looked shocked, as if not able to believe her. She could have easily died from embarrassment at that moment. But more than anything she wanted to see it finished, to never go through this ordeal again. If she could cleanse her soul of the memories maybe there would be a chance of walking away whole. "I wanted to strike back at Thia for her shallowness. To show you what you were missing with me. I'm sorry."

He released her chair and stepped away. It was a long moment before he spoke. "I'm the one who's sorry, Megan. Sorrier than you'll ever know. I was blinded by Thia. Saw you only as her little sister." He swallowed. His gaze seemed to wander for a moment over her face, her hair. At last it met her eyes again. "It never occurred to me that I might have a chance with you."

She drew a long breath.

He ran his hand over his brow, then squeezed his temples. "You mentioned a note. Left inside the room."

"Yes?"

"What did it say?"

"Simply that she couldn't wait any longer. Would I please make her apologies in person."

"This makes no sense." He shook his head.

"Well, if she was late to another meeting . . ."

"No. What I mean is, she also left a note for me. Stuck it beneath my windshield wipers so I couldn't miss it."

"Wait. Let me understand this. Thia interrupted my schedule, begged me to come all the way into town to help, then told you herself after all?"

"No, that's not what she wrote. Not even close." He looked at her intently. "Are you sure you want to hear this?"

A sense of dread raced down her spine. "Yes."

He exhaled loudly, then leaned against the far wall, arms crossed. "She said you had the hots for me. That you had found out about our special place and had forced your way in. Were waiting for me in the room."

Megan felt as if she'd been punched. "That's a lie."

He nodded. "Only one of many, obviously. I know that now." He paused, his gaze not straying from hers. "Thia's message pleaded with me to meet you, talk to you, let you down gently. Said your mooning over our relationship was making it difficult for her to continue seeing me."

Megan wanted to leap from the chair, but wasn't sure her legs were steady enough to hold her upright. "If she weren't dead . . ."

"My thoughts exactly." He stared at the ceiling. "I was pissed that morning. It wasn't the first date she'd canceled. Always at the last minute. Always full of theatrics. Before I arrived, I spent time considering ways to make her pay. Then I saw you."

He lowered his gaze, focusing again on her. "I used you, Megan, to get back at Thia. She said you wanted it. I cared nothing about being a little rough, if it would make you run. If it would convince you to leave us alone." He shook his head slowly. "I wouldn't have forced you. I only wanted to scare you. You seemed so willing at first."

"I thought it was what I wanted." She swallowed. "But I couldn't go through with it."

"I should have stopped as soon as you asked. But I wanted to be free of your interference. To stop Thia's complaining." He moved toward her. "So many times this last year I wanted to explain, but couldn't find the words." He raised his hands then dropped them to his side again. "I still can't. 'I'm sorry' seems so inadequate."

She nodded, feeling her anger slipping away. She'd used him, too. It was time to move forward, but so many questions remained. "How could she do this to both of us? Did we mean nothing to her at all?"

"It wasn't directed at you, Megan." He sat on the corner of his desk across from her. "The sequence of events Thia triggered that day are too difficult to explain. Even if I wanted to, I couldn't tell you."

"I know most of them."

He shook his head. "You only know what appeared on the surface. It ran far deeper."

"I know Thia and Pete were at the Desolation Point hut right before their deaths. And that there was a third person with them." She was guessing, but if she could prod him to tell her more maybe it would help.

He stopped gazing off into space and quickly stood. "What?"

"Rachel has a photo which proves it, taken right before their deaths."

Russell went pale. "Are you saying there's a third person in the picture?" He was in front of her now, less than a foot away. His voice was strained.

"Not in it, but how else could there a snapshot of both Thia and Pete?" She could understand him being surprised, but where was the anger coming from? And the look on his face. It was close to desperation. "Someone else had to be there."

Russell exhaled slowly, then laughed. "The tripod." He
glanced down at her. "Pete's camera had a small, five inch tripod
attached to the strap."

"But . . ."

"You're lucky, Megan." He turned and strode toward the window. With his finger he bent one of the blinds and peered out. His
tone sounded more as if he was talking to himself than to her.
"Let's just say that these are dangerous people." Stopping abruptly, he pivoted on his heel.

Megan was dumbfounded. "What people?"

"No one. Forget what I said."

"No, Carrol. I won't forget. I can't." She sprang to her feet
and joined him near the window. "You know something. More
than what was in your report."

"I don't." He grabbed her wrists and held them near his chest.
"And if you're smart, neither do you."

"But you're honor-bound to reopen the investigation. That's
your job."

"I have no honor. I thought you knew that." He released his
grip. "You need to go."

"But, Carrol . . ."

"Forget what I said. I know nothing and neither do you." He
leaned over his desk and began shuffling papers. "It's all specula-
tion. Don't repeat it. To anyone."

"Rachel will ask."

"Don't tell her anything. Don't tell your houseguest, either."

"Rey is no threat to me."

His tone was cold. "Wise up, Megan."

"I trust him."

"Don't. He's lying to you."

"What?"

"The name he's using, Rey Harrison, is an alias."

She drew a sharp breath. It was as if she'd been slapped.

"Sorry I had to be the one to tell you, but you need to trust no one." He glanced up at her as she backed toward the door. "Think about this, too. Someone wired your snowmobile with a transmitter. Your every movement, your every phone conversation, is being monitored. Be careful. Now go."

❄   ❄   ❄

Scott stomped the snow from his boots then reached for the doorknob. He missed it and nearly fell as the door swung inward. He glanced up, directly into his sister's eyes. His jaw tightened. "You're still here?"

Megan nodded. "Don't worry. I'm leaving."

He noticed her flushed cheeks. Her tone was sharp. What the hell did she have to be so agitated about? She should be showing remorse for the way she'd treated him earlier. Maybe she would if he delayed her a bit. He nudged the door mat with his foot, blocking her path. "So you finished your business with Sheriff Russell?"

"Yes. You can continue your meeting now. Sorry to interrupt."

Something had shaken her. Disturbed her. He hardened his sympathetic reaction, focusing instead on the overdue apology she owed him. It certainly wasn't ready to slip off the tip of her tongue. Not yet, anyway. He didn't need this headache. She'd made her choice. Had Harrison now. No longer needed, nor wanted, a baby brother to coddle.

Funny. He never thought he'd miss the attention.

She laid her hand on his arm. He looked down at her fingers slightly curved against his coat sleeve. Maybe now she'd say it.

"I haven't had the chance to . . ." She paused, as if not knowing how to go on.

Yes, it was coming. He raised his eyes to hers. Admitting fault would be hard, but she was cut from tough material. "A chance to what, Megan?" Damn it, he deserved to hear the words.

She cleared her throat. "To ask how you're feeling. If you want any help." Her voice softened as she squeezed his forearm. "Professional help."

"Shit." He pulled away. "I have better things to do." He shoved past her then closed the door in her face. She watched him through the front door window. He hoped she had regrets. He felt ripped in two. Family loyalty? If it meant anything to her, she wouldn't have turned on him.

He kept walking, slamming closed the door to his private office. He dropped into his chair, leaned his elbows on the desk. He pressed his palms against his temples on both sides. He didn't want her approval, never cared for those soulful looks she gave him. Why did it hurt so much now?

He had to focus on his goals. The new ones. The ones he'd set just this past week. He lowered his head, cradled it in his palms. First, he wanted Sheriff Russell to be proud of him. Damned proud. That would bring more special projects his way. The second was to win big tonight. Yeah. He would earn the respect of his card-playing buddies. Soon the entire town would hear. But all that aside, he could use the money. Lots of it. And on a regular basis, too. Even a big win tonight wouldn't be enough. He needed an steady inflow of bucks. Big bucks.

At first the cost of the cocaine had emptied his pockets. Now he had holes in them that went clear down to his shoes. The freebie of crack Lute had given him yesterday, though appreciated, hadn't lasted long. He'd planned to save it until he could truly enjoy it. Then Megan had practically thrown him out of the sheriff's office. The buzz was already starting to wear off.

Maybe Lute would bring more tonight. Something tugged at his memory. Something about the crack. Oh, yeah. The packaging. The vial had been wrapped in five crisp one hundred dollar bills, secured with a rubber band. And the note, another surprise. A simple request, one easily accomplished. Shit, that kind of work was easy.

He raised his head. That was it. If he could work special projects for both Lute and the sheriff simultaneously, his cash supply would grow quicker. When he had enough, he could stop playing gofer. It was all so clear to him now.

Success was close, he could taste it. He felt lightheaded, kind of like a second rush. Leaning back in his chair, he raised his feet until they rested comfortably on his desk top, then crossed them at the ankles Russell-style.

Tonight. Yeah. It all begins tonight.

❄   ❄   ❄

Megan climbed the stairs to her cabin slowly, as if her snow boots were filled with lead. She couldn't stomach another confrontation right now. The alternative, not knowing, was even worse though.

She paused, glancing toward Grandma Grace's house. The afternoon light was beginning to fade but her neighbor was still planting. Changing flowers in her artificial wonderland of a garden. The floral choice *du jour* was purple. Had she ever seen the purple ones before? They must be new. How nice that Grace had a harmless hobby that kept the real world at bay. Pure heaven compared to what she'd just been through at Sheriff Russell's.

Pushing the door open, she entered the cabin. Her kitchen was deserted. The connecting door to the lower level stood open. She heard Rey moving about downstairs. Humming. Maybe if she walked softly enough across the wooden floor, she could indulge in the solitude a few moments longer. Anything, to avoid facing him.

Pulling off her boots, she placed them quietly on the mat beneath the coat rack. Rey's jacket hung in front of her. Instinctively, her hand reached out to touch it, to bring it to her cheek. It was real, why wasn't he?

"Megan?" His voice rang clear, as if he stood next to her.

Yes, but who in the hell are you? She didn't want to know, not yet anyway. What if he were using her somehow, as Russell and Thia had done? What if his involvement in last week's murder wasn't quite as innocent as it had initially seemed. He wasn't capable of murder, but maybe his injury had been concocted to simply get him inside her home. To watch her. Monitor her actions. Why else would he use an alias? He called her name again, louder this time.

She would face him later, when her encounter with Russell was further behind her. When her heart and soul didn't feel quite so exposed. Bracing herself, she answered him. "Yes. I'm home. I'm going to lay down for awhile."

"You're not feeling well?" He stood at the bottom of the staircase. Only the top of his head was visible from her position by the coat rack. She didn't want to see more. Not his eyes, that could read her so clearly. Not his arms that had held her tightly, so securely, this morning.

"I'm fine. Just tired." Footsteps sounded on the wooden stairs. "We'll talk later." She headed quickly toward her bedroom, making it there in record time. After closing the door, she leaned against it.

Chicken. Idiot. The fantasy was ending. Soon she'd know all the nasty details. Glancing about, her gaze lingered on her desk. Memories came racing back to mind. The way he had stood behind her, reading the daily report on mountain conditions from the screen, his hands resting lightly on her shoulders. Hands that were warm, strong and capable. So representative of him.

Megan closed her eyes and let her head fall back against the solid wooden door. How could she go on from here?

SEVENTEEN

AVE'S ATTENTION WAS drawn to the brilliant flash of color zipping by his office. Based on both the speed and the intensity of neon hue, there was only one person it could be.

"Ali, wait!" He set down the report and hurried to the door. Before calling out again, he realized his mistake and switched to a more professional tone. The one the staff was used to. "Ms. Jeffers?" He stepped into the hallway and stopped abruptly.

Ali was leaning against the wall, less than a foot away. "Yes, Mr. Edwards?" Her smile was mischievous. His deviation from the norm must have amused her. "Is there something I can assist you with, sir?"

His peripheral vision caught the office administrators smiling. He pulled at the knot in his tie and stiffened his spine, shoulders back. "Yes, in fact, there is. Do you have a few moments?"

"For you? Always." She stepped away from the wall. "Lead the way."

Nodding to the eavesdroppers, he retreated into his office. Ali followed him inside and closed the door. He buttoned his suit jacket, wanting to put formality back into the situation, something he tended to forget when she was around.

Ali looked him over as she approached his desk. One side of her mouth curved upward in a smirk. "It won't help, Dave. I swore off proper business protocol after my first week here, remember?" She moved aside his in-basket and leaned one hip against his desk.

His buttoned-down collar seemed to tighten. To his relief she changed subjects. "So, what's up?"

"I spoke with Rey this morning."

"Rey? The name sounds familiar, but I can't quite place the face. Used to work here, right?" She tapped her cheek thoughtfully for a moment, then raised her index finger. "I've got it. The brother I used to see behind the cereal box each morning."

"Exactly."

"Did the lost lamb mention anything about plans to return home?" Picking up his tournament-winning softball, she began to toss it back and forth. "Or should we send his things to Snagtooth?"

Sometimes her style was like a refreshing mountain breeze. Other times, it was closer to a whirlwind. "No departure date yet. Last night Megan's cabin was vandalized."

"You're kidding."

"I'm not." He relayed the details he'd received, including the lack of a suspect. "Rey doesn't feel he can leave just yet."

"That's understandable." She shook her head and sighed. "Despite the trouble, however, I have a good feeling about those two."

So did he, based on his and Rey's last conversation, but he didn't want to jump to conclusions. He grabbed the softball in mid-toss, returned it to his desk then flipped open a folder. "Take a look at this. It just came in this morning." He handed her the facsimiles.

"A list of suspects?"

"No. You'll find it interesting reading, though. The Snagtooth Sheriff has a rather dubious record, to say the least."

She scanned the top sheet. "Let's see. Unreconciled speeding tickets. Allows gambling inside city limits. Poker, specifically." She glanced up. "Nice guy."

"Read on."

She ran her finger down the page. "Okay. Here it mentions irregularities in bookkeeping. Extra, unaccounted for income. Other reporting discrepancies, too." She flipped to the second list. "All in all, nothing too dirty. Not the sort of thing movies are made from, anyway."

"You're right. Small errors. But it's the consistency of the behavior over the last two years that caught my eye." Dave leaned back in his chair. "His first year in office seemed to be strictly by the book. It wasn't until his alias was discovered that the rest came to light."

She nodded. "Where did you get this dirt?"

"I hired a P.I. Bottom line, it seems as if the sheriff's being paid to look the other way. Makes me wonder what else he's capable of."

Ali watched him silently for a moment, then glanced at the final page of the fax. It was a collage of photos spanning the last decade. After a few moments, she squinted at one of the items, then looked up. "Is this him?" She was pointing to the clipping from the *Snagtooth Gazette*.

"Yes. But that one's dated more than ten years ago."

"The face is familiar."

"Of course. You just met him."

"No. Not from this week's encounter."

She was silent. A highly unusual behavior pattern. Dave felt a tingling sensation at the nape of his neck. He stood and came around to her the side of the desk. He glanced at the same snapshot from over her shoulder.

Ali positioned it so the light was better. "It's really nagging at me. Something from a year or so ago. A memory, just out of reach." Her words came more slowly. After a moment, she laid the report on the desk.

He touched her shoulder awkwardly. She turned, but appeared unable to speak. Her lips were slightly parted, her eyes wide. He drew her into his arms without thinking twice. Her head came to rest on his shoulder as he stroked her hair. He spoke softly. "Ali, what is it?"

Her voice was unnaturally calm. He strained to hear her words. "I saw him two years ago."

"Where?"

"Dave," she lifted her head. "Two years ago I was in jail." Her words were barely above a whisper. "Did you know that?"

"Yes. I heard you ran into trouble soon after college." Rey had briefly mentioned how he'd had to post bail for her a few years back. Shoplifting, despite her purse containing every credit card known to man. A cry for help. She'd lived with Rey ever since being released. "That's behind you now."

She attempted to pull away, but he tightened his hold. Eventually her shoulders sagged and her head resumed its natural place against his chest.

"So you were in trouble. That's your business, no one else's. It happens to a lot of people on their own for the first time."

"Right." She tilted her head back until she met his eyes. "I bet you never did. Stories of Dave-the-bad-boy aren't very plentiful around here."

"You'd lose that bet, Ali. But it's a long story. Later, okay?" He held her gaze for a moment longer, then released her and stepped away. Once safely behind his desk again, he dropped into his leather chair. Would she ask, when things calmed down? Could he explain it if she did?

He pulled the facsimile toward him and tried to give it his full attention. "Did Russell visit the jail while you were there?"

Moments passed before she answered. "No, we never actually met."

He was relieved she'd allowed him to change the subject. She perched on his desk again. "His picture, though, hung in my cell. Could have been this exact shot. It was a five by seven. And it was autographed."

His shock must have registered in his expression. Ali quit circling the issue. "My cell mate was named Betty. This is her brother, Rusty."

"Rusty. That's the alias the P.I. uncovered." He expelled a deep breath. "Makes sense, I guess."

"Betty was a hooker. She was picked up for soliciting and drug possession. Cocaine. Bragged to me about what a fine grade powder the cops had confiscated from her."

"Was she worried about what her brother would do when he found out? He was a sheriff, after all."

"No." Ali laughed. "She knew exactly what big brother would do. Get her more."

Dave sat upright. "What?"

"A new supply." Ali exhaled deeply. "Rusty was her source."

❊   ❊   ❊

Dave sat straighter in his high-backed chair. If what Ali was saying proved true, then the beloved Sheriff of Snagtooth was into drugs in addition to his list of other offenses. "Do you know what you're saying?"

"Yes." Ali stood and waved her hand over the facsimile pages. "Pushing cocaine makes the rest of the infractions on that report look like child's play." She sighed. "Betty referred to her brother's temper, as well. We have to get this information to Rey."

"It's been done." He leaned forward, elbows propped on his desk. "Rey needs to watch his back. Megan's, too."

"Oh, God. What if they provoke him?"

"My thought exactly. Russell has a lot to lose, which makes him even more dangerous."

Dave briefed her on the other report he'd received, regarding the mix-up in the name of the helicopter service and the fact he couldn't make a reservation. He reached for the phone. "Let's call him." He dialed Rey's private number. Ali paced. Moments later, he replaced the receiver. "No answer. His voice mail isn't picking up, either."

She came around to his side of the desk. "Call Megan's phone then."

He flipped open his note pad and punched in the number. The line was busy. "We'll keep trying."

"What? We're going to wait?" She leaned down until their noses were only inches apart. "Are you crazy?"

"If I can't get through soon, I'll have the operator break in. We can wait thirty minutes."

"Maybe you can." She straightened, then turned to leave. After collecting her purse she slung it over her shoulder. "I'm going home to pack."

"You can't go to Snagtooth. Not with everything going on there. It's not safe."

"You make your choices, I'll make mine." She faced him, arms locked across her chest.

Dave stood and walked over to her. He rested his hands on her shoulders. "We're on the same side here, Alison."

"Prove it." Her voice was raspy. "Rey has protected me from every bad thing that's come along for the last two years. I can't sit back and do nothing."

"I want to help, but we need to think reasonably." Her eyes were watering. He resisted the urge to pull her close. He needed to remain focused. "The corporate jet's gone at present. It won't be back until nearly eleven this evening. I don't know if we can arrange a special charter at this late notice or not."

"I don't care. I'll drive."

"That would take all night."

She shivered.

He ran his hands up and down her arms. "What makes the most sense is for us to keep trying to reach him by phone. We'll call all night if we have to. If we haven't raised him by morning, we'll fly out first thing. I'll reserve the plane. Preempt whatever else they have scheduled."

She looked at him steadily. Her tone was gently mocking. "Who is this 'we' you keep referring to?"

"I'm going with you."

"Oh, really. Why? Don't you want to stay here and make phone calls?"

"You have to ask?"

"Yeah." She lifted her chin. "I guess I do."

"Rey's the closest friend I've had in years. It's taken me awhile to realize that. I resisted mixing business with my personal life, but he never stopped reaching out to me." He linked his hands with hers. "He's been protecting me, just as he has you. In a little different way, perhaps, but basically the same idea."

Ali raised an eyebrow.

"Later, remember?" He released her. "I'll go home and pack. If I haven't reached Rey by nine, then I'll come over to your place."

"Forget nine." She shifted her purse higher on her shoulder. "We need an earlier start than that."

"I was referring to this evening, not tomorrow morning. We'll take turns calling through the night." He grasped the knob and opened the office door.

She followed him into the hallway. "Don't forget."

"I won't."

"Slumber party. My house. Nine."

"Not a minute later."

She nodded, smiling in that mischievous way of hers as she slowly backed down the aisle. He was somewhat pleased at her reluctance to leave and returned her casual wave. It wasn't until she had cleared the administrators' desk and he caught them staring that his words came back to haunt him.

He winced. The two women sitting at matching oak desks outside his office door kept their eyes carefully downcast, as if absorbed in paperwork. However, neither woman's pencil moved. He didn't hold out hope that they'd missed the last exchange.

❄   ❄   ❄

Lute looked around the cheap motel room with disgust: nicked formica end tables, worn carpeting complete with cigarette burns, orange paisley bed covers not worthy of being called comforters. Some other sap could stay here tomorrow. He was checking out.

Cowboy had called for a change in plans. No pickup today. He was to leave Snagtooth immediately after tonight's game, didn't have to hang around until Harrison was gone. Princess would meet him at the Lost River Airstrip near midnight. By then the deputy had to be dead.

His head hurt. His gut clenched. Too much, too fast. And most of it was his damned responsibility.

Cowboy had been vague as to the reason for the changes. Explaining things wasn't his style. Maybe he could pry the info out of Princess, but he wasn't betting on success. She and Cowboy were tight, despite their history together. Two guesses immediately came to mind: trouble back at home base or his boss wanted to keep closer tabs on him.

Why was he always under the goddamned microscope? Their discussions lately had been only by phone. He'd kept his voice appropriately humble. Hadn't over-stated his role. Hadn't over-stepped his bounds.

Shit. He'd always done whatever Cowboy asked, had the black marks on his soul to prove it. Take tonight, for example. He'd followed instructions. The proof was in the plastic bag tucked into his jacket pocket. Lute felt for it. He rummaged for the aces inside his pocket. Both were destined for the poker game, going away gifts.

Poor kid. He wouldn't force the deputy to take the coke. It was his choice really. Still, his own hands weren't clean, hadn't been for quite awhile.

After checking the closets again, Lute closed his suitcase. He had nothing of value to leave behind, but he didn't want anything traced. Soon he'd be disappearing for good. Only hoped it was to a destination of his own choosing, not a hole in the ground. Not a free fall through the trees.

He swung the bag from the bed and dropped it by the door. Trouble at base camp had to be it, the only plausible explanation. The punk Billy quickly came to mind. He clenched his fists. The kid shot off his mouth at every opportunity. Lute pressed his palms against his ears as the words replayed.

"Lute, branch out on your own."

"Lute, try this great powdery shit."

"Lute, aren't you tired of being kicked around?"

Of course he was, but he wasn't about to take advice from a coke-head. Stealing from the kitchens, what a stupid-assed thing to do. Hell, the cooks probably would have given him some, if the kid had asked.

Not only was he more irritating than the rest of the runners, he was stupider. Even more than Rookie had been. Lute sighed, not realizing until now that he'd retired the name. In honor of a boy he'd personally killed. Sick.

He sat on the lumpy bed, allowing himself to remember Rookie a moment longer and the pathetic hand-made scarf the kid had been so pleased to own. Lute saw it after the other killings last year. It had been dropped on the floor, partially beneath the bed, at the yellow hut. Not wanting it left behind, he'd stuffed it into one of the chopper's side compartments. Rookie'd found it there.

The boy had become attached to it. So what if the fucking initials had matched his own? It was a mistake to wear it. Handknitted by Grandma. Had the kid really wanted the scarf, or had he wanted a grandma? Pitiful. He hoped the boy was buried in it, since the original owner wasn't. Somehow that would seem right. Put it finally to rest.

The kid was dead, move on. And if Billy followed suit, hopefully the new runner, the one Billy recommended, would have more smarts. Seemed like he did. Maybe he would be smart enough to say 'No.'

He stood and stretched. There might be a double-hitter tomorrow. The chances were good. There had been no pickup today. The stash had to be retrieved sometime. Cowboy was too greedy to let it sit beneath the hut, no matter what the risk. Was it desperation making his boss careless, or preoccupation with that construction project Lute had seen notes on?

He unlatched the door for the last time. What was Billy's friend's name? EJ, ER, ET? It didn't matter. Lute would have no more luck remembering initials than he'd had remembering names. The organization would bring the boy in, check him out, sign him up if needed and drop him like a yesterday's garbage when they were through with him. All in a day's work.

He glanced up and down the hallway. Though none of Cowboy's watchdogs were in sight, he knew they were out there. Somewhere. Tracking his every move. Lute turned off the lights and stepped out of the room. He hoped he had it all, because he refused to look back again.

❄   ❄   ❄

Rey knocked on the door to Megan's bedroom. It seemed odd that she had it closed. After all, he'd slept in there just last night. There was no answer. He knocked louder. "I've fixed a dinner tray for you. May I come in?"

"Yes. It's not locked."

He opened the door carefully, balancing the tray with the other hand. Megan was stretched sideways across the bed, leaning on one elbow. She had a sleepy expression that he would like to become used to. He stopped. Were her eyes red?

She'd said she didn't feel well when she came home from town. She'd been crying instead. The pot of tea would make her feel better. And the two cups would tell her he'd come to talk. Pushing the door closed with his foot, he crossed to the PC table next to her bed. He'd seen her use it as an end table last night. "Should I make some room here?"

"Sure. I'll do it." She grabbed a stack of folders and placed them on the floor. She was avoiding his gaze. He sat the tray on the newly cleared space. A second group of papers caught his attention.

The top sheet was the report he'd received earlier from Dave regarding Mountain High Adventures. He'd left it there, planning to share it with her later. The letterhead displayed his corporate logo quite predominantly, something he'd overlooked before. Had she seen it?

This was as good a time as any to tell her. Things were nearing a conclusion, he could feel it. Besides, he couldn't stay away from the office forever, would need to call soon for the jet. Perhaps she would go with him to Seattle until the investigation blew over. And leave Rachel and Granny behind? He sighed. Not a chance.

After filling the cups to cool, he picked up the letterhead. The snapshots of Thia and Pete were beneath it. She'd been looking at them again. He sat on the edge of the bed and faced her.

She was still in a reclined position. Their eyes met. She appeared sad. Not angry. Disappointed. He wanted to reach out to her. She faced him. When she didn't reach for him, he ran his fingers gently along her forearm.

She moved. It was subtle, maybe, but she'd definitely pulled away.

"What's wrong?"

"Who are you?"

He felt his face redden.

"Please." She held up her hand. "I don't care what the actual answer is, just don't lie to me. Not anymore."

"Megan." He didn't let his gaze stray from hers. "It was more a force of habit than a deliberate lie. I always travel under an alias."

"What in the hell are you talking about?"

"This." He handed the facsimile to her. She accepted it. "Forget the text for now. Look at the logo."

"How cute." She lowered the page enough to see him. "It matches your coat."

"And my skis. My long underwear, too, if you look close enough."

Though she blushed slightly, she didn't smile. "No more games. What are you trying to say?"

"Moore Comfort is mine. My company. I let you believe I worked there."

"You own it." Her gaze returned again to the fax. She squinted and read aloud the fine print. "From the desk of Reynold Harrison Moore."

"The third. Don't forget, the third."

"The third, what?"

He pointed to his name. "Right here. Reynold Harrison Moore III."

She looked closer. "I can't believe it."

"It's always struck me the same way." He took the pages from her and set them aside on the desk. "I rather enjoy simply being Rey Harrison. I wanted you to accept me for who I am, not what I'm worth." He stretched out on the bed so that he was laying next to her, face-to-face. "Can you still trust me after this?"

"I want to. I would be lying if I didn't admit that I'm hurt."

"I'm sorry. I could say that the right time never presented itself, but that would be an excuse, not the real reason. I feared our relationship would change. Or rather, that I wouldn't know for sure why you were interested."

She looked at him for a long, quiet moment. "This must be the emotional baggage you were referring to the other night."

"Yes." He didn't touch her, didn't move toward her at all.

"I don't intend to interrogate you over every issue that arises, to make sure you haven't lied through omission." Her voice was stern. Almost Grace's voice. "That's twice now, Rey. I don't know if I could take a third time."

"You will never have to. You deserve that, and more."

"We're through with secrets, then?"

He laid his hand over his heart. "My soul's bare."

"All right." She frowned. Her expression turned to one of teasing. Grinning. She drew a line along the bedspread tracing a pattern. "I've read about your company. Your rise to fortune. I bet you've never scrimped and saved for groceries in your life."

"Never shopped for them, put them away or cooked them either. Actually, I've never been allowed in the kitchen at all." He leaned forward and kissed her forehead. "Not before meeting you."

This time she didn't pull away. He reached out and touched her cheek. She gave up her anger, and leaned into his palm. After a moment, she moved into his arms.

He shifted her position until her head was tucked beneath his chin. "I travel with an alias for safety reasons. A combination of old fears and unyielding habits. Ready for me to tell you this bedtime story?"

She nodded.

"I was kidnapped at age fifteen. Held for ransom. After being released I was shipped off to boarding school, anonymously. Went by the name Rey Harrison for the next ten years at least. Didn't reclaim my birth name until I started Moore Comfort."

"That was short and sweet. Why do I have the feeling you left out the most important parts?"

It was his turn to sigh. "I don't enjoy remembering the rest."

"From what you told me earlier, your father must have died around the same time."

He nodded. "Attempting to rescue me. Instead of following the kidnappers' directions, he traced them to where they held me. I'd cut the ropes earlier, though, using a piece of glass. There was no way for him to know, of course, that I'd been plotting my own escape. I was being held on the top floor of a two story building, but I had more courage than brains back then." He adjusted the pillow under his head more squarely.

"My father had the ransom money. Didn't want to wait until the appointed rendezvous time, the next morning. The police were with him."

Megan shifted position until she was up on one elbow, looking down at him. She was waiting patiently. This was hard to say, but he wanted her to know. "The lookout warned the other kidnappers that my father was outside. When the cops were spotted, the shooting began. I escaped in the confusion."

"How?"

"Threw a chair out the window, then jumped. That's how I hurt my knee originally. I should have thrown a mattress out first."

She frowned. "How can you joke about such a tragedy?"

"Megan, that's where we differ." He pulled her back into his arms. "Dad died saving me. I felt guilty as hell, still do at times, but what's past is over. It can't be changed. I miss him terribly, but I know he'd want me to live. Not let guilt overshadow the rest of my life."

She snuggled against his chest. "I have no idea what Thia was up to on her last day. The more I find out, the more confusing it becomes." He could feel her trembling. "I might have been able to play a different part, if she'd given me the chance."

He put one hand on the back of her head and rocked her slightly. "Nothing can bring her back, Megan. You have to let her go."

"I can't. Not yet."

❄   ❄   ❄

Megan stepped from the tub and toweled herself briskly, trying to flatten the goose bumps. A bright foil packet, half-hidden beneath the dust ruffle, caught her eye. She knelt and picked it up. A remnant from the night before, when the open box dropped and scattered. An amusing moment, but soon forgotten in the passion that followed. She stood and listened. The cabin was still. Where was Rey Harrison Moore III? Had he gone out? The bath, instead of leaving her relaxed, had only increased her anxiety.

She slipped the flannel nightgown over her head and let it fall the length of her body. Despite the fabric being soft and familiar, it chafed her skin. Dread filled her, leaving a heavy feeling in her chest. What would tomorrow bring?

Outside, the wind howled. The sky was as black as gunpowder. Gusts of snow and ice beat against her window.

She needed to be near Rey. It consumed her, added urgency to her every movement. Had he retreated downstairs? It wasn't like him to go for so long without checking on her. She resented that at first, but she was used to it now. Comforted by it. Though he couldn't hold the elements at bay, in his arms the demons would surely sweep past. With him, she could face anything.

She pulled the comb through her hair, then set it and the wet towel aside. She peered into the hall. Her front door was locked and her shades drawn, but no longer was her home secure. Someone had a key. She listened for any sound interrupting the silence.

The events of the last week replayed in her thoughts. She couldn't put them aside. The futile mind games haunted her as she made her way down the hall. Each new face in town swept past her mind's eye. The old faces, too, with new behavior patterns. She could no longer figure it out. Was ready to scream.

A fireplace log fell, startling her. She flinched, edging closer to the wall. Smoke. Crackling wood. She eased around the corner, carefully avoiding the loose floorboards near the kitchen.

Rey was kneeling in front of the fireplace, about to add more wood. Relief flooded through her. He must have heard her sigh, because he paused, mid-toss. "What's wrong?" After setting the log back into the crate, he quickly stood, brushing his palms against his jeans. "You're barefoot. Aren't you cold?"

"Freezing." There was no need to elaborate. She hurried across the room and was with him before daring to breathe again.

"It's okay. We're safe." He ran his hands over her shoulders, then smoothed back her hair. Touched her face.

"Hold me."

"Of course." He wrapped one arm around her. She felt him reach for a quilt with the other. He pulled it across her shoulders, securing the edges, then locked her within his embrace. "You'll be warmer by the fire."

"I'll never be warm again. The coldness has seeped in, touching everything." She shivered. "In the charred remains of the shed, the ripped curtains in my kitchen, the dead bodies in the mountains. Tomorrow, Thia will have been dead one year."

He leaned forward. "No more dwelling on it tonight. Let's think about us, instead." She felt his lips hot against her forehead.

"But the nightmare's repeating itself. Can't you feel it?" A log crackled as it caught fire. Her heart beat faster.

He stroked her hair and pressed her closer. She tucked her head in the hollow between his neck and shoulder. "Jealousy drove me to Russell. My sister didn't deserve his love. I thought I could give him more. In exchange, he would give my life the intensity it was missing. If I hadn't been blinded by envy, she might still be alive."

"She used you." He moved his hands across her back. "Russell used you, too. Forget the past."

"But where does that leave us? With a terrifying present and a future undecided."

"It leaves us here. Now. Together."

Her fingers splayed across his chest. "I love you."

"And I love you."

Tears burned behind her eyelids. "Then make me forget the rest."

❄ ❄ ❄

If forgetfulness was what she wanted, then he would force the night and all its dangers away by the sheer strength of his love.

Her mouth was hot, willing and open against his. He strained to be closer, as if to become not two, but one. She pulled his shirttail free from the waistband, he answered by dropping the quilt to the floor. Her nightgown slid unrestricted up her hips under his fingertips.

Before he had a chance to remove his shirt, her hands were beneath it. Her nails traced a path along his spine, raising gooseflesh on his arms. He tried to unbutton a cuff. She interrupted him.

"Help me with this." She was trying to free his belt buckle. He released it with a swift yank. She needed no assistance with the rest. His jeans bunched around his ankles. Her eyes were dark, her expression intense, fueling his desire.

He claimed her lips again. He pressed her lower body closer, her hips arched toward him. His pulse quickened. A free fall toward oblivion.

Her touch grazed upward along his thigh. He turned and she found him. He closed his eyes. Her palm was cool against his heated skin. She began a steady rhythm. He held on, moving with her, letting her set the pace. His motions became involuntary.

He covered her hand with his, then brought her fingers to his lips. "Not yet." He took a deep breath. Positioning himself between her thighs, he drew one of her legs upward.

He held her knee firmly to his side and traced her skin beneath the nightgown. She was bare, waiting. He touched her. She clung tighter, nails biting into the nape of his neck. Her movements were erratic. Her breath was hot and urgent against his skin. Sounds without words. Then all breathing, all motion, stopped.

Her grasp on his neck loosened as her body sank against his. He kissed her, holding her close until the trembling ceased.

He moved toward the wall beside the fireplace. She leaned against the smooth stones. She pressed her knees against his waist, her lips against his neck. The crackling of the fire faded along with the scent of burning alder. His senses were overwhelmed. Megan.

With a firm grasp on her hips, he entered in one decisive thrust. She encouraged him with words then only with sounds. Faster. Deeper. His vision clouded. He couldn't stop it from happening. He didn't want to.

Was he standing or flying? Flying. And Megan was there with him.

❄   ❄   ❄

Eric looked around his rented, second story room and let out a long sigh. He shut off the tape and leaned back against the headboard. It was all so simple really. And now, thanks to the recording of Sheriff Russell's last phone call, it was obvious, too. Cowboy's arrangements with the flag-waver for tomorrow were all signed, sealed and delivered. He would be gone soon, on to his next assignment. Riding a desk, in the city somewhere. No more home-baked bread. For how long would he miss this place?

He stood and checked his clips. There would be fireworks at daybreak, just as Logan had predicted. Innocent lives would be at stake and identities finally revealed. The most he could do right now was get a good night's sleep. This just might be the last time he laid on a feather mattress for awhile, or awoke to fresh cinnamon rolls. He'd better make the most of it.

Should he try to reach Logan and chance his call being intercepted? Everything was set for tomorrow, only the location was new. He'd leave word for his partner some other way. A safer route.

He stripped off his shirt and jeans, climbed in bed and forced his eyes shut. He'd pursued Cowboy for two years. Why wasn't he feeling exhilaration, knowing the end was near? Instead, he felt as if he'd been punched in the gut.

It all came back to the flag-waver again. He hadn't spotted the scheme. It had been too clever, and too obvious. No, he'd missed it, despite the fact that the guilty party was right under his nose.

❄   ❄   ❄

Five hundred bucks, down the drain. Scott leaned closer and pulled his waste can toward to the bed and stared into it. He'd been ahead most the night. The final jackpot had been so close that he had already visualized the bankroll jammed in his wallet. Now he just saw darkness. If only Lute hadn't pulled that last ace from the deck, the finale would have been his.

Instead, all he had to show for his efforts was a second gift bag of coke and another quick errand for tomorrow. Lute's instructions were clear: take Harrison to one of the huts and hold him there until Lute arrived.

He would exercise his brain, make up something credible. Completing action items for both the sheriff and Lute wasn't really a conflict of interest. Coincidental that both men focused on the same pair.

How his sister got in the middle of it all was too confusing to figure out. At least she would be unharmed if he could convince her not to do something stupid. Manipulating Harrison would be child's play, if the guy thought his actions would benefit Megan somehow.

He lifted his head from the can. Yeah, it wasn't sounding too bad after all. He couldn't lose. Pleasing two bosses would make the rewards roll in faster. He already had the sheriff's trust. He'd been left in charge for tomorrow. Some last minute trip. Perfect. The extra leeway would make fulfilling Lute's request even easier. And with Lute providing the white powder entertainment, life wouldn't be so bad.

Should he celebrate? He grinned, laying back on his bed. Now or later. The choice was his.

Wait. Hadn't he promised the sheriff he'd do something? He frowned, trying to force a coherent thought through the foggy haze. Yeah, early this evening, when Russell had spoken with him about tomorrow's trip.

For one dismal minute, he'd thought that his boss was assigning him extra work. Late night duty such that he would miss the game. Instead Russell had asked him to stay away from the Okanogan forest, except for visiting Megan. He was to keep her home, out of the woods, for the next few days. Scott had readily agreed. His boss must have noticed he was confused, because he'd hurried to explain that he'd be away for awhile. Scott was to be in charge of the office.

If he were truly in charge, then he could decide whether he'd stay behind a desk or venture into the mountains. After all, being the top man commanded a certain amount of authority. It also required sound decision-making ability. The sheriff wouldn't have chosen him if he doubted his judgment.

Speaking of decisions, he pulled the baggie from his pocket. The gift bag from Lute. A good faith gesture. A pre-payment for services not yet rendered. Coke this time, not crack. He'd taken it, not wanting to appear ungrateful. It was just that since he'd switched from snorting to smoking, his nose was beginning to heal.

The plastic sack turned and spun in his hand. Did he want it now? Had he decided? It would erase the memory of tonight's loss. Erase his feelings of betrayal by Megan. Re-knit his broken dreams, if only for one night.

His hand dropped to his chest and his eyelids closed. No, not yet. He'd finish off his crack tonight. He would save this stuff for tomorrow.

EIGHTEEN

MEGAN AWOKE TO unfamiliar yet welcome sensations: a warm, solid chest pressed against her back, a strong arm encircling her waist. They must have slept like this, spoon-fashion, throughout the night. She couldn't remember having the energy to move after finally making it from the living room to the bed.

She ran her fingertips over Rey's forearm, testing to make sure he was real. He responded by pressing her tighter to him. Was he awake? She would never be able to fall back asleep with him so close. Her heartbeat quickened, as did her desire.

Last night he'd proved himself a man of great imagination. In fact, his ideas and her curiosity were nicely matched. She sighed. A long, memory-wracked day lay ahead. The person who'd threatened her by entering her home, leaving her unwanted gifts and warning messages, was still at large. She would venture out there soon, exposing herself to the intruder. Because despite all the dangers, she still had a job to do or others may die.

Thia. Today was the anniversary of her death.

Megan tried to slip free of the protective arms holding her. His grasp tightened. "Going somewhere?"

"Yes." She rolled onto her back. Staying here, like this, forever would be heaven.

He cradled her breast in his palm. "Think again." After nuzzling her ear, he tucked her head beneath his chin and resumed his steady breathing.

They felt so right together. Hardly the millionaire and the forest ranger at all. Hopping out of bed to pour him a bowl of cold cereal seemed laughable. Why not let the maid do it? Even funnier was the fact that he was typically the one fixing meals for her.

Could he run his ski wear company from the wilderness with only a snowmobile for transportation? Not likely. Could she survive in the city without her beloved mountains to race across? Maybe. First, though, she should go for it. See where her dream of being a biathlete might take her. To succeed, the initial step was to try. Give it her all. Then, at least, she would know.

Where did that leave them? At ground zero. Except for one thing. For a brief moment in time, last night, they'd both been hopelessly and emphatically in love. Or in lust. Most likely, a lot of both. She pressed a quick kiss to his neck. "Rey?"

"Hmmm?"

"I can't simply lie here all day."

"We really must straighten out your priorities." His voice was as warm and snugly against her skin as a fleece jacket. "We'll work on that. Later."

She smiled. She loved his half-asleep persona. So uncharacteristic of him. She wiggled her head out from beneath his chin and kissed his unshaven jaw. "My top priorities all take place outdoors."

"Sounds cold." He sighed and stroked her hair. "But if you're game, I promise to give it a try."

Definitely lust. She stopped thinking, stopped planning her work day for a moment and simply indulged herself in the sensation of having him next to her. As she resettled herself against him, he abruptly raised himself to one elbow.

"Sorry. I wasn't thinking." He rubbed his hand over his eyes. "What time is it?"

"Seven." She was no longer interested in rising from the bed. "What are you apologizing for?"

"Your entire day will be off." He glanced out the window. Dark clouds were obscuring the morning sun. "We may be in for another storm today."

"So, I'll skip part of my morning workout." She placed her hand on his shoulder. "I'll make up the time later."

He leaned over and brushed his lips over her forehead. "Forget it. Out of bed. Your training is a promise you made to yourself. I'm not going to interfere. Besides, there's no way to predict what else might surface today."

Though he hadn't explicitly said it, he must be thinking the same thing she had earlier. The danger was still out there.

"All right." She sat up, pulling her half of the sheets around her. "But let's compromise." She looked down at him, still partially hidden beneath the covers. "After the snow pits, would you like to accompany me on my practice runs?"

He grinned lazily. "You have to ask?"

Lingering a few additional moments felt so tempting, with him lying there on her lace-edged pillowcase. She quickly swung her bare feet to the floor and scooted to the edge of the mattress. "Afterwards we'll swing by Desolation Point. I've been thinking I'd like to visit the hut again. I believe Thia and Pete were trying to tell us something in the photo."

"Such as?"

"I don't know. Maybe we missed something. Maybe everyone did." She reached for Rachel's snapshots on her desk, beneath

Rey's e-mail reports. "I was glancing at these again yesterday." She flipped through them, then handed him the stack. "Take a look at the one on top."

He did.

"Thia would have posed for this picture solo, not sat tamely at Pete's side. There's something inside the hut we're missing." She tucked the covers more securely beneath her arms. "Or else Thia would have chosen an outdoor setting, flashing her world-famous smile and showing off whatever ski wear she was being paid to peddle that week."

"Watch it. Now you're traipsing close to my line of work."

"Sorry." She glanced at him. "By the way, did those little black boxers carry the Moore Comfort logo? I didn't have a chance to examine them thoroughly."

With the photos secure in one hand, he sat up. He positioned himself next to her on the mattress's edge and kissed her. "Would you like to?"

His voice had turned husky. She ached for his touch. "Of course I would." She wanted to feel his hands on her again, too. Wanted the world to remain at bay to let them simply enjoy each other for awhile. She lifted the blanket. "Oh, excuse me. You're not wearing them."

"That's it. Now you've really asked for trouble." Her smile was replaced by laughter as he took her by the shoulders and rolled her back onto the bed.

"Wait, Rey. I have work to do."

"You should have thought of that before." He buried his head between her breasts and began nibbling his way toward her navel. The photos spilled from her hand onto the sheets.

She considered not gathering them until later, but knew they'd be crushed within minutes. As she reached for the stack, the top picture caught her attention. Thia and Pete, laying crooked and broken in the snow. The incongruity of the situation that had been nagging at her suddenly became clear. "That's it!"

Rey lifted his head. "Not really, love, but I'm getting very close."

"No, look at this."

He held her gaze as if ready to debate her timing, then stopped. His manner turned serious as he looked at the snapshot. "What, specifically?"

"No skis."

"What do you mean?"

"Neither Pete nor Thia are wearing skis."

"So? Someone could have removed them."

"Wouldn't the first snapshots be taken before the scene was touched?"

"You're right. But their bindings might have released when they fell." Rey shrugged. "It would be unusual for all four to come loose, but still, it's possible isn't it?"

"No. Stop thinking 'downhill' for a moment." Ignoring her state of undress, Megan got up and quickly crossed the room. She donned a bathrobe from her closet then opened the bedroom door.

"Where are you going?"

"Downstairs. Come on."

❋   ❋   ❋

Megan crossed the living room, haphazardly tying her bathrobe. Rey was close behind, his bare feet pounding across the wooden floor. She glanced at him over her shoulder. His shirt hung open and he was still in the process of zipping his jeans. When he looked up, he caught her glancing at him. He smiled. "I hope Rachel doesn't decide to visit this morning."

"At least not until we're dressed. There's no use locking the front door, though. She has a key." She reached the staircase leading to the lower level.

"Wait." He touched her arm. "What did you just say?"

"Rachel has a key. You don't think she had anything to do with the arson, do you?"

"When it comes to your safety, I suspect everyone."

She pulled away, frowning. "Don't be ridiculous."

"All right then, convince me. Who else has a key?"

"Scott."

"Of course." He sighed. "Now I feel safe."

Her brother had many faults, but this was going too far. "You're questioning his involvement, too?" Her voice was louder than she'd intended.

"Megan. There was no evidence of a break in."

"One thing at a time. For now, let's concentrate on the skis."

"All right. Lead the way."

She quickly went down the steps. He followed behind. Once downstairs, she knelt and reached beneath the first twin bed and pulled a long nylon bag free. She opened it. "Thia wore these on her last day. Look at this."

He sat next to her on the floor. She pointed to the release mechanism. "Her bindings were customized. Metal throughout, no plastic clips. Specifically designed not to come apart."

"But what if she were to fall during a race? She could break a leg or tear a ligament."

"Thia worried more about an accidental release at the rifle range. It happened to her once at Nationals, when she was rising from the prone firing position. She lost valuable time and, because of it, the race."

He nodded.

"See these pins?" She pushed back the thick metal bar.

Rey leaned closer. "Yes."

"The toe of her boot has matching holes. Here, I'll show you. Hold this." Handing him the ski she reached for a second bag. She slipped one of Thia's boots onto the pins. "When the bar is clamped down like this," she secured the binding, "the toe is fixed into position. The police report showed nothing bent or damaged in the fall." She glanced up. "This bar could only have been released intentionally."

He frowned and was silent.

She stood. "Here, let me demonstrate."

"I believe you." He put his hand on her arm, stopping her from rising. "It's just hard to comprehend all at once."

He never doubted her. Not her word, not her abilities. It was yet another thing that set him apart from everyone else in her life. A knot formed in her throat. God, she was glad he was here.

His touch was firm and steady. "If your sister's skis landed thirty feet away, that could only mean one thing."

She nodded. "When Thia went over the edge of Devil's Elbow, she wasn't skiing."

❄   ❄   ❄

Sheriff Russell slammed his office door shut. The less anyone overheard, the better. He gripped the phone tighter. "Megan, I told you to leave it alone."

"I can't. Her skis were physically removed before she fell. No way could they have simply fallen off."

"We don't know any more now than we did a year ago."

"The same person who removed her skis might have stolen her scarf. That would explain how it reappeared. Ever think of that?"

"A used scarf is not exactly a hot commodity. Drop it."

"She was my sister. I can't." Her voice caught. "I have to know."

He stared out the window, positioning the receiver between jaw and shoulder. How had he gotten in so deep? When he could speak once again, his tone was soft. "She's dead. I'm sorry but no one, no unraveling of year-old events, can bring her back."

"What about the pictures? Pete must have take them for a reason: to send a message. About the hut."

He paced the length of his office. "They were goofing off, nothing more. I would have noticed if . . ." He winced then cursed silently.

There was a long pause before he heard her voice again. It was unnaturally quiet. "Russell, what are you saying?"

"Nothing. There was no message. And certainly no reason for you and Harrison to head up there today. Stay away."

"You were there." Her words were close to a whisper. "I can't believe it."

"All right, so I saw them. Big deal." His neck ached. He transferred the phone to his hand. "You were also on the mountain that last morning. Afterwards." He cleared his throat, not wanting to reopen the subject again after so adequately closing it yesterday.

That seemed to stop her. He waited, pacing to the door and back.

"This is different. You were the last person to see them alive." Her voice seemed to drift off, as if she were no longer holding the receiver to her mouth. "And all this time, I thought I was."

He spoke to her gently, consolingly. "Okay, I did see them. I admit it."

"Why didn't you tell me?"

"I saw nothing worth mentioning. I felt extraneous so I left."

"Don't feed me that line about Thia and Pete having an affair." She'd regained her composure. Her tone was crisp and strong again across the line. "I won't buy it. Not like Rachel did."

He didn't bother objecting.

"You lied to me, Carrol. After all our honesty on other subjects, you were still lying through your teeth on this one."

"I did not. We didn't discuss my presence at the hut one way or another."

"Don't give me that crap."

He shoved his hand into his pocket and leaned against his desk, crossing his feet at the ankles. "What purpose would it have served for me to mention it after so long?"

"You neglected to put it in your report last year, too." She drew a sharp breath. "My God."

"What?"

"No wonder you knew about the tripod. I should have figured that out yesterday."

He straightened. The hair on the back of his neck was at attention. "Megan, tell me again about the pictures on Pete's camera. How many were there and who else was in them?"

"This is funny, you asking me."

"Listen to me carefully."

"No." Her voice had increased in volume. "It's none of your damned business, Sheriff. You didn't care about them then, why the hell should I share them now?"

Russell had the urge to kick something. His chair. The side of his desk. He didn't want the noise to bring his deputy running. He spoke slowly, enunciating each word. "If it gets out that you have photos, even if you've seen and no longer have them, you're as good as dead. This isn't funny anymore."

"It never was."

His ear hurt. He switched sides. "Sorry for the choice of words." He'd screwed up, big time. How could he get through to her, so there wouldn't be other accidents to regret?

"Nothing has changed, Megan. Your going to Desolation Point hut today is fruitless and dangerous. I've asked Scott to stay away also." He ran his fingers back through his hair. "Hell, I'm scheduled to leave town shortly myself."

"Where are you going?"

"Anywhere, other than here." He walked toward the window again. Bending one of the mini-blind slats, looked out. "If I'm worried enough to warn Scott away, for God's sake don't you think you should avoid the place?"

"You know something you're not saying."

"Megan, my phone's bugged. I bet yours is, too."

"Russell, how long were you there the day Thia died?"

A goddamned one-track mind. Where was she going with it this time? "Why?" He exhaled and let go of the blinds. "Do you think I was fool enough to stick around for the actual event?"

"Were you there long enough to see an out-of-place person? Or some unusual air traffic, such as a helicopter with gunmen, perhaps?"

"No. I came directly back to town."

Another long pause. She was getting too close. His nerves were frayed. He crossed to the desk, dropped into his chair.

When her voice came again, the tone was mocking. "Kind of a long trip for only a few minutes, Carrol. Sounds as if you might have been meeting someone."

His patience snapped. "I had a lot on my mind, as you recall. I needed the fresh air. You of all people should understand that." He waited, hoping she'd accept his reasoning. "Look, if it will make you sleep better, I'll take you up there myself. Someday." He raised his voice another degree. "But not today."

"Thanks for the generous offer, but I'm sleeping quite well, thank you."

Shit. Was she implying what he thought? "All right, today then. I'll come up early afternoon. I'll take a look at the vandalism to your cabin while I'm there."

"How nice." Her tone changed to attack mode again. "That happened two days ago, Russell, the fire was four. I haven't seen you in the mountains all week. Why bother now?"

"I sent Scott. I'm still waiting for his report."

"Right. We'll talk about him another day." He heard her sigh. "Rey and I cleaned up most of the mess. We couldn't wait any longer."

"Did you consider fingerprints? You've all but wiped them out."

"I didn't think it would matter. There's no one to press charges against. No break in. I figured one of two things happened. First, the person was a professional and would wear gloves. Or it was someone I know well enough to give a key to. In the second case, their fingerprints would already be present, right? Rey agreed with that reasoning."

The way she threw his name into every bit of dialogue grated on Russell's nerves. Time to send her guest on his way. With Harrison gone, Megan's activities would be easier to monitor. She would have a much better chance of coming through this alive. After all, they had never actually targeted her, as far as he knew.

"Then consider my visit a neighborly house call. After all, I have good news to deliver."

"Such as?"

"I'm giving Harrison his walking papers. He's no longer a suspect; he can go."

"Rey, leave?"

He hated the way her voice sounded wistful. He kept his tone upbeat. "Not only can, but should. I'll personally escort him out of town. Today."

"Why?"

They were tighter than he'd feared. Maybe consoling her would help. "I know it seems fast, but I believe it's for the best. After all, one of the two men Harrison saw last Saturday is still alive. Need I say more?"

"What are you implying?"

He cupped his hand around the receiver. "The second man may have been here in Snagtooth. There was a stranger in town yesterday who fit the description."

"He's after Rey?"

"My recommendation is that Harrison escape into the anonymity of Seattle. He's been using a false name here the entire time. Unless word has already leaked out on that, he just might be safe if he leaves now."

"Rey's in danger." Her tone was flat, her words repetitive. The difference was, it was no longer a question. He was finally getting through.

"Yes, Megan. Let him go."

❋　　　❋　　　❋

After his workout, Rey found Megan sitting in her room, staring at the floor. Her bed was still unmade. Not like her at all. "I thought you'd still be out in the field. Finished so soon?"

She looked up at him. "I didn't go."

"You've been here the entire time? Megan, what happened?" The photos again? He reached out, took her hand.

She stood, kissed him absently on the cheek, then paced toward the window. More staring. Her expression tore at his heart.

"Please tell me. Maybe I can help."

"No." The same faraway tone. "Rey, you have to leave. Immediately."

"I'm not leaving. Someday, yes, but not now." They hadn't discussed yet how they would continue their relationship, but they'd find a way. Some solution that met both their needs. She was committed to the slopes; that pretty well ruled out his Seattle condo. But he could design ski wear from almost anywhere.

"You have to leave today." She turned away from the window but her eyes remained averted. "Russell said you're free to go."

"Is that right?"

She nodded. "You're cleared of all charges."

"I never signed a single deposition. Never talked to a law enforcement officer other than our good sheriff. I never even saw the charges of which I'm now cleared. Doesn't that seem strange?"

He crossed slowly to the window and stood before her. "This is bullshit and you know it." He softened his voice and reached out to touch her shoulder. "Do we have to play this game or will you simply tell me what happened?"

She looked at him steadily. Her lips moved as if she were about to speak but no words came forth. After a moment, she stopped trying and walked directly into his arms. Her hands pressed tightly against his back, her head lay against his chest. "You're in danger."

He tightened his embrace. "What exactly did Russell say?"

"There were two men in the chopper, the day of your avalanche." Her voice caught. She cleared her throat and tried again. "The boy is dead, but the man's here in town. Looking for you."

He stared at her, so safely tucked in his arms, and kissed the top of her head. "Megan, you don't know me very well if you think I would desert you in the midst of this danger. I can't." He drew back so she'd look at him. "I won't."

"You have to leave."

"Then come with me." He felt her sharp intake of breath. "Not forever. Just for now." He brought his hands to her shoulders and gently massaged the area above her collar bone. "I love you. The rest we'll figure out from the safety of Seattle. Pack whatever you need for a week or so. We'll take off as soon as possible."

"What about my job? Granny? Rachel?"

"We'll tell them, as soon as we're safe." He cradled her head in his palms. "Remember, I'm not asking you to leave your mountain forever. We'll be back. As soon as this is over."

She went still in his arms. Her embrace loosened. Her eyes seemed to search his face. He was no fool. For her to walk away from all she knew and everyone she loved, for her to go with him, was a lot for him to ask. And he was asking her to decide right now. "So, what do you say?"

Stress lines were etched on her forehead. He held his breath, awaiting her response. When it came it was tentative but, thank God, also affirmative. "I'll get my duffel bag."

❆   ❆   ❆

Rey folded his sweat pants and placed them in his bag. His drawer was nearly empty. He would pack Megan's things next. She'd left her clothes and toiletries out on the bed, then dashed off to tell Rachel. He'd offered to pack for her to save time. Once in town, they'd rent a car and drive to Winthrop. Dave could have the jet pick them up there.

He would miss being here. The outside world had ceased to exist for them for a few, precious hours last night. The fire's glow had created the most interesting shadows as it danced across her skin. She had laughed as he chased them with his tongue. The crackling and hissing of the burning logs provided a perfect backdrop, more closely mimicking their urgency than any soft, romantic music ever could.

A new beginning. They would find a way to make it work.

He scooped up the final contents of his drawer and stuffed it in his bag. After securing the flap, he slung his back pack over one arm and climbed the steps. It took a second trip to retrieve his skis and poles. After everything was stacked by the upstairs door, he crossed to Megan's room to use her phone. If he couldn't reach Dave, they would be in for a long drive back to Seattle.

He lifted the receiver. Her phone was dead. He frowned then glanced at the router. The dial was set to Modem. Had it been set incorrectly all night? Did Dave try to reach him? After flipping the toggle switch, he heard the tone and quickly punched in the numbers.

His corporate answering service picked up on the first ring instead of the usual fourth. He frowned as he heard the operator come on the line. He identified himself and asked for Dave.

"The offices are closed, Mr. Moore."

"Why?"

"It's Sunday, sir."

Damn. When was the last time he'd forgotten the day of the week? The Okanogan had done this to him. No rush hours, no morning television news, no *Wall Street Journal.* He smiled. Nice, actually. "Thank you. I'd say this has been a successful vacation for me, wouldn't you agree?"

"Yes, sir." He heard laughter in her voice.

"Please send me through to Mr. Edwards voice mail then."

"Right away, sir."

After leaving a synopsis of the situation on Dave's private line, Rey tried reaching him at home. No response there either. He left a second message at that number. Next he called his own home, attempting to find Ali. At the very least she'd be amused that big brother had thought of calling her in order to find Dave. No answer again.

He switched back to Modem. He connected to his office account. Surely if his partner went away for the weekend, he would have left an electronic note.

There were several. The report on Russell sent a shiver down Rey's spine. Where was he getting his cocaine supply? Here in Snagtooth? Maybe Scott had picked up his habit at the office. Rey couldn't wait to discuss that angle with Megan.

Megan. Rey stopped typing and looked up from the computer screen. His heart hammered against his chest. She had met with Russell alone yesterday, confronting him with more details of Thia and Pete's death. Then another phone call this morning. The sheriff had tried to convince her, through scare tactics, to send him back to Seattle. If Russell were involved with the deaths somehow, and if Megan had provoked him . . .

Rey couldn't finish the thought. Too many ifs. Too many horrific possibilities.

He disconnected the computer, ripped the hard copy of the report from printer and switched the router back to Line. Dave was on his way. Hopefully he was bringing reinforcements.

There was a knock on the front door of the cabin. "Just a minute." He shoved the report into a file folder on top of her desk and stood. As he approached the door, Russell's face appeared in the window.

Sheriff Russell. Alias Carrol the womanizer, Rusty the pusher. Confronting the man was something Rey looked forward to. But not now. Not when the backlash could affect Megan. There was no way to predict what the man might do, or what he might already have done. Rey would get the two of them safely away from here and then deal with the sheriff. With pleasure.

❄   ❄   ❄

Rey opened the cabin door. "Sheriff. Good to see you. I heard about your generous offer." Calm and cool, he reminded himself. No badgering.

Sheriff Russell entered and pulled off his hat. "I hope you're referring to my providing you taxi service to the nearest town."

"Exactly. We're almost ready. Megan will be back shortly."

"We?" Russell stepped forward. "What in the hell do you mean, we?"

"She's going with me. View it as a short vacation, until things settle down. There's been too much anxiety lately." He kept his tone cordial. "While she's gone, Scott can keep her posted on developments."

"Megan's not leaving."

The sheriff was in his face, expression flushed, jaw hard. Rey didn't waver, didn't blink. Instead, he countered with a quiet and steady voice. "And when did you start making decisions for her?"

Russell remained eye-to-eye with him, inches away. After a moment, he stepped back. "When exactly did she plan to return?"

"We haven't discussed a date."

"How do I know she'll come home at all?"

"You don't."

Regret crossed the man's face. Rey hadn't expected that, not after the information Megan had given him. Maybe there was a heart inside that chest after all. He decided to take a chance. "You and I started off at odds with each other and never got back on track. For whatever reason, I'd like to set that straight between us. I love Megan. I plan to build a life with her, wherever she wants, whatever it takes."

Russell pressed a hand to his temples. "All right, Harrison. I mean, Moore. Whoever the hell you are. I guess it is time for us to level with each other." He exhaled slowly. "I care for Megan, too. She's been hurt."

"I heard."

Russell raised his head and looked directly at him. Seemed to ponder the words for a moment. "Yeah. Well, I'm the bastard who did it, but it sounds as if you already know that." Moments passed before he continued. "There were several piss-poor reasons involved. I'd like the chance to make it up to her."

There was some decency. Rey was pleasantly surprised. He took the edge off his voice. "Then let her go."

"That's not what I meant."

"I know. Now let me make myself clear." He waited until he had Russell's full attention. "You had your chance, now it's mine. And I intend to spend the rest of my life making her happy."

"Well, you're off to a real bad start." The sheriff advanced again, his hands clenched. "Megan's been in danger ever since you got here, city boy. You brought it into her home, surrounded her with it."

"That was timing. It had nothing to do with me."

"And now you're leading her by the hand into something much worse."

"What do you mean?"

Russell snorted. "The organization you stumbled into has far-reaching arms. Branch offices, let's say, in your corporate lingo. They've seen you. They're after you. How in the hell are you going to keep yourself safe, much less her?"

"A bodyguard, if needed."

"Megan Jeffers on a leash. Right. She'd wither and die with those restrictions. With her by your side, you double your chances of being discovered." Russell's expression hardened. "They're after you, Harrison, not her. But if they track you down, and she's with you, they'll get her too."

Rey was silent.

"Leave her with me. I know their basic plan. It's almost over. I'll keep her outside the action." Russell shoved his hands into his pockets, then looked down at the floor. "I can't stop what's going down, but I can keep her safe."

That summed up the man's main fault, right there. He wasn't really corrupt, or uncaring. Just weak. "Do you have trouble living with yourself?" Rey winced at his word choice, but at least the tone had been right. Sympathetic.

The sheriff raised his head. "I've made mistakes, I admit it. Small ones, that led to huge sinkholes. As soon as I can manage it, I'm history around here. I'll start over somewhere, clean. But right now we're not discussing me. It's Megan I'm worried about."

Rey nodded as he watched him. The man had dug his own sorry grave, but at least he recognized it.

"She'll be safe, Harrison, I swear it. And when it's over, then you can start this life together that you're planning."

Rey frowned. "Why the big-hearted gesture? What do you get out of it, a clear conscience?"

"I'll level with you. With you gone, not only will it be safer for her, but I get a second chance. It's as simple as that."

Rey paused. Actually, that was excellent motivation. If Russell genuinely cared about her, then he would fight to protect her.

He glanced at his gear. Hers was still unpacked, in the bedroom, her clothes stacked on the bed. The empty bag triggered an image of the two men from the chopper again. This time instead of focusing on the scarf the boy was wearing or on the guns the men carried, a vision of their flat burlap sacks came to mind. He straightened.

The men had been there to pick something up, not to drop off. Were they Russell's drug source? He and Megan had planned to visit the hut again this afternoon. Could he convince Russell to take him there, and leave Megan out of it? Away from danger? How ironic that he was scrambling for a way to visit the Desolation Hut now, when he and Megan had spent all night there just a short while ago.

Stall tactics, that was it. He needed for the sheriff to believe he was cooperating, yet at the same time, delay his actual departure. At least until Dave arrived. Something credible. A trip to the hut sounded perfect.

Rey nodded. "All right. You're making good sense. I'll agree to leave with you, under one condition."

"Name it."

"We stop by the Desolation Hut first."

"Are you nuts?"

"I've been without my tape recorder this past week." True. Dave had it.

"The hut is the last place you should be."

Something big was about to happen, he could sense it in Russell's nervousness. The way he kept shifting his eyes, clenching his fists. Keeping Megan out of the way was sounding better all the time.

She'd be upset if she thought he was protecting her, but actually it would be the other way around. Megan would figure out what he'd done, the farce he'd set up to make the diversion happen. She would call the right people, marshall forces. Instead of protecting her, she'd be protecting him.

He kept his tone unhurried. "The tape has notes on it from last Saturday's field test. Without it," he shrugged, "we'll have to rerun the tests almost immediately."

"Meaning, you'll be back."

"Correct." Bull's-eye. The last thing the sheriff wanted to hear. Rey went on casually, as if the stakes weren't enormous. "It was last used at the hut. It's small and black, could have easily slid under the bed out of sight. I want the chance to retrieve it."

"I'll mail it to you when it's found."

"No deal." Megan's snowmobile sounded in the distance. Rey walked toward the window and looked out. She would be here any minute. Russell's nervousness increased. Rey pressed the advantage. "Do I go or stay?"

The sheriff crossed to the window and stood next to him. Together they watched as the shiny black Vmax pulled into the yard. Russell turned to him. "I don't trust you."

"So? We have a second thing in common."

"And, what was the first?"

"We want the same woman."

After a slight hesitation, Russell nodded. "All right, you son of a bitch. It's a deal."

NINETEEN

MEGAN TURNED ONTO the snow-covered trail that led to her cabin. Her current home. The one she'd be locking up within the hour to travel with Rey to Seattle. The week ahead would be almost as nerve-racking as the one prior. She hoped it would have a happier, clearer ending.

Searching for Rachel this morning had been futile. The Rescue Rangers weren't practicing at their designated spot. A call to the office confirmed that the patrol was dispatched to a real avalanche site, one too far for her to travel to in the current weather conditions. Radioing the team was an option, but there would be no privacy.

She briefly considered leaving a note on Rachel's kitchen table, but preferred not to say good-bye on paper. Neither would she identify in writing what she just learned about Russell. Her cabin had been broken into. Rachel's might be next. The fact Russell had been at the hut the morning of Pete and Thia's deaths, then lied about it afterwards, changed everything. She wanted to share that with her friend in person.

As she came around the last turn, she spotted Russell's snow-mobile. Adrenaline shot through her. She glanced toward the cabin. Two heads were visible in the window. She waved. They must have turned away.

Rey, be careful.

Parking her Vmax near the charred remains of the shed, she hurried up the stairs, then entered. Both men were somber. They'd been talking, but what about? She crossed to where Rey stood and gave him a quick kiss. His response was uncharacteristically cool. Was he surprised by her display of affection?

She glanced at the sheriff. "I wasn't expecting to see you." She unzipped her coat and tossed it on the nearest chair.

"I told you I would be here. I've released Harrison from his obligation to stay. I came right away. There's no reason to delay."

"Great. For once, we're in perfect agreement." She linked her arm with Rey's and looked up at him. "Are we all packed?"

"Not exactly." He tilted his head toward the pile of belongings by the door. Her gaze followed. Only his bags were there.

"You were obviously interrupted." She kept her smile in place and started to move away toward the bedroom. "I'll finish. It will only take me a moment."

His arm, intertwined with hers, tightened. "Megan, there's been a small change in plans."

"Oh?" She hated the sound of that.

"Something urgent at the office. It will keep me occupied most of next week." His eyes were fixed on hers. His tone was precise, business-like. The voice of a CEO. Had he already returned to his other world, without her?

"The details are in the file folder on top of your desk, if you want to know more."

"I don't think I do." Her ears thundered; her heartbeat quickened.

"Please review them anyway. They explain the situation quite clearly."

"I see."

She pulled away. He reached for her hand. At the same time, his expression softened.

"After thinking it over, I decided it would be better if I traveled back ahead of you." With a hint of laughter, he lightened the message. To her it seemed forced. "It will give me time to ready things at the condo. I'll send for you in a few days."

"Send for me?"

"Yes."

She didn't attempt to hide her sarcasm. "And what sort of things are you readying?"

"Your bodyguard, for example."

Her throat constricted. She forced out the words. "Excuse me?"

"A personal bodyguard. You'll need protection round-the-clock until things blow over."

She wrenched her hand free from his. Taking a step closer, she positioned herself so that Russell was at her back. It was humiliating enough that he was observing this, but she refused to look at him. She kept her eyes fixed on Rey. "I need protection in the city, but here I'm free to come and go?" Tears burned in her eyes. She willed them not to fall. "I must have missed something."

Did he meet Russell's eyes for a moment, over her shoulder, or was she imagining things? She suppressed the urge to turn around and confirm it. Instead she searched Rey's face for an answer. What had transpired in the last hour?

He continued, calm and cool. Not the man she knew at all. Certainly not the man she loved. "Sheriff Russell offered to personally watch over you. He's given me his word you will be safe."

A shiver ran through her, raising goose flesh on her arms. It was beginning to make sense. A glimmer of light. It was bullshit, plain and simple. Delivered with the face of a poker player and the voice of a corporate executive. Why, though? Had he learned something new? Something threatening the safety of their plan?

Take it slow, keep him talking. Listen for what he can't say. She added a dose of stubbornness to her tone. "You decided all of this without me."

"Yes. I knew you'd understand."

Definitely bullshit. She'd be pissed and he knew it. Somehow they were trapped. She played along. "Well, guess again."

"What?"

"Send for me all you want." Hands on hips, she stepped forward, her chin raised. "Staying here is sounding better with every passing minute."

She turned toward the sheriff. He was practically smiling. She gave him a share of her playacting. "You said he was free to go, didn't you?"

Russell straightened, his grin disappeared. "He is."

"And he's ready."

"Yes."

"Then what are you waiting for? I have things to do. Such as reading reports. How fun." She tilted her head in Rey's direction, mocking his request, but didn't chance a look at him. "You two can be on your way any time, as far as I'm concerned."

"Well." Russell cleared his throat and backed up a step. "I guess there's no use in sticking around then, is there?"

Rey shook his head slowly. "And since we're stopping by Desolation Point before going into town, the sooner we get started the better."

Megan's blood turned to ice. "The hut? Why?"

"I haven't seen my recorder in days. The last place I used it was at the hut. Maybe it fell on the floor."

She nodded coolly, amazed she could move at all. "It could have slipped beneath the bed."

His eyes met hers. "I plan to check there first."

After a moment, he turned and walked toward his gear. It was as if she were watching him head straight into danger. Was that he wanted her to do?

He put on his coat. "I left Dave a message earlier. He will probably attempt to contact me here within the hour."

She nodded, listening intently.

"Tell him about my revised travel plan."

"All right."

"Then I guess we're off." After picking up his backpack, he approached her for a final time. He touched her cheek. "Take care." After one last brush of his mouth against her cheek, he was gone.

❄   ❄   ❄

Megan's fingers tightened, crumpling the edge of the report. She'd found the print-out exactly where Rey said it would be. It explained Russell's connection with drugs. Her heart pounded as she read the closing line. Dave was coming today. Intended to arrive shortly after noon. It was nearly two P.M. now. Why hadn't Rey waited? Why take such a risk?

She paced the floor of her bedroom. If Russell was a pusher, he could easily be involved in other illegal activities. He'd been sheriff for more than three years. Besides dealing drugs and being somehow linked to Thia and Pete's death, what else had he done?

"Rusty." The alias sounded strange to her ears, though she'd heard it before. It was his high school nickname. Thia had referred to it once when they were thumbing through old yearbooks together. Russell had been a dozen years ahead of them in school. His record as quarterback still remained unbroken. Together they had laughed at the ancient picture of him under the book's section, Snagtooth Hall of Fame.

The second time Thia mentioned his nickname he'd been present. Her sister had never brought it up again. Megan let her thoughts wander back, to other times with Thia. To other memories that might make a difference now.

A shoulder injury caused Russell to lose his athletic scholarship. Years of job hopping followed. No one had expected him to amount to much. But as sheriff, he'd shown them all. It must have taken courage to run for office. Why throw all that away?

Megan froze, afraid to let the next thought come. "Oh, God. No." She tried to force it from her mind before it could fully materialize, but was too late. Scott's habit must have started at work.

Russell wouldn't have forced the drugs on her brother, just make them easily available. Becoming hooked was still Scott's fault. What infuriated her most was that Russell hadn't told her. He'd let it continue, untreated. For that, she could never forgive him.

Megan heard an approaching snowmobile and bent the blinds to peer out the window. Dave and Ali. Thank God. She rushed from the room and yanked open the front door.

Ali waved excitedly. Dave pulled to a stop and released his chin strap. "Where's Rey?"

"Gone." Megan bolted down the stairs, not bothering with her parka. "He left with the sheriff thirty minutes ago. They're headed towards the Desolation Hut." She forced herself to slow down. "Snagtooth, after that. Waiting there for you, I guess."

"Damn. Why the hut?"

"He claimed he'd left the tape recorder there, the one containing notes from your field test."

"I took the recorder with me last Monday. He knew that." Frowning, Dave turned to Ali. "Did he mention anything about it?"

"No." Holding on to Dave's elbow, Ali swung herself off the vehicle. "I told him the notes from the tape had been transcribed. The recorder couldn't be lost."

That confirmed her worst fear. He'd been covering up his true intent. She glanced at the trail he'd taken with the sheriff. Clear, crisp tracks in last night's new snow. Straight up the mountain, directly into danger.

She crossed her arms over her chest, trying not to shiver. "He mentioned it might have slipped to the floor, but he wasn't free to speak. My God. Thia was pointing to the floor." She turned and stared at Dave. "There's something beneath the floorboards."

"What are you talking about?"

She quickly explained the pictures taken immediately before and after last year's murders. "Rey must be planning to check it out, despite the sheriff being with him."

"Let's go in." Ali cocked her thumb in the direction of the front door. "We'll be able to think clearer if our brains aren't frozen."

Dave agreed and led the way. As soon as they had their coats off, he paced the kitchen. Ali pulled out a chair, turned it backwards and straddled it. Megan sat across from her, elbows on table, chin in her palms. She told them about her agreement to accompany Rey to Seattle and the last minute change in plans after his private discussion with the sheriff.

Dave paused by the counter and leaned against it. "He mustn't have seen my report on Russell before he left."

"He did, though. He put it in a folder where I would find it after he was gone."

"Then why would he place his trust in the man?"

Her stomach turned. "It was his method of getting Russell away from the cabin, most likely. Away from me." She paused, not able to continue.

"He protects all of us, so stop feeling guilty. That's how he is, clear through to the bone." Ali gave her a sympathetic grin. "Get used to it. Believe me, there's no changing him. I've tried."

Megan felt warmed by Ali's words. Acceptance. Ali, for all of her outward geniality, was as protective of her brother as he was of her. To be included by Ali in the circle of those who loved, and were loved by Rey, meant a great deal to her.

She had to find him. Help him. She inhaled deeply, trying to stop trembling.

Dave put his hand on her shoulder. "He wouldn't have left without a plan."

"I know that. But . . .?"

"This is how I figure it." Ali stood and braced one foot against the chair. "He had to get Russell away from the cabin before we arrived. Who would go for help if he pulled a gun on all four of us? We'd be stuck." She glanced at Dave. "It's a simple principle: divide and conquer."

Megan's gaze met Dave's. "Makes sense to me."

He nodded. "She has a point."

"So we're supposed to go for help." Megan frowned. "But to whom? The sheriff has been deceiving this community for years. No one would believe us without evidence."

Dave pulled out a chair and sat. "Maybe it would help if we made a list of knowns and unknowns. Such as, why all this focus on one shack? On one specific mountain peak?"

Megan interlaced her fingers in front of her. "That hut's the nearest one to Devil's Elbow, where last Saturday's murder occurred."

"The same teenager also visited the Desolation Hut just hours before he died."

"My God." She leaned forward on her elbows. "That never occurred to me."

Ali pounded her fist on the table. "The boy was in the chopper that triggered Rey's avalanche." She glanced at Megan. "Is it possible for noise to shake something like that loose?"

"Of course." Megan stood. "We've got to do something. Now. But we have to be careful. Granny took in a new boarder on the same day Rey arrived. He could be legitimate, but my guess is he's not. I don't want to run into him accidentally."

"Rey asked me to do a trace on him." Dave paused. Megan held her breath. "There was no record at the University."

"Then Granny's not safe, either."

The sound of another snowmobile captured their attention. Ali started toward the door, but Dave grasped her arm. "Wait. And stay down. It could be the sheriff returning. For us."

❄   ❄   ❄

Megan refused to wait, there was too much at stake. Before the sound of the engine had died she was at the front door, peeking through the curtains. "It's Scott. Thank God."

She glanced at Ali and Dave, suddenly feeling uneasy. Awkward. How much could she say to them without being disloyal to her brother? "Scott hasn't been himself lately." Her voice trailed away as Dave's eyes met hers.

"I know. Rey told me."

Embarrassment warmed her face.

"Megan, we both have experience in dealing with cocaine addiction. First hand experience." Dave didn't look away. "We can help."

She stared at him then at Ali, reading between the lines what they weren't saying. "Thank you."

She watched as Scott stepped from his snowmobile. "Unless he's already high, we should ask for his help. He has contacts we can call. The other deputies. Maybe the Winthrop authorities."

Dave's tone was gentle. "If we do, and if Russell is his coke provider, we're risking a lot."

"I can't believe he would hurt anyone."

"You're about to stake your life on that."

"I know." Her voice was nearly a whisper as she glanced at them standing across from her. "And yours, too."

❋   ❋   ❋

Megan pulled open the door before her brother had a chance to knock. Walking out onto the ice-encrusted deck, she closed the door behind her and faced him alone. "Have you been snorting already this morning?" She hated the desperation she heard in her tone, but couldn't hide it. "Tell me the truth."

"That's none of your goddamned business."

"I need your help. Rey left with Russell thirty minutes ago. They're headed to Desolation Point."

"That's impossible. The sheriff's out of town for a few days."

"No, he was here. We have to find them."

"We?" He looked past her, toward the doorway and scowled. She turned, also. Dave's face was visible through the window. "What the hell are they doing back here?"

"Let's go in. We have to talk about Russell." Would he believe her? How far did his hero worship for Sheriff Russell go? Farther than look-alike boots? Opening the door, she followed him into the cabin. "Brace yourself. You're not going to like this."

She noticed he ignored both Ali's welcome and the nod Dave gave him. He stood rigidly by the door with arms crossed.

Her stomach was in knots. No use delaying. "Scott, we know how you've been getting your cocaine."

His expression turned hard. "You told them?" He tilted his head in Dave's direction.

"They knew about your problem long before I did."

"Right."

"They've both been there. In over their heads, just as you are. They can help." She pressed on, ignoring his derisive laugh. "Right now we need to focus on Russell. He's your supplier, isn't he?"

"That's bullshit."

"Well, this isn't. The sheriff has a younger sister, Betty, who's somewhat of a regular at the King County Jail." Megan repeated what she'd just learned. "Betty admitted to Ali that he was her source and supplies it to all of her friends."

She paused, expecting him to object again. Instead he seemed to be lost in thought. She continued. "That's enough to get him fired and put away for a long time." She waited until his eyes met hers. "As bad as that is, I'm afraid he's in even deeper trouble. And this time, Rey's with him."

She told him what she knew of Russell's presence at the hut before Thia and Pete's murder. His anger at learning about the film in Pete's camera. His attempted cover-up. His threats when found out. Through it all, Dave and Ali stood by quietly. She ended with the similarity of their sister's death to the recent murder.

"Murder?" Scott's face was red, his eyes wide. "Now you're claiming Thia was murdered? Well, I was part of that investigation. There was no proof."

"Thia wasn't skiing when she fell from Devil's Elbow. The bindings were manual release only, remember? The skis landed more than thirty feet away." It felt good to let her anger out. "It couldn't have been an accident, now could it?"

"I can't believe it." He swore under his breath. "How do you know all this, a year later?"

"I have pictures to prove it. They arrived yesterday."

"Murder." He was no longer listening. He shook his head as

he walked away.

Dave came forward and touched her shoulder. She forced herself to take a deep breath. "That's the first I've heard of this, Megan. Rey didn't mention it when we spoke on the phone."

"We discovered it this morning."

"Maybe Thia and Pete had a reason to stop above Devil's Elbow."

"The snow was too deep to traipse around in it. Besides, Thia wouldn't have taken a stroll beneath a cornice." She looked back at her brother. He was tuned in again and frowning.

"Scott?"

"Yeah?"

"Did the report note any footprints on the ridge above the accident site?"

"I don't know."

She tried another tack. "Were you involved in that part of the investigation? Maybe Russell didn't include you for some reason."

"He did so." Hostility flared in his eyes. "But we had other things to take care of, too. Couldn't let all of our time be sucked up into one stupid act of carelessness. Thia and Pete were lovers and weren't paying attention. Leave it at that."

So he'd bought the story, as Rachel had, these past twelve months. Megan looked directly at him. "Did you hear that fairy tale from Russell?"

"Of course." His tone was mocking. "Is it hard for you to accept that Miss Perfect Sister wasn't so perfect?"

"Scott, he fabricated that lie. One of many."

He seemed speechless. Finally she'd gotten through.

"Enough. Rey and the sheriff have over an hour's head start on us." She moved toward the door and grabbed her jacket. "Scott, go into town and get help. Call whoever you have to. Contact the Winthrop office for backup officers. We'll be at Desolation Point."

She turned to Dave and Ali. "Warm up both my vehicles. We'll leave your rental here, it's too lightweight for the terrain we'll be on. I'll grab spare ammunition from the basement and meet you outside. The keys are on the counter near Rey's cookie jar." She'd said that without thinking. His cookie jar.

"Rey's?" Ali lifted one eyebrow. "My brother eats cookies?"

"Not only eats them, bakes them, too." Memories of their earlier conversations around her kitchen table came drifting back. And the shorter talks while wrapped in each other's arms.

Dave reached for the keys and signaled to Ali. "Get your parka. We're leaving."

She followed, retrieving her jacket from the rack. "Rey knows how to cook?" She paused. "Wait. We're rescuing the wrong guy. I don't know this man."

Dave held open the door for Ali. "Save it for later."

Megan noticed that her brother still hadn't budged. His eyes had that far away look in them again. "Scott?"

He glanced her way, slowly. "Yeah?"

"Time's running out."

"Yes." Scott nodded. "Unfortunately, you're right."

❄   ❄   ❄

Scott pulled Megan's front door tightly closed behind him, pausing at the top of the stairs. He was ashamed. Those sad soulful eyes. Megan hadn't understood. Not at all. It made perfect sense to him, but she'd never buy into it. Would never see it his way. Not that any of it really mattered. He'd had a job to do and he did it. For her own good. He'd try to explain it to her again later. But for now, he had to move on.

He glanced out over the frozen lake toward Granny's. Purple flowers today. What fools. His boss wasn't at Desolation Point.

Russell would look at him with pride when he realized Scott had figured out the signal all by himself. His raise would be huge. He could certainly use it. The gift bag in his pocket wouldn't last long.

He descended the cabin steps and joined Ali and Dave by the snowmobiles. "A slight change in plans." He zipped his coat quickly, snapped the collar up and around his neck. He was calling the shots from here on out. "I just contacted the office. They'll send reinforcements in from Winthrop. No need for me to go back into town after all. Megan will wait here for them."

Ali frowned. "Shouldn't we all wait?"

Scott shook his head as he walked across to his sister's Vmax and turned it off. He palmed the key. "No need. We'll rendezvous with her at Cutthroat Peak."

Dave pulled his helmet off. "Just a minute. We're headed to Desolation Point."

"Sorry. They're already gone from there. The sheriff was spotted by air just a few minutes ago, much farther south, and to the east. Cutthroat's his destination now." Scott climbed onto his own vehicle.

Dave didn't appear convinced. He was still glancing back at the door. Bad sign. "Won't Megan need her keys if she's to join us?"

"Oh, yeah. Right. Guess I forgot." He grinned, trying to pretend the mistake had been a foolish one. "I'll just toss them on the counter." He stood and nearly jogged to the cabin. A heavy snow was beginning to fall. Before opening the door, he paused and looked at them. Steadied his voice.

"Stay there, I'll be right back."

TWENTY

L UTE OPENED THE menu and stared blankly at the day's selections. He'd seen them before, they were all bad. Fat, onions and starch, rearranged in various combinations so they'd resemble different culinary delights. No matter what he ordered it would all taste the same, just like the bile rising in his throat.

The laminated cardboard surface reflected the neon colors of the "Good Food" sign flashing behind him in the parking lot. Instead of welcoming people, it warned them. He'd picked this particular greasy spoon to be the meeting place because of the typically high number of empty seats. Disgusting, but perfect.

EJ should arrive any minute. Lute felt sorry for the kid but felt even sorrier for himself. He should have gotten out weeks ago, when the kids first started dying.

Billy was gone. This is why he'd been called back from Snagtooth. A replacement was needed. Lute, Recruiting Officer. He could put that on his next resume.

Though he never really liked the little shit, he winced at the memory. They'd found him in his room with a needle jammed in his arm. What a lonely way to die. Lute's bet was Cowboy arranged it. He swore under his breath. He'd told the kid to stop stealing from the kitchen, hadn't he?

Lute lowered his menu and glanced at Cowboy's thug smoking a cigar by the door to the diner. He would have to see today's assignment through. Then, at first chance, he'd disappear.

A dark-haired youth pushed open the swinging doors and looked nervously around. His hands were shoved into the pockets of his torn jeans. Stupid red tennis shoes. It had to be him.

EJ's eyes never stopped moving, assessing each diner. Lute gazed steadily in the kid's direction, wanting to make eye contact. Finally, the kid pushed back his baseball cap. Their eyes met. Lute gave him a subtle nod toward the bench seat across from him, then raised his menu again. He felt, rather than saw, the kid slide into the booth.

Time to spew the lies, hook him and reel him in. God, he hated this part. He mumbled the agreed-upon pass phrase. EJ responded correctly and on cue. Grimacing, he set his menu aside. The curtain was rising on the first act. "Thanks for coming. I'm Lute."

The kid fidgeted in his seat. "Where's Billy?"

"Couldn't make it."

"Then what am I doing here?" EJ frowned. "He should have canceled. Saved me the effort of coming this far north."

"He's gotten you assigned to a new job. It's too big to be handled by only one man." That much was true. Lute cleared his throat. "He recommended you, specifically."

"Why me?"

"He believed you could do it." Lute leaned forward. "Straight and simple, kid, this is your big chance."

EJ crossed his arms, elbows on the table. He was scowling. "For what?"

"Working the streets is pocket change, kid, compared to what you could be making. Don't you want a larger cut of the action? Billy did."

EJ didn't blink as the seconds ticked by.

Lute shrugged, switching tactics. "Those were his words, not mine. He was the one who thought you might be ready, not me." He glanced around as if bored. As if EJ's agreement wasn't a life or death matter.

EJ wrapped his fingers tightly around his water glass and drew it toward him. He cupped it between both palms. "I don't know."

"What's not to know? Money is money. Afterwards, go your separate way. You'll still have your part of the take."

"And Billy? He'll be along on this job?"

"He was looking forward to it." Another black mark on his soul.

They sat in silence for several moments. Lute dismissed the waitress who'd come to take his order. After she refilled his coffee and drifted to the next table, Lute pressed his point.

"We leave immediately. No waiting around, no changing your mind. Tomorrow, you and I are history." Personally, he planned to disappear forever. "So what do you say?"

The boy expelled a deep breath. "All right. Where do I meet you and when?"

"The when is now. You ride with me." He dug in his pocket and flipped several coins on the table.

"Now?"

Lute tilted his head toward the door. "We ride with him." He signaled a thumbs up to his watchdog.

The man hovering beyond the glass door dropped his smoke and crushed it beneath his toe. Lute stood and curled his hand beneath the teen's upper arm, helping him to his feet. Stepping back, he let EJ and his bright sneakers lead the way. "After you."

❄   ❄   ❄

Scott. How could he do this to her? Megan pulled against the ropes binding her wrists. For her own good. Bullshit. She blamed Russell for this. And Scott, too, for being so weak.

Levering her foot against the bedpost, she wedged her tennis shoe off then slipped free from the rope. She'd done the right thing, choosing in the end to cooperate with him. Letting him overpower her. She would be free quicker this way than if her brother had tied her more securely. Free to find Rey.

She scrambled to sit upright, not wasting time on the knot binding her wrists. After sliding from the bed she ran toward the window. Please God, don't let Dave and Ali leave.

Turning so that her back was against the window, she groped for the cord controlling the shades. She pulled downward, unsuccessfully. Her wrists had almost no mobility. Gripping the cord tighter, she bent her knees and slowly lowered herself toward the floor.

Halfway down, she suppressed the urge to laugh hysterically. Thia used to challenge her to wall sitting contests, reminiscent of this maneuver. They would compete throughout the summer months to help keep their thigh muscles in shape for skiing. Thia was the usual champion, but Megan often came threateningly close. Scott never participated.

Scott. Tears blurred her vision.

When the shade was drawn as far as possible, she leaned right to lock it into place. She fell to one knee then struggled to stand. The vehicles were still in the yard, engines running. Dave and Ali stood beside one, talking. No use screaming, they wouldn't hear her with the engines running.

The sound grew louder. Someone had opened her front door. A draft of cold air blew the hair near her face. Was Scott coming back? A change of heart?

She rushed to the bedroom door. It was open only a crack. Since her hands were still tied, she nudged it wider with her knee. He was leaning just inside the entryway. Didn't want his snowy boots on her floors. Now that was the brother she remembered. "Scott."

He stared at her. Her keys were in his hand. Remorse had deepened the lines on his face.

"Don't do this. Untie me. We'll forget it ever happened."

"I can't, Megan." His tone was strained.

"You can. We'll work this out." She stepped closer. "No one has to know."

He glanced over his shoulder toward the front door. Was he reconsidering?

She pressed him. "We have to stop Russell. Before he hurts anyone else."

He turned back to her. "The sheriff wants to help you. To keep you safe. He's not involved with the other. He knows nothing."

"You mean, with the drugs you're taking?"

"Shit, no. Forget the coke." His gaze darted around the room. His words were as unfocused as his attention. He was talking to himself. "There are others involved. Men with money." His voice was a near whisper. He licked at his lips nervously. "I'm supposed to meet them. And bring Harrison with me."

"But Rey is already with Sheriff Russell. I know where they are. We could go together."

"No. You're to stay here." His eyes widened. "You don't know these men. I do. It's not safe. Think about all the accidents around here lately."

"You know who caused them?"

"Hell, yes."

"Who?"

"I did."

"You?"

He nodded, moving closer. "But you have to believe me, the shed was never supposed to burn. It was to drive Harrison out of town, to keep your nose out of things, also. But you kept getting more involved." His voice shook. "I can't save you if you get too close. The sheriff's right, you have to stay here. Away from the danger."

His words were slow, but decipherable. He was walking toward her. Keep coming, she prayed. Any closer and maybe she could run past him, outside.

"When I saw Russell last evening, he told me he was going out of town. He lied. I don't know why." He shoved his hands into his pockets. "He put me in charge, warned me to stay out of the woods, except for coming to your place. I should have left Snagtooth, too, but I couldn't." He whined with the voice of a small child, his expression begged for her sympathy. "You see, I've taken their money. Their drugs." He pulled a baggie from his pocket. "I'm in trouble, Megan."

She ached for him and for the misery he'd caused. She tried to reach out, touch his arm, but her hands were still bound. "I can help."

He stared at her. Were her words getting through? His expression swiftly changed from contrite to hardened. "No more mothering me, bailing me out. This time, I'm taking care of myself. I've got a plan."

His mood swings were causing her head to pound. "What kind of plan?"

"Instead of bringing Harrison with me, I'll meet up with him. With Russell, at the hut. That will be good enough. It has to be." Clenching the plastic baggie, he shook it at her. "When this is over, I'll stay clean. I swear."

If only that were true. "Ali and Dave? What about them?"

"They'll go with me. I'll drop them somewhere." His hand fell to his side. "I can't leave them with you, they would go straight to the authorities. Same as you would." His shoulders slumped. "With you it's always black and white. I could have reasoned with Thia."

"Thia?"

"Sure. She had problems. Wasn't as perfect as she pretended to be. Had flaws, like me."

That was an understatement. Megan kept her tone soft, reasonable. "Of course she did. We all do."

"We had a lot in common. Bet you didn't know that. A taste for fame and fortune. Someday it will come my way as it did for her. A different path, maybe, but still it'll happen." His voice trailed off again. "I just hope it lasts longer."

His eyes were fixed in a faraway stare as though seeing through her. Could she squeeze by him yet? "Scott, don't talk like that." She moved closer, slowly, not to cause alarm.

"You were the oddball among us, Megan. Thia and I went after our dreams, tried to make the good things happen. You wanted the world to come begging at your doorstep, asking you to be a part of it."

She flinched.

He shook off his daze and glared at her. "You have more dedication and talent than our sister ever had." Sweat gleamed on his forehead. His fists were clenched. "Explain to me, this once, what are you so damned afraid of? What are you waiting for?"

It was time. Though trembling from his hurtful words, she bolted forward. She made it past, several steps, before his hand caught her arm. She screamed. He pulled a bandanna from his pocket and secured it over her mouth. Though he'd switched his hold, she still couldn't wrench free.

He drew her back toward the bedroom, his fingers digging into her tender skin. The ropes, now taut on her wrists, bit into her flesh. He pushed her inside and closed the door. She could hear him dragging something across her wooden floor, probably shoving it under the knob.

Her door opened inward. How pathetic. How sad.

No use in opening it, it would make him furious. She was better off like this than lashed to the bed. She would follow, once he left the yard. If he left the keys. If not, she'd contact Granny.

Leaning backward against the wooden frame, she tried to stop the tears pooling in her eyes. Where had she gone wrong? Was he still listening? She wiggled the bandanna free. So much for his knot-tying ability. "I never knew you resented me this way, Scott. What did I do?"

"You took Harrison's side against me. Never gave me the chance to explain."

"Tell me now." Hurt swelled in her chest. Even the simplest movement made her ache.

"No." His words were soft, barely audible. "It's too late."

She sank against the door. Her breath caught in her throat.

All was quiet except for the humming of the engines. No footsteps. He was still there. Had to be. What would it take to reach him? "No matter what you've done, no matter what you're doing now, I still love you. I always have."

She waited. Finally his voice filtered through the wood. "I know. I've always counted on that. I just didn't realize how much. Until now."

"Scott." Tears dampened her cheeks.

After a moment, his tone hardened. "Stay put. If you don't, I can't help you." His voice grew dimmer. He was walking away.

The snowmobiles quieted to a soft purr as the front door closed.

❊　　　❊　　　❊

Rey stood before the Desolation Point hut, gripping the door handle with his gloved hand. So much had happened since he'd first stumbled across this hut eight days ago. Even if he could, he wouldn't undo the chain of events. They'd led him to Megan.

He looked over his shoulder. Sheriff Russell stood near the snowmobile, scanning the horizon. Expecting visitors? If so, Rey didn't like the odds. He would take only a hurried look around the inside of the hut. Then he'd allow Russell to take him back down the mountain. He would invent an excuse to wait for Dave and Ali in Snagtooth. They would bring Megan. He didn't think Russell would go so far as to force him at gunpoint to leave town.

He squeezed the handle and shoved the door inward. The homeyness of the interior struck him again. Just like Granny's parlor: comfortable, warm, and inviting. Crocheted seat cushions on hand-carved chairs. Crocheted doilies. Worlds away from the ugliness of the drugs.

Recalling the photo of Thia and Pete and their positions in the room, Rey chose one of the twin beds. It was the same bed he and Megan had spent the evening on, trying to escape memories of the vandalism. That realization gave him a slight chill. He sat as Thia had before, looking across the room. What had they seen to cause their dead-pan expressions? Something out the window?

The helipad was visible. The ski trail was not. If a copter had arrived while Pete and Thia were here, they might have snapped a picture of it. He ruled that out. That left the indoors. Thia's hand pointing to the floor.

He looked down. Nothing but a gold braided rug. Maybe the pointing finger had no importance, but he had nothing else to go on.

Russell had not yet come inside, but would shortly. Time was running out. Scooting the rug aside with his foot, Rey examined the wooden planks. Worn and filthy. A sharp contrast to the fluffy, bright bedding and the crisp, lace-trimmed curtains. Granny must draw the line at sweeping. Either that or the hut had a lot of foot traffic.

The groove running along the plank nearest the bed was wider than the others. Rey followed it until he saw a perpendicular cut on the wood. Pushing the rug further out of the way, he saw a second cut three feet away from the first. His heart pounded.

He dropped to his knees, reaching for the knife in his pocket. Standard Boy Scout issue, nothing special. It would never be able to lift a section this size without bending the blade. He would try, though. Inserting the tip into the corner of the rut he pried at the edge. Still no luck. He pushed the blade in deeper.

The door swung open, the sheriff entered. Rey had no time to react, no time to pretend his actions were meaningless. Within seconds Russell's gun was drawn. The sound of laughter filled the cabin. "Well, let me guess. Your tape recorder's down there."

"No."

Russell dropped the humor from his voice. "You just made a big mistake."

"Only one? I'm having a good day, then." Rey attempted to stand. The sheriff released the safety on his weapon. "Drop the knife, then get up."

Rey laid it on the rug, then shook his head as if amused. "You've got the gun, Sheriff. I'd be a fool to . . ."

"You've been one all along. You were almost out of here. Is this why you insisted on coming up here?"

The question was rhetorical. Russell signaled for him to move aside. He did. After Rey was several yards away from the fake inset and the knife, Russell kicked the open blade under the bed. It slid across the floor until it thumped against the wall.

Russell eased his finger off the trigger. "You screwed up, big time."

"And what about you, Rusty? When did things first go wrong for you?"

The sheriff's eyes widened for an instant before he reclaimed his composure. Just long enough to confirm Dave's report.

Rey shoved his hands into his jacket pockets. He didn't know if they trembled from adrenaline or fear. Didn't know if his entire body shook or just his hands. Other than his brief stand-off with Scott, it had been twenty years since someone had pulled a gun on him. Then, he'd mustered enough nerve to jump from a second story window. But the sense of youthful immortality had died within him that day. Died along with his father. He had too much to live for now to be reckless.

He forced his tone to be casual. "That's right. I know about your alias, just as you discovered mine. Up until now, your crimes have been small. Indiscretions you could probably walk away from if you chose to resign from public office. Why don't you?"

"I don't know what the hell you're talking about."

"Walk away from this drug running operation. I'll help you find legal help. Someone discreet. You could start over in some other line of work."

The sheriff's breath was coming faster. He pulled at his collar, glancing around the room. Rey stepped closer. "Stop, Russell, before it's too late."

"I can't." He turned toward the window, the arm with the gun dropping slightly to his side. "There's no time. We'll never get down this mountain before they see us."

Rey heard the faint hum of chopper blades. He moved toward the glass. Russell steadied his aim once again. "Stay where you are."

"Listen to me." Rey didn't move an inch. "They don't need to know I'm in on their game. We'll use the story about the lost tape recorder."

Russell's laugh was sharp. "There's enough cocaine right now beneath these floorboards to finance you, me and the entire Snagtooth community for life. They've been trying to get at it for over a week now. Ever since you and your buddies arrived and scared them off. The word on the airwaves is that the pickup is today, no matter what."

"So we'll let them retrieve the drugs, then call the authorities." Rey shouted to be heard over the whirring blades. "They'll be arrested when they try to land back at the origin."

Russell shook his head. "They'll kill me for bringing you here." He looked up, absently. "Unless." He leveled his gun at Rey again. "Get over there."

"What?"

"Sit on the bed. I'll play it like I did before."

"Before?"

"Thia wouldn't leave the drugs alone either. Had to come up here, investigate. Brought Pete Aldridge with her. Stupid fools, both of them." He wiped his forehead against his sleeve. His hand with the gun didn't waver. "Last time, I was able to walk away. Maybe it'll work again."

Rey's heart pounded as he sat on the edge of the mattress, where Pete and Thia had sat. Was the nightmare repeating itself? He fought the urge to clench his fists, to grip the bedspread. "Megan was right, then. It was murder."

"Megan." Russell's exhale was close to a sigh. "So stupid for me to regret something that never was."

Beyond the window, the chopper descended the final stretch. The Mountain High Adventures logo was familiar, forever imprinted in his memory.

Russell adjusted his position so that he could also watch, without releasing Rey from his sight. "Megan should have left her sister's death in the past. Not asked questions. Not flashed those photos around town. She'd be better off." The sheriff's voice had changed from threatening to resigned.

Rey's throat tightened, his words were strained. "She knows nothing. Was only guessing. I was the one who wanted to come back up here today."

"You're lying. I spoke to her earlier."

"She's innocent."

"Then use your last breath ruing the fact you involved her. Unfortunately, though, to Lute it won't matter."

"Who?"

"That's the only name I know. There's the boss, of course. And the boy they killed last week. Hell, I almost forgot about the one they killed yesterday."

A chill ran down his arms, his spine. "Yesterday?"

"Yeah. Didn't drop him in my woods, though. Just told me about him so I'd get the message loud and clear. No more screw-ups. Anything else you want to know, you can ask Lute himself." Russell motioned toward the window with the tip of his gun. "Here he comes."

❄   ❄   ❄

The kitchen drawer held the carving knife upright. Megan pressed herself firmly against it. Within moments her hands were free. She rubbed her wrists then ran them under cold water to stop the numerous small cuts from bleeding. The hydrogen peroxide could wait. Rescuing Rey couldn't.

She entered her bedroom and opened her rifle case. She still needed to reload her clips. Leaning the Anschütz against the foot of her bed, she quickly donned her long underwear and woolen socks. The afternoon sun was going down, leaving behind the gray light of dusk. The wind was picking up. It would be dark soon and harder to stay on the trails at the speed she had in mind. She stepped into her ski pants, tucked in her turtleneck and pulled a long, thick sweater over everything. Now for ammunition.

Crossing the living room, Megan flipped on the light switch and quickly descended the stairs to the bunk room. The boxes she wanted were in a fireproof case in the closet. She knelt and scooted it forward. A cold draft stirred the hairs on the back of her neck. Frowning, she glanced toward the basement door. It was closed and bolted. The sound of wood creaking overhead drew her attention.

The floorboards near the front door were the only ones she recalled being loose. The draft chilling her upper body confirmed her suspicion. Someone had just entered her cabin. Who?

She tilted her head toward the staircase, listening. Not Rachel. She would call out. If Rey had returned, he wouldn't slowly move from kitchen to bedroom, without a word. And his boots, with their rubberized soles, wouldn't make that tapping noise. She flinched with each footstep.

The stranger coughed. Definitely a man. Her hand gripped the bed post. She had to do something. Simply turning off the lights would do no good. If the intruder searched down here, he'd simply flip them back on.

There were lamps situated on end tables on either side of the bed Rey had been using. Luckily they were off and cool. The overhead light wasn't, however. She'd have to work fast. Megan reached under one of the shades and twisted the bulb. She slipped it into her pocket, came around the bed and repeated the action with the second. It dropped, hit the edge of the table, and shattered. Had he heard that? Yes. The footsteps overhead stopped.

Could it be the same person who had vandalized her home just days ago? Maybe, unless Scott had done that, too. If the man had arrived a few minutes earlier, she would have been upstairs with no ammunition. Now she had the ammo, but no rifle. The footsteps moved again, this time toward the living room. Toward her.

Megan climbed on the bed and balanced the balls of her feet against the dipping of the mattress. The blackout curtains on the windows were drawn, thank God. That would save her precious time. She pulled her sweater over her hand, then reached high to twist the third bulb free. It took several attempts but at last the room was plunged into near darkness.

The only light visible now was the one upstairs, reflecting harshly against the dark, wooden steps like a slender knife blade. The connecting door must be open a crack. A break for her, albeit a small one. Maybe the intruder would think she was out, instead of hiding downstairs.

More movement. Was there anything nearby with which to protect herself? She scrambled off the bed, trying to think. She had a pocket knife. A lot of good that would do if her stalker was armed. She thought of her two pistols. It was too dark and too late to start pulling out drawers to look for them. If she had them with her now, could she actually use them? Would she be able to pull the trigger on another human being? Of course she would.

Probably.

Damn. What a time to not know if she could actually kill someone. She'd simply have to shoot him in the leg while she figured out the rest. She frowned. Why think about that at all when she was unarmed?

No, wait. There was Thia's rifle. The one she'd never used, never touched, and tried not to think about. For the first time, she was thankful for her father's offering. If only she could find it, in time. In the dark. Her jaw clenched tightly. Would her clips fit Thia's newer model? Just in case, she'd stuff loose ammo into her pocket and hope Thia's own clips were stored with the rifle.

The phone rang upstairs. She would give away her position if she picked it up. She listened hopelessly as it rang a second time. The intruder's heels clicked rapidly against the hard wood floor. The ringing abruptly stopped. He'd answered her phone? Bold of him. But then breaking and entering took a certain type of personality anyway.

Time to focus on finding the rifle. The man upstairs was talking softly into the receiver. That placed him either in the kitchen or her bedroom. It had to be the kitchen from the sound of it. Directly in bird's eye view of the connecting door downstairs.

More low, husky murmurs. She's not here, were the only words she could distinguish. That was enough. Her fingers tingled as goose bumps rose along her arms, down her legs. The man breaking in was someone the caller knew. Someone who wouldn't arouse suspicion by answering her phone. Who?

No time to think, every minute was precious. She dropped to her knees and began searching for the rifle under the bed by touch. The second twin produced results. She dragged the box quietly across the floorboards.

Her fingers fumbled for the latch on the glass case. It opened. Silently she lifted the lid and removed the weapon. She felt for the clips, finding three. Good. Were they damp? Would they work?

She found the ammo canister and silently prayed that the box on top wasn't past its expiration date. Opening it, she stuffed a handful of shells into the pocket of her ski pants. The intruder replaced the phone receiver and the footsteps began again. Damn.

She located the end table between the beds. The phone. Picking up the receiver she was thankful for the illuminated buttons. She punched autodial for Rachel. Her friend picked it up on the first ring.

"Hello?"

"It's Megan." Her whisper sounded more like a frog's croak. She steadied her voice as she heard footsteps approaching. "No time to explain. Call me back."

"Sure, but . . ."

"Just do it. And keep whoever answers on the line." Megan depressed the receiver hook, but left her finger on it.

The sliver of light on the stairs widened to a full arc. She held her breath until the phone rang. Would he answer it again? Yes. As hoped, the intruder backed away from the connecting door.

Megan released the hook as he picked up. She heard the muted hello. Mitchell. The raspy quality was unmistakable.

Rachel's voice kicked into high gear, causing Megan to briefly smile. She laid the receiver on the bed and covered it with a pillow. After scrambling to her feet, she headed toward the back door, Thia's rifle firmly in her hand.

It felt strange to carry it, as if she were depending on her sister all over again. Was that where the intense guilt was coming from, because Thia hadn't been able to rely on her in return?

She'd shoot Mitchell another day, when she was more sure of her equipment, and of herself.

❄   ❄   ❄

The dead bolt slid free easily, but the door itself stuck. The lower entrance hadn't been used in days, not since Rey moved in with her upstairs. Megan grasped the handle tightly with her one free hand, refusing to release the rifle. She had to jar the door open, there was no other way out.

Mitchell was still talking into the phone. Rachel was stalling him, allowing her a few precious moments more. Her pulse was pounding in her ears. She couldn't make out the words. Could only hear the slight buzzing from extension hidden beneath the pillow. Then he raised his voice.

"Megan's here? Where?"

Don't Rachel. She winced as she heard his reply, could guess what had gone in between. "Thanks. I'll get her and call you back."

Why, Rach? Her best friend. Her confidante. One of two people having a spare key to the cabin. Maybe Scott hadn't broken in at all. God, it hurt. Tucking the rifle under her arm, she leveraged her full body weight against the door. It swung open just as she heard her name called from the upper floor.

The voice was definitely Mitchell's, if that was his real name. Fear chilled her blood as she thought of him living close by all week. And Rachel. She couldn't dwell on that. He was shouting now, bounding down the stairs.

There would be time later for assigning blame, for restitution and for healing. Right now, she needed help. Who was left? Who was trustworthy, and also within reach?

Oh, God. Her next task crystallized, as soon as it came to mind. She needed to warn Granny.

❄   ❄   ❄

Megan emerged from the outside stairwell, bracing herself against the blowing ice and snow. Grandma Grace's shiny red snowmobile was parked down the trail, behind the burned remains of shed. Close enough for the light from the kitchen window to reflect off the hood. Not near enough for the sound to warn her of his arrival due to the direction of the storm.

Should she take the time to search for Granny's extra ignition key or run? She had no choice, he would come after her if she left the vehicle behind. The odds were in her favor. Mitchell would be forced to walk, thus giving her more time.

She ran toward the vehicle and snapped open the storage compartment. Her pulse raced, but not from exertion. She felt beneath the towel, the water bottle, other odds and ends. The spare key was still there. As expected, Granny had not taken her advice. Bless her stubborn soul.

Slinging Thia's rifle and harness over her shoulder, Megan climbed on and fired up the vehicle. She sped eastward across the snowy field toward the lake, ducking her head against the wind. No helmet.

The oncoming storm had forced an early darkness. The purple snow crocuses along the frozen shoreline were illuminated by the porch light. Silly, but welcoming just the same. Expected. Normal, when nothing else was.

She pulled up to Granny's back door. After stepping off the vehicle, she shoved the spare key into her pocket, twisted the knob and raced inside. "Grace! Where are you?"

"With my sewing, dear. I wasn't expecting company."

Megan ran down the hallway, careful not to trip on the throw rugs. When she turned left into the parlor, she was still out of breath. She shifted her rifle strap higher on her shoulder. "We can't stay here."

Granny lowered her glasses. "A beer? Don't be silly." Her eyes twinkled in amusement. "I do have a little Peppermint Schnapps, though. Look above the stove. Behind the cooking sherry."

Granny sat amid scraps of fabric in varying shades of lavender. Some covered the dining room table, more littered the couches and chairs. A wall to wall purple mess. Megan came closer, so she could be heard distinctly. "We have to leave. Let's find your coat."

"I can't go out. This place is in an uproar." She waved her hand eloquently over threads and needles. "Now sit down and tell me what all the hollering is about. Is your tail on fire about something again?"

Megan counted to five then leaned forward. "Grace." Another pause. "We've got to get you out of here."

"For whatever reason?" Her wispy gray brows were furrowed.

"It's about Mitchell. Your boarder. He's coming back any minute."

"My Eric? I should hope so. We're having pot roast for dinner." She smiled. "He loves anything with gravy, you know."

"No, I don't know. And neither do you." Megan circled around the sewing table and seized Granny gently by her upper arm, urging her to stand. "Come on."

"But I lent him my scooter. I have to stay."

"I've got your scooter." Persistently, she led the older woman from the room.

"But . . ."

"That's right. He's on foot. Half frozen, if I had my wish. It would slow him down."

"That's a very unneighborly thing to say."

"He can sue me later. Come on."

Megan selected a tweed jacket from the coat rack and handed it to her friend. "Button that. You'll need a hat and gloves, too."

"Now just a minute." Granny dug in her heels.

"I'm sorry. I promise to explain later." For the first time Megan was glad that the woven throw rugs slid easily across the highly polished floor. She used them as if they were People Movers at the airport, scooting Granny closer toward the door.

"I'm not going anywhere."

"Grace, Eric was ransacking my house." Someone outside called her name. Mitchell. Time was up. They'd never make back it to Granny's snowmobile in time. They had to hold out until Rachel could alert the police. Her heart sank. She'd forgotten, momentarily. No one would be calling anyone for help.

"I believe that's Eric now."

"I know." She glanced quickly around at the pristine rooms on either side of her, then remembered the mess in the parlor. "This way." She led the older woman back down the hall. Anyone in their right mind would enter the sewing room last.

Granny tapped her on the arm. "There's something you ought to know."

That was an understatement. She'd been suffering from a major knowledge-gap these last twelve months. "We'll talk later, okay?" She pulled a chair aside to make a pathway, then guided her friend through the cleared space and into the closet.

The shelves were crammed, but they were narrow. There was plenty of room to stand after Megan moved a grocery sack full of purple fabric and quilt batting out of the way and tossed a second one out the door.

The women stood side by side in the darkness with Megan's rifle between them. They were dressed in coats, hats and gloves. The heat was stifling.

Granny broke the silence. "This is ridiculous."

"Shhh." Mitchell called her name again. It was no longer muffled. He was too close.

Granny piped up again. "Now listen here. This is my home. Eric is . . ."

"I know exactly what he is." Megan's voice was barely above a whisper. It was useless listening for footsteps in a house covered with throw rugs. "Grace, I don't know all the facts yet, but there's something desperately wrong here in Snagtooth. The sheriff's involved, my brother Scott, too. Rachel also plays a part in it. But Mitchell's the ring leader. It all centers around the hut at Desolation Point, the same place Thia was before she died."

"I know."

"We have to keep quiet."

"All right, dear, but I feel very foolish."

Megan's scalp tingled as she heard furniture being moved aside. Had he already made his way to the parlor? She reached for her rifle. Still unloaded. Maybe she could crack him over the head with it. She fumbled in the darkness, touching the contents of shelves, feeling for anything that could be used as a weapon. There was nothing sturdier than the stem of an artificial flower.

The closet door opened. Light flooded in, hurting her eyes. Megan turned, hoping she could raise the rifle fast enough. Mitchell's hand came forward. A quick flash of silver caused her to flinch. It wasn't a gun.

In his palm was his badge.

❄   ❄   ❄

Megan's first rational thought was that someone was pulling on her sleeve. She glanced down at Granny.

"I was trying to tell you, dear. Eric's one of the good guys."

"But, how did you know?"

Mitchell stepped forward. "I have the same question."

Grace made a dismissing sound then walked out of the closet with her chin held high. "You don't think I would have let you stay here without checking you out, do you, young man? The DEA, right? I may be old, but I'm nobody's fool." She picked up the brown paper sack Megan had tossed from the closet and began restuffing it.

"Let me do that." Eric bent down to help her. "How did you find out about me, Grace?"

"The equipment you lugged upstairs when you moved in was a dead giveaway. But actually, your phone was your downfall."

"I carry my phone with me."

"Not when you shower, you don't." Granny knelt and stuffed more fabric scraps into the bag. "It's registered to a very nice man named Logan, I believe. We had a long chat." She grinned. "He sends you his best."

"My partner." Eric frowned and shook his head. "When this is over, he's a dead man." He stood then held out his hand to Grace.

She laid her hand in his. He pulled her to her feet. "But he was so pleasant, Eric. Do remember to be kind."

The front door swung inward. Rachel burst through. "Megan? Granny? Where is everyone?"

"In the sewing room."

Rachel came around the corner. "Eric, good. You found Megan."

Megan crossed the room and stood in front of her friend. Her heart beat faster. "Care to explain why you gave away my location?"

"I ran into Eric in town this morning. After eavesdropping on his call, he decided it was to his benefit to explain who he was." Rachel glanced over at him. "Right?"

He nodded.

"When I called your cabin, he was desperate to find you." She shrugged. "When you called me back, you didn't give me a chance to get a word in."

Megan felt a heavy weight lift from her chest. "I'm sorry. I shouldn't have doubted you."

"It's okay. I knew you'd put it together eventually." She glanced around. "Where's Rey?"

"He left with Russell. They're headed to Desolation Point." She brought her friend up to speed on the events of the afternoon. "Scott's taken Dave and Ali somewhere. Could be the same destination, I don't know." She purposely left out the part where her brother had tied her in her room. Her escape had been an easy one. It should remain solely between them.

"It depends on where this afternoon's action is." Eric scowled as he paced the length of the room. "If Rusty is as crooked in life as he is on paper, we need to find him. I'm not sure Desolation Point is the right place, though." He stopped pacing and looked over at Grandma. "Grace, where do you think they're headed?"

"Wait a minute." Megan stood in front of him, hands on hips. "What exactly are you accusing her of?"

"Every successful drug running operation needs a system for flagging pickups and deliveries." He pointed to Granny. "Grace is their flagger."

"Don't be absurd." Megan walked closer to her friend. Rachel followed suit, standing on her other side. The older woman raised her chin defiantly.

"Okay. A consensus of one." Eric softened his tone and addressed his landlady directly. "Grace, why did you set out the snow crocuses today?"

"Because the Cutthroat Peak hut is purple. I wanted to warn the heli-skiing operators to stay away from yesterday's avalanche area. They can see my flowers easily from up above." She pursed her lips. "Unless it's overcast, of course."

Megan reached out and touched Granny's arm. "There were no avalanches reported in that zone."

"I only know what Sheriff Russell tells me. He calls religiously with your afternoon report. I set up the signs before the morning runs start. Have for the last year or so, except when I'm under the weather."

"Grace." She stepped around in front of her oldest and dearest friend. "I file my reports overnight. There are no afternoon reports."

Granny blinked. "Then . . ." She glanced from one person to the other. When her gaze traveled back to Megan, she stopped.

Eric stepped forward. "You're their official flagger, Grace. You signal both sides of the operation. The Canadians drop off; the Americans pick up."

Granny's face turned beet red. She opened her mouth to speak, but no words came.

Eric laid his hand on the older woman's shoulder. "We'll discuss it later. Right now, we need to get up there." He turned to Rachel. "Would you stay here with Grace?"

Granny stepped on his foot, hard. "I don't need a baby sitter. Rachel's the best darned rescuer around. You'd better take her with you. Why her patrol . . ."

"Grace, I need you here to contact Logan for me. To explain things. Tell him to get here as quickly as possible. Rachel will lead him to me after he arrives."

Granny looked admonished. Megan stifled the urge to smile. Turning away, she zipped her coat. "I'm going after Rey."

"I figured you were. We're going together." He was moving down the hallway already. "Grab your rifle. Sometimes, I can't shoot worth shit. I've been watching you practice. If you're half as accurate under pressure as you are during target practice, then their butts are nailed."

That sounded good, very good. She glanced at Thia's Anschütz. It seeming fitting, her sister's rifle being used to bring down her own murderers. She grabbed it and followed Mitchell out the door.

TWENTY-ONE

UTTHROAT HUT LOOKED a hell of a lot better on the inside than the out. Scott had thought twice about going in. The freezing wind blowing snow up his nose had convinced him. He stared out the window, still trying to warm himself.

Why wasn't Lute here? Or the sheriff for that matter? Granny's flower garden had clearly pointed to Cutthroat Peak.

Such an obvious scheme, really. He'd caught on days ago, after picking up the receiver on his multi-line office phone and listening in on the sheriff's conversation. His boss had been relaying the next day's avalanche warnings to Granny Grace.

Why did she need to know? The old bat didn't ski. None of the data was accurate anyway. It wasn't until Russell started talking about the new line hut and how Granny had decorated it purple, that it had all started making sense. That, and Lute's comment to look for the flowers.

He'd done his part. The curtains gripped in his right hand were purple. So where in the hell was Lute? Holding the others here would be difficult without help soon.

So far they'd bought his story. The guy, Edwards, wasn't so bad. Kind of the nervous sort but easy to ignore. The woman was a different story. She kept blabbering at him. Confusing him. Compounding his headache.

The coke Lute had given him was burning a hole in his pocket. He closed his eyes and touched the plastic bag, imagining the rush. Like soaring downhill on an untouched slope. Skis piercing through mounds of virgin white powder. He would be unmatchable. Unstoppable. Content. He sighed.

Edwards stopped pacing. Scott could sense the man standing behind him. Staring, no doubt. No one would sneak up on this deputy and get away with it. He turned quickly. "Back off."

Edwards flinched. "You never answered my earlier question. Why are we here instead of at Desolation Point? That's where Rey and the sheriff were headed."

Scott took note of the respect in the man's voice and relaxed. "We're waiting."

"But they left the cabin before us. If this was their destination, they would already be here."

His temples were pounding. Edwards was trying to trick him, to confuse him. Like the sheriff had done. "We're staying. Lute said the flags are never wrong."

"Lute? Who's Lute?" The woman was speaking now. Moving toward him from across the room. What was her name? He couldn't remember. She stood next to Edwards, sticking her nose in.

Shit. She was driving him crazy. They both were. He held the baggie in his left pocket again. The plastic felt good against his palm. Soothing. The coke would calm his nerves. When he was alone, he would relax and enjoy it.

Something rough poked at his finger. The edge of the note he'd found stuffed inside the bag. Lute's note.

The request had been totally unexpected. Come to the pickup area. Bring Harrison. He'd tried. Unfortunately, Harrison had already left the cabin with the sheriff. He frowned. Sheriff Russell, who was not out of town despite his saying he would be. No, Scott didn't want to think about that again.

The woman waved her hand in front of his face. Scott had forgotten they were there. "Is Lute a Snagtooth deputy, like yourself?"

"Leave me alone." He tried to back away, but the wall was behind him. When they attempted to block his way, he got fierce. "Stay there and shut up."

Brushing past them, he crossed the room. The heels of his boots thudded each time they connected with the wooden planks. Maybe he'd take a turn pacing for awhile.

"Does Russell know we're here?" The woman again. "Does anyone?"

Ali, what a pain in the ass. Yeah, that was the right name. Ali. It was coming back to him.

He'd had no choice but to bring her along. Edwards, too. They'd gotten in his way. He glanced over his shoulder at them. Ali's hand was curled around Edwards' coat sleeve. The gesture reminded him of his sister.

Megan clung also. In her own way. With words. That's why he had to get himself out of this mess without her help. This time he would show her he could stand on his own.

Leaving her behind had been the surest way to keep her out of danger. The fact he'd had to tie her up to do it seemed harsh. He'd never forget the look on her face as he closed the door. It hadn't been fear. No, more like disappointment.

Dave stepped forward. "Enough indecision. We're leaving. If you want to stay longer, fine. Do so. Ali and I are getting out of here."

"You can't."

Dave moved again. Seemed to lunge at him. Scott drew his Smith and Wesson and clicked off the safety. "Stop right there."

Copter blades hummed in the distance. Thank God. Lute would know what to do. He'd take over. Scott signaled toward the window. "Too late. Company's coming." His vigil would soon end.

Edwards peered out through the thick glass. "This is who you're waiting for? High Mountain Adventures?" He turned quickly. "Are you crazy? These guys are drug runners."

What? His gun wavered for a moment. That didn't make sense. Lute was his friend. They played poker together, did favors for each other. Edwards was tricking him again. He brought his weapon level with the man's chest. "They told me to come here and I did."

"But why?"

"I don't care. I owe them. Stay inside if you don't want to be involved." With his free hand, he reached into his pocket for his gloves. Wrong one. This one held the coke.

Ali rushed him. Pulled at his arm. "Don't go out there."

Was she nuts? He could have shot her. "Leave me alone." The bag of cocaine fell to the floor. He paused, glancing at it once, then shoved her aside headed for the door.

Once outside, he ran toward the landing strip. The chopper passed low over the hut. He clicked the safety on and shoved his gun into his holster so he could wave.

What the hell? The bird was ascending. They couldn't leave without him. He ran further onto the landing site. "Wait. I'm here."

The helicopter circled back and hovered. Scott stood in the center of the snow field, arms outstretched. The aircraft door opened. Through the clatter of the blades, he heard Ali shout his name.

He squinted against the whirling air and flying ice chips. Lute? No, someone else. It was too damned hard to see. The storm clouds parted, allowing the late afternoon sun to peek through. It bounced off the metallic side, blinding him. He shielded his eyes.

The chopper drifted left, changing the angle. He'd been wrong. The light was reflecting off the barrel of a gun, pointing directly at him.

❊   ❊   ❊

A thick clump of trees stood on a rise, uphill from Cutthroat Hut. Eric pulled his snowmobile into the center, hoping it would provide adequate coverage. He motioned to Megan to pull alongside him. They cut the engines. Had the High Mountain Adventures pilot spotted them?

Megan stepped from the vehicle she'd borrowed from Granny. "They're definitely here. My Vmax is parked to the side of the hut. Scott's vehicle, too." She pulled off her helmet. "I'm going to get a better look."

"Stay down."

"But what if the helicopter lands? Scott, Dave and Ali are inside."

"Then we'll be right behind them. Hold on while I try to contact my partner."

"Make it fast. In the meantime, I want a better view of the front door." Crouching, she headed toward a group of firs to the left. "There's Scott."

"Where?"

"Leaving the hut." She pointed. "God, what's he doing? He could be killed."

Not if he's in on it, Eric wanted to say. Instead, he walked toward her. The sharp crack of gunfire made him flinch. He dove to the ground. Megan did the same. He crawled the rest of the way to her before drawing his gun. They hid behind a single, wind-tortured tree for cover.

More shots. Scott fell. Wasn't it always this way? They got the kids first. One minute he'd been running foolishly in plain view, the next he was gripping his belly. But at least this time, the victim was still moving. Eric watched as he rolled in the snow, from his side onto his back.

Megan started to rise but he grabbed her sleeve. "Don't. They'll fire at you, too." He dragged her backwards further into the trees. More camouflage.

She tried to jerk away. " He's my brother."

"They're leaving. Hold on. We'll get you there as soon as it's clear." His radio crackled. "Logan, fire up the chopper and get your ass in the air. We have one man down."

"I'm already airborne, buddy. I'll call the medics."

Logan was good, damned good. "Let me give you the coordinates."

"I have them. You're at Cutthroat Peak, right? Rachel Aldridge is with me, told me you're there with the ranger lady. I verified your location via the Vmax transmitter."

"Lucky guess. She's not driving it. I'll explain later."

"We'll be right there."

"Over."

Eric watched as Megan, standing next to him, waited silently. He'd thought she'd be gone in a flash as soon as his attention was diverted. Instead, she merely stared at the scene, poised as a runner would be awaiting the starting signal.

He shoved the radio into his pocket, trading it for binoculars. "Let's make sure there's no further company in-route."

"What transmitter?"

"I installed it a few days ago. Sorry, but it couldn't be helped. You're all over this damned mountain, I had no other way to keep track." At her outraged expression, he merely shrugged, pulling the caps off the lenses. "If it's any consolation, you spoiled several pickups. Must have driven Cowboy crazy."

"Who's Cowboy?"

"The bastard behind all the drugs."

"Then I'm glad I helped make his life miserable."

He lifted his binoculars skyward. "Especially the day you parked at Smuggler's Peak for several hours." He could almost feel her staring at him. Lowering the glasses, he moved forward. "Let's go."

❄   ❄   ❄

Fifty meters never seemed so far. Megan was breathing hard as she dropped to her knees in the snow next to Scott. He was alive, thank God. She opened his jacket. Blood had seeped onto his shirt and was spreading. He'd been hit just below the waist.

He opened his eyes. "Sorry, Champ."

His nickname for her. She hadn't heard it, except in sarcasm, since they were kids. "Save your strength." Lifting his head slightly with one hand, she pulled the hood of his parka up. Protection against unnecessary heat loss.

Mitchell arrived, bringing the space blankets and emergency kit from her vehicle. She slipped the insulation under him. After applying a dressing lightly on top of the wound to catch the blood flow, she pulled the blanket further around him.

"How did you get here?" His voice was barely audible but the words were clear. Shock hadn't yet set in.

"I arrived the same way you did."

"Stole the nearest snowmobile and followed the flowers?"

"Exactly. Now, no more."

He closed his eyes.

Tears clouded her vision. She pulled his blanket tighter. "You'll be at the hospital soon." She glanced around for something with which to elevate his feet. Nothing. Mitchell was gone. Inside the hut, she prayed for the medics to hurry. Scott needed more help than she could give him.

Scott was talking again. She leaned closer to hear.

"I wanted so much. It's a long story."

"Tell me later." She smoothed the hair away from his forehead, tugging the ribbed band of his ski hat further down. "It will give us something to do while you're confined to a hospital bed." She kept her tone light. "It will keep your mind off the flimsy robe that drapes open when you walk."

"Sounds wonderful." He tried to smile.

She bit her bottom lip to keep it from trembling.

"Never wanted to hurt you."

"I know that." She checked his pulse. It was fast. Unsteady.

"So much trouble. The shed fire. Your house." He grimaced.

She stroked his cheek. "At least now I can stop blaming Rachel."

"Rachel? She's your best friend."

"The two of you were the only ones with keys."

"You accused her instead of me?"

"Don't paint me lily white on this, Scott. Of course you crossed my mind."

"Should have broken a window." His grin was lopsided, his eyelids were at half mast. "Bigger suspect pool."

His arm movements had dislodged the blanket. She pulled the edges together again. Nothing to do but sit and wait. It was a helpless feeling.

"They paid me a lot of money." He groaned and shifted. She put her hand on his chest to still him. "Needed money. Needed the drugs, too."

Mitchell startled Megan by kneeling next to her. Dave and Ali positioned themselves on Scott's other side. Mitchell brought forward a plastic baggie containing a grayish white substance, a sight which was familiar to her now. "This yours? You dropped it inside the hut. Edwards found it."

Scott nodded. "It's mine."

Mitchell's voice was steady, his tone more factual than condemning. "You're a lucky man, Deputy. I heard Cowboy ordering Lute to cut this particular batch of coke with drain cleaner. A farewell gift, I believe he called it. If you had ingested it you'd be dead."

"God." Her brother stared at the bag, eyes wide open, lips parted. Megan gripped his arm. Another close escape.

Dave dropped to one knee. "Will he make it?"

"He's holding on." She paused, not trusting her voice, and cleared the lump from her throat. "Scott never meant any harm."

Dave nodded. "Any word on Rey?"

"Not yet."

Finally, there was the sound of a helicopter in the distance. It was music to her ears. Her only hope was that it wasn't another variation of High Mountain Adventures. She waited. Rescue was painted predominantly on the side.

It hovered then descended slowly on the landing strip. The door opened immediately. Within minutes, the medics had taken Scott's vital signs and strapped him securely to a back board.

Megan stood aside as they performed their tasks. Efficient. Capable. She was no longer needed. "What will happen to him afterwards?" She watched as they lifted and carried him to the waiting chopper.

Mitchell spoke calmly, slowly. "I've interviewed both witnesses. The deputy caused no bodily harm. No one's pressing kidnapping charges."

She glanced at Dave, then Ali. "Thank you."

"We still have drug possession, vandalism. We'll discuss those later on, when he's stable."

The forward and rear doors were opened wide. Scott was placed prone into the helicopter. The team was ready for take off.

Eric turned to her. "There's room . . ."

"I know." It was killing her to stay, but he would receive excellent care. And he didn't need her mothering him anymore. They would start over, bury the past and forge a new relationship. One that worked better for both of them. If he lived.

She watched until the helicopter lifted then turned to Mitchell. "Let's find Rey."

❄   ❄   ❄

The side window was fogged over. Lute brushed the sleeve of his coat across it and peered out. The vehicle parked next to Desolation Hut belonged to Russell. He didn't have a clue as to why the sheriff was there, but it didn't bother him. The man was harmless.

Princess landed the chopper on the snow pack. When would she leave Cowboy's organization? Ever? Once this pickup was over and he was sunning his pasty white flesh on a Mexican beach, he wouldn't think of those left behind. Time to save his own miserable ass.

The last time he was here, Rookie had been alive. He hadn't known Billy. Now both were dead and some new kid sat next to him. EJ, Billy's friend, was holding on to the door for dear life. Punks, all of them. Not worth him worrying about. He had to forget he'd liked this one on sight. He nudged the kid and handed him an empty burlap sack. "Let's go." He wrenched the door open and got out.

EJ followed. Lute waited for him to come around the side of the aircraft. When the boy did, he suddenly stopped. "Someone's here."

"I know."

"But the vehicle says, 'Sheriff.'"

"All right, so you can read. Come on." Lute trudged along, toward the hut. Each footstep should feel lighter. He was closing in on his freedom. Instead, the thought of possibly more trouble, and the usual solution, depressed him.

"Is this where we're meeting Billy?"

Lute grimaced. "We'll talk later. We've got work to do."

Cowboy's instructions had been clear: don't return without the shipment. The sheriff had better cooperate. Lute drew his weapon and pushed the door inward. Russell stood mid-room, his own gun leveled at the guy in the corner.

Rey Harrison.

Lute glared at Russell. "What the hell is he doing here?"

"I couldn't shake him. He got too close, figured it out. The drugs, the location, everything. I had to bring him."

He stepped forward, entering the hut. EJ followed, keeping close to his side and his mouth shut. Good. Lute walked past the sheriff, past the pointed gun, until he stood before the man sitting on the bed. The one he'd been both pursuing and avoiding for days. "Harrison. At last."

"Unfortunately."

He scanned the room. "The ranger's not with you?"

"She knows nothing about this."

"Why don't I believe that?"

"It's true."

Lute unzipped his coat slowly. He kept his shoulders back and his tone sharp. "Where is she?"

"At home. I'm on my way out of town."

"Not any longer." He pointed across the room to the pair of carved wooden chairs. "Russell, tie him to one of those. I'll radio Cowboy. We'll wait for his instructions."

Stall tactics. A plan formed in his mind. He'd grab the stash and direct Russell to stay behind, holding Harrison captive. If they went to the cops later, he didn't give a shit. He'd be in Mexico by then.

Russell moved forward to grab Harrison's arm. Lute watched them make eye contact. It lingered. They were planning something.

He motioned for Russell's gun. "I'll stand guard while you secure him." After a slight hesitation, the sheriff handed over his weapon. Lute pulled a length of rope from one of the sacks. Russell accepted it then dragged a chair to the center of the room.

EJ leaned closer. "Are you going to kill him? I didn't sign up for any killings."

He'd forgotten the boy was there. There was no good answer. He ignored him.

The boy tried again. "Billy's not here. Maybe he's at another hut."

"Kid, your friend's dead. Overdosed. Tough break." From the loud squeaks he guessed EJ had sunk onto a bed. Lute didn't take his eyes off the action across the room.

Harrison was seated on a monstrosity carved from a tree trunk and embellished with a gold seat cushion. Russell lashed him to the arms of the high-backed chair, without the slightest degree of roughness. Out of character, from what Lute had heard.

"Now his feet."

Russell nodded. Lute tossed EJ his burlap bag. "Pop the floor-boards then fill these. Divide it evenly. Don't take all day."

"What do you mean?"

"There's a fake floor over there, under the rug." Keeping the gun firmly pointed at the other two men, he stowed his own weapon then dug in his coat pocket. He tossed the boy an eight inch pry bar. "Use this."

"You mean, by the bed?"

"Here." Lute walked over to it and scooted the rug aside with his foot. Russell lunged forward. Must have been waiting for the slightest diversion. His boots against the wooden floor alerted Lute before the sheriff made it halfway.

Lute fired, striking him high in the shoulder. Russell fell, cursed and grabbed his injured side. The scent of gunpowder filled the air. Soon it would be mixed with the nauseating odor of blood.

"You fool." He hit him full force with the butt of the gun. Russell lay moaning, holding his jaw. "Forget the bags, kid. Grab the other chair. Tie him back-to-back with Harrison. Arms first."

EJ hesitated then approached the sheriff slowly. The man's expression had the boy scared. Damn. This could get them all killed. Lute strode over and shoved the gun in Russell's face. "If you so much as breathe, it will be your last. Now kid, do your job." Lute watched as EJ looped and secured the ropes. When he was through, he stepped back.

"Nice knots. Were you a Boy Scout?"

EJ nodded. His hands were shaking.

Lute wished there was a way to get the kid out. But he'd stayed alive so far by not being a hero. He'd be stupid to change that strategy. "Let's load up and get the hell out of here."

He set the gun aside, knelt and pried at the false floor. It opened. He grabbed the first bag. A gust of bitter cold wind swept across the hut, blowing his hair.

The draft wasn't from the crawl space. Dread traced an icy finger down his spine.

Shit.

Cowboy stood in the doorway.

❋　　❋　　❋

It was deathly calm. The purr of the chopper outdoors provided background music. Princess had never shut off the engine. She'd expected, as he had, a quick exit. Their helicopter must have muffled the sound of the second aircraft approaching. Lute heard it lifting off, though, leaving Cowboy behind. With him.

His boss walked further into the hut, reached back and closed the door behind him. The latch clicked into place. His gaze never strayed from the scene. Lute swallowed hard. Russell's gun was on the floor, several feet away.

Pausing, his boss glanced at him kneeling by the hole. Then at the kid. Only the motion of the Stetson's brim told Lute which of them was under the microscope. A slight nod acknowledged their presence. Their efforts. The fact his attention moved on indicated, good job.

Cowboy crossed the room, toward the captives. The heels of his alligator boots tapped a steady rhythm on the wooden planks. No outward aggression, no hurried movements. As always, he scared the shit out of Lute. The puckered scar on his left cheek only enhanced the overall image.

"Quite the party you have going on here, Lute."

"Sorry for the delay. We're getting this stuff loaded now." Lute kicked into high gear, tossing the first of the one kilo sacks to EJ. The kid placed it inside the burlap bag with care and awaited the next. They couldn't have done better had they practiced.

Circling the men tied to the chairs, Cowboy paused by Russell's side. The sheriff had to twist his head to see him. He moaned at the effort. Blood stained his shirt from shoulder to waist.

Cowboy hooked his thumb into his belt loop, thin leather gloves and all. "Surprised to see you here during a pickup, Rusty. You're paid to guard the drops. Did our signals get confused?"

Russell made another wordless sound. That seemed to piss off Cowboy. His tone turned harsher.

"Now that I think about it, there have been a lot of mistakes lately. An unforgivable amount. A delegation problem on your part, turning over errands to the deputy too early. In retrospect, I think you'll agree that he wasn't quite ready for the responsibility."

Lute kept pulling sacks from beneath the floorboards, trying to ignore the chill in his boss's voice. EJ kept his gaze glued to the task of loading the bags.

Cowboy shifted his weight to one leg. "Let's see. First the shed. Lute had to eventually set the fire himself. Then the cabin. A very small time operation." Leaning closer to Russell, his words slowed. "I expect more for my money."

Russell nodded. He must have learned it was better to be silent.

"Good. We understand each other." Cowboy tilted his head toward the gun at EJ's feet. "That's a fancy piece. Is it yours, boy?"

EJ shook his head. "No, sir."

"Bring it here."

Not letting go of the sack, EJ leaned over and picked up the weapon. He stretched his hand toward Cowboy, as if not wanting to get closer.

Cowboy palmed the weapon, turning it over. Examining each detail. He checked the rounds. Each gesture precise. Deliberate. Lute had never seen his boss touch a gun in the entire time they'd been together.

"One bullet missing. Interesting." Holding the gun aloft next to his scarred cheek, Cowboy squinted and looked down the barrel. "I smell the gunpowder. Lute must have shot you with your own gun. Am I right, Sheriff?"

No answer. The man's expression was pained. Probably couldn't answer if he wanted to.

Cowboy continued to survey the room through the gun sight, moving it only an inch at a time until it was aimed toward Russell. Then he paused. "Good job, Lute. Nice touch. Except for one thing." The brim of the hat lifted. "You missed."

The weapon fired, blowing off most of the sheriff's head. Lute flinched but didn't look away. Tried to pretend that Cowboy doing his own killings was an everyday occurrence. Harrison had leaned forward, was straining against the ropes. Too late, of course, to miss the gore.

Lute's heart thundered in his chest. He forced back the bile that rose in his throat. EJ didn't fare as well. He puked down the hole, all over the plastic bags.

Though the retching was pathetic it was damned convenient. And it just might save the kid's life. Yanking EJ's collar, Lute lifted him until they were eye-to-eye. "Go outside." And keep going, he wanted to add. The boy obeyed, stumbling to the door. He chanced one final, terrified look over his shoulder.

Lute snarled and motioned angrily. "I said, get out of here." He was relieved when the door shut again. Good luck, kid.

Cowboy stood in front of Harrison. "And you, Mr. Harrison. Or is it Moore?" Lute noticed the man's eyebrows raise slightly. "That's right. We found out." Cowboy paused. "We sent a man to your condo today. Your sister wasn't home. Maybe she'll return later."

Rey stared straight into Cowboy's eyes. Lute had to admire him for that. Too bad the man didn't know that once he'd seen the eyes, death was next.

Cowboy leaned closer to him. Each word seemed carefully chosen and delivered. "You've been trouble since Day One. Too bad you didn't die in that avalanche. Would have saved me a hell of a lot of grief."

He straightened and addressed Lute. "Maybe we should use the Devil's Elbow site, again. It's fitting. We used it the last time anyone got this close to our operation. Remember?"

Harrison interrupted. "That would be Pete and Thia, correct?"

The fact that Harrison spoke, shocked the hell out of Lute. That he'd returned Cowboy's cool, detached tone told him the man had balls of steel. Challenging him, not prisoner to warden but equal-to-equal. He had more courage in his thumb than Lute had in his entire body. Though misplaced and hours too late, still he bet the man slept good at night.

"Brave." Cowboy nodded slowly, maintaining eye contact. "I never found out their names. A pretty woman. Strong, athletic. Was able to hold onto the copter's door for quite some time. Didn't want to jump, despite the fact her boyfriend showed her how."

Harrison didn't so much as blink. Like an old time stand-off, but only one was armed. Lute had watched long enough.

Flipping the bags over, he wiped them once against the ground to remove some of the puke then shoved them in the burlap bag. When they were all accounted for, he stood. "That's it." He tied the bags, keeping his face diverted from his boss. He couldn't save Harrison; could only help himself now. "I'll take these back to the chopper."

Cowboy's tone was sharp. "Toss them outside and come back in. Get the boy. There's one more task before we leave."

Lute's pulse beat faster, a knot clenched his gut. "What do we need the kid for?" He swallowed. What the hell had he been thinking? There were no medals on his chest.

Cowboy repeated his request calmly. "Get the kid."

Lute followed orders. He found EJ sitting on a stump, shivering. Why hadn't he run? Stupid shit.

Within minutes, they stood inside the Desolation Point hut again, facing Cowboy. Harrison, tied to the chair, was amazingly still alive.

Cowboy looked around the building, examining the interior, seeming to nod his approval. "This has been a good place. Has worked well for us."

What his boss was driving at? The chummy tone of voice had Lute on guard. He waited.

"Yes, I just might miss this place." When Cowboy's once-over was complete, he refocused his attention on Lute. "Burn it."

"What?"

"You heard me. Take that reserve tank of camp stove fuel and burn it."

"But, Boss . . ."

"Lute, come here."

No anger. A matter-of-fact tone, spoken crisply and cleanly. Speechless, Lute walked closer. EJ hung by the door. Cowboy laid his arm casually across Lute's shoulders. He must already be dead, because it was what he imagined hell would feel like.

Cowboy pushed his Stetson back. There was a permanent dent in his forehead where the hat usually rode. "You've been my right hand man for quite awhile."

Lute nodded.

"Well, let me share something with you. This is it. Afterwards we're parting ways. I'm flying south." He drew a slow breath. "The operation's yours."

Lute stood motionless, absorbing the words. Wondering what the fuck was going on. Behind him, he could hear EJ's teeth clattering.

"I want this finale to be really special. You see, this isn't the first time that Harrison and I have tangled." Cowboy moved, taking Lute with him, until they were both looking at the other man. "About twenty years ago, I had him right where I wanted him. Could have killed him anytime. There was going to be money, enough money to swim in."

His voice had built to a crescendo, then like a bubble it burst. Cowboy's torso sagged in mock disappointment. Harrison's expression never changed. So it hadn't surprised him. A case of mutual recognition. His boss' arm lay heavier on Lute's shoulder. He waited.

"Then my run of good luck suddenly changed. Harrison escaped. And all he left for me to remember him by was this." He touched the scar running down his cheek.

No wonder Cowboy had been so relentless in his pursuit of this one skier. The man had witnessed practically nothing, yet Cowboy had refused to let it go. Lute should have seen the clues. Recognized the uncharacteristic behavior. Forgotten about the shipment and taken off.

"Simply shooting him just wouldn't do the trick, now would it?" He removed his Stetson and placed it on Lute's head. "Now tie the kid up, throw him down the hole and torch the place. Let's head home."

Cowboy walked toward the door. EJ stared, terrified as the boss drew nearer. The kid was waiting for his execution. Eventually Cowboy passed by the boy. The kid's relief was painted briefly on his face as his eyes sought Lute.

Could he do it? Kill this boy and burn Harrison alive? Did he believe that, if he followed through, he'd walk out the door a free man?

Cowboy turned. His gaze met Lute's. "Well?"

Taking off the loaned hat, Lute tapped it against his thigh. He glanced once at Rey off to his side and then chuckled, as if amused by the situation. It worked. Cowboy relaxed his stance. Hooked his thumbs once again in his belt.

Lute tossed the Stetson like a Frisbee toward his boss' face and reached for the gun in his waistband at the same time. "I've had enough of your bullshit." He squeezed the trigger.

❄   ❄   ❄

The Desolation Point Hut was a barely a silhouette against the darkened sky. Next to it a single helicopter parked on the snow field. A second chopper had taken off a quarter hour before, flying

454

over her while she and Mitchell were en route. Fear had run through Megan at the thought of being too late. Of the hut being empty. Thank God she'd been wrong.

Mountain High Adventures. We meet again.

The blades of the cold steel bird revolved sluggishly against the building storm. She steered her vehicle onto the flats but behind a large mound of snow, out of view of the chopper. Mitchell pulled alongside her. Two sharp popping sounds had her turning toward the open front door. More gunfire? They switched off their snowmobiles' engines. Between the howling wind and whirring of the helicopter, she doubted anyone had heard their approach.

A solitary figure ran from the structure, braced against the wind, toward the waiting aircraft. A man. He climbed in. The chopper slowly rose from the glacier, foot by agonizing foot as the wind tossed it around. The thick coating of ice on the blades hindered lift off. It barely cleared the ground.

Mitchell touched her shoulder. "Look."

She turned. The hut was on fire. Adrenaline pumped through her, but for an instant she couldn't move. Fear had hold of her. She wrestled herself out from under its grip. Rey was inside.

Dave and Ali pulled up on a single snowmobile. Dave was on his feet as soon as the vehicle stopped. She ran to them. "Rey."

He nodded. "I know. Let's go."

Mitchell caught her by the arm. "You can't."

"Don't try to stop me." She wrenched away.

"We'll switch places. I'll get Harrison. You shoot down that chopper."

"Me?"

He reached beneath his knee length coat and retrieved his gun. He shoved it at her. She refused.

"There's no time to argue. You do it. I can't."

"All right. But I won't have a chance in hell with your gun. Now go." She pulled off her glove and felt for the butt of Thia's rifle, still slung over her shoulder. The stock was firm and smooth. Reassuring beneath her fingers. Before today, Megan hadn't touched it in over a year. It had been longer ago that she'd fired it. Thia's aim had been rock-steady. Would hers be, too? It was now or never.

Swinging the rifle from her shoulder, she positioned it in front of her. Mitchell and Dave ran ahead. Ali stood to one side, her fists clenched, her face hopeful. As much as she feared for her brother, she was staying to provide moral support. Megan acknowledged her with a nod of thanks.

Carefully but quickly she loaded the clips, watching the chopper struggle. It was thirty meters away, hovering near the cliff's edge. Hoping to catch an up-draft, she guessed. They'd let it sit too long. That was in her favor. She raised the rifle to shoulder level. Yanking off her goggles, she squinted against the blowing ice pellets. Her best bet was to take out the pilot.

Five shells, one target. Much better odds than the usual five-to-five ratio. But this target was moving. Still, she could do it. She lifted her cheek off the stock.

Thia was gone. But with her older sister's rifle clenched in her hand, they were no longer competitors. It had to be now.

She glanced skyward again. The chopper hovered forty meters away, directly overhead. Ten shy of her usual target. The wind shifted. Ali whispered a prayer. Megan squinted, imagining a bulls-eye on the window beneath the aircraft.

Slow the pulse. Shoot between beats. Focus. She drew a single, steadying breath and let it out slowly. Waiting.

The pilot appeared. Megan fired, emptying her clip by rote. The copter instantly spun left, as if the throttle had been slammed into. A quick downward spiral then a crash into the mountain side.

The fuel tank ignited. Explosions of heat and flashes of light forced her backward. She covered her ears.

Flames leapt. Metal twisted and crumpled. Hissed. Finally settled in a heap against the stark white snow. Then silence, except for the crackle of fabric and plastic being consumed. The smell of gasoline burned her nostrils.

Megan jammed the butt of the rifle into the snow and leaned against it. Her head cleared, her ears stopped ringing. She glanced up. The hut.

"Oh, God. Rey." Dropping the rifle, she ran.

❄   ❄   ❄

Rey stared at the false floor. The drugs were gone. EJ was down there instead. Dave's protégé. EJ's involvement explained his disappearance from the cocaine abuse program.

Lute's death replayed in Rey's mind. It had happened quickly, he was still reeling from the shock. The bullet hole Lute shot through the Stetson had sent Cowboy over the edge. He'd been livid, insane with anger. The veins near his temple had bulged as he rolled Lute's dead body across the floor with his booted foot, screaming at him.

After pushing him into the hole Cowboy had ordered the boy down to keep the dead man company. He'd ridiculed him with how Lute always had liked the rookies. Best they stay together. Sick. Rey would never forget the fright on the boy's face as Cowboy slid the cover back over the opening. Then he'd hauled the heavy wooden bed on top to keep it in place. The man's breathing had been erratic as he'd spread white gas around and tossed his flaming lighter into the corner.

Cowboy. Rey had never known his kidnapper's name. Had only imagined how the slice in his cheek would have healed. It was a hideous scar. He must have hated that. A constant reminder of how he'd lost out to a mere kid. Cowboy must have also escaped that day. The young punk had emerged as an unscrupulous criminal.

Though twenty years had passed, the hard cold gleam in his captor's eyes was still the same. Their message: this time, no escape. It was predictable that Cowboy hadn't treated him to the same bullet-to-the-head treatment the sheriff received. It would have been too easy.

The flames were moving closer. Rey struggled against the ropes on his wrists and legs. Dried blood itched the nape of his neck. It nauseated him to think about what it was. The thickest rope still lashed him to the dead sheriff. Ever since Russell had taken the bullet, that particular rope had been the tightest, cutting into his arms.

The door burst open. Mitchell. Dave followed him in. Their attention was immediately drawn to Russell. His partner paused mid-step, before continuing forward.

Mitchell was on his knees, already working the ropes. Dave took the other side. "You're in one fine mess."

"Thanks." Rey's throat was parched. He could hardly speak. "Where's Megan?"

"Outside, taking care of the chopper."

"You left her with Cowboy?"

Mitchell glanced at the growing fire. In addition to the walls burning, the table in the corner had caught fire. "She's shooting down his helicopter." He continued to work the ropes. "My hand's not worth shit when it comes to firing."

"Great." An undercover agent who couldn't shoot. That was a heavy load on Megan. "She's all right, then?"

Dave nodded. "She's great. A hell of a lot better than you are."

Mitchell was cursing. "I need something to cut this with. We'll never untie it in time." He scrounged in his pocket, retrieved a pocket knife and started on the rope at chest-level. Not only did it bind Rey to the sheriff, but it held the two wood-carved chairs together. Mitchell sawed furiously.

Rey leaned toward his partner. "Listen. EJ's beneath the floorboards. I don't know how he ended up connected to all this. We'll find out later. Move the bed. There's a pry bar in the corner. Go."

Dave scrambled to his feet, shoved the bed aside and had the floor board free in seconds. He reached in and helped the boy out. He hugged him tightly then pointed to the body laying next to him on the frozen ground. "Who's that?"

EJ stared into the hole. "His name's Lute." He swallowed hard. "Cowboy killed him."

A loud crackling sound drew Rey's attention. The fire in the far corner had devoured the wall and crept up to the roof. The noise level increased. The heat intensified. Rey yelled to be heard. "Dave."

His partner seemed to force himself to look away from the floor and toward Rey. "The man is dead. Get EJ out of here. Take him to safety." Dave nodded and ushered the boy to the door.

The first rope drooped against his chest. Mitchell shoved the second chair out of the way. Russell's body flopped like a broken doll. Rey's arms ached as the circulation returned. His wrists were still secured. He rubbed his fingers together as best he could. They were sticky where the blood hadn't yet dried. His feet were in worse shape, totally numb. The fire continued to move across the roof, snapping and hissing. A second wall caught fire. Heat burned his face.

Megan squeezed by Dave and EJ and raced inside. Eric yelled at her. "Help me here. Find something sharp. Anything. The roof's about to fall in. Work on his ankles."

She flinched as ceiling fragments dropped beside her. "What are you doing?"

"Cutting the ropes."

"Forget it. Step back."

Rey's eyes widened as Megan brought her boot up and jammed it against the wooden chair arm. It splintered, broke off in his lap. One hand was free, though still attached to a strip of wood. He would be bruised tomorrow, if he lived.

Mitchell arched his eyebrow then stepped back. He repeated her kicking maneuver as Megan examined the ropes at the base of the chair. "Tip it on its back. The ropes might come off that way."

Rey braced himself for the thump. Scooting the rope free turned out to be a futile effort.

A section of roof fell and crashed to one side of them. Megan glanced up. She looked terrified. Her eyes met his. They would never make it. "Go."

"What?" She leaned closer to him.

"Go while you can."

"No way." She grabbed Mitchell's sleeve as she stood. "Let's push it out the door, as is."

Rey watched the crumbling ceiling go by as he was shoved head first toward the door. He shifted his gaze back to Megan. She was by his feet next to Mitchell, straining as she pushed the awkward chair. They bumped him over the threshold and let go. He crossed his arms over his face and hoped the log wouldn't roll as he slid across the snow pack.

He slammed into the side of her snowmobile. Though his elbow ached like hell, he was alive. He saw the crumpled remains of the Mountain High Adventures helicopter. Cowboy wouldn't be able to hurt anyone again.

Megan was the first person to reach him. She knelt next to him in the snow. "Rey. You're all right." She kissed his face, pushing his hair away as if to get a better look. He tried to hold her but the broken chair arms were in his way. Immediately she dug for her pocket knife and began working on the ropes binding him to the wood.

"The Okanogan is very hard on me, love, but I still want to start my recovery over, right here."

"Here?"

"Actually, it was your cabin I had in mind. As enamoured as I am with your wilderness, it's a bit cold outdoors." One rope was free. He hugged her to him. "I'll stay for as long as you want. I love you."

"And I love you." She started on the other side. A mischievous glint appeared in her eyes. "Are you saying that the timing is finally right for us?"

"Yes. All of our distractions are over." The downed helicopter burning in the distance illuminated the jagged mountain peak behind it. Desolation Pass. As wild and fierce as its name. He pointed toward the flaming mound. "Did you shoot that down?"

Ali joined them. She took Megan by the wrist and raised it champion-style. "Damn straight she did. She was great."

"I never doubted her."

Ali let go of Megan and patted him on the shoulder. "This is the second time you haven't made it safely down the mountain. I guess the mulled wine is still out of the question."

"We'll discuss it later."

His second arm was free. Smiling, he drew Megan close and kissed her. "You made the shot."

"Yes. I used Thia's rifle."

"Poetic justice."

She relaxed against him, her head on his chest. He wanted to hold her this way forever.

Three men approached slowly. Though they were silhouetted against the orange hue of the burning cabin, he recognized them instantly: Dave, EJ, and Mitchell. The first two were close together, Dave bending toward the younger man. The rescue process was beginning again.

Ali hurried to Dave's side. They were close enough for Rey to overhear them. Introductions. Mitchell, as usual, walked alone. He'd be removing his things from Grace's shortly and be on his way. A rescue copter was already approaching.

Rey waved the man over. "Mitchell, thanks. I had you pegged wrong. Sorry."

The agent shrugged. "No sweat. If you'd guessed right, I wouldn't have been doing my job." He pointed toward Dave and Ali. "They were a tremendous help. Their patience with Deputy Jeffers probably saved his life."

Rey hugged Megan tighter. The circulation in his wrist was returning. The nightmare was ending. He glanced back at Mitchell. "Will you be leaving soon?"

"Not until after dinner." He checked his watch. "Damn. Grace will have my hide for being late again." He smiled. "I wouldn't consider going, though, without sampling her stew one more time. I'll save the news that she won't be arrested until after dessert. Besides, I think she's invited Rachel to join us. Said my table manners have improved just enough to have earned the pleasure of Rachel's company." He leaned closer. "I think I have a dinner date."

Rey laughed. "Sounds like the Granny Grace I know. One last favor before you go."

"Anything."

"Would you mind freeing my feet?"

Megan lifted her head. "Yes, please do." She turned back toward Rey. "Then we'll take care of the rest, together."

ABOUT THE AUTHOR

MARY SHARON PLOWMAN lives in Issaquah, Washington with her three children: Jessica, Jennifer and Brian. She has been an avid reader since her Nancy Drew days, when she secretly longed for Ned to kiss Nancy. The idea for *White Powder* came from her desire to create a romantic suspense novel about a strong heroine coping with the rugged North Cascades wilderness. In addition to being an author, Sharon works as a Program Manager for The Boeing Company in the area of electronic commerce. Her current writing project is a romantic time travel adventure set during World War II.

Goodfellow Press

Novels from Goodfellow Press are smooth and seamless with characters who live beyond the confines of the book covers.

Hedge of Thorns by Sally Ash. A gentle story unfolding like a modern fairy tale, of painful yesterdays and trust reborn.
ISBN 0-9639882-0-4 $7.99/$8.99 Canada.

This Time by Mary Sharon Plowman. A man and a woman with differing expectations and lifestyles, take a chance to love.
ISBN 0-9639882-1-2 $7.99/$8.99 Canada.

Glass Ceiling by C.J. Wyckoff. Facing career and emotional upheaval, Jane Walker makes a bold choice to explore East Africa with an unorthodox man.
ISBN 0-9639882-2-0 $9.99/$10.99 Canada.

Bear Dance by Kay Zimmer. A man betrayed and a woman escaping painful memories struggle to overcome the barriers keeping them apart.
ISBN 0-9639882-4-7 $9.99/$10.99 Canada.

Homework: Bridging the Gap by Kay Morison, Ph.D/Susanne Brady. Empowers parents, teachers and students to solve the homework dilemma.
ISBN 0-9639882-5-5 $12.99/$15.99 Canada.

Ivory Tower by May Taylor. An old house is given second life by a group of young entrepreneurs who, while investigating its mysterious past, discover new meaning in their own lives. ISBN 0-9639882-3-9. (released 1997)

The Inscription by Pam Binder. Time is not an obstacle for an immortal Scottish lord and his present day American love. ISBN 0-9639882-7-1 (released 1997)

Mātūtū by Sally Ash. On the rugged New Zealand coast, an English violinist and an American writer discover healing and love, helped by an old Maori legend.
ISBN 0-9639882-9-8 (released 1997)

Cookbook from Hell by Matt Buchman. A moderately irreverent fantasy providing an alternate view of religion gently wrapped around a pair of love stories.
ISBN 0-9639882-8-X (released 1997)

For information on Goodfellow Writing Seminars call 1-800-853-2153.

Your comments and suggestions are welcome. Write us at:
Goodfellow Press • 16625 Redmond Way, Suite M20
Redmond, WA • 98052-4499